graceful
waters

a novel by

BL Miller
&
VH Foster

GRACEFUL WATERS

ISBN 1-933113-08-1

THIS TRADE PAPERBACK ORIGINAL IS PUBLISHED BY **INTAGLIO PUBLICATIONS**, GAINESVILLE, FL USA

FIRST EDITION: OCTOBER 2003
SECOND PRINTING: INTAGLIO PUBLICATIONS, SEPTEMBER 2004

CREDITS

EXECUTIVE EDITOR: STACIA SEAMAN

COVER DESIGN BY DONNA IRENE ROBERTS

Acknowledgements

There are many people who have helped me. Their kindness and willingness to give of themselves is awe inspiring.

A special big thanks to Donna Roberts for creating the cover design for this book. She was on a tight deadline at work, but still, she squeezed me in.

Gypsy helped me out in ways too numerous to mention. Hugs and kisses to you, Gypsy.

Radclyffe suggested that we take *Graceful Waters* to BookEnds Press and StarCrossed Productions. Thanks for all the help and advice, Rad. You're a dear.

My friend Polly Robinson was a big fan of this story. She had told me that she'd read it three times, so I asked her if she would write a small blurb for the back cover. She did, and I loved it. Thank you, Polly.

I would also like to thank Michelle De La Rosa for all the help with my website. You are a webmaster extraordinaire.

Kathy Smith, you've been great to work with. It's been a pleasure.

Stacia Seaman, an editor par excellence. She worked beyond the call of duty by working on *Graceful Waters* when she was ill. Thanks, Stacia.

I would also like to thank all the pups who sent feedback on the early version of this book. There were so many of you kind souls, and your comments and questions helped me know we were on the right track.

And last, but not least, my friend, BL Miller. This story was her brain child and I was happy when she asked me if I would write it with her. She is a dear friend and a wonderful writer.

Thanks to everyone. I love you all. ☺

Verda

VHFoster@AOL.Com
http://verdas-kaleidoscope.womenwhoroar.com/

GRACEFUL WATERS

The booming voice of the bailiff cut through the din of the courtroom. "All rise, Family Court of Iroquois County is now in session. Honorable Judge Grimm presiding." Grace stood next to the public defender, her hair a rainbow of pink, green, white, and blue with blonde roots. "Be seated." The bailiff sat after the judge took the bench.

"Miss Waters," Judge Grimm said, looking squarely at Grace. "This is not the first time you've appeared before me, but it will be the last. You have no regard for the rights of others, and no amount of community service or probation is going to change that." Grace rolled her eyes. "I know you think this is all some kind of fun little game, but your playtime is over, young woman," he said, his voice rising with anger. "You assaulted a teacher and that kind of behavior cannot be tolerated. I agree with the school board's recommendation that you not be allowed to return to Iroquois High School. Since the district attorney has decided not to charge you as an adult, the question before this court then becomes what to do with you."

"Who cares," Grace said, then rolled her eyes at the reproachful look from her court-appointed lawyer.

"Indeed, Miss Waters," the judge said. "It's clear you don't. It is also clear to this court that your mother is unable to maintain any type of control over you, and releasing you to her custody again will only result in allowing you the opportunity to add to your already lengthy record. Therefore, the sentencing will be as follows; the minor Graceful Lake Waters is remanded to the custody of the state until the age of eighteen, which I understand to be in six months."

"Big fucking deal," Grace said, ignoring the stifled cries of her mother sitting in the row behind the defense table.

Judge Grimm's face turned beet-red. "That's enough from you. I was going to send you to Crestwood, but after listening to you, I think something more than a minimum-security youth facility is in order. I'm sending you and that smart mouth of yours to Sapling Hill."

"You had to open your mouth," her lawyer whispered.

"Big deal," Grace said, flipping her middle finger at the judge before the handcuffs were put on her by the bailiff. "Boot camp for girls. Who cares?"

"Oh Grace," her mother said as the bailiff passed her to the corrections officer for the youth facility.

DAY ONE

The parking lot was full of upset parents waiting for the corrections officers to take their teenage daughters away to the Sapling Hill Youth Facility for Girls, better known as the Girl's Boot Camp. Grace had spent the two weeks since sentencing at Crestwood, unable to see her mother. Now she had only a few minutes before she would be put on the bus and sent north to what other teens had described as "hell with lots of trees." To her annoyance, Edna Waters spent those minutes crying at the sight of her daughter in an orange jumpsuit and shackles.

"That's right, make a scene," Grace said, rolling her eyes as her mother pulled out another tissue.

"I'm supposed to be happy that my only daughter has been incarcerated?" her mother said, dabbing at the tears that spilled out of her eyes.

"It's six months, Ma. I can do that standing on my head." Grace turned her head to let the wind blow the pink bangs out of her eyes. "Look at it this way, you're always complaining you don't know where I am or what I'm doing. Now you'll know."

"Shackles," her mother said, referring to the restraints keeping Grace's wrists pinned to her sides. "If your grandfather had lived to see this."

"Yeah, yeah, I know I'm a huge disappointment and a disgrace to the family," the teen said, drawing a look from a nearby guard.

"If you would just realize how much better things could be," her mother said. "If you would just get some direction in your life."

"I've got direction." Grace turned back to her mother, her fists clenched. "I don't need you or anyone else telling me how to act and what to do. I can handle everything just fine by myself."

"That's enough," the burly guard said as he approached the pair. "Mrs. Waters, it's time for you to say good-bye now." He glared at Grace. "Maybe you'll clean up that smart mouth of yours and learn some respect at Sapling Hill."

"Yeah and maybe I'll grow up to be president too, right?" She jerked her wrists against the restraints. "You don't give a shit anyway, so get the hell away from me, you lousy pig."

The corrections officer grabbed her arm. "I think you'll sit up front with me," he said. "Mrs. Waters, did your lawyer explain the visitation to you?"

Grace's mother nodded and pulled out another tissue. "He said maybe after the first two months."

"They'll send you a letter to let you know," he said. "Let's go, you smart-mouth punk."

"What's the matter? Can't get any unless you chain them up?" Grace taunted as he pulled her in the direction of the bus. "Then again, maybe you ain't got one to get up in the first place."

"Oh yeah, that big mouth of yours will be real welcome at Sapling Hill," he said, jerking her to stop in front of the bus where another officer stood with a clipboard in hand. "This is Grace Waters," he said. "She's going up front."

Grace was furious by the time the bus pulled through the high gates of Sapling Hill. A well-aimed glob of spit had earned her a gag that brought laughter and comments from the other teens. Now the bus had stopped and everyone was off except her. The guard who put her on the bus, and whom she had spit upon, was now talking to a tall woman with short black hair and wearing military fatigues. The woman nodded several times, then stepped onto the bus.

"Well, Waters, it seems you're going to be this group's hard case." The imposing woman stood in front of Grace and towered over her. "You listen up and you listen close, little girl. Playtime is over!" she shouted into Grace's ear, startling her as the shackles that held her to the seat were removed. "Now you get your ass off this bus and line up. Move it!" Grace ran off the bus, the screaming woman right on her heels. "Move move move!" When the teen reached the end of the line, she turned and stood facing the bus.

"All right, ladies," the tall woman said. "Welcome to Sapling Hill Rehabilitation Facility. I am Instructor Carey. You will refer to me as Instructor Carey or ma'am." Carey paced back and forth in front of the three dozen girls. "Nothing else will be tolerated. Do I make myself clear?" She was met with a chorus of "Yes, ma'ams" and "Yes, Instructor Carey," except for Grace, whose mouth was still gagged.

Carey walked down the line until she stood in front of Grace. "This is Waters," she said in a loud, clear voice. "Waters didn't know enough to keep her mouth shut. As you can see, she was punished." Reaching around Grace's head, Carey untied the knot and removed the gag. "This is Sapling Hill. You have a chance here to turn your life around. The other instructors and I are here to help you. If you accept that help, you will leave here a different person. If you don't," she stared directly at Grace, "this will be the saddest five months you've ever had."

"This is bogus," Grace said to the girl standing at the next cot.

"Word up," the girl said. "I'm Latisha Jones." She held out her hand.

"Grace Waters." She reached out, shaking the hand in dark contrast to her own. "What'd you do to get here?"

"Set fire to the school library," Latisha said. "You?"

"Threw a chair at a teacher," Grace said. "He had it coming, though."

"You get five months?"

"Six," Grace said. "After I get out of here I have to serve another month, probably at Crestwood."

"I'm done after here," Latisha said. "Girl, that's one funky 'do."

Grace ran her fingers through her multicolored hair. "Works for me. Better than dreadlocks," she said, referring to the style Latisha was wearing.

"Jones."

They turned to see the imposing Instructor Carey approach. "This is not macramé class and your head isn't a planter. Get those beads out of your hair now. Waters, let's go."

Rolling her eyes, Grace put her hand on her hip. "Where?"

"Drop and give me ten pushups, now!" Carey yelled, causing Latisha to jump back and the other girls in the barracks to stop what they were doing to see what the commotion was about. Grace lowered herself to the floor, though not as fast as she knew the screaming woman would have liked. "When I tell you to do something, you say, yes, ma'am or yes, Instructor Carey!" she hollered. "Four, five, six, keep going. Seven, eight, nine, ten. Stand up."

Grace felt the anger rise in her along with the embarrassment of being reprimanded in front of the other girls, but knew enough to stay quiet this time. Clearly Instructor Carey was not someone to mess with. "Now let's go."

Grace remained quiet as Instructor Carey led her to the administration building, not wanting to draw any more pushups. "We're going to do something about that hair of yours," Carey said as she unlocked the door labeled "Barber."

"No way," Grace said. "You're not fucking touching my hair."

Carey was immediately at her right side. "Did I ask you a question?" she yelled into Grace's ear. "Drop and give me ten! You don't get to make the decisions around here, do you understand? Do you understand?"

"Yes, ma'am," Grace said as she pushed up with her arms.

"What do you think people think when they see that rainbow on your head? They see a freak, not someone to take seriously. Is that what you want people to think of you?"

"No, ma'am."

"I don't care what trash your parents let you get away with, you don't swear at the instructors here. Do you understand?"

"Yes, ma'am." *Bitch.*

"All the way up, all the way down, Waters. You don't take shortcuts here," Carey said. "Nine, ten. Stand up." Grace did as she was told, giving the instructor a dirty look for making her do pushups. "Get your ass in that chair, and I don't want to hear one word from you unless I ask a question, got it?"

Grace rolled her eyes and slowly moved into the chair. "Yes, ma'am," she said, doing her best to be as disrespectful as she could with the word.

"We can do this easy or we can do this hard, it's all up to you, Waters," Carey said. "You can follow the rules and do what you're told, or spend all day doing pushups and being yelled at. You make your own bed here." She put a short length guard on the electric clippers. "Now you're going to sit still, and that smart mouth of yours isn't going to say a word unless I ask you a question."

Grace gave her a murderous look as the clippers were turned on.

"What you're thinking is written clearly on your face." Carey shut the clippers off. "You think I'm the biggest bitch living and you'd love to take a shot at me." The dark-haired woman gripped either side of the barber chair, her face only inches from the teen. "Do it and you'll never be that unhappy again. Now wipe that look off your face and sit up straight."

Grace clenched her jaw and stared hard at the door opposite her as Instructor Carey wrapped a plastic robe around her neck. *Damn bitch.* She became even angrier as multicolored locks of hair fell to the floor. "You wanna leave some?"

A firm hand clamped down on her head, keeping her from moving it. "Move your head again and I'll shave you bald," Carey said. "And when I'm done, you're dropping for ten for that smart mouth of yours. Want to try for twenty?"

"No, ma'am."

"Then sit still and keep quiet."

Walking back to the barracks, Grace ran her fingers through her now short blonde hair. "Fucking bitch," she said, rubbing arms sore from all the pushups. Seeing Latisha standing with several other girls just outside the barracks, Grace headed over to join them.

"Damn, girlfriend, you got chopped," Latisha said.

Grace self-consciously rubbed her hair. "The bitch wasn't happy until she damn near scalped me," she said. "What'd I miss?"

Latisha shook her head. "Nothing. See that girl over there? She got into it with the short instructor."

"Yeah," one of the girls standing next to them said. "And Gage started screaming and yelling at her and the wimp started crying like a baby." The girls laughed at the incident and Grace joined in, knowing full well that no one could make her cry.

"All right, girls, let's line up," Instructor Gage said as she approached. "Arm's length apart, I want to see you nine across and four deep." Other girls began to assemble and Grace quickly made her way to the back row. Suddenly she felt a firm hand slap down on her shoulder. The look from the girls around her left no doubt as to who it was.

"You're going up front where I can keep my eye on you," Instructor Carey said. "Let's go." Grace knew better than to object.

Now up front, Grace had an unobstructed view of three of the instructors. Carey was the tallest; her short black hair barely peeked out beneath the olive drab cap, while mirrored sunglasses kept her eyes hidden. Next to her was Gage, her complexion several shades darker than Latisha. Standing slightly behind the other two was Donaldson, a tall, short-haired blonde with an angular face, whose light blue eyes were in constant motion, moving from one girl to the next.

"Quiet," Carey said, causing a silence to fall over the group. "As you know, you were not allowed to bring any personal effects, other than what you're wearing." The mirrored sunglasses turned in Grace's direction. "This is the last time you will wear those clothes. You will be provided with everything you will need to wear while you are here. And before any of you get any ideas, bras and panties are required, not optional." Grace wondered how they were going to enforce that rule; not that she would ever violate it. Ever since she had started to develop, her nipples had been too sensitive to rub up against a shirt all day.

Instructor Gage stepped forward, the petite woman barely coming to Carey's shoulder. "You will be divided into four squads. Count off and line up with your squad. You will be known as Alpha, Bravo, Charlie, and Delta squads in that order," she said over the counting. "Let me explain how your days will go, ladies. At 0600 you will wake up. You'll have half an hour to shower, dress, and make your bunks. At 0630 you will report here for inspection. Whenever you are told to report to formation you will come here and assemble with your squad. You will have morning mess between 0700 and 0730. At 0735 there will be barracks inspection. From 0800 until noon you will participate in physical training or field training. In the future we will refer to these as PT or FT. After lunch you will have classes, mentoring sessions, or studying time until dinner. After that, you'll have three hours for studying or rec time. Lights out is 2100 hours. That's nine p.m. for those of you unfamiliar with military time."

"You will attend classes and training according to your squad assignment," Instructor Carey said. "The schedule will be posted on the bulletin board outside the mess hall. You will have one-on-one counseling sessions with your assigned mentor. That schedule will also be posted on the board. There are no weekends here, ladies. Monday, Wednesday and Friday are Schedule A and Tuesday, Thursday and Saturday are Schedule B. Sunday is not a day of rest. On Sunday your mornings will be the same as they are on A and B schedules with the exception that you may be excused from the morning run if you wish to attend chapel. The afternoons will be spent in studying or doing your homework unless you receive privilege."

"Privilege," Instructor Gage said, her voice much higher than Carey's. "What do you think privilege is? Just like the real world, privilege is something you earn. If you are on privilege, you will be allowed to spend your free time in the rec room or at the athletic fields. You'll be allowed to have visits from your family."

"No way," Grace said when she saw the khaki dress uniform. "We're not in the fucking army."

"You got a problem?" Instructor Gage said, approaching rapidly.

"No, ma'am."

"Then cut the chatter and keep moving."

Grace filed forward, stopping at the counter where Inspector Carey was waiting.

"Name?" the dark-haired woman asked without looking up from her clipboard.

"Waters, ma'am."

The instructor turned around and grabbed a neatly folded stack of khaki slacks and shirts with Grace's name patch already sewn on. "Shoe size?"

"Eight, ma'am." Instructor Carey pushed the clothes into Grace's arms, then added a pair of black boots and white canvas sneakers with thick soles. "Move on to the next station."

Moving on, Grace found herself in front of Instructor Donaldson.

"Bra size, panty size."

"Thirty-two C, four, ma'am." Two sport bras and three pairs of panties were added to her pile.

"Into the next room, strip and shower, then change into your dress uniform and report to formation. Make sure you stand with your squad," the blonde woman said. "Next. Bra size, panty size."

Grace entered the next room where Instructor Mitchell was waiting. "Strip. Clothes go in this bag, footwear in the box. What's your name?"

"Waters, ma'am," Grace said as she put her foot on the bench and began untying the laces.

"Let's go, Waters. You don't have anything I don't."

"Listen up," Instructor Carey said. "You've received two sets of tee shirts and shorts. The blue set is for PT, the white set for sleeping." She stopped in front of Grace. "Waters, when would you wear the blue set?"

"PT, ma'am."

"You have been issued several undershirts," Carey continued, moving on down the line of bunks. "When you report to morning formation you will wear your dress uniform. That consists of the following: your boots, neatly polished with the laces not touching the ground, one pair of white socks, panties, bra, one pair of khaki slacks neatly creased down the front and back, one khaki web belt with the buckle polished, your khaki cap, one undershirt and your khaki shirt with the sleeves neatly pressed." Reaching the end of the bunks, she turned around and began walking back. "When you are told to report to FT, or field training, you will report in your BDUs. BDU stands for battle dress uniform. That's the camouflage shirt and pants with the olive undershirt and olive cap. Classes and meals will be attended in your dress uniform only." Once again she stopped in front of Grace. "Waters, what makes up the dress uniform?"

"Khaki shirt and pants, ma'am."

"Drop and give me ten," Carey said. "Anyone else want to try?"

I hate you. Grace lowered herself to the concrete floor and began to count pushups.

"We survived day one," Gage said, opening a can of soda and leaning her hip against the desk.

"It's going to be a long term this time, Sue," Carey said, leaning back in her chair. "I just feel it." She looked at the stack of folders on her desk. "We still have to finish up the mentoring assignments."

"How many are left?"

"Twelve," Carey said. She sighed and reached for the top folder. "All right, Jennings, Christine. Sixteen, assault with a deadly weapon, declared PINS after cracking her father's skull with a lug wrench. Psych eval suggests sexual abuse."

"I'll take her," Gage said.

"All right, that's one down, eleven to go," Carey said, reaching for the next folder. "Bowen, Jan. Seventeen, oh this is nice, armed robbery, possession with intent to sell, assault, three different trips to Crestwood. Sent to a foster home after step-father arrested for sexually abusing minors. Psych eval incomplete?" She flipped the top page to see the supplemental information. "She attacked the psychologist at Crestwood but has a long history of receiving counseling." She looked at Sue.

"Wonder what that shrink said to tick her off." Running her thumb along the corner of the rest of the pages, Carey let out a low whistle. "Seems like everyone has something to say about her."

"Three trips to Crestwood says a lot by itself," Gage said. "Let's set her aside for now. Who's next?"

"Lopez, Maribel..."

The two instructors went back and forth selecting the girls they would be responsible to mentor and counsel. Carey picked up the last folder, surprised by its thickness. "Waters, Graceful." She raised an eyebrow and looked at Gage.

"You have to admit her mother was clever," Gage said.

Carey smiled and shook her head. "Her mother should have called her Stormy. I thought I was going to have to strap her into the chair to get that clown hair off of her. All right, let's see the distinguished record of Smart Mouth. Seventeen. Assault, vandalism, possession of drugs on school property, the list goes on." She flipped through the pages. "Look at this transcript. A's and B's freshman and sophomore years, then she went right to C's, D's, and F's first quarter of her junior year."

"What's the psych eval say?" Gage asked.

"Incomplete. Don't tell me she attacked her shrink too." Carey looked through the pages until she found the report. "She refused to say anything to the psychologist." She closed the folder and set it on her stack. "I'll take Waters, you take Bowen."

"You sure?" Gage asked.

"I'm sure," Carey said. "I have a feeling about Waters."

Grace draped the towel over her shoulder and picked up her toiletry kit. "This is so bogus," she said.

"Word up," Latisha replied. "What do they think we're going to do with a Bic?"

"Nothing," Jan said. "Gage just wants to get a look, that's all." They stepped into the changing room and opened their assigned lockers. "Gets a thrill figuring out who's a natural blonde."

"How am I supposed to shave my bikini area if she's right there watching?"

"Turn your back to her," Grace said, kneeling down to unlace her boots. "Then all she'll see is your ass."

"Yeah," Jan said. "That's wide enough to keep her from seeing anything."

"Bite me, Bowen," Latisha said. "I'm not the one who had to go back and get larger-sized pants."

"That's not my fault," Jan said. "Crestwood gave them the wrong size. I told you that before."

"Uh-huh, sure," Latisha said.

"Are you girls going to stand there and chatter all day?" Instructor Gage called out from the shower room.

"No, ma'am," Grace said, pushing her pants and panties down together, then sitting on the bench to pull them off. "Babysitting in the shower," she added in a lower voice. "Way bogus."

"Well," Jan said. "Let's go show Short Shit what we've got."

As they entered the large shower area, Instructor Gage stood near the entrance with a clipboard and a box of safety razors by her side. "Name?"

"Bowen, ma'am," Jan said. Gage looped a plastic tag on a razor, then labeled it with permanent marker. "Shaving allowed only in stations one through four," she said as she handed Jan the razor. "Name?"

"Waters," Grace said, looking around the tiled room, ten showerheads spaced along three walls, while a towel rack and privacy wall took up the fourth. She rolled her eyes. *Of course, pukey green with little windows way up high that no one can squeeze out of. Like anyone is going to try and run away while buck naked in the shower.*

Setting her towel on the rack, Grace walked past Jan at station one and took station two while Latisha took the one next to her. "Hot water?"

"Lukewarm," Jan said, soaping her underarms. "So what's the deal with having to shave right here?"

Grace turned on the water, setting it as hot as it would go. "Guess they don't want us to slit our wrists or something."

"With these little things?" Jan asked, holding out the blue razor. "Next thing you know they'll take away bar soap for fear we'll carve it into a gun."

Grace rinsed her hair, then reached for the shampoo dispenser mounted on the wall between each shower station. "No hair dryer, no makeup, no nail polish, can't even wear jewelry."

"Word," Latisha said. "My holes are going to close up, but they don't care."

"I'm surprised they let Hathaway keep her glasses," Grace said. "Don't they know they have metal screws?"

"You have a commentary, Waters?" an authoritative voice asked.

"No, ma'am." Grace said, sharing a look with Jan and Latisha. *I have got to learn to watch what I say when the Goon Squad's around.*

DAY TWO

G race kept her eyes focused on the flagpole as the instructors walked up and down the rows of girls. To her dismay, she found herself face to face with the imposing Instructor Carey.

"Two hits for Waters," she said. "No undershirt, laces touching the ground." Grace shifted her weight from one leg to the other and rolled her eyes. "Drop for twenty!" Carey yelled into her ear.

Grace dropped to the ground, fighting to keep her thoughts to herself. *Damn bitch. You think it's so fun to do pushups? Get that tall ass of yours down here and do them and see how you feel, Queen bitch.* When she finished, she rose and glared at the flagpole, wishing it would magically collapse and land on Instructor Carey.

"All right, report to the mess hall. Barracks inspection in thirty minutes," Instructor Carey said, and mirrored sunglasses looked in Grace's direction. "I've seen the barracks, and some of you should think about skipping breakfast."

"Ten hut," Instructor Carey said as she and Gage entered the barracks. "Line up at the foot of your bunk. Bowen, sneakers go to the left of the footlocker, not the right. Jennings, hats aren't worn indoors." She stopped at Grace's bunk. "Obviously your mother never taught you how to make a bed," she said, reaching down and ripping off the linens with one firm tug.

Grace watched her bed linens drop to the floor. *Damn.*

"Make it again," the dark-haired instructor said. Grace reached down and took the sheet, then spread it out over the cot and began to tuck it in around the sides. "Hold it," Carey said, pulling the sheet free. "Watch me. Do the blanket and sheet together. Tuck the bottom in first, then make a sharp corner here," she demonstrated. "Then the sides. No wrinkles and you can bounce a quarter off it."

"Yes, ma'am," Grace said, thinking it silly to worry about how a bed was made.

"Now you do it," Instructor Carey said, stripping the bunk again.

"Yes, ma'am." Picking up the linens, Grace spread them out over the bed. She tucked the bottom in, then made a less than perfect corner and pushed the blanket under the sides.

"Think if I took out a quarter that it would bounce on that?" Carey asked.

"No, ma'am." *Who cares?*

Instructor Carey then gripped the top of the blanket and pulled the linens off again. "Now do it correctly."

"Yes, ma'am." *Bitch.* Grace jerked the blanket up from the floor.

"Ten hut!" The teen jumped to attention, the blanket still gripped in her hand. "You'd better learn to curb that smart-ass attitude of yours, and I mean right now!" she yelled into Grace's ear. "Do it right and you wouldn't have to do it again. Do you understand?"

"Yes, ma'am."

"I'm not sure you do, Waters. But you will. Now you drop and give me ten. Now!"

Grace hit the floor. *Fucking bitch.*

"Count out loud, Waters."

"One," *I hate you.*

"Two," *I hope you get hit by a bus...*

"Three,"...*and after they hit you...*

"Four,"...*they back up and ...*

"Five," ...*run over you again...*

"Six," *I hope I'm driving the bus.*

"Seven," *Why can't you leave me alone?*

"Eight," *Fucking bitch.*

"Nine," *Drop dead.*

"Ten, ma'am."

"Now get up and make that bunk properly," the instructor said.

"Yes, ma'am." Grace reached down and picked up the blanket again, this time making sure not to snatch the linens.

"All right, Alpha and Bravo Squads, fall in." Carey stood in front of the group of girls. "The four hours between barracks inspection and lunch are reserved for your physical and field training. On A schedule you'll have PT with me and on B with Instructor Gage. There is more to gain from PT than just sore muscles. You will gain confidence and a sense of accomplishment, both of which are sorely lacking in each and every one of you. How many of you think you can run five miles?" She paused and looked from girl to girl. "Don't all raise your hands up at once. You'll be doing five miles easy before you're through here." Grace rolled her eyes and put her hand on her hip. "Waters, you have a problem?"

Grace straightened up. "No, ma'am."

"Are you sure? You don't seem happy about the idea of PT."

"PT is fine, ma'am."

"Then it's the five-mile run that caused that little display of attitude?"

"No, ma'am."

"Then I have to assume your unspoken commentary was for no reason," Carey said calmly as she walked over to the teen's side. "So since you disrupted for no good reason, drop and give me ten pushups right now!"

Grace lowered herself to the ground.

"Do you like doing pushups?"

"No, ma'am."

"Then you like being yelled at," Carey said. "Is that it? Do you need to be yelled at?"

"No, ma'am."

"Are you sure?"

"Yes, ma'am."

"Then you better adjust that attitude of yours, and quick," Carey said. "Because I'm not going to put up with it. Do you understand?"

"Yes, ma'am."

"Seven, eight, nine, ten. Now get up and show some respect."

Grace stood up and straightened her cap. *Bitch.*

"All right, we're taking a nice easy one-mile run, girls. Start stretching."

Stretch this, Grace thought as she limbered up. As soon as the dark-haired woman's back was to her, the teen flipped her the middle finger.

"Man, she's got it in for you," Jan said in a low voice.

"She's a fucking bitch," Grace said. "I'll never make it through this dump if I have to put up with her."

"That's not chatter I hear, is it?" Instructor Carey said, causing all the whispering conversations to stop. "Must be done stretching then. All right, line up and get ready."

"Grace, sit here," Latisha said, moving over to make room on the bench. "Did you see the schedule for classes?"

"I saw it," Grace said as she swung her legs over the bench and sat down. "Any idea what PF stands for?"

"Not a clue, but Gage is teaching it," Latisha said. "I know SD is Self-Defense."

Grace rolled her eyes. "Great, Carey's teaching that one."

"Yeah, another excuse to beat up on us," Jan Bowen said. "Grenner said that Viking Donaldson told Delta Squad that SR is Sexual Responsibility."

"Oh no," Grace groaned. "Don't tell me they're going to do that whole 'be good girls and keep your legs closed' bullshit."

"Sounds like it," Jan said. "What's the matter, Waters? Your legs so far apart they're in different zip codes?" The table erupted in laughter.

21

"Fuck you," Grace said lightly, unaware of the dark-haired woman coming up behind her. "At least I don't go to the kennel looking for dates."

"Oh no, you didn't just say that," Latisha said.

"Bite me, Waters."

"Naw, I'm trying to cut down on fat," Grace said, drawing more laughter at their table for several seconds before it suddenly stopped and everyone looked at a spot just behind her. She rolled her eyes, knowing that once again she had been caught by the queen bitch.

Carey squatted down so she was eye level with them. "Do you ladies think you can find something more constructive to talk about?" she said, looking around the table and pausing when her eyes landed on Grace. "Unless you would rather write a nice long essay on how incredibly unladylike it is to imply that someone has sex with dogs."

Grace rolled her eyes. *Can't you find someone else to pick on?* When the instructor walked out of earshot, Grace saluted with her middle finger. "Aye aye, Captain Carey, ma'am," she said, drawing giggles from the girls at the table.

"She's just worried there won't be any Dobermans left for her," Jan added, causing even more laughter. She held her hands up like a begging dog. "Woof woof."

"Oh shit," Latisha said. "She's coming." The girls settled down and did their best to appear interested in their lunches when the instructor returned.

"Why is it that out of all the tables in here, this one is the loudest?" Carey said. "You girls must have too much pent-up energy. I'll tell Instructor Gage to work you a little harder tomorrow during PT."

"All right, settle down," Carey said as she closed the classroom door. "This is the infamous SR on the schedule. SR stands for Sexual Responsibility and for the next five months we will be studying just what that means, and what effect your sexual activity can have on your life." The dark-haired instructor sat on the desk. "Now this isn't high school and you certainly aren't a group of choir girls. I expect most, if not all, of you are no longer virgins. Put your hand down, Jones, I'm not asking if you are or aren't. Now, tell me what you think sexual responsibility means. Waters."

Oh sure, pick on me. "It means being responsible about sex, ma'am."

"Give me an example, Jones."

"Using a condom," Latisha said.

Carey slapped her hand on the desk and stood up. "Next to abstinence, a condom is the single most effective way to prevent both pregnancy and sexually transmitted diseases. Bowen, give me another example of being responsible about sex."

Jan smirked. "Making sure your parents aren't coming home soon, ma'am."

Carey gave her a mirthless smile that Grace recognized instantly. "Bowen, do you think this is funny?" the instructor said as she slowly made her way over to the girl's desk.

"No, ma'am."

"Well then why don't you take a minute and think of a better answer? Oh, and while you're thinking, drop and give me ten!" Carey's eyes turned and landed on Grace. "Waters, since you think you gave such a brilliant answer, why don't you give us another one while we're waiting for Bowen?"

Damn it, Jan; don't piss her off. "Not going someplace alone with someone you don't know, ma'am," Grace said.

"Good answer," Carey said. "Why?"

Great. Why didn't you move on to someone else? "Because something might happen that you don't want to happen, ma'am."

"Now, Bowen, see if you can condense Waters's long-winded answer into one word," Carey said. "What can happen?"

"Rape, ma'am."

"Nothing funny about that is there, Bowen?"

"No, ma'am."

"Rape is the number one violent crime committed against women," Carey said. "You will be taking self-defense class while you're here, but it's always best to avoid a situation rather than having to fight your way out of one."

Oh, spare us the lectures, Grace thought, slumping in her seat and resting her chin on her hand.

"Waters, when you're in my classroom you will sit up in your seat like a young lady," Carey said. "Now drop for ten. Hathaway, give another example of sexual responsibility."

While Mo, the youngest of the squad, gave her answer, Grace lowered herself to the floor and began her pushups. *You witch. You miserable rotten bully bitch from hell. Drop for ten. Drop for twenty. Why don't you drop for a while and see how it feels?* She continued to mentally curse out the instructor, forgetting to count at the same time.

"Waters."

"Yes, ma'am."

"Are you feeling guilty?"

Grace paused, arms fully extended, and looked questioningly at her. "Ma'am?"

"You've done fifteen pushups. I hate to tell you, but you can't bank them for credit later. Take your seat."

Ah damn. "Yes, ma'am."

"Just your luck you have mentoring with me right after SR," Carey said. "Sit down." The instructor tossed her cap on the hat rack and settled behind the desk. "I said sit." Grace rolled her eyes, then flopped into the chair. Carey jumped out of her seat. "Stand up! That is the last time you pull a stunt like that, do you understand?"

"Yes."

"Yes, what?"

The eyes rolled again. "Yes, Instructor Carey."

"You think people don't notice that little commentary you make with your eyes?" Carey said, sitting on the edge of the desk so she was eye level with Grace. "From now on, every time I see those eyes roll, you'll owe me twenty pushups." She walked behind the desk. "Now, sit down like a civilized young woman should." Grace sat down and watched as Carey opened a folder. "Quite a distinguished record for seventeen," she said, lifting the top page to see the continued list of offenses. "Vandalism, assaulting a teacher, assaulting other students, possession of marijuana, expelled from school." Carey closed the folder and looked at her. "You're on the fast track to the State Correctional Facility for Women," she said, tapping the folder.

Grace shrugged her shoulders. "Whatever."

Carey rose from her seat. "Drop and give me twenty!" Grace moved fast, hitting the floor as the instructor continued to yell at her. "Let's refresh your memory. You will answer and address me as Instructor Carey or ma'am." She knelt down next to Grace. "Do you understand this time?"

"Yes, ma'am."

"You will only speak when a question is asked, or if you have permission. Understand?"

"Yes, ma'am."

"Whether you like it or not, you will learn to respect authority," Carey said. "And for the next five months, each and every day, I am the authority! If I tell you to do something, you do it with no questions and no lip. Do you understand?"

"Yes...ma'am," Grace said, her arms screaming from the exertion.

"Your mouth shouldn't make promises your body can't deliver, Waters. Let's go, seven more." Carey returned to her seat and opened the folder again. "Interesting transcript from your high school. Seems like you went from an angel to the devil reincarnated in just one year. You threw a chair at a teacher?"

"Yes, ma'am."

"Why?"

"It...just happened, ma'am."

"Committing an act of violence against a teacher isn't something that just happens," Carey said. "I'll ask one more time. Why?"

"He pissed me off, ma'am," Grace said as she finished the final pushup.

"I piss you off too, don't I?"

Grace hesitated, then answered. "Yes, ma'am."

"Did you know Mr. Henderson sent a letter with your records?"

"No, ma'am."

Carey pulled out the handwritten note. "It seems he actually thinks very highly of you. At least he did when he had you for Earth Science during your freshman year. Says here that he thinks you're bright but you just don't apply yourself. In fact, he says he was telling you just that when you decided to throw the chair at him." She tossed the note back in the folder. "Nice way to treat someone who's trying to help you. You have anything to say about that?"

Grace stared at the faceted glass egg. "I don't care, ma'am."

"Well I have five months to make you care, Waters," Carey said. "And if I have to be a boil on your ass to make you care, I will. Trust me."

Grace walked down the hall of the administration building, running into Latisha just outside of Instructor Gage's classroom. "Hey."

"Hey, girlfriend. Where were you?"

Leaning against the wall, Grace turned her head and glared in the direction of Carey's office. "I had my mentoring session with Queen Bitch."

"Ooh, too bad," Latisha said. "I have Mitchell for mentoring. She's pretty cool."

"Lucky you," Grace said, pushing off the wall as others arrived for class. "Come on, we'd better not be late. I don't need Gage on my ass, too."

"Take a seat," Instructor Gage said. "This is Personal Finance. If you think this will be an easy class, you are sadly mistaken. You will learn about managing your income and expenses, how to plan for the future, financing and credit, and investing." Gage paced back and forth in front of the class. "Abusing credit is the easiest way to get yourself in trouble. Letting someone else use your credit is another. If someone asks you to put a bill in your name, get a cell phone for them, charge something on your credit with a promise to pay it back later, you run as fast as you can. Waters, how long does a negative mark stay on your credit report?"

"I don't know, ma'am."

"Seven years," Gage said. "Think about how long that is. Most of you were under the age of ten seven years ago. Can you imagine paying now for something that happened when you were ten? That's what a negative mark on your credit report is. Bankruptcy stays for ten. As juvenile offenders, your records are wiped clean at age eighteen. You get a fresh start, a new life. When you are irresponsible with your money and credit, there is no magic way to wipe the slate clean. Jones, if a bank approves you for a credit card, would you take it?"

"Yes, ma'am," Latisha said.

"You would." Gage turned and walked back to her desk. "I'm going to ask that question again in a week. We'll see if your answer changes."

"You have a class now?" Grace asked as they left the classroom.

"No, you?"

"No."

"Going to study hall?"

"It's either there or back to the barracks," Grace said. "Any idea who's in charge of that?"

Jan brushed up against her. "No one," she said. "No one knows if we're there, no one knows if we're not."

"No way," Grace said. "They must have hidden cameras or something. There's no way they trust us to just go in there and study."

Jan looked stricken. "You think?"

"I don't know," Latisha said. "But I'm not gonna take the chance."

"I'm with you," Grace said as they started walking down the hallway. "Carey's on my ass enough."

"She sure is," Jan said. "Guess you shouldn't have spit at that fat guard on the bus. Got you pegged from the start that way."

"It wouldn't have mattered," Grace said. "That bitch has it in for me." She touched her shorn locks. "Look what she did to my hair."

"I heard that short girl, Sally Dawson, had to be treated for lice," Latisha said.

"Damn, I'm glad her bunk is down at the other end of the barracks," Jan said.

"Really," Grace said. "She can keep her bugs to herself."

When they arrived at the classroom reserved for study hall, several other girls were already there. "Okay, Jan, what's your problem with math?" Grace asked as they claimed a table for themselves.

"Percentages and fractions suck," Jan said.

"Yeah, like your mother," one of the girls standing near the teacher's desk said.

"Fuck you, Grenner."

"Naw, I wouldn't wanna take that job from your daddy," Grenner said.

Jan jumped from her seat, shoving the larger girl against the desk. "You got a problem?"

"At least I know what a fraction is, stupid," Grenner said, looking to make sure her friends were standing behind her.

"Come on," Latisha said. "Let's go back to the barracks and study there."

"Stay out of it, vine head," Grenner said. "You too, Blondie."

"You got a fucking problem?" Grace said, moving to join Jan.

"I don't know where you little prissies came from, but if you want to stay in one piece, don't screw with me."

The door, which had been ajar, flew open and the doorway filled with the large blonde instructor. "Well, if it isn't a group of little girls trying to play king of the mountain," Instructor Donaldson said as she entered the room and stood between the two groups of girls. "Let me make it easy for you," she said, her eyes darting from girl to girl. "At Sapling Hill, the only kings of the mountain have the word Instructor before their names, got it?"

"Yes, ma'am," several girls said.

"What's that? Waters, I didn't see your lips move."

Grace rolled her eyes. "Yes, Instructor Donaldson, ma'am."

"You just don't know when to shut that smart mouth of yours up, do you? Waters, drop and give me ten pushups. Bowen, Jones, go sit down. Grenner, Dawson, find something to do before I find it for you."

"Yes, ma'am," Grenner said, giving Grace and Jan the evil eye before scooping up her books and moving to the far table. Everyone in the room knew it was not the end of the situation. The only question was when and where the next battle would be.

"All right, ladies, let's get lined up around the mat," Carey said as she moved to the center of the blue padding. "I'm here to teach you how to defend yourself against an attack. By the end of this series, you'll know exactly what to do to get away from an attacker. Now, since you get five minutes at each end of class to change, we're going to get right to business." She shook out her arms, then looked at Grace. "Waters, front and center."

"Yes, ma'am." *I'm dead.* Grace stepped into the middle, stopping two feet away from the taller woman. Carey walked behind her, then turned Grace to face the others. "When you attack your opponent, it's important to know if it's a man or a woman. On a man, there are four key areas, eyes, throat, groin, and knees. On a woman, it's eyes, throat, and knees. Insteps are also a good point of vulnerability, especially if you're being held from behind." A strong forearm wrapped around Grace's throat. "Waters, I'm a mugger. Give me your purse and you won't get hurt. What do you do?" Reaching up, Grace grabbed the muscular arm and did her best to dislodge it, her efforts completely ineffectual. "Now, if I had a weapon, you'd be very unhappy by now," Carey said. "The first thing you do is try and avoid the situation. If that's not possible, decide what's more important, a few dollars or your life. If they want the money, give them the money. Now Waters, I'm a mugger. Give me your purse and you won't get hurt. What do you do?"

"Give you my purse, ma'am," Grace said, wishing the instructor would let go of her and pick on someone else.

"Now I'm not a mugger but a rapist. I don't care about money. What do you do?"

"I try to get away, ma'am," Grace said, the arm around her neck tightening and her body pressed against the solid woman behind her.

"Think you can get away from me?"

"No, ma'am," Grace said, feeling the pressure ease, as the instructor pulled away from her.

"Sit down, Waters. When you are faced with a situation where you are in danger, the ultimate goal is to survive," Carey said. "If the opportunity is there to escape, by all means do it, but if it isn't, or a weapon is involved, your life comes first."

"So we should just lie there and get raped?" Jan asked.

"That's a choice only you can make," Carey said. "But if the choice comes down to being raped or being killed, I choose life. Now, knowing some self-defense moves can help."

"So's carrying Mace," Grace said in a low voice.

"What was that, Waters?"

Shit. "I was just saying that Mace is good for defense, ma'am."

"You think so?" Carey smiled knowingly. "Waters, stand up."

Damn. Grace stood up and moved to the center of the mat while the instructor walked over to a supply locker and opened it, removing a small canister. *Great, what's she gonna do? Mace me?*

"Any weapon, whether it's Mace, a gun or anything in between, can be turned against you." She tossed the canister to Grace. "It's empty," she said. "But it will work for our purposes. Waters, now you have a can of Mace. What are you going to do?"

Why me? "I would spray it in the attacker's face, ma'am."

"And what if it's windy? Or the attacker is right on top of you? Mace won't work then."

"I'll spray him before he gets too close, ma'am," Grace said.

"All right, we'll see," Carey said. "Waters, I'm a mugger."

Grace gripped the canister, ready to spin and aim it at the older woman's face, but when she raised her arm, it was caught in a firm grip and the teen found herself flat on her back. "Oof."

"Now I have a weapon to use against you," Carey said, holding up the canister that had fallen out of Grace's hand upon impact with the mat. "And now Mr. Mugger is mad. Still think Mace is the answer, Waters?"

"No, ma'am," she said, looking up at the imposing woman.

"Get the idea, Waters?"

"Yes, ma'am."

Instructor Carey stood up and addressed the class. "A weapon is only good if you are the one in control. Why bring something into the situation that could be used against you? Waters, go sit down."

That's it, I'm not saying another word unless Queen Bitch calls on me.

"Any idea what kind of meat this is?" Grace asked, pointing at the oval patty.

"Mystery meat," Jan said, stabbing hers with her fork. "Processed, formed, nutritionally sound, tasteless mystery meat."

"Wonderful," Grace said, glancing around to make sure no instructors were within earshot. "It'll go good with the instant potato flakes and lima beans."

"I think they have someone who knows what kind of food we like and makes sure they never serve them," Latisha said, adding a copious amount of salt to her food. "We can't even get salsa around here."

"I'd kill for a taco day," Grace said, sniffing the unidentifiable meat before taking a bite. "Or ice cream."

"How about soda?" Jan added. "I'm getting tired of milk, juice, and water. And that excuse for coffee they serve is undrinkable."

"Really," Grace said, burying the piece of meat in her mashed potatoes. "Someone should tell those idiots in the kitchen not to use the dishwater to make coffee." Seeing activity at the table where Alpha Squad was sitting, she nudged Jan with her elbow. "What's going on?"

"I don't know, but there's Scary Carey," Jan said.

"Uh-oh," Latisha said. "She looks pissed."

"At least it's not at us this time," Grace said. "Look, she's talking to Grenner."

"More like she's yelling at Grenner," Jan said. "Yup, there she goes. Ten or twenty?"

"I know that look," Grace said. "Twenty." She winced when she saw Instructor Carey kneel down to continue her tirade as Grenner did her pushups. "She's really pissed."

"Word," Latisha said. "Ooh, Scary's turning red."

"Do you girls have nothing better to do?" Instructor Gage asked. The teens quickly turned in their seats and looked down at their trays. "That's what I thought."

Grace waited until Gage was out of range. "Damn," she said. "We always get caught."

"At least it wasn't for whatever Grenner did," Jan said. "Look, she's still yelling at her."

"Hey, Grace," Campbell said. "I didn't think it was possible for someone to piss off Carey more than you do."

Grace gave a false smile and scratched her cheek with her middle finger. "I've seen her drop you a few times."

"Yeah, but you hold the record."

"I want to know what she did so I don't do it," Jan said. "Look, she's finished."

"Doing pushups," Grace said. "Queen Bitch is still yelling at her." She took a bite of her food, watching the dark-haired instructor finish her tirade. Just watching those pushups had made her arms ache. *I'm glad it's not me this time.*

Grace groaned and sat up, the light coming through from the sodium lamp outside providing little illumination.

"Psst, you up?" Latisha whispered.

"We're all up," Mo said from the bunk on the other side of Grace. "How can you sleep through all that?" Loud snoring was heard from the other end of the barracks. "Sounds like a damn bulldozer."

"I'm up, Latisha," Grace said, pushing off the blanket. "Every time I start to fall asleep, Godzilla over there starts up again."

"Esa muchacha le van a poner una almohada sobre la cara si no para."

"Lopez, you know we don't speak Spanish," Grace said.

"I say that girl is going to get a pillow over her face if she doesn't stop," Maribel Lopez said, moving from her bunk to flop across Grace's.

"I'll help," Jan said, joining the crowd and sitting on the edge of Latisha's bunk. "I woke her up twice to tell her to knock it off."

"Which one is it?" Grace asked, propping her pillow against the wall to use as a backrest.

"Campbell," Jan said. "Grenner's not too far behind either."

"Be quiet," a voice in the darkness said. "Some people are trying to sleep."

"How is it you can sleep through Campbell's snoring, but our talking is too much?" Jan said. "Shut up and roll over, Rosetti."

"Dammit, there's no way I can handle tomorrow with no sleep," Grace said. "Campbell! Shut the hell up!"

"Wha—what?" Campbell said, her voice thick with sleep.

"Your snoring is enough to wake the fucking dead," Jan said.

"Shut up, Bowen."

"Piss up a rope, Rosetti."

Grace slammed her head into the pillow and rolled her eyes as the bickering continued. "We're never going to get any sleep." The springs squeaked as Jan joined Mo and her on the bunk.

"I snuck a deck of cards back from the rec room," Jan said.

"And just how are we supposed to see them?" Mo asked. "It's not like we can turn on a light."

"Word," Latisha said. "Viking or Short Shit would be on us faster than ugly on Dawson."

"You'd better have those cards back before they do inspection tomorrow," Grace said. "Queen Bitch will drop your ass."

"You mean Scary?" Jan snorted. "I've handled worse than her. A few pushups ain't gonna make me change and be a choir girl."

31

DAY THREE

"Stop hogging the mirror, Waters."

"Bite me, Rosetti," Grace said, checking her appearance and adjusting her collar. "I'll be damned if I'm going to do any more pushups today."

"Just our luck she's in charge of Bravo Squad," Latisha said, tucking her shirt into her pants. "I'd rather have Donaldson than Scary Carey. Grace, how do I look?"

"Like a Hershey Kiss reject," Grace said, moving away from the mirror. "But you shouldn't get any hits."

"Don't worry," Jan said. "Scary will find something, she always does."

Someone outside yelled for formation. "More fun at Sapling Hill," Grace deadpanned. "Time to face the queen bitch."

The noon sun was bright, forcing Grace to squint as the instructors moved through the rows. Suddenly the sun was gone, eclipsed by her nemesis. "Think that bunk of yours will pass today, Waters?"

"Yes, ma'am," she said, seeing a distorted image of herself in Carey's mirrored sunglasses.

"We'll see," Carey said. Grace waited endless seconds before the instructor moved on. "Waters, no hits."

"All right, ladies, we're going to take a little run today," Instructor Gage said. Groans went up within the crowd. "What's that? You want two miles instead of one?" Grace rolled her eyes, unaware that the ones hidden behind mirrored sunglasses were watching her.

"Waters, drop for twenty!" Instructor Carey said as she came storming over. "You have a problem, Waters?"

"No, ma'am," Grace said, unhappily noting the instructor she despised was now only inches from her, black boots shining from the early morning sun. The temptation was there to spit and ruin that perfect shine but Grace knew the consequences would be most unfortunate for her.

"I'm tired of you interrupting formation," Carey said. "Now what's your problem?"

"Didn't get...any sleep last night, ma'am. Campbell wouldn't stop snoring."

"And you don't think it's fair that we're going to make you run and do all the other things scheduled for today because you didn't get your beauty rest, is that it? Do you think Mr. Employer is going to care that you didn't get a good night's sleep?"

"No, ma'am."

"Getting your sleep interrupted is a fact of life, Waters," Carey said. "We all have to do things we don't want to do, including going to work after a rough night." The boots moved out of Grace's vision. "And for those of you that are keeping your bunkmates up, I suggest you report to the infirmary for those nose strips before someone decides to give you a pillow party."

Grace stood up, wiping the small stones from her hands as the instructors began inspecting their squads. Straightening her shirt, Grace looked forward as Instructor Carey came into view. *Just keep walking, bitch. My shirt is ironed, my belt is straight. There's nothing you can give me a hit for.*

"Waters, two hits. Crooked hat, laces touching the ground."

"Pick up a workbook and take a seat, I don't care where," Instructor Donaldson said as they entered the room. Grace took one of the soft-cover books and headed for the back corner of the room, the place where she was least likely to draw attention. "We're starting with Chapter One," the tall blonde instructor said. "If this part seems easy or familiar to you, keep working ahead. If it seems too hard, you might want to think about going to the remedial math class, but your tests scores all indicate you should be able to handle this level of math. Here are the rules. You will have homework, every night. I expect that homework to be done. No excuses, no exemptions."

While the instructor they called Viking was talking, Grace opened the workbook and looked at the problems. *Oh please. I knew this stuff in ninth grade.* She began filling in the answers, finishing the chapter in just a few minutes. Out of boredom, she started working on Chapter Two when she heard her name called. "Yes, ma'am?"

"What's an integer?"

"Any whole number, ma'am."

"Can a fraction be an integer?"

"No, ma'am."

"Can negative seven be an integer?"

"Yes, ma'am." *Oh please move on to someone else.*

"Very good. I see you paid attention in at least one of your classes." Instructor Donaldson turned her attention to Latisha, allowing Grace to go back to filling in answers in the workbook.

"Sit down," Carey said as Grace entered the room. "I read your essay. The only thing you want to get out of this experience is to do your time so you can get back to...let's see..." She looked down at the paper. "Oh yes, running your life. You think you've been doing a pretty good job so far?"

"When I'm left alone, yes, ma'am."

"Really?" Carey leaned back in her chair and laced her fingers together. "How much money do you have in the bank?"

Grace shook her head. "None, ma'am."

"Own any real estate?"

"No, ma'am."

"Extremely rich relatives to which you are sole heir?"

"No, ma'am."

Carey's eyes burned into Grace. "You're giving me a great deal of no's. Tomorrow I want you to tell me the positives. What you have managed to accomplish."

"Yes, ma'am."

"What do you want out of life, Waters?"

Grace focused on the crystal egg sitting in the front center of the instructor's desk. "To be left alone, ma'am."

"And how do you plan on accomplishing that?"

Grace shrugged. "Once I'm out of here, I'll get a place of my own and do what I want."

"You'll need a job to pay for it," Carey said. "That means you'll be working for someone else. Not going to be left alone that way."

"I'll start my own business so I don't have to answer to anyone else, ma'am."

Carey leaned back in her seat. "You think that's so, hmm?"

"Yes, ma'am."

"You'll have customers to answer to, suppliers, employees, bankers, the list goes on and on."

"I'll figure something out, ma'am."

"Until you do, get used to answering to other people," Carey said. "You were a peer tutor?"

"Yes, ma'am," Grace said, surprised by the change in subject.

"Two years," Carey said. "You didn't sign up for it when you became a junior, why?"

Grace paused, thinking through her answer before speaking. "I didn't feel like it, ma'am."

"You didn't feel like attending class or doing homework either," Carey said. "Started skipping classes the first week."

What? Do you have a day-by-day report of my life? "Yes, ma'am."

"You missed two days as a freshman and none as a sophomore. See a pattern here?"

Still staring at the egg, Grace shrugged. "I was sick, ma'am."

"I doubt that," Carey said. "So what happened between tenth and eleventh grade?"

"Nothing. I just decided I didn't like school anymore, ma'am."

"Look at me," Carey said. "I have a feeling school had little or nothing to do with it. I took a closer look at your grades. You aced almost every test but never turned in homework and skipped classes, that's why you failed so many courses." The instructor let out a breath and reached for paper and a pen. "All right, we'll do it this way. Since you can't come up with any productive goals, we'll come up with some together. Goal number one."

Oh great, Grace thought to herself. *Why didn't I just put some bullshit on that paper instead?* "To do better in school, ma'am," she said.

"Let's be a bit more specific," Carey said. "You'll get your GED."

"What?" she yelped.

"You heard me," Carey said. "And you owe me ten. Try again. Goal number one?"

"To get my GED, ma'am," she said, looking down at the egg again. *Fuck. I can't believe I did that. Ten pushups for forgetting ma'am.*

"Goal number two?"

Grace thought about it but came up with nothing. "I don't know, ma'am."

"Forget about academics. Your mouth and your attitude get you in trouble, so goal number two will be to learn how to deal with situations in an appropriate manner. By the way, sixth period on your B schedule will be Anger Management."

"I don't need anger management, ma'am."

"Oh yes you do," Carey said. "You're looking at me right now like you'd like to come over this desk at me and you're going to say you don't need Anger Management?"

"I just need to be left alone, ma'am."

"Which isn't going to happen, so you'd better learn to deal with it," Carey said. "Sit up. Are you going to slouch in your boss's office?"

"No, ma'am," Grace said as she straightened up.

"Then don't think of doing it here."

Grace put her face under the stream, rinsing off the dirt of the day. "I'm telling ya, Jan. If Campbell and Grenner didn't go get those nose things, I'm going to kill them myself."

"I'll help," Jan said, soaping her upper body. "You didn't grab your razor."

"Naw," Grace said. "My hair doesn't grow that fast. I won't need to shave my pits for a few days."

"Speaking of shaving, did you see Rosetti?"

Hitting the shampoo dispenser, Grace pushed a healthy amount onto her hand. "No. What about her?"

"She's bald down there. Shaves it all off."

"Why bother?" Grace asked.

"Maybe she doesn't like getting her hand covered with short and curlies," Jan said.

"Hey, girls."

"Hey, Latisha," Grace said as the younger teen stepped up to the shower next to her.

"What's up?"

"Nothing," Jan said. "Just talking about Rosetti and her bald spot."

"I shaved there once," Latisha said. "Itched like hell when it grew back in."

Grace looked at the area in question. "You've got the Black Forest going on there. What'd you use, a lawn mower?" Jan laughed while Latisha flipped her the middle finger. "Just kidding," she said, putting her soapy head under the water. The chatter died down as others entered and the sound of running water increased. *Make sure no one notices,* she thought as she covertly stole glances of the other girls, making them brief and infrequent for fear her guilty pleasure would be discovered. Ever since she'd found a magazine left around by one of her mother's boyfriends, Grace had found breasts fascinating. Of course, it was not something she would ever admit to anyone else, nor would she ever speak of just how good a shower felt on her nipples. Adjusting her position, Grace closed her eyes and enjoyed the sensation of the pelting water. *Maybe I can sneak into the bathroom for a little while,* she thought, rinsing the rest of the soap from her body before she became too aroused. She would have wished for more time but Jan and Latisha shut off their showers within seconds of each other, forcing her to reluctantly do the same.

DAY FOUR

Instructor Carey blew the whistle. "All right, enough chatter. Hathaway, you know the shirts get tucked into the shorts." She held the basketball up. "Obviously you know what we're going to be doing. The focus here will be on teamwork, not trying out for the WNBA. No Harlem Globetrotter bullshit, no hanging from the hoop." She walked to the center of the basketball court. "Five girls from each squad. Let's go." She held the ball in one hand and the whistle in the other. "All right, play nice, play fair and have fun." The two squads moved into position on the court or on the benches. "Ready?"

Grace won the tip-off and the game was on. A quick pass from Jan to Campbell resulted in the first basket, but was answered quickly by a three-point shot by Lauren Grenner for Alpha Squad. Carey ignored the street talk between the two teams as the lead went back and forth with Grace and Jan scoring the most points. Unfortunately, ignoring the talk also meant she missed the comment Grenner made when she blocked Grace's shot and sent the ball down court for Rosetti to make the basket. She did notice when guarding became nudging and was just about to intervene when an elbow flew.

"Foul on Grenner," Carey said.

"I didn't do nothing," the heavyset redhead protested.

"All right, that's it," Carey said. "Grenner, drop for twenty. Jones, go get the ball."

"It was an accident, ma'am," Grenner said as she lowered herself to the ground.

"Bullshit," Grace said, rubbing her jaw.

"Waters!" Carey said, glaring at the blonde teen. "I don't need your help. Grenner, that was no accident. You owe me a two-page report on sportsmanship and fair play."

"Yes, ma'am."

"Waters, if I thought washing your mouth out with soap would help, I'd need a bar the size of Kansas. Do you think civilized young women swear like that?"

Grace rolled her eyes, knowing she was about to get a lecture. "No, ma'am."

"Drop for twenty!" Carey shouted. "I've warned you before about that stunt with your eyes." She knelt down next to the teen. "You will break that habit, do you understand?"

"Yes, ma'am."

"Do you?"

"Yes, ma'am!"

"Grenner, you need to learn to keep your hands to yourself."

"Yes, ma'am."

"You two better get over this, and quick, or you'll be very unhappy little girls. Do you understand?"

"Yes, ma'am," they said in unison.

"Let's go Waters, you're holding up PT," Carey said as Grace continued to do pushups. "Now," she said when the teen finished and stood up. "Take your free throws. Grenner, I'm not going to warn you again."

ONE WEEK

Grace set her tray down on the table, then lifted her legs over the long bench and sat down. "Z-burgers again," she said, looking at the cheeseburger on her tray.

The dark-skinned girl sitting next to her chuckled. "Damn straight. I know I'm going to fall asleep in class again."

Grace smiled. "I hear you, Latisha. It doesn't help we have the most boring class right after lunch."

"Better than PT," Latisha said, popping a lukewarm French fry into her mouth.

"I don't know," Grace said. "I'm not happy about running three miles right after breakfast." As she lifted the cheeseburger to take a bite, a sharp elbow caught her in the back of the head.

"Sorry, accident," Grenner said, though the girl with her began giggling.

"Bullshit," Grace said, rising to her feet and turning to face the bully. "What's your problem, Grenner?"

"Sit down, Waters," the redhead said. "'Fore you get your ass kicked all over the floor."

"It was a basketball game, Grenner. It's not my fault you suck." The normal din of chatter stopped, replaced by the sound of the nearby girls moving their trays away.

"Is there a problem here?" Instructor Gage said, setting her hands on her hips. "Grenner and Dawson, go find a place to sit. Waters, sit down. Since you two seem to have so much energy, you can do trash detail today." Grace exchanged an angry glare with the heavyset redhead and her shorter sidekick before sitting back down on the bench.

Grace kept a wary eye on Grenner and her friends as everyone readied for bed. She exchanged a concerned look with Latisha. "Trouble," she whispered. As expected, the redhead walked down the aisle, stopping in front of Grace's bunk.

"Bitch," the redhead said. "You're lucky Gage was there."

"Go away," Grace said. "I'm not getting in any more trouble because of you."

"Oh you've got trouble, Waters," Grenner said.

"Ten hut!" Instructor Gage shouted from the doorway, causing the girls to scatter back to the foot of their own bunks. The diminutive black woman strolled down the aisle, stopping in front of Grenner. "You just don't learn, do you?"

"I wasn't doing nothing, ma'am," Grenner said.

"Obviously you must have been sleeping during English class," Gage said. "You can write a report for me on double negatives."

"Yes, ma'am."

"What were you doing by Waters's bunk?"

"Nothing, ma'am," Grenner said. "Just talking, ma'am."

"Drop and give me twenty," Gage said. "I don't tolerate lying."

Grace swallowed, knowing she was next. She contemplated what to say when it was her turn. Tell the truth and make the situation worse or lie and hope things would calm down. When the instructor stopped in front of her, Grace made her decision.

"What was Grenner doing by your bunk?" Gage asked.

"Talking, ma'am," Grace said.

"Talking about what?"

"Nothing important, ma'am."

Gage tapped her booted foot on the concrete floor. "I didn't ask you if you thought it was important or not, Waters. What did she say to you?"

"I don't remember, ma'am," Grace said, knowing Gage knew it was a lie.

"Drop," Gage said. "I'll let you know when to stop."

Grace dropped to the floor. "Yes, ma'am."

"Jeez, Gage is in a mood this morning, isn't she?" Jan said as she arrived at the table and sat down next to Grace.

"I think she sleeps on a bed of nails," Grace said. "Either that or she's not getting any."

"Well, look at her," Jan said, smothering her waffles with syrup. "Who would fuck her?"

"Donaldson," Rosetti chimed in. "That Viking looks like a great big dyke."

"Yeah," Jan said. "Or Scary. She probably can't get any either." She brushed her shoulder against Grace's. "You gonna eat that?"

Grace stabbed one of her waffles with her fork and put it on Jan's plate. "I don't know how you can eat so many of them," she said. "Tastes like cardboard to me."

"Anything tastes good if you put enough syrup on it," Jan said, grinning before she shoved a piece of waffle into her mouth. "You sfill gomma help me wiff mulpfying factions, wight?"

"Yeah, study hall before math," Grace said, reaching for her lukewarm coffee. "You've got the homework done, right?"

"Mose of ip." Jan drained her milk carton. "I didn't get the last ten or so."

"No prob. We'll get them done before you have to go to Mitchell's class," Grace said, bringing her carton to her lips. A hard bump from behind sent milk over her face and down her shirt.

"What the..." She knew from the giggling who it was before she turned. "What's your problem, Dawson?" she said, seeing Lauren Grenner standing next to the smaller girl.

"It was an accident," Sally said, her smirk telling a different story.

Grace jumped to her feet. "Bullshit."

"Goon Squad," Jan warned.

"What's going on?" Instructor Gage asked as she crossed the room.

"Dawson hit my chair," Grace said.

"It was an accident," Sally said.

"It was, I saw it," Grenner said.

"You two have no business being near Bravo table," Gage said. "Put your trays down and both of you drop for ten. Waters, are you done eating?"

"Yes, ma'am."

"Then go get changed and you can spend your study period writing a paper about the proper way to deal with a confrontation."

Grace glared at Sally and Grenner as they did their pushups. "Yes, ma'am."

ONE MONTH

"It's too fucking hot for PT," Jan said.

"They're trying to kill us," Grace said. "Two miles a day is too much. Here they come." The girls snapped to attention as the instructors entered the formation area, having changed into the PT shorts and shirts.

"Ten hut," Instructor Gage said. "It's really hot today, isn't it?"

"Yes, ma'am," a chorus of voices rang out.

"I bet you'd love it if we didn't run two miles today."

"Yes, ma'am."

"Good. Because we're not running two miles, we're doing three. Now spread out and start stretching."

"I told you so," Grace whispered to Jan.

"Damn bitches," Jan whispered back.

"Of course they can run it with no problem, they've been doing it for years probably," Grace said. "Four weeks and they're kicking us up to three miles."

"Goon Squad loves to stick it to us," Jan said. "It's in their job description to be assholes."

"Cut the chatter," Instructor Carey said. "Unless you'd rather have four?"

"No, ma'am," the group said quickly.

"All right then. Everyone ready? Let's go."

Once on the trail, the girls found some relief from the beating sun thanks to the trees and the shade they provided. Still, the extra mile took its toll, slowing even the fastest girls down. Grace found herself doing barely more than a slow jog during the last half-mile. "Come on, Waters, pick it up," Instructor Carey's voice came from somewhere behind her. "You'll be glad you did when you get over that hill."

"Yes, ma'am," she said, willing her legs to keep moving. *Why? Am I going to drop dead of a heart attack when I get there?* The hill seemed insurmountable and her pace slowed to a walk.

"Move it, Waters."

"Yes, ma'am." *Just a few more feet. A little more. Then I can rest.* Step by step she made it to the crest of the hill, convinced she wanted nothing more to do than collapse on the grass past the finish line.

Convinced, that is, until she saw what lay just beyond, a crystal clear lake as blue as the sky.

"Let's go, girls," Instructor Donaldson said from her perch sitting against a shady tree. "Jump in, the water's fine."

"All right," Jan said as she reached the top of the hill. "Hey, there's a lake up here."

Grace heard the shouts of those behind her as she dropped to the ground and whipped off her sneakers and socks. "Jan, hurry up," she said, stuffing the socks into the sneakers.

"I'm hurrying," Jan said, flopping to the ground next to her. "Keeping your shirt on?"

Grace nodded, standing up and wiping the sand off her shorts. "I'm not getting sunburned."

Jan's blue shirt came off. "I don't care," she said. "Let's go."

Within minutes Sapling Hill Lake filled with screaming teens. The girls took turns splashing and dunking each other, Grace giving as good as she got. She looked up just in time to see Instructor Carey swing from a rope connected to an overhanging limb, tucking into a ball and crashing into the water with a great splash. Several girls squealed at the new toy and began scrambling for the bank. Grace swam to the inlet away from the others, able to watch the action without being in the way. *Oh no,* she thought when she saw Instructor Carey coming toward her.

"So," the dark-haired woman said, treading water just a few feet from her. "Was it worth the extra mile?"

"Yes, ma'am," Grace said, tapping the bottom of the sandy lake with her tiptoe to keep her head above water.

"Why aren't you running up to use the rope like everyone else?"

Think fast. "Um...it's nice and shady here, ma'am."

"Don't think you're going to hide here all day," the instructor said. "I'd better see you moving around and participating."

"Yes, ma'am," Grace said, consciously not rolling her eyes. *As long as I don't have to go near that rope.*

"Enjoy it while you can, this won't be a daily event."

"Yes, ma'am," Grace said before the dark-haired woman pivoted and swam away. Dunking underwater to cool off, she swam over to where several other girls were tossing around a volleyball.

"Grace, over here on our team," Latisha called, waving her arm and like most of the dark-skinned girls, covered on top with only her sport bra. "Beyond Chambers is a goal for us and beyond Jennings is goal for them. Got it?"

"Naw," Grace said. "I'll watch for now." She waded over to a rock that jutted up from the water and climbed on it. From her vantage she could watch the game and still see the girls using the rope. She enjoyed the view for several minutes before sensing someone watching her.

Looking around, she came eye to eye with Instructor Carey, who was treading water out in the deeper section of the lake. *Better start moving before she decides to move me,* Grace thought as she pushed off into the water and started swimming around. She did not get far before the dark-haired woman reached her.

"You're a little fair skinned to be lying around soaking up the sun, aren't you?"

"Yes, ma'am," Grace said, letting her toes sink into the soft lake bottom. Instructor Carey stood as well, the difference in height causing the water to stop mid-torso on her.

"I'd prefer to see you in the water," the older woman said, apparently unaware of the way the wet shirt clung to her. "It's easy to lose track of time and get a nasty sunburn on a day like this."

"Yes, ma'am," Grace said, forcing herself to look up at the instructor's face and not where her eyes wanted to focus.

"You haven't been on the swing yet."

"No, ma'am."

"Any reason why not?"

"I was watching the volleyball game, ma'am."

"You should try it."

"Maybe later, ma'am," Grace said, looking away to the lake before her eyes betrayed her, but making sure to catch a quick glance in the process. "I think I'll swim around for a while."

"We'll be spending the rest of PT here," the instructor said, causing Grace to smile. "Try to spend as much of it in the water as you can. I'm already seeing some pink on your cheeks."

Grace knew the color was not from the sun. "Yes, ma'am," she said, looking back to the dark-haired woman and waiting expectantly for her to say something. To her surprise, Instructor Carey smacked the water, sending it splashing at her.

"Just cooling you off, Waters."

Grace reacted quickly, slapping at the water and trying to dart out of the way. "Self-defense, ma'am," she said, using her arm to send up a large amount of water before slipping beneath the surface to avoid the endless deluge aimed at her. She came back up with her hands held up. "I surrender, ma'am," she said, closing her eyes as a few more slaps of water came her way.

"I knew there had to be a way to get a smile on that face," Carey said. "It doesn't have to be gloom and doom all the time. Go play."

"Yes, ma'am." The teen turned and headed toward the volleyball game, stopping after several yards to see where the other woman had gone. *It's a shame you're such a bitch,* she thought, watching Carey leave the water and take the path leading to the rope. *Otherwise you wouldn't be so bad to look at.*

SIX WEEKS

"All right, girls, settle down," Instructor Carey said. "Bravo Squad, it seems that Alpha Squad thinks they can beat you. Can they?"

"No, ma'am," the squad said in unison.

"And Bravo Squad is going to show that we know the meaning of good sportsmanship and fair play?"

"Yes, ma'am!"

"Jan, you're captain. Pick your starting lineup."

The game started off peacefully enough, Bravo Squad taking the early lead and steadily widening the gap as Grace, Jan, and Latisha combined for most of the baskets. When Alpha Squad called a time out, Bravo huddled together near their bench.

"Lauren's getting too many shots off," Jan said. "Grace, you and I are going to double-team her, keep her covered so they're forced to pass to Dawson. She can't handle the ball worth shit. Mo, you keep her covered."

"Now wait a minute," Mo said, pushing her glasses up on her nose. "Are you trying to say that I suck as a guard so I have to cover the worst player they have?"

"You're faster than Dawson," Grace said. "You'll be able to keep her covered best." She held her hand out. "Bravo ready?"

"Let's go, Bravo!" they shouted in unison, knowing from the look on Alpha Squad's faces that it annoyed them. As soon as the whistle blew, Grace and Jan moved to cover the best player on the Alpha Squad. Where she went, they went, isolating her from the rest of the team. A slap by Mo knocked the ball out of Alpha's control, allowing Latisha to get it and lay it up for two more points on Bravo's side.

"Lay off, Waters."

"Just playing the game, Grenner," Grace said. "Get over it."

"Just back off. You too, Bowen."

"Tell someone who cares, Lauren," Jan said. "Stop whining."

"You'll be the one whining when I kick your ass all over this court," Grenner said.

"You and what army, fat ass?" Jan said.

"If Scary wasn't around..."

"You'd be running like a chicken," Grace said, shifting to block Grenner from being able to accept a pass from Dawson. Together with Jan, she kept the heavyset redhead from getting the ball, allowing Bravo to lengthen their lead. When the ball went out near the Bravo basket, Grace stepped offside and readied herself to do something she had seen once at a college tournament. Grenner had her back to her, expecting Grace to pass the ball to Jan or Mo, but instead she aimed for the heavyset bully's back, then stepped into the court and caught the rebound, turning and sending up a shot that was nothing but net. "Yeah!"

"That's not fair," Grenner said, giving her a shove.

"Stop whining, crybaby," Grace said as they readied for Dawson to throw the ball in. A steal by Mo caused everyone to change direction and head down court, but when Grace came to a halt, Grenner did not, tripping over the blonde's outstretched leg and slamming onto the asphalt.

"You fucking bitch," Grenner said, lunging at Grace and knocking her to the ground. The whistle blew loudly as Instructor Carey came running over.

"Grenner you drop for twenty, then sit on the bench. Waters, are you all right?"

Grace rubbed her elbow and glared at Grenner. "Yes, ma'am."

"This isn't some corner lot, Waters. Wipe that look off your face or you can sit on the bench. We don't play street-fighting basketball here."

"Yes, ma'am." She looked at her elbow, deciding that while the skin was scraped it was not bad enough to require a bandage. She caught Grenner's eye and smirked. *Serves you right, you stupid bitch. It's just a damn basketball game.*

"You sure no one's coming?" Grenner said.

"Clear," Dawson answered, running back from the double doors.

"Okay, help me with this," Grenner said, bracing herself against the side of her stand-up locker. "I'll tip, you reach in and grab it."

"Don't drop it on me, Lauren."

"Shut the hell up, Sally. I'm not going to drop it. Just be ready. This thing's heavy," Grenner said. "On three. One, two, three." She pushed on the locker, tipping it up just enough for Dawson's hand to slip underneath and pull out the sharpened butter knife that had been hidden there. "Okay, I'm dropping it."

"Okay," Dawson said. Grenner dropped the locker, then took the knife.

"Go watch the window," Grenner said.

"You'd better be quick, Lauren," Dawson said. "I don't want to get caught."

"Shut up and watch the window," Grenner said, heading for Jan's bunk. "I'll teach those bitches to fuck with me." The first stab was at Jan's pillow. "How do you like this?" Crude but effective, the sharpened knife cut through the bedding and eventually the mattress, Grenner laughing as the linens were reduced to ribbons. After finishing with Jan's bunk, she turned her attention to Grace's. "Trip me, will you? Make me look stupid in front of everyone? Think you can hit me with the ball and get away with it?" She laughed maniacally as she turned the bedding into shreds. "Laugh at me and get away with it, huh?"

"Someone's coming," Sally warned.

"Shit." Grenner hid the knife in her pants. "Come on," she said, heading for the far door. "We'll hide it in the woods and go back for it later."

"I'm telling you, she slammed me on the mat."

"She did not, Jan," Grace said, reaching for the door. "She put her leg out and you tripped backwards."

"Yeah," Latisha said. "It's not Scary's fault your weight makes you fall harder."

"Come over here and say that, Short Shit," Jan said, juggling her books to free up a hand to take the door. "At least I knew what a simile was."

"But you didn't know what a homonym was," Grace said, opening the door wide enough for Jan to catch, then stepped inside. "Gage loved 'the opposite of homyn-her' though. What the hell?"

"What?" Jan said, bumping into Grace's back. "Oh shit."

"Ooh," Latisha said, drawing the word out. "Someone messed up your cribs bad."

The girls walked to their respective bunks. "Look at this," Grace said, holding up the tattered remains of her blanket.

"How the hell am I supposed to sleep on this?" Jan said, pulling the shredded linens back to reveal the mattress beneath. "Half the stuffing's out of it."

"Same here," Grace said, still stunned by the damage. "Anyone else's bunk hit?"

"No," Latisha said, returning from the far end of the barracks.

"You think it was Lauren?" Grace asked, dropping her ruined pillow.

"I don't know, but whoever it was, I'm going to kick her ass," Jan said, kicking the end of her bunk.

"What happened?" Grenner said as she and Dawson entered the barracks, followed by the rest of Alpha Squad.

Grace caught a glint in Grenner's eyes and knew that her guess was correct. "Like you don't know," she said.

"What makes you think I had anything to do with it?" Grenner said, walking past to reach her own bunk.

"Yeah, I wonder," Grace said as the door opened and more girls arrived. "It's not our fault you suck at basketball."

"You'd better watch what you say," Grenner said, throwing her books on her bunk. "I'll kick your ass."

"Fuck off," Grace said, readying herself for a fight. "I'm not afraid of you."

"I'm gonna jump you so hard your momma's going to feel it," Grenner said.

"Go ahead and try," Grace said, stepping away from her bunk and into the aisle. "Or do you want me to wait while you find your knife? Better yet, since you're too much of a frigging coward to fight someone face to face, why don't I turn around?"

"That's the only way your momma got anyone to fuck her," Grenner taunted.

"Uh-oh," Latisha said, moving away from the two of them. "You shouldn't talk about someone's momma like that."

"Stay out of this, you black bitch," Grenner said as she approached, Dawson right behind her.

"You got something to say, Dawson?" Jan said as she reached Grace's side. "I'll knock your ass back to whatever hole you came out of."

"You dumb bitch," Grace said. "Does your mother even know who your father is, or does he know you as just a squirt after a cheap fuck?" That was all it took for Grenner to snap and lunge at her. They fell back onto the concrete floor while Dawson decided to back away rather than face the bulky Jan Bowen. Grenner landed several good punches before Jan was able to shove her off Grace. Leaping to her feet, Grace readied herself for round two only to be stopped by yelling from near the door.

"Scary and Gage are coming," Lopez said, making a mad dash to her bunk. Grace walked over to her destroyed bunk, trying to slow her breathing down and straighten her shirt, which had become untucked during the melee.

"Does someone want to explain why we're the only ones in the mess hall?" Carey said as she entered. "What's going on?"

"Grenner trashed our bunks, ma'am," Jan said, pointing at the mess.

"I did not," Grenner said, then added, "Ma'am."

Instructor Carey whispered a few words to Gage, who then left the barracks. "Ten hut." The girls snapped to attention. Walking down the aisle, she stopped in front of Grace. "What happened, Waters?"

"Bowen and I walked in and found our bunks like this, ma'am," she said, willing her hands not to curl into fists as her anger refused to ebb. "Grenner did it, I'm sure of it, ma'am."

"Bowen."

"Yes, ma'am."

"What happened?"

"Just like Waters said, ma'am. We were in study hall and came back to put our books away before dinner. Jones was with us. We came in and saw our bunks cut to pieces, ma'am."

Grace watched as Carey walked back up the aisle, stopping in front of Grenner. "And where were you?" the instructor asked.

"Dawson and I were playing one-on-one at the court, ma'am."

"Uh-huh," Carey said. She turned to the other girl. "Dawson? You know nothing about this, right?"

"Right, ma'am," Dawson said.

"Fine," Carey said, walking back down to Grace's area of the barracks. "Report to the mess hall."

Grace looked quizzically at Jan, who shrugged her shoulders. As they were leaving, Instructors Gage and Donaldson entered the barracks and started opening lockers.

"Dinner will be silent," Instructor Mitchell said as they entered the mess hall. "Pick up your tray, get your dinners, sit down, eat, then report to the formation area." Grace picked up her tray and silverware pack, exchanging looks with Latisha and Jan. "Not one word from any of you," the instructor continued, moving a chair to the center of the room and sitting down on it. "I don't even want to hear your forks hitting the trays. I know it may seem impossible for some of you, but you'll survive not talking for a few minutes."

After eating their meals in silence, the girls reported to the formation area where the other three instructors were waiting. "Ten hut!" Carey yelled, startling many of them. "Two pieces of state property were destroyed today, cut up by a knife or razor. Now we've searched your bunks and lockers, but were unable to find it." Carey removed her mirrored sunglasses. "Here's your one chance. Whoever did it or knows who did it, step forward." She waited until the count of three. "I'm not going to begin to tell you how disappointed I am that one or more of you would do this, or that someone is hiding a weapon. Alpha Squad, take a step forward and spread out." The girls of Alpha Squad moved until they were two arms' lengths from each other. "Anyone who commits a crime while here can expect to be treated like a criminal," Carey continued as the instructors converged on the squad. "Hands on the back of your head, fingers laced together, eyes front." The instructors searched the girls thoroughly, going so far as to have them remove their boots lest a small blade be hidden inside.

All four squads were searched, but again there was no sign of a knife or razor. The four instructors huddled and talked at length, then turned to face the girls. "Report to the barracks," Instructor Donaldson said. "Put your bunks back in order, then report to your squad instructor's classroom. Bowen and Waters, throw your blankets and mattresses into the dumpster near the mess hall."

"So what are we going to do?" Instructor Gage asked, settling into one of the chairs in Carey's office.

"I don't know, Sue," Carey said. "It's not like we have spare mattresses lying around."

"Can't we take two from the infirmary?"

Carey tossed her pencil on the desk. "I wish I could, but then we'd be in violation for having less than one infirmary bed available for every ten girls."

"So let them sleep in the infirmary," Gage said.

"Can't," Carey said. "State law mandates an instructor or nursing professional be on site in the infirmary whenever someone is in there."

"So one of us will have to stay in the infirmary with the girls?"

"Every night," Carey said. "Unless someone really gets hurt, and then the nurse could keep an eye on them."

"Carey," Gage said. "I don't want to give up my bed. You know my back hates those cheap mattresses."

"But only one of them is mine," Carey protested. "I shouldn't have to give up my cabin either."

"Think there's any chance we can talk Judith or Marilyn into doing it?" Gage asked.

Carey shook her head. "Not even if we offered them money," she said. "I'll watch them tonight. Tomorrow I'll call and get new mattresses sent up." Carey leaned back in her chair. "It really bothers me that we didn't turn up that knife."

"I know," Gage said. "Unless it's hidden somewhere on the grounds."

"It must be," Carey said. "We turned the barracks upside down and searched every one of them. Unless it was dumped right after the crime."

"I don't know about that," Gage said. "On the street, sure. Knives are as easy to get as candy. Here, though, a knife is too valuable to just throw away."

"Meaning it has to turn up eventually," Carey said. "Let's keep an extra eye on Lauren Grenner and Sally Dawson for the next few days."

"You think they did it?"

"They're as likely as anyone else. Grenner, Bowen, and Waters got into it during PT and the word is that Dawson is Grenner's toad." Carey laced her fingers and put them behind her head. "I'll have Marilyn lean on both of them but I doubt they'll crack. I just want that knife before one the girls gets hurt."

Working together, Grace and Jan hauled their shredded mattresses out to the dumpster while Latisha followed with the blankets, sheets, and pillows. When they finished, the girls joined the rest of Bravo Squad in Instructor Carey's classroom. Knowing the instructors were mad, they sat quietly until Carey arrived.

"There is a weapon being hidden by someone," Carey said. "If you know something, this is the time to come clean." Several seconds passed in silence. "If you think protecting your buddies is the right answer, you're sadly mistaken." Brown eyes focused on each girl in turn. "If I find out you knew who did this and didn't tell me, I will make you the sorriest girl on the planet." She waited a few seconds more. "All right, Bravo Squad dismissed. Waters and Bowen, stay." Once the other girls were out of the room, the instructor spoke. "Other than suspicions, do you have any proof that Grenner was involved?" Carey asked.

"No, ma'am," Grace said.

"No, ma'am, but she didn't seem surprised by it either, ma'am," Jan said.

"That's not enough," Carey said. "All right. Waters and Bowen, report to the infirmary at 2100 hours dressed for bed."

"Yes, ma'am," both said, getting out of the classroom as quickly as possible.

"So we have to sleep in the infirmary?" Grace said as they left the administration building.

"That's not the worst of it," Jan said. "I broke a rib when I was at Crestwood and they had to have a nurse stay in the infirmary the entire time I was stuck in there. Any bets Scary's gonna be our bunkmate tonight?"

"Damn," Grace said. "Please don't punish me like that."

"You? Scary dropped me twice today."

"Dropped me three times," Grace said. "Getting so I just see her coming and my body wants to hit the floor."

Carey unlocked the infirmary, reaching in to flick the light switch. "Either of you snore?"

"No, ma'am," Grace and Jan said in unison.

"Good." Carey hefted a roll bag and stepped inside. "Bathroom is down the hall, beds are in there," she said, pointing at the large room opposite them. "You have five minutes each to get done what you need in the bathroom and then it's lights out. Go on, pick out a bunk."

"Lucky us," Grace whispered as she and Jan entered the large room that held the infirmary's beds.

"So if someone's sick, they're gonna put them in here with us?" Jan asked, pulling back the covers on a bed near the window, completely unaware that the instructor had followed them into the room.

"The beds have casters so if we have to move one into a different room, we can," Carey said, dropping her roll bag on the bed opposite Grace's. "But I'll get new mattresses up here tomorrow so it won't be an issue."

"Maybe Grenner did us a favor," Jan said. "That old mattress was lumpy as hell...uh, ma'am."

"That 'favor' will end up costing the state over two hundred dollars per bunk," Carey said, unzipping the roll bag and pulling out a pair of light blue pajamas. "That, when the two of you actually begin working, will be two hundred dollars each of your taxes being flushed down the toilet because of this foolishness. Two hundred dollars that could be used to provide food and shelter to homeless people, books to the schools, transportation and meals to the elderly, or a dozen other good things that would help people instead of being used to replace equipment destroyed for no good reason." She jerked the blanket back, revealing the stark white of the infirmary sheets. "So don't think anyone did you a favor, Bowen."

"Yes, ma'am," Jan said.

"Well, ladies? Don't just stand there, if you need the bathroom, go now," Carey said.

"I'm all set, ma'am," Jan said, crawling between the sheets.

"Me too, ma'am," Grace said. *And if not, I'll hold it 'til morning.*

"I'll be right back," Carey said, picking up the pajamas and a toiletries kit. "Try not to destroy the place while I'm gone."

As soon as the instructor left the room, Grace went over to Jan's bunk. "I'm going to kill Grenner for this."

"Yeah, who knows how many days it's going to take the stupid state to get new mattresses up here," Jan said. "And we're going to have to put up with Scary or Short Shit."

"This is so bogus," Grace said. "We didn't do anything wrong and we have to spend the night with Queen Bitch five feet away."

"I just hope she doesn't snore," Jan said.

"Fuck," Grace said. "That would be my luck."

"Office of General Services, how may I direct your call?"

Carey had been listening to music for so long it took a second for the words to register. "Yes, this is Joanna Carey, head instructor for Sapling Hill Youth Facility. I need to get two mattresses shipped up here right away."

"Hold please." Click.

"I've been holding," she said to the teeth-grating music.

"Purchasing. How may I direct your call?"

"This is Joanna Carey, head instructor for Sapling Hill Youth Facility. I need to get two mattresses shipped up here right away."

"Hold please." Click.

"Oh, you have got to be kidding," Carey said, leaning back in her chair.

"Purchasing, Miss Dunphy."

Carey decided to save her breath until she was sure she was talking to the right person. "Are you the one I talk to about getting some supplies?"

"Where are you calling from?"

"Sapling Hill Youth Facility."

"When was the voucher submitted?"

"I haven't," Carey said. "It's an emergency order."

"You have to submit a voucher."

"How long would it take after that?"

"Miss, there are procedures that have to be followed. What facility are you calling from?"

"Sapling Hill."

"Please hold." Click.

"Argh," Carey growled.

"This is Mrs. Smith. How can I help you?"

"Mrs. Smith? I was just talking to a Miss Dunphy."

"I'm Miss Dunphy's supervisor. Who am I speaking with?"

"Joanna Carey. I'm head instructor at Sapling Hill Youth Facility." Carey hoped having a supervisor meant there was a way to get the mattresses quickly.

"Miss Carey, according to our records, you submitted a rather sizable order just three months ago. Is this something that you didn't receive?"

"No, we've had two mattresses destroyed and we need to have them replaced," she said.

"Were the items lost as a result of fire or other natural disaster?"

"No, vandalism."

"And the items you're requesting have not been approved on a voucher yet, is that correct?"

"Not yet," she said. "But I can fax a voucher to you if you want."

"Well we can certainly add to your fall purchase request."

"You've got to be kidding," Carey said into the phone. "I need those mattresses now, not with the next shipment of supplies."

"I'm very sorry, Miss Carey, but Sapling Hill Youth Facility is budgeted for supplies to be issued once every six months for use during that period. A request for purchase has already been approved and processed for this period. Any vouchers submitted now that are not a result of an OGS backlog or error will be processed for delivery in August."

"August? August? What am I supposed to do with two girls who don't have a bed to sleep in for the next four months?"

"If you would like to submit a voucher for new mattresses for the next dispersal, we'll be happy to process it. Is there anything else I can help you with?"

"Is there any way I can get emergency funds so I can go out and buy the mattresses myself?"

"All purchases must be approved by the General Accounting Office."

"I get the picture," Carey said. "Bye." Hanging up the phone, she ran her fingers through her short black hair and sighed. Another night of sleeping on the infirmary mattresses was just not an option. The remaining choice was only slightly better.

"Ten hut," Carey said as she and Instructor Gage entered the barracks. "Waters, pack your gear into your footlocker. Bowen, you too." Grace moved quickly, packing everything but her uniforms into the footlocker. "All right, you two. Let's go. You have new housing from now until the end of the term."

Oh great, Grace thought as she slung her uniforms over her shoulder and reached for one of the handles for her footlocker. To her surprise, Instructor Carey took the other end. The four left the barracks, Jan Bowen and Gage heading west while she and Carey headed east. "Ma'am, may I ask where we're going?"

"You'll see," Carey said. They walked beyond any area that Grace was familiar with, up a winding path that opened into a small clearing with a cabin. "The choice was between the infirmary or here, and frankly I prefer my recliner to those hard-backed chairs." Carey opened the door of her cabin, then reached for the footlocker. "Go inside, find the kitchen, and sit down in a chair."

"Yes, ma'am." *Oh damn, I'm dead.* She quickly located the small kitchen and sat down.

Carey put the footlocker in the corner of the living room. "You can change out here or in the bathroom," she said, heading for the bedroom. "Hang your uniforms in the closet in the living room. Give a shout when you're decent."

"Yes, ma'am," Grace said, going to the living room and opening her footlocker. *I'll never survive.* She pulled out her sleeping shirt and shorts. *My arms are going to look like Popeye's from all the pushups she's gonna make me do.* After removing her khaki shirt, she hung it on the hanger, then stripped off her undershirt and sports bra. *I'll never survive four months here with her.* The pants were exchanged for the white shorts, then hung up with the shirt for the next day. Grace took a moment to look around. Half of the square cabin was taken by the bathroom and instructor's bedroom, while the other half was the living room and kitchen. The front door opened into the living room with the small closet she had used in one corner and a soft blue recliner in the other corner. A tall reading lamp sat on the table next to it, and the couch faced a false fireplace. A simple wooden coffee table took up the center of the room. It was functional but woefully lacking in terms of any personal effects. No paintings hung on the walls; no pictures adorned the mantelpiece. *Nice place, but you wouldn't know who lived here.* "I'm dressed, ma'am," she said, deciding she had taken enough time.

Carey stepped out of the bedroom dressed in light blue pajamas, the initials JC monogrammed on the breast pocket. "You get the couch," she said, settling into the recliner. "Sit down." Grace sat on the couch. "Rule number one. Don't touch anything unless you have permission, especially anything in my refrigerator."

"Yes, ma'am."

"Two, you don't use the phone or listen to the answering machine."

"Yes, ma'am."

"In the bathroom is the linen closet. You'll find fresh towels there. I'll get you clean sheets and a blanket. Each day, you'll strip the couch down, fold your bedding, and set it on your footlocker."

"Yes, ma'am." *This is hell. I've died and gone to hell.*

"I don't want to find water on the bathroom floor or toothpaste in the sink."

"Yes, ma'am."

"This..." Carey tapped her hand on the armrest. "Is mine. You can use the couch to sit on."

"Yes, ma'am."

"Did you get all of your homework done?"

"Most of it, ma'am. Everything that's due tomorrow, ma'am." *Oh great, here it comes. From now on, I'll be studying and doing homework from the beginning of free time until lights out.*

"Your math is all done?"

"Of course, that's easy," Grace said, then realized her mistake. "Ma'am."

"Good," Carey said, standing up. "I'll get your bedding while you get your workbook."

"Yes, ma'am," Grace said, waiting until the other woman had gone to the bedroom before rolling her eyes. *I am so dead.* Reluctantly, she walked over to the footlocker and retrieved her math workbook. *Fifty pushups, easy.* Setting the book on the coffee table, she returned to her seat on the couch and awaited her fate.

"Here you go," Carey said when she returned to the room. Grace took the blanket, pillow, and sheet.

"Thank you, ma'am," she said, surprised when she saw Carey open the drawer on the lamp table and remove a pair of glasses.

"This it?" Carey asked, picking up the workbook. The small black-rimmed glasses looked odd to Grace, who was used to seeing mirrored sunglasses or nothing at all on the instructor.

"We had to do through page forty-two, ma'am," Grace said, hoping the instructor would see that work was done and leave it at that.

"Really?" To Grace's dismay, her mentor flipped through the pages, stopping where Grace had finished during study time. "So why is yours done through page one-fifty-seven?"

Grace looked down at the carpet. "I was bored in study class and I only had my math book, ma'am."

"Are you bored in math class?"

"Yes, ma'am."

"And it never occurred to you to mention this to anyone? Look at me."

Grace looked up and found herself captured by curious brown eyes. Instructor Carey did not look angry or upset, merely puzzled by her decision. "I um...I figured there was only Remedial Math and regular Math and since I'm already in regular Math..." She shrugged her shoulders. "My homework's always done when Instructor Donaldson wants to check."

"Is she aware you're so far ahead?"

"No, ma'am," Grace said. "She doesn't check my homework anymore. I guess she figures I do it so she doesn't have to check."

"Do you get anything out of class?"

"Not really. I'm usually working way ahead of whatever they're doing," she said. "But I give the right answer when she calls on me."

"When she calls on me, ma'am," Carey said. "All right, it's almost 2100 hours. We'll talk about math tomorrow. You can go to bed right after you do ten pushups."

"Yes, ma'am." *Oh yeah, I'm in hell.*

The smell of fresh coffee filled the air as Grace slowly woke up. When she opened her eyes, it took several seconds for the unfamiliar surroundings to make sense. With a soft groan, she sat up and rubbed her face. "Morning, ma'am."

"Good morning, Waters," the instructor's voice came from the kitchen. "You have another half-hour before wake-up."

The option of catching more sleep was tempting but Grace did not want to appear lazy. "That's okay, ma'am. I'm up now, ma'am."

"I put a set of towels out for you in the bathroom."

"Thank you, ma'am." After a good healthy yawn, Grace went to her footlocker and removed her toiletries and last clean set of underwear. *Guess I'll be at the laundry during first free period.* After she set them on the carpet, she folded the bedding and placed it on top of her footlocker. Collecting her things, Grace headed for the bathroom, stopping just before the door. "Ma'am?"

"Yes?"

"In the barracks, we have the shampoo dispenser, ma'am," she said, turning to see her mentor standing in the kitchen, a white mug with a multicolored logo in her hand. "Did you want me to go get some, ma'am?"

"No," Carey said. "Use mine for now."

"Yes, ma'am."

"Fresh razors are in the top drawer of the vanity. Waters, I'm going to trust you not to need supervision. Don't make me regret that decision."

"Yes, ma'am."

"Don't lock the door."

"Yes, ma'am."

"Hang your towel neatly over the shower door when you're done."

"Yes, ma'am."

"Don't touch my conditioner or my body oil."

"Yes, ma'am."

"And the bathroom had better look as clean when you leave it as when you went in."

"Yes, ma'am." *What do you think I'm going to do? Have a party in there?*

Grace stepped into the bathroom, amazed at how bright and airy it seemed. A skylight graced the slanted ceiling and pale yellow tiles allowed the sunlight to bounce all over the room. Opening the top drawer of the vanity, she found the package of razors. *I'm glad she's not gonna watch me shave,* she thought as she stripped off her clothes and stepped into the shower stall. It was then that she realized in all the times she had taken a shower while at Sapling Hill, Instructor Carey never had shower duty. *Must be nice being in charge.* A smile came to her lips as she turned on the water. *Of course if I was in charge, I'd volunteer for shower duty.*

Steam rose as she took her time scrubbing under nice hot water. A corner bench built into the stall made the perfect place to put her foot as she washed between her legs, being much more thorough than she ever could with others in the same room. *For someone with short hair you sure have enough things,* she thought, looking at the full shower caddy. *Shampoo, conditioner, cream rinse, mousse, body lotion, body oil...guess you believe the commercials.* Rinsing her hair, she reached for the shampoo and poured a healthy amount on her hand. *Strawberry, nice.* She basked in the privacy after a month of community showers for as long as she dared, then rinsed and turned the water off. *Nice shower. I could get used to this.* Opening the frosted glass door, she stepped on the yellow mat and toweled off.

After dressing, Grace looked around the bathroom. A red toothbrush sat in a ceramic holder built into the tile. *I'm surprised you don't have one of those fancy electric toothbrushes,* she thought, opening the medicine cabinet to find the usual assortment of toiletries. *Must not worry about your teeth as much as you do your hair.* Beneath the vanity she found cleaning supplies. *Well, I'd rather clean one toilet than ten. I'll probably end up having to keep the whole cabin clean or do her laundry or both.*

Grace returned to the living room, unsure now of what to do until morning formation. After putting her things away, she sat down on the couch and laced up her boots.

"Do you drink coffee, Waters?"

"Yes, ma'am," she said, turning to see Carey open a cabinet and pull out a red mug. *Real coffee,* she thought excitedly, loathing the brown liquid that came from the large urn in the mess hall. Grace quickly jumped to her feet and entered the kitchen. "Thank you, ma'am."

"This is the only mug I want to see you using. Cream and sugar?"

"Cream, ma'am."

Carey opened the refrigerator, pulling out a pint of half-and-half. "I tried the mess hall coffee once," she said, then scrunched up her face. "Tastes like they filter it through dirt."

Grace smiled. "We figure they use the swamp water, ma'am," she said, taking the pint, putting a splash into her coffee, then handing it back.

"You may be right about that," Carey said, leaning against the counter. "I was on duty on a cutter off the coast of Connecticut and we ended up reusing the grounds two or three times. It still tasted better than the mess hall coffee."

Taking a sip, Grace hummed at how good it tasted. "Oh, this is great," she said, taking a larger swallow. "Ma'am," she added belatedly.

"All right, let's make a deal before you ma'am me to death," Carey said. "Here in the cabin you can skip the ma'am, but you slip up out there and I'll drop you for ten, you got it?"

"Yes, ma'am, I mean yes. A cutter, that's a ship, right?"

Carey smiled and shook her head. "That's one way to put it."

"Were you in the Navy?"

"Coast Guard," Carey said, holding out her mug, which Grace now realized sported the Coast Guard emblem. "And that's enough about me.

Now, let's talk about you and math." She drained her coffee mug. "What do you want to do about it?"

"About it?"

"Do you want to stay in math class?" Carey asked. "Or would you rather have free period?"

Grace finished her coffee, surprised at how quickly she drank it. "I don't mind being in class," she said, looking from her empty mug to the coffeepot. "I'll just work some more in the workbook." Taking a chance, she gave the instructor a small smile. "I didn't think it was a good idea to do my English homework in math class."

Carey reached for the coffeepot. "That's probably one of the brightest ideas you've had since you arrived here," she said, pouring the aromatic brew into her mug. "I know I'd drop you for twenty easy if I caught you doing your homework during SR." She held out the coffeepot. "Maybe I should be checking to see if you're really taking notes?"

"Thanks," Grace said, holding her mug out. "I'm taking notes. Ask Instructor Gage. She checks."

"She checks to see if you're taking notes for Sexual Responsibility?"

"Um, would you mind if I...?" She pointed at the refrigerator. "It's part of English class. Note taking and studying. We have to show her that we're taking notes in our other classes. Well, except for Self-Defense. Thanks," she said when Carey handed her the pint of half-and-half.

"So do you want to stay in math class or not?" Carey asked.

"No," Grace said. "I'd rather use it as a free period."

Carey sipped her coffee. "I'll speak with Instructor Donaldson."

"Instructor Carey?"

"Yes?"

"Um...about barracks inspection?"

Carey took a sip of coffee before responding. "Your footlocker is here and you're using the closet as you would the big locker in the barracks. Since you don't have a bed to check, make sure the sheets and blanket are neatly folded and centered on your footlocker." She had another sip. "I'll have to think about what chores I can assign you."

"Yes, ma'am."

Grace took her place next to Latisha. "Hey."

"Man, how did you survive a night with Instructor Scary?"

Looking at the group of leaders, she spied Carey. "It was okay," she said, turning to spot Jan standing behind her. "How'd it go for you?"

"It sucked," Jan said. "Gage snores worse than Campbell."

Grace rolled her eyes. "Wonderful," she said.

"Yeah, and how do you tell an instructor that?" Latisha asked.

"Better figure out a way to make some earplugs," Grace said.

"So what happened with you?" Jan asked.

Grace shrugged. "I can't touch anything. She probably has a fingerprinting kit to check and make sure I don't."

"I'm going to kill Grenner for this," Jan said.

"Save some for me," Grace said. "I thought it was bad enough dealing with Queen Bitch on A schedule when we have two classes with her. Now I have to spend free time with her watching every move I make." She deliberately looked away when the dark-haired woman's head turned in her direction. "See?"

"Just like having Big Brother on your ass," Jan said. "All right, she's looking somewhere else now."

Grace looked back. "More like Big Sister," she said. "Big Sister Queen Bitch from Hell."

"Marilyn, do you have a minute?"

"Sure, Carey," the tall blonde instructor said.

"Let's go in my office," Carey said, leading her down the hall. "I wanted to talk to you about Waters."

"Sure, I don't have my grade book with me but she's been passing the tests with flying colors," Donaldson said as they entered the office.

"Did you know she's over a hundred pages ahead in her workbook?" Carey said as she sat down behind her desk.

"I knew she was ahead, but not by that much," Donaldson said, settling in a nearby chair. "Is there a problem?"

"I'm thinking of releasing her from math and letting her have it as a free period. She can do her math independently and turn it in to you."

"We all had to take classes that we didn't like, Carey," Donaldson said. "If this was high school..."

"If this was high school, we'd have an advanced class to put her in. What are you going to do when she finishes that workbook?"

"I don't know," Donaldson said. "We only have the two math workbooks, remedial and standard. Once she finishes that workbook, I'd be just as happy to have her out of class. Teenage girls with nothing to do tend to be disruptive. Right now she sits in the back of the class, keeps quiet and doesn't cause any problems."

"That won't last if she gets bored," Carey said. "And I bet our chances of getting a better math book for her are just as good as they were at getting a new mattress."

The tall blonde laughed. "It would be startling what we could get done if it wasn't for bureaucrats."

"Amen to that," Carey said. "Whenever you feel like releasing her from class, go ahead. I'll note it in her records."

"She's not going to stop tutoring, is she?"

Surprised, Carey looked up at her. "Tutoring? I didn't know she was. When is this going on?"

"You didn't know? Every time I see her in study hall she's helping someone with their math," the blonde woman said. "I know Jones and Rosetti are both getting help from her, and she might even be helping some of the girls in Judith's class."

"Was this your idea?" Carey asked.

Donaldson shook her head. "Not mine. Maybe Sue had something to do with it."

"Or maybe our little Miss Waters decided to do it on her own."

"Stranger things have happened. Speaking of math, I have to get ready for class," Donaldson said. "You know, Carey, once she finishes that workbook, she'd probably be ready to take the GED."

"She's not eligible," Carey said. "She either has to be out of school for one year or her kindergarten class has to graduate first."

"Yeah but wasn't she a senior? They graduate in June," Donaldson said. "Anyway, I have to go. Are you covering lunch today?"

Carey nodded. "Sue and I are."

"Have fun," the blonde said. "Nothing like a mess hall full of teenage girls to give one a migraine."

"I'll bring my aspirin," Carey said. "See you later."

Once Donaldson closed the door, Carey opened her Rolodex and flipped through the small white cards. Finding the one she wanted, she dialed the number, then opened the bottom drawer of her desk and pulled out a thick file folder.

"Iroquois High School, Main Office."

"Yes, I'm looking for a Mrs. Hamlin. I understand she's a math teacher there."

"I'll transfer you to the math department. Please hold." Click.

"That's not surprising," Carey muttered to herself.

"Math Department, Mrs. Black speaking."

"Mrs. Hamlin, please, this is Joanna Carey from Sapling Hill Youth Facility. I need to speak to her about one of her former students."

There was a pause. "Mrs. Hamlin is not in a class at the moment. Hold on and I'll see if she's in the teacher's lounge." Click.

"What, no music?"

"This is Deb Hamlin."

"Mrs. Hamlin, this is Joanna Carey. I'm an instructor at Sapling Hill and I wondered if I could talk to you for a few minutes about one of your former students."

"I have so many students that I'm not sure how much help I can be, Miss Carey. Is Sapling Hill the girl's boot camp?"

"Yes. I'm hoping you'll remember this one. Graceful Waters. She's a senior this year."

"Oh yes, I know Grace Waters. Of course, it's hard not to know someone who is forcibly removed from school after throwing a chair at a teacher."

"It's one way to make an impression," Carey said, leaning back in her chair.

"That it is. If it wasn't for her behavioral problems, she'd be a wonderful girl. Very smart, at least as far as math is concerned."

"I see that from her transcript," Carey said. "She's almost finished with the math course we have available for her here and we still have four and a half months of session left."

"What can I do to help?"

Carey sat up. "This is what I was thinking..."

"Oh, bullshit."

"Bite me, Campbell," Rosetti said. "It happened."

"No way. The drummer?"

"The drummer and one of the roadies," Rosetti said.

"Slut," Grace said, dodging a friendly swat.

"Screw you, Waters."

"Viking's coming," Latisha said, closing the door and scrambling to her seat. Instructor Donaldson opened the door.

"Waters."

"Yes, ma'am?"

"Collect your things and come with me." Donaldson closed the door.

"Ooh, what'd you do?" Latisha asked.

"Not a clue," Grace said, scooping up her books and papers. "See ya later, I hope."

"I understand you and Instructor Carey talked about letting you out of class?"

"Yes, ma'am," Grace said as she followed Donaldson down the hall.

"I hear you only have twenty or so pages to go before you're done with the workbook?"

"Yes, ma'am."

"I have a test I want you to take." The blonde instructor unlocked one of the unused classrooms. "I'll come get you after class," she said, holding the door open.

"Yes, ma'am." Grace went in and sat down at the desk where several papers were waiting. Turning over the blank cover page, she began filling in the circles next to the answers she thought were correct. *She thinks I'm going to finish this in forty-five minutes?*

Despite her reservations, Grace did finish it in time, double-checking her answers as the instructor walked in. "Are you finished?"

"Yes, ma'am."

"What do you have now?" Donaldson asked as she took the paper and sat down at the teacher's desk.

"Free period, ma'am."

"You have homework to do?"

"Yes, ma'am."

"You can do it here as easy as study hall. Get cracking."

"Yes, ma'am." Grace pulled out her English notebook, deciding the test must be a final exam so she could be exempt from math class. *So why do I have to be here while Viking grades it?*

Completely engrossed in what she was doing, Grace was startled when Instructor Donaldson called her name. "Yes, ma'am?" *Damn, give a person a heart attack why don't you?*

"Did you take your SATs in February?"

"No, ma'am."

"Why not?"

Embarrassed, Grace looked down at her paper. "Why bother? Even if I wanted to go, I can't afford college, ma'am."

"Uh-huh," Donaldson said, lacing her fingers together. "You know you just took a sample SAT test? Just the math section, of course."

"I didn't know, ma'am."

"How do you think you did?"

"I think I passed, ma'am."

Donaldson walked over and handed her the test. "I would say so too, Waters. Seven sixty out of a possible eight hundred."

"It was the problem with the exponents and square roots, wasn't it?" Grace asked, flipping through the pages to check. "I knew it. I didn't know how to do that one so I guessed, ma'am."

"The answer is B, by the way," Donaldson said. "You did very well, Waters. Better than most high school students. That's an outstanding score. If that had been the real test, you'd have something to be proud of."

"Thank you, ma'am," Grace said, closing her notebook. "Instructor Donaldson, can I go now, ma'am?"

"One more question, Waters. If you had the opportunity to take the SATs, would you?"

"I guess so, ma'am," Grace said. "It didn't seem that bad."

"Keep working on your math workbook," Donaldson said. "Turn it in to me when you're finished with it."

"Yes, ma'am." Grace gathered her things and left, thinking the test to be a waste of time.

Grace lay in the darkness, listening carefully for any sign that Instructor Carey was awake. Wiggling her hips, she checked one last time to make sure the couch would not squeak and give her away. Closing her eyes, she rubbed her nipples through the thin cotton tee shirt, her lips parting as she felt the hardening beneath her fingers. *Oh yeah, that's nice.* Keeping her left hand on her breast, Grace reached down and pulled her shirt free from her shorts, then brought her fingers to her mouth. Wetting them thoroughly, she reached beneath the shirt and let out a quiet sigh as wet fingers touched her painfully erect nipple. In her mind, a faceless mouth was pleasuring her, giving her sensitive nipples just the right amount of friction and pressure. The shirt was pushed up, revealing her breasts to the night air. Wetting her fingers once more, she continued to play with her nipples until the need became too much. Pausing long enough to make certain Carey was still sleeping, Grace pushed her shorts and panties down to her ankles. Her faceless lover moved down, touching her in the most intimate of places. *Oh yeah.* Without thirty-five other girls to possibly wake up and see her, Grace felt safe pulling her knees up and spreading her thighs. Her fingers became the faceless woman's fingers, teasing and pleasing, promising more but holding back until Grace could take it no more. Arching her back, she let out the softest of gasps as she crashed over the edge, frantically rubbing with her palm to prolong the orgasm. Eyes closed, Grace basked for several minutes in the relaxing feeling, her overheated body cooling down and her breathing returning to normal.

Grace jumped when she heard the papers slap against Carey's leg. Looking up, she immediately recognized her handwriting on the top paper. *Uh-oh.*

"When did you do your homework?"

"Um...during last free period yesterday."

"After AM?" Grace nodded. "Did you read over this before you turned it in?"

Oh shit. Why? "No."

"Apparently." Carey looked at the paper. "How did the attack on Jane Doe move from the park at night to her bedroom during the day?" She tapped the paper. "You said here she should have locked her bedroom door and snuck out the window."

Oops. "I...I must have confused it with one of the other case studies," Grace said. "I'll do it over."

"You turned it in, you live with the grade," Carey said. "There were three case studies assigned; the one with the girl drinking and walking through the park, the woman working late and going to her car in the parking garage, and the woman with the flat tire. Which one of those has a bedroom?"

Grace tried to think fast but nothing would come to her. "I...I guess none of them. I must have been thinking of something someone said in AM."

"Is that your answer?"

"Yes, ma'am," Grace said, wondering if she was about to get dropped for her lie.

"Is there something you want to talk about?"

"No."

"I can't help you if I don't know what's going on," Carey said.

"There's nothing going on," Grace said. "Really."

"Uh-huh," Carey said. "You wouldn't be here at Sapling Hill if there was nothing going on."

"Sue, got a minute?" Carey asked, motioning the shorter woman away from the mess hall door.

"Be quick," Gage said. "I can hear the din rising already. If I leave them alone for too long we'll have a food fight on our hands."

"Does Grace participate in AM?"

"Sometimes," Gage said. "It depends on the subject. Why?"

"Something she wrote has me wondering," Carey said. "Does she ever say anything about being abused or molested?"

"Waters?" Gage shook her head. "Mention sex in any form and she clams up and stares at the floor until class ends."

Carey looked at the mess hall, the noise inside growing. "Anything happen in AM yesterday?"

"Nothing worth mentioning," Gage said. "Waters seemed preoccupied but participated when I called on her."

Grace was putting her clothes in the washer when the laundry-room door opened. "Hey, Jan."

"Hey," Jan dropped her stack of clothes on the adjoining washer. "Time to get those whites white and the brights bright."

"I hope you're not calling these bright," Grace said, poking at Jan's rolled-up pair of khakis. "They don't know the meaning of bright around here."

"You gonna hang out?"

Grace reached for the laundry detergent. "You think I'm going to take a chance and leave my clothes where Grenner can get her hands on them?" She poured the liquid in the washer, then closed the lid and set the dial. "With my luck I'd come back and find a gallon of bleach on them."

"I just know she's the one that unhooked the springs on Christine's bunk," Jan said, stuffing her clothes into the washer. "Yet another thing no one can prove that bitch did."

Grace handed her the detergent. "Her and her toadie Dawson," she said.

Jan bumped her. "You know we owe them for trashing our bunks," she said, pouring a healthy amount of soap into the washer. "If I could get that fat ass alone, I'd kick her ass."

"And get yourself put on restriction," Grace said. "Think the instructors are hard on us now? Get caught going after Grenner and see how they can be." She pushed herself up to sit on the washer. "I don't need to give Carey any more reasons to drop me."

"Yeah, well you're not the one who has to wear earplugs to bed," Jan said, hopping on her washer. "Gage dropped me three times last night. Oh!" She scooted closer. "Guess what I found in her bedroom."

"You snooped in her bedroom?" Grace said. "If she had caught you, your ass would be grass."

"You're telling me you haven't looked around when Scary wasn't there?"

"No, not really," Grace said. "I peeked in her room once but I didn't go in or anything." She gave a conspiratorial smile. "So what'd you find?"

"Let's put it this way," Jan said, holding her hands several inches apart. "It's about this long and takes batteries."

"You're kidding," Grace snorted. "That is so gross."

Jan laughed with her. "I told you she couldn't get any. Bet Scary's got a matching one in her room."

"I'm not checking," Grace said.

"Yeah, well," Jan said, swinging her legs and banging the heels of her boots against the washer. "You can't say anything, you know. If it got back to Short Shit, she'd know I was in her room and she'd kill me."

"I won't say anything," Grace said. "If they ever thought we were looking around when they weren't there, we'd be stuck in the damn infirmary until graduation." She smirked. "I get to have real coffee. Not the shit they serve in the mess hall."

"Cool," Jan said. "Hey, did you check out the shower yet? I assume the cabins are the same."

"Of course," Grace said. "You think I've been bathing in the lake or something?" She nudged Jan with her shoulder. "What about it?"

"I mean have you, you know...checked it out?" Jan leaned closer. "Put it on the pulsating head. It's great."

"You mean..." Grace smiled and looked away. "Pervert."

"Well? It's not like anyone else is gonna give it to you here." Jan shrugged her shoulders and banged her heel against the washer again. "Whatever, you'd like it. Gotta take advantage of the few extras we can get out here. Hey, did you catch those stand-up comedians last night?"

"What are you talking about?"

"On TV, they had a four-hour marathon on that comedy channel."

"Oh," Grace said. "Carey doesn't have a TV."

"Too bad for you," Jan said. "Short Shit doesn't care if I watch TV once my homework's done."

"Wanna trade?"

"Short Shit for Scary with no TV?" Jan shook her head. "I'll keep my pair of tens and you keep your queen of bitches."

"Thanks a lot," Grace said. "The only time I catch a break is when she's on late duty and doesn't get back to the cabin until after lights out."

TWO MONTHS

"Ten hut," Carey said. "All right, I know some of you are very excited, but this is formation. Parents will be arriving at approximately 1000 hours. I expect all of you to be on your best behavior. Those of you who are not expecting anyone should be in the rec room or your barracks unless you have permission from an instructor to be somewhere else."

Grace stepped into what usually was her English classroom, excited about seeing her mother after so long an absence. Her excitement quickly turned to anger when she saw the portly man standing near the window. "What's he doing here?"

"Grace, oh Grace, it's so good to see you," her mother said, rising from the chair and enveloping her in a hug. "Look at you. You cut your hair."

"They cut it for me," Grace said, glaring at the man. "I don't want him here."

"Honey, Bob asked to come," her mother said. "He cares about you."

Stepping back from her mother, Grace jammed her hands into her pockets and formed them into tight fists. "I don't want him here."

"Now, Gracie, I know we've had our problems, but things will get better," he said, moving away from the window and closer to her.

"Stay away from me," she said, backing closer to the door. "Ma, why did you bring him? You know I hate him."

"Grace, Bob and I have reconciled," her mother said.

"You've what? Are you nuts?"

"We're getting married this fall," Bob said. "Right after you come home."

Anger welled quickly within her. "No way. No way in hell I'm living with you again. Ma, you want him, fine. I'll find someplace else to live."

"Grace, please," her mother said. "Please, just sit down and let's talk, okay?"

"Sit down, Gracie."

The fists became tighter. "Don't you tell me what to do, you son of a bitch," Grace said.

"Please don't fight," her mother said, taking a tissue out of her pocketbook. "I've missed you so much, Grace. Please, come sit down and talk to me."

Grace pulled her hand out of her pocket and reached for the door handle. "Not as long as he's here."

"Where do you think you're going?" he said. "I drove almost three hours to bring your mother here."

"Then wait in the fucking car and I'll talk to my mother," she said.

"Who the hell do you think you are talking to me like that?" Bob said, moving quickly to capture her wrist in a painful grip. "Now you sit your ass down and you visit with your mother."

"Bob, let her go," her mother said. "Grace, please."

Grace tried but could not help crying out in pain as he forced her down to her knees. "Let...go."

"Are you going to listen to your mother?"

Grace nodded quickly. "Yes."

"I thought this place was supposed to make you better," he said, shoving her arm away. "You're still the same smart mouth you were then."

Still kneeling, Grace rubbed her reddened wrist. "Go to hell, you son of a bitch."

Bob moved fast, his hand swinging back to catch Grace in the side of the face before she could react. Stars filled her vision when her head smacked against the painted concrete wall. "I oughta take you over my knee and spank you until you can't sit for a week," he said.

The door opened. "Excuse me, what's going on here?" Instructor Donaldson said from the doorway.

Grace slowly rose to her feet, her head pounding from the impact. "Request permission to return to my barracks, ma'am," she said, holding her sore wrist.

"Grace, please don't go," her mother said.

Her nose throbbing, Grace wiped her lip only to have her fingers come back bloody. Facing her mother, she made no attempt to stop the flow. "This doesn't bother you, does it?" she said, her eyes angry slits. "Why should it? Nothing else he does bothers you." Turning her head, she wiped her face on her short sleeve. "You want to see me next month, don't bring him. I'll never step in your home as long as he's there."

"You see what we have to put up with?" Bob said.

"Grace, come here," Donaldson said, taking a step forward into the room and putting her hand on the teen's elbow. "Mrs. Waters, please wait here."

"What? I drove almost three hours to bring her up here," Bob said. "Just let us handle this."

"I can have the state police up here in five minutes to arrest you for striking her," Donaldson said, seeming every bit the Viking protector to Grace. "Now wait here."

Carey took a deep breath before nodding for Donaldson to open the door. Her dark eyes took in first the teary woman, then the angry man standing by the window. "Excuse me," she said. "I'm Joanna Carey, head instructor here at Sapling Hill."

"I'm Edna Waters and this is my fiancé Bob Garvey," the woman said. "Is Grace all right?"

Carey clenched her jaw, holding back the biting comment that came to her lips. "She has a bloody nose but it doesn't look like anything's broken. Mrs. Waters, would you come with me please?" The man moved away from the window. "Just Mrs. Waters," she said.

"Sit down, please," Carey said as she entered her office.

"He didn't mean to hurt her," Mrs. Waters said. "Sometimes Grace says things that—"

"A grown man just gave your teenage daughter a bloody nose," Carey interrupted. "It doesn't matter what she said." She sat down at her desk. "And the fact that you are defending your fiancé over your daughter is frankly rather sad."

"You don't understand," Mrs. Waters said. "Bob loves her. He never means to hurt her. They've been scrapping for years."

"How old was she when he first came to live with you?" Carey asked, suspicions forming in her mind.

"She was, let's see...he moved in late May and she was in tenth grade...she was fifteen. Always a difficult age for girls," the woman said.

"Was she a problem before that?"

"No," Mrs. Waters said. "She had her moments, but it was hanging around with her friends and picking up their bad habits that got her into trouble."

Certainly not your lecherous boyfriend. "Can you think of any incident that happened the summer between her sophomore and junior years?"

"No," the older woman said.

"Mrs. Waters, has Grace ever claimed to have been abused by any of your boyfriends?" Carey watched the woman's eyes flicker away.

"Why, no. She's never mentioned anything like that," Mrs. Waters said. "Has she mentioned anything to you?"

"It would explain her sudden change in behavior," Carey said, avoiding the question.

"I told you, it's her friends," Mrs. Waters said. "She thought her father could do no wrong and has always scrapped with any man that tried to take his place, but nothing has ever happened like you're trying to imply, Miss Carey."

Knowing she would never get through to the woman, Carey made a notation in Grace's folder, then closed it. "Mr. Garvey committed an act of assault against your daughter. Both the instructors and medical staff here are required by the state to report any incidents of suspected child abuse. Your standing by and doing nothing is tantamount to neglect, and as head instructor, it's my job to protect these girls. As such, any future visits by you will be done on a supervised basis, and Mr. Garvey will not be allowed on the property."

"You can't do that," Mrs. Waters protested.

"Oh yes, I can," Carey said. "The state, not you, is Grace's custodial guardian and I am in charge of this facility. If you want to visit, those are the rules."

"Can I see her now?"

"She's waiting for the nurse to come up to examine her," Carey said. "She won't be finished before visiting time is through." Carey rose from her chair. "If you'll come with me, I'll take you back to your boyfriend so he can drive you home."

"Marilyn?" Carey said as the sedan pulled out of the parking lot and the door to her office opened.

"Yes." Donaldson said. "They had a few choice words for you."

"I'm sure," Carey said, making sure the car was out of sight before turning away from the window. "I'm going to head back to my cabin and get Grace a clean shirt."

"Taking the cart?"

"No, I think I need to take a good hard run," Carey said. "And we wonder how these kids get so screwed up."

Carey rapped her knuckles against the doorframe. "I brought you a clean shirt."

"Thanks, ma'am," Grace said, taking the cotton shirt. "Are they gone?"

"Yes," Carey said, stepping into the room and sitting in the chair next to the bed. "We're barring him from coming on the property and she can only see you with supervision."

Grace sat up and pulled the bloody shirt off. "I don't want to see her," she said, reaching for the clean shirt. "Can I make it so she can't come here anymore, ma'am?"

"We can talk about it," Carey said, averting her eyes from the half-clothed teen. "Grace, I have to file an incident report on this."

"Covered," the teen said, allowing Carey to stop looking at the wall. "What good is it going to do?" She crossed her arms. "Ma'am," she added belatedly.

"It allows me to have an order issued keeping him away from you," Carey said.

"That's all I want," Grace said. "I want to be as far away from them as possible, ma'am."

"Relax with the ma'am for now," Carey said, running her finger along the edge of the teen's eyebrow. "Nice lump there. That'll smart for a few days."

"Why did she have to bring him?" Grace said, sounding far younger than she was. "Why is she marrying him?"

"You'd have to ask her that," Carey said. "And if she does marry him, you're going to have to learn to deal with it."

"I'll deal with it, all right," Grace said, crossing her arms over her chest. "I'll be eighteen in a few months. I'll get my own place and the hell with her."

"That's one option," Carey said. "But it's expensive to live on your own, especially with not even a high school diploma."

"So I'll get my GED," Grace said. "It's one of my goals anyway, right?"

"It is," Carey agreed. "Your kindergarten class graduates in a month or so. Any time after that you can take the test."

"I want to take it," Grace said firmly. "I'll do whatever it takes so I don't ever have to go back and live there."

"Do you want me to check into the SATs? If you do decide to go to college, you'll need them."

"Sure."

"What happened before Instructor Donaldson entered the room?"

Grace gave a mirthless smile. "I need to spend more time in SD. Obviously I didn't move fast enough. The son of a bitch hit me. Knocked me into the wall."

"Is that how you got the bump above your eye?" Carey asked. Grace nodded. "I'll make sure they do an X-ray just to be on the safe side."

"I don't like being in the infirmary," Grace said. "My nose stopped bleeding. Can't I just go back to the cabin?"

"I wouldn't make you stay for just a bloody nose," Carey said. "But I don't want to take a chance with that bump on the head." She took a quick look around the room. "I don't like infirmaries either," she said. "I spent lots of time in one when I was a kid and it wasn't as nice as this."

"What happened?"

"You really want to know?" At Grace's nod, Carey chuckled. "All right. When I was thirteen I went to summer camp." She held up her index finger. "Just once. My parents refused to send me again."

"What happened?"

"Let's see. On day one I twisted my ankle. Once I was off crutches, I fell off the top bunk and cracked a rib. Then I leaned against the go-kart and accidentally put my hand on the exhaust manifold. I was thrown from a horse, fell out of a tree, tripped over a root during a nature walk, and caught my hair on fire during a bonfire." She was pleased to see her story had the desired effect as Grace laughed. "There were one hundred six tiles on the examination room ceiling."

"Oh that sucked," Grace said through her laughter.

"It did," Carey said. "So I know how boring it can be to sit in a place like this. Do you want me to bring you something to read?"

"You mean homework?"

"I meant a book. I have a few paperbacks at the cabin. Unless of course you'd rather do homework."

"No," Grace said quickly. "I'm caught up on my homework and a book would be nice. What kind?"

"I have a few sci-fi and a couple best sellers. I'll bring a few and you can choose."

"Thanks," Grace said.

"I have some paperwork to get done," Carey said as she stood up. "I'll get the books but then I need to get back to the office." She rolled up the bloody shirt. "I'll toss this in the washer while I'm at the cabin. Don't want the stains to set in."

"Instructor Carey?" Grace looked down at her hands. "Thanks, you know, for getting the shirt and something to read and..." She twisted her fingers together. "And coming to see if I was okay."

"Of course I would come see if you were all right," Carey said. "Grace, I really wish things had gone better for you today. I know how much you were looking forward to seeing your mother."

Grace shrugged. "I should have known better. Nothing ever goes right for me."

"That's not true," Carey said. "You're here, and while I know you think this is a punishment, you can turn it into an opportunity to make your life better." She walked to the doorway. "You've already made some significant changes, even if you can't see them yourself. And asking about the SAT and GED shows you finally care about your future." She lightly tapped the doorframe with her knuckles. "You're making progress, Grace. Don't let this set you back."

Grace took her seat in the loose circle of chairs, finding herself between Christine and Instructor Gage. *I knew I should have got here early.* "Hey," she said to the overweight teen next to her.

"Hi, Grace."

"All right, girls," Gage said. "Let's settle down and get started. We left off last time talking about how to recognize your buttons. Often it is those closest to us that, whether intentional or not, press the most and the biggest buttons. Waters, who pushes your buttons the most?"

"No one, ma'am."

"Really?" Gage turned her chair so she was facing Grace more than anyone else. "You think no one can push your buttons?"

"Not anymore, ma'am," Grace said, knowing she'd just made a challenge but determined to win.

"You're sure you want to go there, Waters?" Gage asked.

"Yes, ma'am."

"What about your mother? Does she push your buttons?"

"No, ma'am," Grace said, looking down at the deep green carpet.

"She never says anything to upset you?"

"No, ma'am."

"Never does anything to upset you?"

Grace hesitated, sensing where Instructor Gage was going. "Sometimes but it doesn't matter anymore, ma'am."

"Really? Why?"

"Because I'm not going to see her anymore, ma'am."

"You're going to cut your mother out of your life? Must be a good reason."

"Doesn't matter, ma'am." *Come on, move on to someone else.*

"Obviously your mother did something to push your buttons. What was it?"

"I'd rather not say, ma'am."

"You don't get that choice in here, Waters," Gage said. "What did she do?"

"She decided to marry a jerk, ma'am," Grace said, not wanting to use the real name she had for him and risk earning pushups.

"And why is he a jerk?"

"He...he just is, ma'am."

"Why?"

"Because..." Grace curled her hands into fists. "He lies and she believes him, ma'am."

"Did she believe him over you?"

Grace stared hard at the carpet. "Yes, ma'am."

"And you're feeling anger at her now?"

Grace's nostrils flared. "Yes, ma'am."

"What did he lie about?"

Grace shook her head, jaw clenched.

"Answer me."

"It's not important, ma'am," she said through gritted teeth.

"It's worth cutting your mother out of your life because she believes a lie he told her about something that's not important?"

"He lied and she believed him," Grace said. "That's all that matters, ma'am."

"Watch that tone with me, young lady," Gage said.

"Sorry, ma'am."

"Parents can make mistakes, believe the wrong person," Gage said as Grace continued to stare at the carpet. "Beneath the anger you're showing there's a little girl who's hurting very badly right now."

*Don't listen, don't think about it, don't...*Grace flinched when she felt the instructor's hand on her back.

"It's all right to talk about it in here, Grace. What happened?"

"It doesn't matter, ma'am." *Don't think, don't feel.*

"It does matter."

"No it doesn't!" Grace screamed. "It could have been about anything. I told the truth, he lied, and she believed him. Nothing else matters." She took a deep breath. "Ma'am."

"You think that's going to save you?" Gage asked. "Unclench those fists, relax that jaw and you get yourself calmed down," she said. "You have no reason to blow up at me. You can think about that while you do ten pushups after class."

"Fuck," Grace said under her breath when she saw Gage and Carey talking. "I'm dead."

"What'd you do?" Jan asked.

"Blew up in AM," Grace said. "Bet she's telling Carey all about it."

"That's the problem with staying with them," Jan said. "Gage does a mentoring session on me every friggin' night."

"She's gonna grill me worse than the cops do when they got a murder suspect," Grace said, dropping her fork on her tray. "I'm going to be doing pushups until my arms break." Grace looked down quickly when brown eyes turned in her direction. "What are they doing?" she whispered.

"Coming this way," Jan said. "You're bacon, my friend."

"Thanks," Grace sighed, readying herself for an earful of angry instructor.

"Waters, pick up your tray and come with me," Carey said.

"Yes, ma'am."

"Good luck," Jan said.

Grace followed Carey to the trash bin where she dumped the rest of her dinner, then set the tray on top with the others. "You can start talking at any time," Carey said, opening one of the double doors.

The sooner I talk, the sooner you'll drop me for ten or twenty.

"We have three hours until lights out," Carey said.

"I don't have anything to say, ma'am."

"Really? Hmm, sounded like you had a great deal to say in AM today."

I knew Gage would tell her. "Not that much, ma'am."

"What did he lie about?"

"I don't want to talk about it, ma'am."

"You're only making it harder on yourself, Grace. We want to help you but we can't if we don't know what's going on."

"He hit me, ma'am."

"How?"

Grace shrugged. "With his hand if he could reach me. Throwing something if he couldn't." *That's it. Stay focused on that. She doesn't have to know about anything else.*

"And your mother didn't believe you? She had to have seen the marks."

"Oh, she believed he hit me," Grace said. "She also believed his reasons why I deserved it, ma'am."

"Why didn't you say this in AM?"

Because all I could think about was him standing there saying he didn't touch me. Hitting me didn't seem that important. "I...I guess I was too angry to talk about it, ma'am." Looking up, she realized they were at the cabin.

"Have a seat," Carey said, gesturing at the steps. "Since you're calmer now, start talking."

Grace sat down and stared at the path. "He's a bum. Sits around saying he's disabled and collecting checks when he really is just a jerk who smokes his weed and watches TV." She glanced out of the corner of her eye at Carey. "Oh yeah, he sits right there in the living room with his pot and his pipe."

"So your mother knew about it?"

"She knew," Grace said. "My mother deals with things by ignoring them and hoping they'll go away."

"Did he ever offer any to you?"

"First time I got high was with him," Grace said.

"Is he where you got the marijuana you were caught with?"

Grace nodded. "But I could have gotten it anywhere, you know. It's not like it's hard to find."

"Do you smoke a lot of it?"

"Well, not lately," she said, gesturing around her. "I know what you mean. When he first moved in he let me smoke with him every day after school before Mom got home from work. I stopped smoking with him after a while but he left baggies in my room so I still had some. But after he left, I only smoked it if someone gave it to me."

"You're smart enough to know that numbing your feelings doesn't make them go away," Carey said. "You're also smart enough to know how easily drugs can mess up your life or even take it away altogether if they're abused."

"I know," Grace said. *But it was the only way to deal with him.*

"There are other ways to numb yourself," Carey said. "Hiding behind your anger and pushing people away are two that you excel at. Someone touches a sensitive subject with you and you resort to anger or violence to get the subject changed. Sound familiar, Miss I Like Throwing Chairs at Teachers?"

Grace looked down. "Yes, ma'am."

Carey smiled. "Oh, you do remember the word, don't you?" Grace went to move but stopped when she saw her mentor's upraised hand. "Sit. Obviously you think the rules for the steps are the same as inside the cabin and I'm not in the mood to watch you do pushups." She rested her wrists on her knees. "I'm more interested in what's going on in that head of yours."

"Nothing, ma'am," Grace said, deciding it was better not to push her liberty.

"I can see the gears turning from here," Carey said. "I get the feeling you're being selective about what you're telling me. Grace, did anything else happen when you were alone with him?"

"No, ma'am," she said, her gaze focused on a stone near the bottom step. *Oh, please change the subject.*

"Did he ever touch you sexually?"

"No, ma'am." *Don't look at her.*

"You know it's safe to tell me if he did."

"Yes, ma'am."

There was an agonizing silence as Grace waited for the instructor to speak. "All right, enough of this," Carey said as she stood up. "I'm hungry and you have homework to do. You can apologize to Instructor Gage tomorrow."

"Yes, ma'am." Grace waited a second, then followed her into the cabin. She went straight to her class books and started her homework in the hopes the conversation would not be continued.

"You threw out half of your dinner," Carey said from the kitchen. "Did you have enough to eat?"

Grace shrugged. "I don't care for macaroni and cheese."

"I didn't ask that."

Oh, she's offering. Grace smiled and went to the kitchen. "Do I have to answer before I find out what it is?"

Carey smiled and opened the refrigerator. "I'm not making anything fancy tonight. There's sandwich meat or help yourself to hot dogs." She pulled out a plate of leftovers and put it in the microwave. "Don't even think about touching the cheesecake if you want to keep your fingers intact."

"I won't, I promise."

"One can of soda," Carey said, programming the microwave and pressing the start button. "I know how many are in there."

Grace went to the refrigerator and looked at the offerings. "How about grape?"

"How many do I have?"

Yeah, you know how many are in here, Grace thought, her smile hidden from the older woman by the refrigerator door. "Three."

"Fine," Carey said.

"Can I have some potato salad?"

"Go ahead. Did you have any fruit today?"

"Orange juice with breakfast," Grace said.

"There's some grapes in the crisper," Carey said.

Grace selected the items she wanted and set them on the counter. "That smells good," she said, referring to the aroma wafting from the microwave.

"And surprisingly it's also nutritionally balanced," Carey said. "Speaking of which, why didn't you eat your spinach yesterday?"

"It was mush," Grace said. "Pasty green mush."

"The joys of mass food production," Carey said. "I suffered through it in the Coast Guard." The microwave dinged. "Something else you have to look forward to when you turn your life around. No more food from vats."

"Amen," Grace said. "I should put that on my goals list for Personal Finance."

"Either add lettuce and tomato to that sandwich or finish up the broccoli in the little container on the second shelf," Carey said as she carefully removed the hot plate from the microwave. "And remember, you don't want the others to think you're getting any special privileges."

"Food? What food?" Grace said, adding lettuce and tomato to her sandwich. The last thing she planned to do was tell anyone she was getting extra treats, snacks, and drinks when everyone else was suffering with food from the mess hall.

"That's what I thought you'd say." With the plate now cooled, Carey picked it up and leaned against the counter to eat. "So have you thought any more about college?"

"I haven't even finished high school yet," Grace said, mimicking her mentor's actions and leaning against the sink as she ate her sandwich.

"You will. It's one of your goals." Carey took a sip of her soda, then sat the can down on the counter. "Answer my question."

"I've thought about it, a little. There's no way I can afford it."

"Don't be so sure of that," Carey said. "If you want to go bad enough, there's always a way to find the money."

"Like you said before, I don't have any rich relatives on the verge of dropping dead."

"I'm sure I didn't put it in quite those terms," Carey said. "There are other ways to get money, Grace. Student loans, grants, work relief from the school where you put in so many hours working on campus in exchange for a break on tuition, the list goes on."

"Where did you go to college?"

"The Coast Guard Academy."

"Well I'm not interested in joining the military," Grace said. "I've had enough of ten hut as it is."

Carey chuckled and turned on the water to rinse her plate. "I'd have to agree," she said. "I can't see you in the service. I can, however, see you in college. Speaking of which, how are you doing on those practice SAT questions Instructor Donaldson found for you?"

"Okay," Grace said. "My scores for the verbal part are lower than the math."

"How much lower?"

Grace finished chewing before answering. "Out of a hundred test questions, I got sixteen wrong."

"Any particular area giving you the most trouble?"

"Relationships," Grace said. "You know, A is to B as what is to what."

"Ah," Carey said with a smile. "I disliked that part too. Keep working on it. As a matter of fact, instead of trying to be ten chapters ahead of everyone else in your classes, concentrate on those SAT practice tests this week."

"Why?"

"Because I said so." Carey took another drink of her soda. "I know, not an answer you like. I was able to reserve a slot for you for the next test but I'm still waiting for approval for the transportation. The test is this coming Saturday."

"Oh." *This Saturday? Three days away?* "I don't think I'll be ready by then."

"You'll do fine."

"Uh-huh," Grace said dubiously.

"You will," her mentor insisted. "You're just nervous."

"Dismissed," Carey said. "Waters, stay behind." Grace remained where she was, wondering if it had anything to do with the IJCF van that was parked near the administration building. Once everyone else was gone, Carey stood next to her. "Today is the last day to take the test until October," she said. "So I'll ask you again, do you want to take the SATs?"

"What happens if I fail it, ma'am?" Grace asked.

"You can't fail it. If you aren't happy with the score, you can take it again in October." A firm hand clasped Grace's shoulder. "Now I need to know. Do you want to go?"

"Yes, ma'am," Grace said, not wanting the opportunity to pass until October.

"All right," Carey said. "Go change into your PT shirt and sneakers. You can keep the khakis on since I don't think you want to go in BDUs or your shorts."

"Actually the BDU pants would be better, ma'am."

"Fine. Go get changed and meet me in my office."

"Yes, ma'am."

"You're not putting her in a jumpsuit?" was what Grace heard as she reached the office door. She paused, waiting for Carey's answer.

"She's going to take a test, not appear in court. It's bad enough you have to use the shackles. I'm not sending her into a test room looking like a convict any more than I have to."

"Suit yourself," the deep-voiced woman said. "Don't worry, she won't go anywhere."

"One more thing. When you get to the school, can you take the shackles off before she has to go inside?"

"Now you're asking too much. Why don't I give her twenty bucks and the bus schedule, too?"

"You have to take the handcuffs off for her to take the test."

"I only have to let one hand out."

"It's your call, of course, but I would take it as a great personal favor if you would do this."

There was a pause during which Grace held her breath, hoping the corrections officer would give in.

"Shackles to and from, leg irons there. So where's the delinquent?"

Grace tiptoed back several steps, then approached again and knocked on the door. "Instructor Carey?"

"Come in."

Entering the room, Grace saw the face that belonged to the gravely voice. It was not a corrections officer that she had ever seen before, but it was clear from the squinted eyes and pinched lips that the woman did not like her. "I'm ready, ma'am."

"Almost," Carey said, opening her top desk drawer. "You're allowed to bring two number two pencils," she said, putting the items on the desk. "Officer Baker will take you to Mohawk High School where you'll take the test, then you'll be returned here."

"I'll be waiting right outside the classroom," the corrections officer said. "Attempted escape carries an automatic six months at Crestwood, or if you're old enough, the women's facility in Irwin."

"I won't try to escape," Grace said, doing her best to keep any attitude out of her voice.

The guard looked at her from head to toe, then shook her head. "I'd rather have her in a jumpsuit."

"I'll take full responsibility," Carey said, then her brown eyes locked on Grace. "She'll be a model young lady."

"Yes, ma'am," Grace said, snapping to attention.

"Search and shackle, let's go," the guard said, grabbing Grace's arm and muscling her face first against the wall. "I know you know the position."

Grace closed her eyes, finding the situation humiliating, especially in front of her mentor. *Hey, watch those hands*, she thought to herself as they closed around her breasts and felt for any foreign objects that could be hidden in her sports bra. It took longer than Grace felt was necessary, but she knew better than to say anything. Finally every inch of her upper body was searched. Now the meaty hands slithered up her left leg, reaching the apex and pressing up hard enough that she was forced to go up on her toes before the procedure was repeated on her other leg. *Getting a good feel, you bitch?*

"Turn around, wrists together out in front of your body, legs shoulder length apart." Grace opened her eyes and turned around, putting her hands as instructed. She looked over to where Instructor Carey was standing, surprised to see her mentor looking out the window. *She doesn't like this either*, she thought to herself. Chains went around her waist, secured by a lock that the guard felt the need to jerk hard to prove it was secure. Grace lost her balance but recovered quickly, refusing to let the corrections officer get the best of her. "Left arm down at your side." The handcuff was slapped on, then locked into position. Her right wrist was held in a punishing grip as the final restraint was applied. "The prisoner is ready for transport," the guard said. "If you'll just sign the release forms."

Carey turned away from the window and crossed the three steps to her desk. After taking the clipboard and scrawling her name across the bottom of the form, she handed it to the corrections officer. Picking up the pencils, she walked over to Grace. "Good luck," she said, opening the side pocket of Grace's camouflage pants and putting them inside. "Good luck."

"Thank you, ma'am."

"Just do your best. I know you'll do good."

"I will, ma'am."

"Hey, where's she going?" Jan asked, jabbing Latisha as Grace was led out of the administration building in shackles, Instructor Carey right behind her. "What happened?"

"I don't know," Latisha said. "She didn't say anything to me."

"Did she do something?"

"Not that I know of," Latisha said. "Instructor Mitchell, what's happening to Grace?"

"You don't have enough of your own business to mind?" the instructor said. "Get stretching. Instructor Carey will be with you in a few minutes."

"Yes, ma'am," Latisha said.

The small windows provided Grace with only a view of passing trees and utility poles. While she hated the shackles, she found the seat restraints to be even more loathsome. *Get some decent shocks on this thing,* she thought as the van went over another bone-jarring bump, bouncing her on the metal bench on which she was restrained. All the questions on the practice test fled her mind and even the simplest equation seemed an insurmountable task. She decided the verbal part was a total loss, having no idea what was on it or even what to expect beyond multiple choice answers. When the trees gave way to buildings and the van slowed, Grace found her hands starting to sweat and rubbed them on her camouflage pants. *It's just a test, right? Nothing to get worked up about. Just a test Viking expects me to ace. What if they ask questions I don't know? FOIL, outer, inner, no—first, outer, inner, last. That's it. Now what's that for?* The van slowed to a stop, causing nervous anticipation to well up within her. *What am I doing here? Everyone else has been in study groups, or at least did some studying for this. I'm gonna bomb, I know it.* The single large door on the back of the van opened, flooding the cabin with sunlight. Officer Baker turned the key to unlock the mesh gate, then stepped inside.

"You try to take off and I'll break your legs, you got that?"

"Yes," Grace said as the seat restraints were removed. "I'm not gonna try anything."

"I've heard that before," the corrections officer said, backing out of the van. "All right, come out slowly." As much as Grace disdained the woman, she was nonetheless appreciative of the steadying hand that helped her step down. "When I release your handcuffs, keep your hands still until I tell you otherwise." The cuffs were removed, then the chains that met at her waist. "Hold still." Another set of leg cuffs were put on her, the chain shorter than the one required for use with the shackles. Finally the first set of leg cuffs were removed and Officer Baker stepped back. "Since there will be a proctor in the room, I'll wait in the hall."

Grace looked at the question again. *Wolf is to pack as blank is to blank: horse to saddle, goose to flock, fox to lair, dog to sled or lion to cub.* Grace tapped her pencil rhythmically against her chin. *I hate these questions. Wolves run in packs. Dogs run with sleds. Is that what they mean? No. It's supposed to be a clear relationship. That's what the instructions said. Flock. A goose flies in a flock. A single to a group. That's got to be it.* Grace let the pencil hover over the circle, reading the question once more before filling in her answer. Thumbing the remaining pages, Grace let out a long breath. *I'll never make it.* Without thought she shifted her feet, causing the chain to scrape against the floor. *Damn.* Several heads turned but just as quickly went back to their own tests. Tapping her chin with the pencil, Grace looked at the next question. *Down is to goose...What is it with all these questions about geese? All right, down is to goose...*

"All right, settle down," Carey said as Bravo Squad entered the classroom. "Take your seats and get those pens out from behind your ears. We have a lot to cover today."

"What happened to Waters, ma'am?" Jan asked.

"I hope you were worried more about your homework than what's going on with someone else," Carey said. "Now, we were talking about the types of sexually transmitted diseases. Bowen, what's the cure for herpes?"

"Um, penicillin, ma'am?"

"Bowen, drop for ten. Campbell, cure for herpes."

"Surgery, ma'am."

"Campbell, drop for ten. Hathaway, cure for herpes."

"There is no cure, ma'am."

"Good, I was beginning to think that for some reason the writers of your text forgot to include it," Carey said. "Do you girls need to go back to the barracks and pick up your brains? Jones, what are the visible symptoms of herpes?"

"A rash, ma'am?"

Carey slammed her book on the desk. "Jones, when were you planning on studying?"

"First period study hall, ma'am."

"And did you even open your book?"

"Yes, ma'am."

"Really? Did you read it?"

"No, ma'am."

"So what were you doing?"

"I was asking if anyone knew what happened to Grace, ma'am."

"If Waters wants you to know what happened, she'll tell you when she gets back," Carey said, seeing smiles form on many of the faces in the class now that they knew Grace would be returning. "Now since obviously Hathaway seems to be the only one who did any reading, you can all sit here and read not only what I assigned for today but through the end of the chapter. Next class will be a test."

"And...time. Please put your pencils down and remain in your seats," the proctor said, closing his pocket watch and rising from his seat. "After I collect your exam, you may leave." Grace remained in her seat, not wanting to have everyone see her leg irons. Only after the last student had left did she get up from her seat, her legs groaning after being in the same position for so long.

Stepping into the hall, Grace was surprised to find it deserted. *Maybe she went to the bathroom. I'd better stay right here.* Leaning against a locker, she waited until the proctor left the room. "I'm sorry, miss, you have to leave now," he said.

"I'm supposed to wait for the guard to get me," Grace said, wiggling her leg and making the chain jangle.

He pulled his pocket watch out again and checked the time. "I don't know what to tell you, but I need to lock up the school."

What am I supposed to do? "Sir, can you just wait here a minute and I'll check and see if she's in the ladies room? Please, if she shows up and I'm not here, I'm gonna be in big trouble."

He sighed and shut the classroom door. "The ladies room is down the hall on the right side. It's the only one available during testing times."

"Thanks," Grace said, moving as fast as her leg chains would let her. The bathroom was halfway down the hall but when she opened the door and called out, no one answered. Now very nervous, she checked each stall before returning to the hallway. "Did she show up?" she asked, even though she could clearly see only the proctor was standing in the hallway.

"No. Come on, miss, you'll have to wait outside."

There was no sign of the IJCF van when she went outside. An hour later she was still sitting on the high school steps. She thought about calling Sapling Hill and letting them know what was going on but there was no pay phone in sight and she was afraid not to be right there when the corrections officer did show up. So she sat there, her feet on the step below with the chain slack hidden behind her feet. Passersby would see nothing more than a teen sitting on the high school steps waiting for a ride. When the van did pull up, an angry Officer Baker greeted her. "Let's go, get down here," the woman yelled from the curb while opening the rear door of the van. Grace worked her way down the steps, mindful of the short chain that hobbled her usual gait. "I thought it was a four-hour test."

"Three," Grace said, letting her hands rest at her sides in preparation for the shackles. "It ended about two hours ago." The guard moved quickly, wrenching Grace's arm up behind her back and slamming her against the mesh door.

"Did I ask you a question, you little bitch?"

Grace smelled alcohol on the woman's breath.

"Now stand still." Grace gritted her teeth as the drunken woman's hands moved over her torso, then up to her breasts.

"Having fun?" Grace said, her anger flaring.

"I'm just making sure you're not hiding anything," the corrections officer said, backing up and easing the pressure of the mesh against Grace's cheek. "Turn around." The shackles were applied, then the wire mesh door was opened. "Get up there." The leg chain made it impossible for her to just step up, forcing Grace to go in butt first, then roll up on her knees. As she was about to push herself up onto the seat, the guard was there, pushing Grace off balance and causing her to fall against the hard steel edge of the bench.

"Ow, shit!" Grace said as she tumbled to the floor, her shackled wrists making it impossible to break her fall. Officer Baker grabbed her by the upper arm and pulled her up onto the bench seat.

"Stop your whining." The restraints were secured, then the crouched guard stepped out of the van. "I'm not listening to your mouth all the way back." Grace heard the driver's door open and close, then the burly woman returned. "Give me a reason," she said, holding a wide roll of duct tape.

No fucking way, Grace thought to herself, staring hard at the floor knowing that if she looked up and saw the mocking look on the guard's face she would lose her temper.

"I had to spend my whole day waiting around for you," Officer Baker said, stepping into the van and crouching down in front of her. "Beautiful day like today where I could have been relaxing at home and I had to be called in because you wanted to go take a test and get away from the hill for the day."

Don't say anything. Don't look. Just stay quiet.

"Huh? What's that? Don't have anything to say now?"

Grace shook her head. *Just get up front where you belong, you fucking bitch.*

"That's what I thought," the guard said, backing up out of the van. "You just remember, one word and I'll shut your mouth for you." The wire mesh gate slammed shut.

There was a short knock, followed by Gage opening the door. "I just spoke to IJCF. They haven't heard anything."

"So where is she?" Carey asked, turning away from the window. "It's a little over an hour to Mohawk. Three hours for the test, then back here. Six hours tops." She looked at her watch. "Eight and a half hours so far."

Gage pointed at the window. "Here they come."

Carey stormed out of the office, Gage on her heels. "Where have you been?" she asked as the corrections officer stepped out of the van.

"Flat tire," she said. "Radio doesn't carry too well up here." Officer Baker inserted the key in the lock, then opened the rear door. "Couldn't even raise a tow truck."

"Really," Carey said, looking at the two tires visible to her. "You had the phone number for here. Why didn't you call?"

"No phones nearby," the guard said, opening the mesh door and stepping inside. Carey strolled around the van, returning to the rear just as the burly woman pulled Grace out. "Do you want me to search her?"

"We'll take care of it," Carey said. "Just get those manacles off her." She was bothered by the way Grace refused to look at her or any instructor. "Waters, how did the test go?"

"Okay, ma'am," the teen said without enthusiasm.

"Do you need some help?" Carey asked the guard, who was taking far longer than she liked.

"It would be easier if she'd hold still," Officer Baker said, releasing the last ankle cuff. "Keep your arms down at your sides." There were a few clicks, then the guard stepped back with an armful of chains.

"Waters, follow Instructor Gage inside," Carey said, gripping the clipboard tightly.

"Yes, ma'am."

"What a day," Baker said, reaching out for the clipboard. "I told you she should have been in a jumpsuit. Nothing but trouble all the way up and back."

"I'll take care of it," came Carey's tightlipped reply. "Officer..." She looked down at her copy of the transport form. "Baker."

The smile left the guard's face. "Like I said, trouble. You know how these girls are. You can't believe anything they say."

Carey stared at her for a moment, knowing her eyes conveyed her feelings about who the real liar would be, then turned and went inside.

Entering her office, Carey found Grace sitting while Gage stood behind the chair. "What happened?"

"I'm not sure, ma'am," Grace said.

"Then tell me what you do know," Carey said, taking her seat and reaching for a blank pad of paper.

"I got to the school and she let me go inside and told me she'd wait for me in the hall," Grace said. "When the test was over, she wasn't there, ma'am."

"What do you mean she wasn't there?" Carey asked, putting her hands on the desk and rising from her seat.

"I was sure she said she'd be in the hallway but she wasn't, and then after an hour the man had to lock the school up so I sat on the steps outside and waited until she showed up, ma'am."

"How long were you sitting there?"

Grace shrugged. "I'm not sure. I think around two hours. She must have lost track of time drinking at the bar, ma'am."

"What bar?"

"I don't know, but when she came to get me, she was drunk, ma'am."

"How do you know that?"

"I smelled it on her breath, ma'am."

"And you don't know how long you were sitting there?"

"I don't have a watch, but it was a long time, ma'am. Two, maybe two and a half hours."

"And you sat on the steps?" Gage asked. "You didn't go anywhere?"

Grace shook her head. "I thought about going to a pay phone to call you, but I didn't see any and I didn't want to be caught walking around, ma'am."

"So when was the flat tire?" Gage asked.

Grace looked confused. "I don't know anything about a flat tire, ma'am."

"From the time you got into the van until you were dropped off here," Carey said, exchanging looks with Instructor Gage. "Did the van stop at all?"

"No, ma'am."

"She was left unattended," Gage said.

"She was left unattended," Carey repeated, sinking back into her chair and rubbing her forehead. "All the tires looked the same. I didn't see where any had been changed recently." Clicking her pen, she circled Baker's name on the transport form. "Waters, what happened remains private, do you understand?"

"Yes, ma'am."

"You can talk about going to take the SAT, but nothing about what happened with that woman. I mean it, not one word."

"I won't say anything, ma'am."

Carey took a deep breath, then slowly exhaled. "You were left unsupervised in a public place. I'm afraid I have no alternative. You have to submit to a strip search."

Grace frowned, but nodded. "Yes, ma'am. Ma'am?"

"Yes?"

"Would it be all right, I mean Instructor Gage can watch me, but would it be all right to go to the bathroom first, ma'am?"

"Actually that's a good idea," Carey said. "Pick up a specimen bottle on the way."

"I'll have to watch and search the stall afterwards, Waters," Gage said. "Let's go."

"Come back here when you're done," Carey said, opening her rolodex. "Sue, make sure I'm off the phone first."

Gage nodded. "Okay, Waters, let's go."

"Yes, ma'am." As soon as the door was closed, Carey began dialing. "Iroquois Juvenile Correction Facility."

"This is Instructor Carey at Sapling Hill. I want whoever is in charge, right now!"

"Sit," Carey said when Grace and Gage entered the room. "I take it everything was fine?"

"Nothing found but two well-chewed pencils," Gage said. "I have the urine sample tagged and in the holding fridge."

"You understand we're going to do a drug test on that urine, don't you?"

"Yes, ma'am."

Carey pulled out a form and scribbled Grace's name on it. "Did you have any coffee, poppy seed bagels, over the counter medications, cigarettes, or anything else I should know about?"

"Just the coffee I had this morning in your cabin. Other than that, no, ma'am."

"What did you eat today?"

"A breakfast sandwich, ma'am."

"What else?" Carey asked, looking down at the form.

"Nothing, ma'am."

"What?" Carey's head shot up, catching the same astonished look in Gage's eyes. "It's almost 1700 hours. What did you have to drink?"

"I had some water from the school fountain while I was waiting, ma'am."

"Do you want something from the mess hall?"

"No, ma'am. I can wait for dinner, ma'am."

"Instructor Carey, you should know I observed a red mark on her back running from her right shoulder diagonally to her left hip," Gage said.

Carey rubbed her left temple, knowing the slight pain would turn into a massive headache before the night was over. "How did it happen?"

"Robocop shoved me when I was getting in and I fell against the bench, ma'am," Grace said.

Carey looked at Gage. "How bad is this mark?"

"It's red, but the bruising around it doesn't look too bad," Gage said.

"Are you in pain, Waters?"

Grace shook her head. "No, ma'am."

"Tell me, in detail, exactly how you got that mark," Carey said, exchanging concerned looks with Gage.

"When she finally showed up, she put the shackles on me and I got in the van," Grace said. "When I turned around to sit down, she shoved me and told me I shouldn't have been allowed to go to take the test in the first place. That's when I hit the bench. Then she pulled me up and pushed me onto the seat, ma'am."

Tearing off the paper she had been writing notes on, Carey pushed the pad and pen over. "Start with coming into this office this morning for transport and put down every single detail until this minute. If you sneezed, I want to know about it. If you bumped your foot against a step, I want to know. Every detail, and don't even think about exaggerating or adding things that didn't happen."

"Yes, ma'am," Grace said. "Ma'am?"

Carey exchanged a concerned look with Gage. "Yes?"

Grace looked at her with all seriousness. "I didn't do anything wrong, I didn't mouth off to her or give her any trouble, I swear it. And I didn't go anywhere. I really didn't, ma'am."

"Don't say anything else until you have that statement written," Carey said. "Sue, stop by the mess hall and pick up a dinner for her, then get Marilyn. I need both of you to make observation reports." She reached for the Rolodex. "I'll call for the nurse."

"You think that's really necessary?" Gage asked.

"She was injured while outside of our custody," Carey said. "I'm not explaining to the brass why there's a report of an injury with no medical documentation."

"Do you want anything?"

Carey used her thumb and forefinger to rub her temples. "A king sized aspirin," she said, picking up the phone. Gage left, shutting the door behind her.

"Fuller Medical Group."

"Yes, this is Joanna Carey of Sapling Hill. I have a girl here that I need to have examined."

"This is the service. I'll notify the nurse on call."

"Thank you." Carey hung up the phone. It was the part of the job she hated the most, being an administrator when what she wanted to do was mentor the teen sitting across from her. She wished she could just tell Grace she believed her, but she had to remain completely neutral until the investigation, if there was one, was complete. Despite having her own paperwork to do, Carey watched as Grace filled one page, then started on another. When the teen finished, she set the pen down and looked at Carey expectantly.

"Everything in there is exactly what happened?"

"Yes, ma'am."

The door opened and Instructors Gage and Donaldson entered, setting a dinner tray on top of the file cabinet. "Grace, the statement you just wrote is a true and accurate representation of what happened today, is that correct?"

"Yes, ma'am."

"And that entire statement is in your handwriting, is that correct?"

"Yes, ma'am."

"Has anyone helped or told you what to write other than my original instructions?"

"No, ma'am."

Carey looked at her watch. "It's 1745. Waters, write down the date and time, sign your full legal name, then hand it to Instructor Gage."

"Yes, ma'am."

Carey handed the observation forms to her blonde coworker. "She's going to eat first, then take her in the back and do a visual."

"Do you want a picture?"

Before Carey could answer, she saw Gage nodding. "It's a good idea," she said, opening the top drawer and removing the key to the supply locker where the camera was kept. She wanted to ask how the test went, how Grace felt, but that was impossible at the moment. "Grace, other than your back, are you injured anywhere else?"

"I don't think so, ma'am."

"All right. Go ahead and eat," Carey said, taking Grace's signed statement from Donaldson. As she read it over, her headache worsened. As much as she believed what Grace said had happened, she knew it would come down to the teen's word against a corrections officer. Marking her initials in the lower left hand corner of each handwritten page, Carey made a notation in her incident report referencing the statement, then finished filling in the various parts of the form. When Grace finished eating, Carey had her escorted to another room to strip and have the mark on her back photographed. Then it was more paperwork as the nurse arrived with forms of her own both before and after examining Grace. When the evening ended, Carey had a stack of papers, a headache that refused to go away, and the promise that the next day would be just as bad when the corrections officer's report was turned in.

It was almost lights out by the time Grace was allowed to leave the infirmary and return to the cabin. The illumination from inside told her that Instructor Carey was already there. *Please don't want to talk about it,* she thought as she climbed the steps. *I just want to go to sleep and forget about the whole damn day.* Stepping inside, she found the dark-haired woman sitting in the recliner. "Hello, ma'am."

"Come sit down," Carey said, gesturing at the couch. "Are you still hungry?"

"No," Grace said as she sat down. "I'm fine."

Carey leaned forward, putting the footrest down and resting her elbows on her knees. "Grace, talk to me."

"I've already told you what happened," Grace said.

"Not about that," Carey said. "The test. I remember how stressful it was for me to take the SAT."

"I've never taken a test that hard," Grace said. "I thought I'd never finish it."

"How do you think you did?"

"I don't know. I think I did okay. On the math part anyway." She shook her head. "The verbal was really hard. I um...I didn't finish the last section," she admitted. "He called time and I still had five questions to go."

Carey smiled and leaned back in her chair. "Only five? You never saw someone fill circles in so fast when I took the test. I think I had twenty."

"You guessed at the last ones too?"

"Yes, they say not to but I panicked when the proctor called time," Carey said.

"Me too." Grace smiled, feeling a little better.

Carey steepled her fingers. "The investigation precludes me from talking to you about what happened with Officer Baker, but I will tell you that I'm proud of the way you restrained your mouth. At least when you returned. I could tell you were angry."

Grace nodded. "I was, but I knew you'd be upset if I lost it."

"I would have," Carey said. "You're showing real progress, Grace. The last time you were dropped off by a correctional officer you had to have your mouth gagged. I'm not saying that to embarrass you. I'm reminding you of where you've been and how far you've come." She snapped her fingers, making Grace look at her and not the coffee table. "You realize it's been over a week since you've made me drop you?"

"Six days," Grace corrected. "Remember, I caught my toe on the corner of the couch."

"You're right," Carey said. "I've been around sailors with much cleaner language than you use." Resting her elbows on the armrest, she laced her fingers together. "There was a time when I doubted you could go six hours, much less six days."

"Me too," Grace said. "It seemed like everything I did got you mad."

"Some things made me mad," Carey said. "The eye rolling for one."

"I've been real good about that," Grace said.

"You have," the instructor said. "I don't take joy in disciplining you, Grace. I do it because you need it, because you've broken a rule, or because you've been disrespectful either to yourself or to someone else."

"Instructor Carey? Thanks for not making me go in a jumpsuit." Instead of looking at the coffee table like she usually did, she met the brown eyes squarely. "I know you didn't have to do that and...well...I just wanted you to know I appreciated it."

"You're welcome," Carey said, giving the teen an approving smile. "I never thought I'd hear that from you." She pushed the footrest down and stood up. "You want a soda?"

"Oh yeah, that'd be great," Grace said.

"Come on," Carey said. "Talk to me nicely and there might be a pint of cherry vanilla in the freezer that we can share."

"So does that mean you're going to college?" Latisha asked.

Grace stabbed at the green beans. "Where am I supposed to get money for college? Rob a bank?"

"What about loans and all those things they give to us poor unfortunates?" Jan asked. "My cousin got to go to cosmetology school and they even gave her money for the bus and lunch each day. Maybe you could do something like that."

"Are you kidding?" Rosetti said. "You remember her hair when she came in here? She looked like a mad troll."

"Fuck you, Rosetti," Grace said. "I only had three or four colors in it. Besides, I'm not into playing hairdresser."

"So there's got to be other ways," Jan said.

"Yeah, maybe I'll win the lottery. Of course you have to be eighteen to buy a ticket, so that's out." She snapped her fingers. "I know, I'll win a scholarship for wayward girls who get expelled from school. Forget it, Jan. College isn't for me."

"But you're the smartest one here," Jan said. "If anyone can get to college, it's you."

"Why would I want to spend four more years in school?" Grace asked, jabbing a piece of meat and popping it into her mouth. "I couldn't wait to get out of high school. You know, even the ones who get scholarships still have to work. Why not just work full time and get the money?"

"Have a kid," Lopez said. "They paid for my sister's apartment, she gets the Medicaid, and they pay for her to go to college," Lopez said. "Even paid for her day care."

"That's because she has a kid and is on welfare," Grace said.

"Well there you go," Jan said. "Go screw around, have a kid, then let the state pay for you to go to—uh-oh."

"And I couldn't figure out what we were going to talk about in SR today," Instructor Carey said from behind Grace's chair. "Thanks, ladies."

Grace remained quiet until she was sure the instructor was out of earshot. "Damn. How does she do that?"

"I don't know, but I bet she's got a dart board in her office with your picture on it," Jan said.

"Since you girls found the topic so interesting at lunch, let's talk about what it means to have children." Carey sat on her desk, her hands curled around the edge. "In this state, half of all families on welfare started with teenage pregnancy. Why?" Brown eyes scanned the room. "Rosetti."

"Because teen mothers can't afford it, ma'am."

"It." Carey shook her head. "You make a baby sound like a car. It's a baby. A living, breathing, extremely expensive and needy human being. There is not a single one of you who can afford to take care of yourselves much less a baby, and if you think Mr. Wonderful is going to step up to the plate and take financial responsibility, or any responsibility, think again. In cases when the mother's age is between sixteen and twenty, less than half of the fathers are identified on the birth certificates." She pushed off the desk and walked between the rows of desks. "Now if the cost isn't enough to convince you, think about the baby's health. Teens are twice as likely not to receive adequate prenatal care as women in their twenties, and almost three times less than women over the age of thirty. Waters, give me an example of what can happen without proper prenatal care."

"Um, birth defects, ma'am."

"Such as?"

"Being retarded, ma'am."

"Mental retardation is a good one. Campbell, name another."

"Physical defects, ma'am."

"Low birth weight and underdeveloped organs are also what teen mothers can look forward to," Carey said. "Children of teen parents are twice as likely to be victims of child abuse and neglect. Jones, is that what you want for your children?"

"No, ma'am."

"Rosetti, what about you?"

"No, ma'am."

"Having kids doesn't seem like a big joke now, does it?"

"No, ma'am," the group said.

"So let's talk about money, since Maribel seems to think having babies is the answer to financial problems. Think kids are cheap? Waters, you have an extra nine hundred dollars lying around?"

"No, ma'am."

"That's how much diapers cost for a year, if you look for sales and buy the cheapest ones," Carey said. "Bowen, feel like dropping a thousand for formula?"

"No, ma'am."

"Let's say you want to finish school, or if you're old enough, work full time. If you're lucky, child care will run between six and eight thousand a year. Working full time at McDonald's will earn you less than twelve thousand gross, and in this state, nine thousand net. So out of the nine thousand you can possibly hope to earn, there's no chance of making ends meet. Lopez, still sound like a good idea?"

"No, ma'am."

"Not so appealing now, is it?" She looked around. "Jones."

"No, ma'am."

"Good. Try to remember that when Prince Charming doesn't want to spend a few bucks on condoms. Any questions?" Nine heads looked everywhere but at her. "I should have known better than to ask. All right, open up your books and turn to page one thirty-seven. We'll start the chapter on abortion."

Grace closed her book, too bored to read another word. "I can't believe you don't have a television."

"When would I have time to watch it?" Carey asked. "When I'm not working with you girls, I'm here grading papers, planning lessons, or doing administrative work. Either that or sleeping. Why clutter the place with something that would only collect dust?"

"You have to take a break sometime," Grace said. "I can't read any more."

"There are other things you can do to pass the time besides zone out to the television," Carey said.

"Like what?"

"Sociable things, like play cards or chat with friends. You're not on restriction, Grace. You can go to the rec room."

"I don't feel like it," she said. "Do you have a deck of cards? I can play solitaire."

"I'll get them," Carey said, rising from her seat. "What games do you know how to play?"

"Poker, crazy eights, rummy, the usual," Grace said.

"Do you know how to play cribbage?"

"No."

"Too bad. It's a fun game," Carey said as she disappeared into the bedroom, returning a moment later with a deck of cards. "How about gin?"

"Yeah, it's like rummy only you don't put your cards down until you go out."

Carey smiled. "Or until your opponent goes out," she said, handing the deck to Grace.

"Kinda hard to get into a game like that during free period because it's so noisy in the rec room," Grace said. "Besides, it takes a while if you're keeping track of points."

"Fine," Carey said, following her into the kitchen. "You can practice your math skills keeping score." She went to the refrigerator and retrieved two cans of soda. "Paper and pens are in that drawer over there."

"Okay," Grace said. "Play to five hundred or a thousand?"

"I'm not in the mood to pull an all-nighter," Carey said as she sat down. "Five hundred."

Grace wrote JC and GW on the paper, then set it aside and started shuffling the cards. "Oh, did you want to deal first?"

"No, you go right ahead." Carey took a sip of soda. "So did anything I said in SR today sink in?"

Grace started dealing the cards. "I'm not planning on having kids," she said.

"In the near future, or ever?"

"I don't know," the teen said. "They're so messy, and changing diapers?" She shook her head. "Doesn't sound like something I wanna do."

Carey chuckled and picked up her cards. "That's one way to look at it."

"What about you?" Grace dared to ask.

"Crossing that line again," Carey said, discarding the nine of hearts. "If I did, it wouldn't be soon enough for my mother. She's been dying to be a grandmother for years now. Your turn."

You didn't answer the question, Grace thought as she picked up the card. "I'm an only child so I guess my mother's not gonna become a grandmother either."

"It's good that you realize how important a decision it is to make a baby," Carey said, laying her cards down on the table. "Gin."

Grace stared in disbelief. "That was too quick," she protested.

"That's the way the cards were dealt," Carey said, reaching for her soda. "Add them up, Waters."

"Face cards are ten, right?" Grace asked, holding a handful of them. She frowned at the answering nod. "You sure you don't wanna play to a thousand?"

Carey reached out and tilted Grace's cards to see. "You had the queens," she said. "I was looking for them."

"You can have them now if you want them," Grace offered, mentally calculating the score. "One seventeen."

Carey clapped her hands together and gathered up the cards. "You catch me with a good hand and you'll be able to make that up," she said. "While I'm shuffling, you can get the snacks out of the cabinet next to the refrigerator."

Grace jumped up quickly. "Great." She knew from looking around when Carey was working late tour exactly what was in that cabinet.

Carey dealt out the cards. "Use a napkin to wipe your hands," she said. "I don't want potato chip grease all over the cards."

"I will," Grace said as she grabbed the bags of chips, pretzels, and chocolate chip cookies. The teen had been eyeing the cookies for days but had not dared help herself to any. "Do you want bowls, or can we just eat out of the bags?"

"Either way," Carey said.

Grace decided to forego bowls, not wanting to wash them afterward. Setting the snacks on the table, she picked up her cards, sorting them by suit. "What a lousy hand."

"Mine's no better," Carey said.

"You could tell me what you need and I could see if I have it," Grace said, picking up the top card of the deck. *Oh, that helps.* She debated for a few seconds before discarding the ace of diamonds.

"Well that's not one of them," Carey said, reaching for the deck. "What are you looking for? Not aces, apparently."

"We're probably looking for the same cards," Grace said as she helped herself to a cookie, then took her turn. *That helps too.*

"Could be," Carey said as she picked up a card. "I'm not telling, though. Pass the pretzels."

Grace pushed the bag over, then snared another cookie. "You must have all the spades because I don't have any," she said as she pulled yet another helpful card from the deck. *Ooh, I just need the seven.*

"Maybe," Carey said, grinning as she took her turn. "I guess you'll just have to wait until I go out."

"Or until I go out," Grace said, smiling as she tossed a card on the discard pile and laid her hand down. "Gin."

"Good job," Carey said, quickly figuring out the total points in her hand. "Eighty-five."

"I'm catching up," Grace said, scooping up the cards. "I knew you had the spades."

"And you've had half a dozen cookies so far," Carey said, reaching over and moving the box out of the teen's reach. "Save some for another time."

"They're good," Grace said. "I love chocolate chip."

"So do I, and I'd like a few before the box is empty," Carey said. "Now deal."

Grace smiled. "Yes, ma'am." She doled out the required number of cards, then drained the rest of her soda.

"You couldn't have dealt me a worse hand if you tried," Carey said. "What a mess."

"Good," Grace said, smiling at the cards she was holding.

"Oh really?" Carey smirked and drew a card from the pile, then debated for several seconds before choosing her discard. "Don't get too confident, Grace."

"I won't." *Hah,* she thought as she drew a card. *Come on, Carey. Give me the ten of hearts.* "Your turn."

"You should never play poker," Carey said. "Waiting on one card, aren't you?"

"Maybe."

"Uh-huh, your turn."

Please be the ten of hearts. Please be the ten of hearts. "Yes," she exclaimed. "Gin." She rubbed her hands together gleefully and picked up the pen. "How many?"

"Let's see, sixty, seventy, seventy-seven, eighty-five, ninety-two. Ninety-two."

Grace passed her cards over. "That puts me in the lead."

"Not for long," Carey said. "I have a feeling this hand's going to be mine."

"This is fun," Grace said, picking up her cards. "We should do this again sometime."

Carey sorted her cards. "We'll see. I have to admit I expected you to demolish all the snacks by now."

Grace eyed the box of cookies. "I would have but you took them away," she said. "And the chips make me thirsty." She picked up her empty soda can and wiggled it. "I don't feel like water."

"I can just imagine what you are in the mood to drink," Carey said, tossing out a card. "One more and while you're at it, grab me a grape, would you?"

"Sure." Grace set her cards face down on the table and went to the refrigerator. *This is great,* she thought to herself. *I never thought I'd be sitting at the kitchen table playing cards with her.* "Instructor Carey? Do you play chess?"

"Yes. Do you play?"

Grace nodded, then realized she could not be seen through the refrigerator door. "Oh yeah. I tried to teach Jan but she doesn't have the patience for it."

"I don't have a chess set," Carey said. "And you're letting all the cold air out."

"Sorry." Grace took the two cans and closed the door. "There's a set in the rec room," she said as she handed the older woman the soda.

"I'll check and see if Sue has one," Carey said. "Your turn."

"Cool." The teen quickly sorted her cards. "So can we?" she asked as she drew a card.

"Can we what?"

"Play again sometime," Grace said.

"Does playing cards equate you being allowed to inhale all the cookies?"

"It doesn't have to but..." Grace gave her best puppy dog look.

Carey rearranged her cards, then set them down and reached for the box of cookies. "As long as your homework is done and you continue to act like a young lady and not a hoodlum, I'm sure I can be persuaded from time to time." She took a cookie, then pushed the box across the table to Grace. "One more." She watched her grin and reach in for another cookie. "You know, when you're not giving me death glares and scrapping with Lauren Grenner, you can be a very likable person."

Grace looked down at her cards. "She's the one that starts it."

"And you feel obligated to finish it," Carey said. "You have to learn to walk away, Grace. One of these days you'll come up against someone much worse than Grenner could ever dream of being, and the fight won't be with words but weapons." She snapped her fingers, causing Grace to look up from her cards. "I don't like seeing you hurt, especially when it can be avoided. By the way," Carey smiled and laid down her cards. "Gin."

"Have a seat," Carey said. "Since nothing escapes the eagle eyes of a Sapling Hill girl, I assume you saw the car that arrived today?"

"Yes, ma'am," Grace answered, wondering if it had anything to do with the incident on the day of her SATs.

"That was the district supervisor for the IJCF. He would be my boss's boss." Carey sat in her chair and did not look happy. "Grace, it went up to the attorney general and it's his opinion not to pursue any charges or reprimand against Officer Baker."

"They believed her over me," Grace said angrily. "I didn't do anything wrong."

"Remember where you are, Waters. You owe me ten."

"Yes, ma'am."

"And yes, they believe a corrections officer with no history of abusing prisoners over a teenager who threw a chair at a teacher and spit at another corrections officer. There's just not enough overwhelming evidence to make them think differently."

"But I'm not lying," Grace said, leaning forward in her seat. "Ask the man that gave the test. He'll tell you, ma'am."

"He was asked," Carey said. "That only suggests that she was not on the premises the entire time you were there. It doesn't substantiate any charges of abusing a prisoner while in custody."

"So is she even going to get in trouble for that?" Grace asked. "What about being drunk?"

"Since they didn't have her submit to a blood test until the next day, we can't prove she'd been drinking, and in light of her contention that you slipped out with the other students and went out a different door so you didn't see her..."

"No. There was one door and she said she'd be in the hall. I sat on those steps forever before she pulled up. I saw her pulling up. She wasn't there," Grace said, her voice rising. "Ma'am."

"Lower that tone," Carey said. "If you had been an honor student who was picked up and received rough treatment, the powers that be would be all over this. The problem is your record automatically makes your testimony suspect."

"So no matter what happened, I'm the one who gets punished, right, ma'am? I'm the one who gets strip searched and questioned and drug tested and monitored and treated like a criminal." Grace folded her arms across her chest. "It sucks, ma'am."

"It does," Carey said. "But we're not punishing you for anything that happened that day, Grace. You had to be examined because you were left unattended in a public place. What if you had sneaked in drugs? Whose ass do you think would be up on the flagpole?" Grace's scowl faded now that she understood why she had been subjected to a search and drug test. "The pictures were to protect you," Carey continued. "To show you had been injured and that it wasn't just a wild claim by a teenager looking to get out of trouble. Look at me. Grace, I know you understand how bad credit can affect you for years after you get everything straightened out. It works the same way in the correctional system."

"So I'm being punished because of what I did before, ma'am."

Carey shook her head. "It's more like Officer Baker isn't being punished because of what you've done before. She gets a free pass, but she's on notice that another complaint won't be so quickly dismissed."

"So what am I supposed to do?" Grace asked. "Just pretend it never happened, ma'am?"

"Is obsessing over it going to help?" Carey asked. "Let it go, Grace."

"Yeah, let it go," Grace said, her hands squeezing her upper arms and her eyes focused on the egg-shaped paperweight. It was happening again. She told the truth and it made no difference. "Let it go, let them do anything they want. It doesn't matter because no one will believe me. I tell the truth and it's like I don't know what I'm talking about or I'm lying or I'm confused and it didn't happen or he didn't mean anything by it or—"

"Wait a minute," Carey interjected. "He?"

Grace looked up at her. "What, ma'am?"

"You said he didn't mean anything by it," Carey said. "Who is he?"

Stricken by the slip of the tongue, Grace tried to recover. "I...I...I didn't mean he, ma'am," she said, her gaze lowering until she was looking at the paperweight.

Carey steepled her fingers. "Grace, what happened the summer before your junior year?"

Taken aback by the question, Grace looked away, her mind quickly going back to that fateful summer. "Nothing, ma'am."

"You know you just earned twenty," Carey said. "Look at me. Try again."

Grace wiped her palms on her thighs, quickly figuring out what to omit. "I got a new bike for passing tenth grade and I spent most of the summer hanging out with my friends, ma'am."

"You hung out with your friends all day and all night?"

"Not all the time, ma'am."

"And you were living with your mother?"

"Yes, ma'am."

"Was anyone else living there with you?" Carey asked, her dark eyes seeming to be able to see into the teen's soul.

Grace hesitated, then bowed her head and nodded. "Yes, ma'am."

"Look at me," Carey urged, leaning forward in her seat. "Who?"

Grace glanced up quickly, then looked at the egg again. "My mother's boyfriend, ma'am."

"The one that was here?"

"Yes, ma'am."

"What happened?"

Grace looked away, feeling the old pain flaring up inside. *Does she know? No, she can't. No one knows. She thinks he just hit me. So why is she asking all these questions? I can't tell her. I can't tell anyone.* "He had a fight with my mother and she threw him out, ma'am."

"When did she throw him out? At the beginning or end of the summer?"

"End, ma'am."

Carey rubbed the bridge of her nose, then slowly blew out a breath. "Grace, nothing you say here will be repeated to anyone. Do you understand that?"

"Yes, ma'am."

"He can't hurt you anymore," Carey said, her voice gentle. "Tell me what he did."

"He hit me, ma'am," she said, falling back on her previous answer.

"He did more than that, didn't he?" Carey asked softly.

"Gave me pot, ma'am."

"I'm not talking about that and you know it, Grace. What else did he do to you?"

"He...he..." Grace felt the tightening in her throat and the sting in her eyes. "He was an asshole, ma'am." She saw a small smile on the instructor's face.

"I don't doubt that a bit," Carey said, her smile was quickly replaced by a more serious look. "Tell me," she urged.

Grace put her elbows on her knees and buried her face in her hands. "Please, ma'am." She heard the creak of the chair, then felt the older woman kneeling next to her.

"I know it's scary," Carey said softly.

Grace sniffed. "Yes, ma'am."

A gentle arm reached around Grace's shoulders. "You can do it. You're a very strong young woman. I know you can."

The tears refused to stop streaming from her eyes. "I can't, I just can't, ma'am. Please don't make me." It was getting too hard. The feelings were too close to the surface. Her emotions were slipping out of her control.

"Tell me."

"No!" Grace jumped from her seat and bolted to the door only to be stopped by an even faster Instructor Carey.

"Sit back down."

"Stop asking me about it." Grace said, angrily wiping at her eyes.

"Grace—"

"No! Leave me alone." Grace grabbed at the door handle but was no match for the older woman's strength. The door refused to budge. "I'm not talking to you anymore," she said. "Let me go."

"You sit back down in that chair right now."

It would have been the right thing to do, but Grace was too upset and too far away from being in control to think clearly. She shoved the chair, knocking it over. "You can't make me!"

"You drop right this instant! Now!" Grace dropped, her palms flat on the short emerald green carpet. "That behavior is completely unacceptable. Do you understand?"

"Y-Yes, ma'am," Grace said as she started her pushups, the tears trickling down her cheeks.

"I don't care how upset you are. You do not walk out on a mentoring session, and you do not throw things!"

"Yes, ma'am."

"Now apologize."

"I'm...sorry, ma'am."

"Stand up." Grace looked straight ahead as the instructor stood at her right side. "Now you pick up that chair and you sit down and don't ever try a stunt like that again."

"Yes, ma'am." Grace righted the chair and wiped her face against her shirt as Instructor Carey returned to her own seat.

"And you wonder why I've put you in an anger management class?" Carey asked rhetorically. "You can't resort to violence to avoid dealing with your problems."

"Yes, ma'am."

"Now," Carey gentled her voice. "I don't enjoy yelling at you but you can't lose control like that. Look at me. The longer you hold it inside, the more it's going to hurt."

Grace sniffled and swiped at her face. *Please stop.*

"You will get to a point where you have to talk," Carey said. "When you do, I'm here. Instructor Gage is here. We'll listen."

"I know, ma'am."

"I hope you do," Carey said. "Grace, I only want to help you. If he touched you sexually, the fault is his, not yours. No matter what he said. Look at me." She steepled her fingers. "Tell me what to do to help you."

Grace fixed her stare at the paperweight, shutting down as she had with the psychologist at Crestwood. It was the only way she had to protect herself from feelings too painful to bear. "Nothing, ma'am."

"I'm over here," Carey said, reaching out and taking away the paperweight. "I can't help you if you don't let me." She waited but Grace refused to respond. "All right, go wash your face and get ready for whatever class you have next." The teen rose and headed for the door. "Grace, this isn't the last time we'll be having this conversation."

"Yes, ma'am."

"It's too hot to be in BDUs," Jan grumbled, lifting her olive cap and wiping her brow. "They should at least let us get out of the camo shirts."

"Word," Latisha said, fanning herself with her hat. "Scary's coming."

"All right, girls, line up," Instructor Carey said as she arrived, also dressed in camouflage pants and shirt. She set the box she was carrying on the ground. "I bet you're wondering where Alpha Squad is. Instructor

Gage came in early today so we could have this exercise. You have to work as a team to succeed at this task."

We're screwed, Grace thought to herself.

"There are four identical courses and the squads are going against each other for the best time," Carey continued. "There are blue flags hidden in this section of woods." She pointed at the trees behind the squad. "When you reach the finish line, each one of you must have a blue flag in your right side pocket. If it's in your shirt pocket, you lose. If it's in your left side pocket, you lose. One person missing a flag, you lose. Any questions so far?"

"No, ma'am," Bravo Squad said.

"When you have all nine flags, continue north until you reach the water tower. I'll give you further instructions then." Carey knelt down and opened the box. "Jones, pass these out." Taking one of the canteens, she stood up and unhooked her belt. "Loop it through your belt like this," she demonstrated. "I suggest you put it back here, not on the side where it would bounce against your hip and get in the way of your arm."

"Better it bounce off my ass," Jan said in a low voice to Grace.

"What good are empty canteens?" Grace asked as she took the plastic container and canvas carrying case. "Maybe we fill them at the water tower."

"So why give them to us now?" Jan said. "She could have had the box waiting at the tower."

"Yeah, but then we'll be timed," Grace said, tightening the web belt.

"So? We're probably gonna lose anyway," Jan said. "Christine always holds us back on these things."

"Enough chatter," Instructor Carey said, ending all the conversations. "Remember that teamwork will get you to victory and if the goal of being the best isn't enough for you, the winning squad gets a special treat, courtesy of your instructor." She removed the mirrored sunglasses, hooking them through her shirt pocket. "I bet a pint of ice cream would taste real good after a hard day of PT and classes, wouldn't it?"

"Yes, ma'am!" they shouted excitedly.

"Then I suggest you work hard and as a team to get the best time," Carey said, reaching for her whistle. "Bravo Squad ready?"

"Ready, ma'am," several girls said.

Carey blew her whistle. "Go."

"If you find one, help someone else," Campbell said as they split up and looked high and low for the elusive blue flags. Grace found one quickly, shouting out to let the others know. Some flags were hidden in the brush, others tacked up on the trees. The team spread out, covering the wooded area and finding the last flag dangling from a high branch.

"Well how the hell are we supposed to get it?" Jan asked as several made unsuccessful jumps at the flag taunting them from above.

"There's gotta be a trick to it," Grace said. "She said we had to work as a team to accomplish the goals."

"But we can't reach it and there's nowhere to hold onto so we can climb the tree," Jan said.

"If we can get some weight on that branch, I bet it'd come down to where we can reach it," Grace said, walking under the branch and studying how it arched and dipped. "Here. If we can get someone up to it, the weight should make it drop."

"It's at least twelve feet high," Jan said. "No one can jump that high."

"We can build a pyramid," Maribel said. "Like the cheerleaders do."

"You're definitely on the bottom, Bowen," Rosetti said.

"Bite me," Jan said, kneeling down and bracing herself. Grace knelt down next to her, offering her back for the next tier. Some of the girls argued about who would be a support and who would try to reach the branch. In the end, after much grumbling and time wasting, it was decided that Latisha would make the jump, being the lightest of the squad. Campbell took position on Jan's left side while Mo removed her glasses and became the fourth in the bottom layer.

"Watch that knee, Maribel," Grace said, wincing when the teen's knee pressed against her spine.

"I don't know if I can do this," Campbell said, adjusting her hands to lock her elbows. "Easy, Thompson, that's my friggin' back."

"Hey, it's high enough with two rows," Latisha said.

"Then hurry up and go," Grace said, feeling the strain of two girls' knees on her back. She felt the weight shift as Latisha climbed over the others to get to the top.

"Okay, I got it," Latisha said. "It won't come down far enough."

"Someone else get up there," Jan said. "And hurry the hell up."

There were several grunts and groans as Rosetti made the journey and gripped the branch. As Bravo Squad had hoped, the limb dipped enough for the last flag to be retrieved. "I'm letting go," Latisha said.

"I...can't hold on," Campbell said a split second before her arms gave out, sending the pyramid of teens tumbling down. Since they were in the middle, Jan and Grace took the worst of it, squashed between the ground and two layers of girls blindly pushing with their arms and legs to get out of the heap.

"Nine buckets, one spigot, one barrel," Carey said as the teens entered the clearing. She pointed at the knothole near the top of the barrel. "Your goal is to fill the barrel until water starts to come out of the hole. Once I say clear, go west two miles along the dirt path, clearing each obstacle," Carey said. "It's going to be a long hot run, ladies. You should think about that."

"Once she says clear," Grace said. "Let's fill our canteens from the barrel."

109

"Take off our canteens, then fill them and put them back on?" Jan shook her head. "That'll waste too much time."

"We don't have to take them off," Latisha said. "Just unsnap it from the case."

"Or loosen the belt and dunk the canteen in," Grace said. "Doesn't matter if we get wet. It's hot as hell already and we haven't even started running."

"Let's go, ladies," Cary said, "time is ticking away and so are your chances at getting ice cream." The teens scrambled to the buckets, then lined up at the spigot to fill them.

"Let's make a relay," Thompson said, handing her near-full bucket to Latisha and taking an empty one from Grace.

"Yeah, like those old bucket brigades they used for fires," Jan said, spreading out to make the chain from the tower to the barrel. "Don't fill them up so high because it's splashing out."

"Half full," Grace said. "It'll be lighter and easier to carry that way." She grunted as she took the nearly full bucket from Thompson and passed it to Jan. "Watch it, it's heavy."

"Jeez, Thompson, make it lighter, will ya?" Jan said as water sloshed over the sides of the metal buckets. It took a few tries to get a rhythm going but once they did, Bravo Squad had no trouble making their bucket brigade work.

"We're halfway there," Mo yelled. "Keep 'em coming."

"I can only fill the bucket so fast," Thompson said.

"So what are we supposed to be learning from this?" Jan asked. "Filling a barrel doesn't seem like a skill I'm going to be needing in the future."

"Well duh-uh," Grace said, handing her a bucket. "Think about it. If we each took turns filling a bucket and hauling it over there, we'd be tired and it'd probably take longer. Remember Carey said teamwork was the key. We're learning teamwork."

"Carey, huh?" Jan said, nudging her with an elbow. "What happened to Queen Bitch from Hell?"

Grace shrugged. "She's been easing up on the bitch lately. Even sat down and played cards with me the other night."

"You let her win, right?"

Grace passed another bucket. "I didn't let her win, she won because she plays gin better than I do."

"Uh-huh," Jan said. "Take my advice, if she asks you to play anything, let her win."

"Why? She's probably not a sore loser."

"You really wanna take the chance to find out?" Jan shook her head. "Why didn't they just let us play a game of softball or something? We have a ball field and never get to use it."

"I heard the state took the bats away after one girl cracked another girl's head open arguing balls and strikes," Thompson said. "Therefore we get to fill buckets with water."

"Almost there," Mo yelled. The squad moved faster, hoping each time a bucket was dumped that the water would be high enough to start coming out the hole.

"Get ready to fill your canteens," Grace said, reaching between bucket passes to loosen her belt.

"Clear!"

"Let's go," Jan said, the girls dropped the buckets and raced for the barrel. Water sloshed about as they pushed the canteens underwater and waited for the air bubbles to stop.

"Watch it," Latisha said when someone splashed water on her.

"Don't worry about it," Grace said, bracing her hands on the side of the barrel as the last canteen was filled. "It's so hot you'll dry in no time." Taking a deep breath, she closed her eyes and dunked her head. *Oh that's cold*, she thought, staying underwater for several seconds before standing up. "That felt good," she said, running her fingers through her wet blonde hair. She happily let the excess run down her back, soaking her shirt and pants.

"Come on, Grace, let's go," Jan said, waiting for her at the edge of the clearing near the trail.

"I'm coming," she said, running to catch up to the others.

The first obstacle was a pile of logs placed across the trail. It barely slowed them down and soon they were upon the second, and much more challenging, barrier. The squad stopped, unsure of what to do. "How the hell are we supposed to get past this?" Grace asked, staring warily at the wall made of cargo netting.

"Guess we climb," Jan said, grabbing hold and putting her foot on the bottom rung. As soon as she took her weight off the ground, the loose netting began to sway, taking her off balance. "Oh, no way." She jumped off and stood aside as Latisha tried with the same results.

"We have to keep the ropes from moving," Grace said, checking the slack in the netting. "If two of us hold it still, everyone else should be able to go up and over."

"And then what?" Rosetti said. "How are those two gonna get over?"

"Two of the people that make it over hold the net on the other side for them," Grace said.

"Well let's do something," Thompson said. "We're wasting time standing around here."

"Let's go," Grace said, tugging on the cargo netting. Rosetti grabbed the other side, creating the tension needed. There was enough room for two girls to go up at the same time, finding it much easier when the cargo netting didn't move around.

"Go, go," Jan urged, hooking her foot in the net when the first pair was halfway up. "You know they're doing this just to torment us."

"Watch, we'll probably lose by a couple of seconds," Grace said as Jan and Thompson began climbing. Looking further up the trail, she spotted the dark-haired figure leaning against a tree. Brown eyes met hers and Grace swore she saw the barest of smiles directed at her before Carey looked away. "Come on, let's go," she said to her teammates, hoping to raise their enthusiasm. Finally it was she and Rosetti left to conquer the netting. *I can do this,* she told herself as she grabbed hold. *Just don't look down.* "You'd better hold it tight, Jan."

"Don't worry, Maribel and I got it," Jan said. "Now climb."

Easy for you to say, she thought as she began to climb. Rosetti was faster than her, over the top and starting to come down the other side by the time Grace was halfway up. Gripping tightly with her hands, she moved her foot and pushed up. The wooden bar that marked the top of the netting wall was getting closer, which meant the ground was getting further away. *Don't think about it, just keep climbing.*

"Hurry up, Grace," Latisha yelled. "We're losing time."

Grace made the mistake of glancing down at her friend. *Oh God, this is really high up. Just keep looking at the bar,* she thought, forcing herself to look up. Still, the fear of falling from such a height was too much for her to take a chance, and she continued her slow pace until her hand touched wood. *Made it.*

"Okay, now just roll over the bar and scramble down this side," Jan encouraged.

"Come on, Waters, move your ass."

"Bite me, Lopez," Grace snapped, leaning her upper torso over the bar. "I'm working on it." *Don't look down. Don't look down. On three just roll over the bar and start going down. One, two...three.* Closing her eyes, Grace pushed herself the rest of the way over the bar, then dropped to the ground several feet below, rolling as she landed.

"Jesus, Waters," Rosetti said. "You sure took fucking long enough."

Grace stood up, twisting her arm to see the tear in the camouflage shirt and the abrasion on her elbow. "We'd better win," Rosetti said as they headed up the trail. "Or I'll kick your ass."

"Get in line," Grace said, unsnapping the canteen from her belt. "I don't hear them yelling, so it looks like we're running for a while." Grace took several swallows, letting some run down her face and soak her shirt.

"Hey, I hear something," Rosetti said.

"It's them," Grace said. "I hope this is the last obstacle."

"Why? Then we have the dead run to the finish," Rosetti said.

"It's better than climbing that net back there or crawling over logs." Grace spotted the rest of the squad as soon as they crested the hill.

"Hurry up," Latisha said as the pair approached, the rest of the squad busily scrambling beneath netting staked a few inches off the ground. "Watch your canteens. Everyone's getting stuck by them."

"No problem," Grace said, unsnapping her canteen. "I'll carry it." She dove to the ground, wiggling her head and arms beneath the netting. *I'll bet this one was Carey's idea,* she thought as she used her elbows and feet to push herself along. *Did it ever occur to them that all this crawling around is going to ruin our clothes? She's gonna kill me already for tearing out the elbow of my camo shirt.* She quickly felt to make sure the loose button was still attached. *I'll probably lose that too before this is over.* It was slow going but much easier than scaling a rope wall, and soon the trio was on the way with the rest of the squad toward the finish line. Unfortunately the finish line was two miles further down the trail, and not one canteen had water in it by the time they spotted the finish line.

The squeals were loud as Bravo Squad realized they were the first to arrive. "Line up and show me those flags," Carey said, standing just beyond the finish line. "Good job," she said, blowing the whistle and pressing the button on her stopwatch. "Congratulations."

The teens yelped and gave each other high fives, talking excitedly amongst themselves. Grace walked over to Carey. "So now we get ice cream, right, ma'am?"

"Yes, you do," Carey said, looking at her. "Your shirt is filthy, not to mention the rest of you."

Grace smiled. "That's what happens when I have to crawl around on my belly, ma'am."

Carey grabbed hold of the teen's arm. "Nice scrape. Any water left in your canteen?"

"No, ma'am."

Carey unhooked her own canteen. "Take that filthy thing off," she said, unscrewing the plastic cap. "All right, hold your arm out."

"It's not that bad," Grace said, then remembered and added, "Ma'am."

"Good catch," Carey said, giving the teen a knowing smile as she used one hand to hold Grace's arm still and the other to rinse out the abrasion. "What happened to you at the second obstacle?"

"I was holding the net for everyone else, that's why I was last, ma'am," Grace said.

"I watched you," Carey said.

Grace looked at the ground. "I don't like climbing things, ma'am."

"What I saw wasn't a question of like and dislike," Carey said, letting go of the teen's arm and tightening the cap on her canteen. "You were scared."

"I'm afraid of heights," Grace admitted. "That's why I wouldn't go on that rope at the lake, ma'am."

Carey clapped her on the shoulder. "We'll work on that. In the meantime, pass the word I don't want any gloating winners. The others are going to be here any minute and I better not see any taunting or chest thumping, got it?"

"Yes, ma'am. I'll tell everyone."

"Twenty pushups if I see anything remotely like that," Carey said.

"Yes, ma'am." Grace walked over to where her friends were standing.

"Hey," Jan said. "I didn't see you drop but I bet Scary was pissed that you tore your shirt, huh?"

"Naw, she didn't seem pissed to me," Grace said, buttoning her shirt. "She did say we'd better be cool around the others when they come in. Said she'd drop us for twenty if anyone razzes them about losing."

"But that's the fun of winning," Latisha protested. "So when do we get the ice cream?"

"Dunno," Grace said. "Hey, I hear them coming. I'd better tell the others to watch what they say." Instructor Gage entered the clearing and walked over to where Carey was standing. Grace warned the others, then joined Jan and Latisha to await Alpha Squad's imminent arrival. As expected, Lauren Grenner and the others were unhappy to see Bravo Squad standing around. "Poor baby," Grace whispered to Jan.

"Yeah, all that work for nothing," Jan whispered back. "Can you imagine that fat ass getting up over the cargo net?"

"Probably had the rest of them pushing from below," Latisha chimed in.

"Hey, keep an eye out for the Goon Squad," Jan said. "I don't want to get dropped for twenty."

"Hell yeah," Grace said. "Especially for picking on Grenner."

"Oh look, here comes the toadie," Jan said as Sally Dawson walked over to them. "You need something, Toadie?"

"How the hell did you get here before us?" the short teen asked.

"Guess we work better as a team," Grace said.

"You cheated," Sally accused, slamming her fists on her hips. "You had to."

"Right," Jan scoffed. "We cheated with Scary watching us the entire time. Get a life, Dawson."

Grace spotted Instructor Gage heading their way. "You'd better walk away, Dawson."

"Fuck you, Waters," Sally said, completely unaware of Gage's approach. "Either you guys cheated or that fucking bitch made your course easier than ours."

"Ten hut!" It took all of Grace's strength not to smirk at the shocked look on Dawson's face. "Is there a problem here, Dawson?"

"No problem, ma'am."

"Really? Well, why don't we just go see if Instructor Carey thinks there might be a problem with the way you like to disrespect her." Gage took hold of Dawson's arm. "Let's go."

Jan waited until Gage and Dawson were out of earshot before speaking. "Bye Toadie. Have fun."

"Make sure you tell Carey how you think she helped her squad cheat to win," Grace added. She nudged Jan with her elbow. "Here comes Delta."

"And Charlie," Latisha said, pointing at the trail where Instructor Mitchell appeared. "Guess our break is over."

"Oh well," Grace said, rising to her feet. "Guess we'll go find out when we're going to get our ice cream."

"As soon as Scary's through with Toadie," Jan said, standing up at the same time Latisha did.

"Serves Dawson right," Grace said. "She shouldn't have accused Carey of cheating." The trio began walking over to where another cluster of Bravo Squad teens was standing.

"All right, girls, line up with your squad," Instructor Gage said, a folded-up piece of paper in her hand. Grace took position where she could keep an eye on Dawson's continued berating by Carey. The petite woman began pacing back and forth in front of the squads. "The race for the flags was won by Bravo Squad. The water barrel, Bravo." She looked down at the paper. "Log pile by Alpha and the cargo net was won by Delta Squad."

"Thanks, Waters," Mo mumbled from behind Grace.

"Charlie Squad took the belly crawl and Bravo won the dead heat," Gage continued as Dawson rejoined her squad. "Overall winner is Bravo Squad. Congratulations."

Jan nudged Grace with her elbow. "So where's the ice cream?" she whispered.

"All right, girls," Instructor Gage said. "We're going to give you the rest of PT to get yourselves cleaned up and ready for the rest of the day. Dismissed." Dirty, dusty, and tired girls began tramping down the hill toward the barracks.

"Go on ahead," Grace said to Jan. "I'll catch you at lunch."

"Okay." Jan bumped against Latisha. "So, which flavor?" she asked as they walked away.

Seeing Carey speaking with Instructor Mitchell, Grace waited near the edge of the clearing. The two women spoke at length, making the teen wonder if she should wait until later to ask, but then Carey looked over, spotted her, and held up one finger to indicate Grace should wait.

The instructors exchanged a few more words, then walked over to where she was standing.

"Yes?" Carey asked as Instructor Mitchell kept walking down the trail.

"What do I do about my shirt, ma'am?" Grace asked.

"You waited to ask me that?" She put her hand on Grace's shoulder and pointed her in the direction of the trail. "I don't think it's bad enough to warrant a new shirt, but it does need to be patched," she said as she removed her hand and they began walking. "I have some camouflage patches in my sewing kit."

Grace fingered the button dangling by a thread. "I gotta fix this too, ma'am."

"Actually I see at least three buttons that could use some tightening up," Carey said. "Remind me tonight and I'll take care of it."

"I know how to use a needle and thread," Grace said. "Ma'am."

"Glad to hear it," Carey said. "However, a needle falls under the same rules as razors and there's nothing more boring than sitting there watching someone sew. I'd rather do it myself." She snapped her fingers. "Oh wait. I'm pulling night tour so I won't be back until after nine."

"I won't do anything with the needle but fix my shirt, ma'am."

"I'd love to say yes but I can't," Carey said. "You won't need your BDU shirt tomorrow anyway so it can wait."

"Okay."

Carey stopped. "Three...two..."

"Ma'am," Grace said quickly.

"You're lucky I'm in a good mood today," Carey said as she resumed walking.

"Would you have really dropped me, ma'am?"

"What do you think?"

"Um...out here by ourselves?" Grace shook her head. "I think you'd take pity on me after all the hard work I did on that obstacle course, ma'am."

"Maybe," Carey said. "And maybe I've been getting soft when it comes to you. Just keep an eye on it, Grace. I don't need any instructors telling me I'm letting you get away with something or playing favorites." The trail emptied out near the administration building. "I've got to get some paperwork done before afternoon classes. I'll see you in class."

"Yes, ma'am."

Though lights out was almost an hour before, Grace was still awake and sitting on the couch when Carey came in. "Hi."

"You should be sleeping," Carey said, kneeling to untie her boots. "Then again, why should tonight be any different from every other night I work late duty."

"Everything okay?" Grace asked. "You're not usually this late."

"I had to catch up on some paperwork in the office," Carey said, setting her boots neatly by the door and heading to her favorite chair. "You girls are going to get a break tomorrow. I'm too tired to write up the test I was planning for SR."

"Cool."

"Don't get too excited," Carey said. "You're only going to get a day's reprieve." She rubbed her face and yawned. "Maybe two."

"Why did you have to work morning PT and the late shift?" Grace asked.

"All four instructors worked morning PT," Carey said. "Two of us still had to cover from dinner to lights out and it happened to be my turn."

"And you're doing PT tomorrow, right?"

"Uh-huh. We're going for a nice long run. Excuse me." Carey covered her mouth as another yawn hit.

"You should go to sleep."

"I am," Carey said. "Right now. Lie down. I'll get the lights."

"Okay, thanks," Grace said, slipping between the covers. "Good night, ma'am."

"Good night, Grace."

"Um..."

"What?" Carey said.

"When you say a nice long run, you mean three miles, right?"

Carey chuckled and made her way through the dark to her bedroom door. "Good night, Grace."

"You know you have an evil laugh, Instructor Carey?"

"Do I? Good. Save your strength for tomorrow. You'll need it."

"All right, girls, enough chatter," Instructor Donaldson said, causing them to come to attention. "You've had a month of three-mile runs. Those days are over!" Blue eyes darted from girl to girl. "You have grown both in body and spirit. I know you can do five miles." Several groans went up from the group. "And after everyone does twenty and stretches we'll get started."

Instructor Carey stepped forward, her eyes hidden behind mirrored glasses. "Now drop!"

Oh sure, Grace thought as she hit the ground. *Not bad enough we have to run five miles, let's wear our arms out first.*

117

Since Grace ran faster than Latisha and Jan, they quickly became separated as the line moved up the slight incline. She paid little attention to those behind her, concentrating instead on the tall figure in camouflage leading the pack. *Oh sure, it's easy for you. You didn't have to do pushups first.* She passed the three-mile mark, the crystal blue lake taunting her as sweat rolled down her face. *Two more miles to go. I'll never make it.*

Reaching the finish mark, Grace slowed down, then walked around to cool down as the other girls began trickling in. Bit by bit, everyone crossed the mark but one who was still out of sight. "It's Jennings again," Latisha said. "That fat ass ain't gonna make it."

"She's still at least ten minutes away," Grace said, looking down the road and seeing no one.

"Yeah, and every fucking minute we have to wait here is that much less we have once we get back to barracks," one of the girls standing near her said.

Grace turned to face her. "You try running five miles with an extra forty pounds strapped to your ass and see how easy it is, Rosetti."

"Suck my left tit, Waters."

"You gotta get Grenner to let go of it first," she said.

"Are you kidding?" Rosetti snorted. "I'd become an Amazon and cut it off before I'd let her near me. Besides, I'm not into dykes."

"Amen to that," Latisha said.

"I'm going to go see where she is," Grace said, kneeling down and making sure her laces were tied securely.

"Why bother?" Jan said from her position lying on the ground. "Save your energy. Donaldson will get her here sooner or later."

"Yeah, well..." Grace began running down the trail, finding Jennings half a mile down the road with Instructor Donaldson barking at her heels.

"Hey...Grace," Jennings huffed. "What are you...doing here?"

"Thought you might want some company," Grace said. "The finish line is just over that hill." She ran alongside the overweight girl, slowing her pace to match.

"Let's go, Jennings," the blonde instructor said. "Waters, five miles isn't enough?"

"Just giving Christine a hand, ma'am," Grace said. "Come on, it's just a little more."

"I'll never make it," Christine huffed.

"Yes you will." Grace moved ahead slightly to keep herself in the other girl's vision. "Really, you're almost there." Once she matched the larger girl's pace, she sped up just a little bit. "Stay with me, just a little further." She smiled when Christine matched her pace. "Don't take a breath with each step," she said. "Try to slow your breathing down or you'll pass out."

"Let me...stop here," Christine practically begged, her breath coming in short pants.

"Come on, you can make it," Grace said, slowing down just a bit. "Listen, you don't want Grenner to have any more excuses to hassle you, do you?"

"That...damn...bitch," Christine huffed.

"Yeah," Grace encouraged, turning backwards to face the other girl. "Just a little more." They crested the hill. "See? I told you," she said when the finish line came into sight. "After all you've done so far, this last little bit is a piece of cake."

"It's about time," Grenner complained as Christine crossed the finish mark.

"Doesn't matter how long it takes," Grace said. "She did it, that's what counts."

"Stay out of it, Waters."

"Make me, fat ass." Catching movement out of the corner of her eye, Grace turned and walked away from her adversary. "Christine, you did a great jo—oof." She went face first into the ground, aided by a solid shove from Grenner.

"Grenner! You drop and give me twenty right now," Carey said as she approached. Grace stood up and brushed herself off. "Someone want to tell me what happened?"

"Lauren was giving me a hard time for being last, ma'am," Christine said.

"So why were you the one eating dirt?" Carey asked Grace.

"I told Grenner to stop picking on her, ma'am," Grace said.

"And what were you doing over here?" the dark-haired instructor asked. "I saw you sitting with Bowen and Jones ten minutes ago."

Instructor Donaldson walked up to them. "What's going on?"

"That's what I'm trying to find out," Carey said, looking pointedly at Grace.

"I went back to see how Jennings was doing, ma'am."

"She did," Donaldson said. "Last half mile or so."

Carey's features softened. "Why?"

"Um..." Grace looked around, seeing everyone in the near vicinity paying attention. "I just...I thought it was a good idea at the time, ma'am."

"Marilyn, can you...?"

"Sure," the blonde instructor said. "All right, girls, let's go."

"You stay," Carey said, putting her hand on Grace's elbow.

Guess it wasn't such a good idea after all, Grace thought as she watched everyone else depart.

"Now, the answer you didn't want to give in front of everyone else."

"She's always getting picked on for being fa—overweight, ma'am," Grace said. "I just thought if I went back and ran with her that she wouldn't feel so bad."

"You mean you thought about someone else instead of yourself for a change?" Carey said. "Mark it on a calendar. Could be the start of bigger and better things." At first Grace thought her mentor was picking on her until she felt a hand rest on her shoulder. "Good job, Grace."

"Um, thank you, ma'am," she said, pleased at the compliment.

"All right, let's go before you miss calisthenics."

"Yes, ma'am," Grace said. *Wouldn't want to miss that,* she thought sarcastically as she followed Carey.

Carey poured a cup of coffee and walked to the table where Grace sat with her nose in one of her books. "How was AM today?" she asked as she pulled out a chair and sat across from the girl.

"Okay," Grace said, looking up from the textbook she was studying.

"Hmm, you must not have had to say anything," Carey said.

"Christine did most of the talking today," Grace said.

"Lucky you," Carey said. "What was the topic?"

"How anger is used to hide fear," she said.

"And you didn't have anything to say?" Carey took a sip of her coffee. "Of all the topics, I would think that would be an excellent one for you to take a closer look at."

"Yeah, well, we ran out of time so..." Grace shrugged.

"And you're not going to fool me into thinking whatever you're doing is due tomorrow," Carey said. "You think I don't know you're ahead in everything you have a textbook for?"

"I-I-I...how did you know?" she asked in a resigned voice, knowing it was useless to deny it.

Carey smiled shrewdly and laced her fingers. "I didn't." She paused. "Until now."

"What made you think so?"

"You're too bright to have to spend that much time with your nose in a book," Carey said. "Have you always done that? Read ahead?"

Grace nodded. "It made it easy for me with class because I knew what the teacher was going to talk about so I didn't have to pay that much attention. As long as I didn't disrupt class, the teachers left me alone."

"Instructor Donaldson said something to me about that," Carey said. "Shame I don't let you get away with hiding in the back of the room in my classes, hmm?"

"Can't hide in SD," Grace said. "Though I think you pick on me more than anyone else."

"You do, do you?" Carey reached for her coffee. "I wasn't aware of that. Why didn't you say anything before this?"

Grace shrugged. "I don't know. I figured you did it deliberately."

"I'll try not to single you out so much," Carey said apologetically. "Do I do that in SR?"

Grace thought about it. "Maybe a little."

"And maybe you'd love to be called on less often," Carey said. "I think I give you some breaks in SR." She smirked at the teen. "I've seen that panicked look on your face when I've asked a question and was deciding who to call on."

"Thanks," Grace said, watching as Carey finished her coffee in several long swallows.

"I need to get one of those things that you put the mug on and it keeps the coffee warm," Carey said as she put the empty cup on the coaster. "So why do you look like a deer caught in the headlights whenever the subject of sex is brought up?" She pointed at the teen. "Just like that."

Grace looked down. "It's embarrassing."

"You don't have to be embarrassed to talk about sex," Carey said. "It's part of life."

Staring at the table, Grace smiled nervously. "I've never talked to anyone about it."

"Well, Grace, your mother—"

"Asked me when I got my period if I had any questions," Grace answered before Carey could finish. "I told her no, she handed me a box of pads and that was the end of it."

"What about your father?"

"He left when I was seven," Grace said.

"Oh." Carey was quiet for a moment. "So what you know you've learned from health class and your friends?"

Grace leaned back and looked at her mentor. "Pretty much. I've seen some magazines too," she said, feeling a blush coming to her cheeks.

"You're seventeen and it seems silly to ask, but do you have any questions?" Carey asked.

"Um, no. I don't have any questions," Grace said, knowing she'd be too embarrassed to ask even if she did.

"Grace, I know it's easy to get wrong information from your friends," Carey said. "That's why you have SR three times a week."

"I know."

"Then also know if you do have a question, I'd rather you come to me and ask than to rely on what girls your own age think, or even worse, to do something you might regret later because you were too afraid to talk to me."

Grace nodded. "Okay."

"Did what I said stop at all before it went in one ear and out the other?" Carey asked. "I mean it, Grace. Believe it or not, I was seventeen once and I do know how scary it can be. I'm your mentor and that doesn't stop once you leave my office."

Grace smiled. "I'm well aware of that, trust me," she said.

Carey returned the smile. "You're a tough nut to crack. I need all the time I can get with you." She rose from the table and picked up her coffee mug. "You need to look at why the topic of sex bothers you so much." A devilish grin came to her lips. "Maybe I'll have you write a paper on it."

"Oh, please don't," Grace asked. "I'll be good, I promise."

Carey chuckled and walked to the coffeepot. "Now I know what to punish you with instead of pushups," she said. "Don't have a heart attack, Grace; I'll let it go for now, but seriously, you need to take a look at your fears. More coffee?"

"No thanks," Grace said, hearing the sound of Carey rinsing out the coffeepot seconds later. *Now can we please change the subject?* "So what's for PT tomorrow?"

"Ah, speaking of fears." Carey returned to the table. "You're going to conquer your fear of heights tomorrow."

"Huh?" She was sure she did not hear correctly. "Heights?"

"Heights," Carey said as she settled into her chair. "We're rappelling off the wall behind the ball field."

Grace's eyes widened. "That big wall?"

"It's not that big," Carey said. "Four stories."

"And you want me to jump off the side of it?" She shook her head vehemently. "I can't do that."

"You will tomorrow," Carey said. "And you're not jumping off the side, you're walking down it with a rope to keep you in complete control. It's very easy."

"I'd rather run ten miles than do that," Grace said.

"Too bad for you, tomorrow we're rappelling," Carey said. "And next week we're going to start using the obstacle course which has a swing rope over the swamp, so you need to get over that fear and quick."

"I can't do it."

"Yes you can," Carey said. "And tomorrow I'm going to prove it to you."

"They've got to be kidding," Grace said, looking at the harness warily. "This is going to keep me from falling?"

"Sure," Latisha said excitedly. "I bet it'll be fun."

"I don't think throwing myself off the top of a building with nothing to stop me but a rope and harness is fun," Grace said, nervously opening and closing the D-ring. "You go ahead."

"She's gonna make you go, you know," Latisha said.

"I know," Grace said. "But I can put it off for a few minutes, can't I?"

"Let's go, Waters."

"Yes, ma'am," Grace said, certain she would be seriously injured before this was over. She moved closer to the edge, her heart pounding harder when she saw the pavement below.

"Step up to the mark," Carey said. "I'll check your harness."

Grace hesitated, then stepped forward. The pavement looked so far away. "Oh God," she whispered.

"You'll be fine," Carey said, tightening the harness. "Everyone else has done it." A handle with a hook on the end was used to pull the rope over. "Here you go, put the rope through the ring and wrap it three or four times."

"What happens if I slip?"

"What happens if I slip, ma'am," Carey corrected, putting the rope in her hands. "If you feel you're going too fast, use your right hand to brake."

"What if my hand slips off...ma'am?" Grace asked, wiping her palm against her fatigues.

"Grace," Carey said gently. "Your hand won't slip because you're going to stay focused, and once you do it, you'll wonder what you were afraid of. Come on, set the rope and lock that ring."

Grace wrapped the rope around the D-ring once, then again, amazed at how much her hands were trembling. "I can't do this, ma'am."

"Yes you can," Carey said. "That's it, one more. Good, now lock the ring."

"What if the harness breaks, ma'am?"

"The harness won't break."

"I'm scared of heights, ma'am."

"Then this is a great time to learn to conquer your fears. Step forward."

"What if the rope breaks?"

Strong hands gently squeezed her shoulders. "I checked the rope, Grace. Every inch of it. I checked your harness. You need to trust me when I tell you that you can do this. Now step forward to the black line."

The black line was only a few inches from the edge, giving Grace a clear view below. "Oh God," she said, quickly moving back until she slammed into an immovable force. "I don't want to do this, ma'am."

"Grace," Carey said, her breath warm on Grace's ear. "Do you trust me?"

"Yes, ma'am," she said, feeling the heat of Carey's body against hers, then the loss when the instructor moved back.

"You know I would never make you do anything I didn't think you were capable of?"

"Yes, ma'am."

"Grace, trust me. Use your left hand to guide and your right to brake. When you step off, get your feet under you and flat against the building. It's just like walking, only gravity is going in a different direction. Grace, you can do this. I know you can. Now step up to the mark."

Grace took a deep breath, then gripped the rope. "Yes, ma'am."

"All right, now bring your right hand back and grab hold of the rope. Step out and plant your feet against the wall. You can do it."

When she looked over the side, the ground seemed even further away than before. Grace thought her heart was going to pound its way out of her chest when she put her right foot on the edge of the building. *On three. One...two...okay, everyone else has done it. It can't be that bad. One...two...three.* Pushing off, Grace scrambled to get her feet between her and the wall.

"Get your feet under you," Carey called from the top of the building. "You're doing great."

Great was not how Grace would have described it. Terrifying was a better word in her mind. Clinging to the rope for dear life, she tried to calm down and pay attention to what she had to do. *Feet flat against the wall, straighten up so I'm almost standing sideways.*

"That's it, Waters," Carey's voice came from above. "Straighten up a little more. That's good. Now ease up on the brake and slowly walk down."

Grace shook her head vehemently.

"Unless you plan on being a monkey and climbing back up, you have to go down," Carey said. "Ease up just a little." Grace did and found herself slipping, but gripping the rope stopped the downward descent. "That's it," her mentor encouraged. "Controlled slippage. Ease up again."

"Come on, Grace," Latisha's voice called from below. "It's really fun."

Bullshit, Grace thought to herself as she slowly made her way down the wall. When she was close enough, she let go of the rope with her right hand and dropped the last three feet to the ground. "Thank God that's over."

"See? I told you it was easy," Latisha said. "Come on, let's get back up there."

"Oh no," Grace said, looking up, way up. "You go. I'll stay down here."

"You have to go back up or she's gonna come get your ass," Latisha said. "You know that."

"She can't make me do that again," Grace said, her heart rate slowly returning to normal. "Once was bad enough."

"What's the problem, Waters?"

"Nothing, ma'am," she said, fighting the urge to roll her eyes. "I'm afraid of heights, ma'am."

"I just watched you scale down the equivalent of a six-story building," Gage said. "I'd say you're well on your way to conquering that fear. Get back up there and do it again."

"Yes, ma'am," she said in a resigned voice, following Latisha and Jan to the stairs. "Please just shoot me now and get it over with." When they reached the top of the wall, Grace deliberately lagged behind, letting everyone else take their second turn before her.

"Let's go, Grace," Carey said. "You've already made it once."

"Isn't once enough?"

"You really want me to answer that question?" Carey asked. "Get over here."

Grace grunted in frustration and tore the paper out of her notebook.

"Problem?" Carey asked, leaning against the archway between the kitchen and living room.

"Just PF homework," she said. "We're supposed to figure out how much our monthly income has to be and set a budget."

"That should be easy enough for a math whiz like you," Carey said. "Just write down your expenses, add them up, then you'll be able to do your budget."

"It's not that easy," Grace said. "We're supposed to use it to figure out how much income we need to have and I can't figure it out."

"Just use all that algebra you've learned," Carey said, entering the kitchen and sitting down next to her at the table.

"How?" Grace said.

"Get a fresh piece of paper," Carey said, rising from her seat and going to the refrigerator. "You want some real life uses? Let's try this one. X equals the amount of money you need to live on." She returned to the table with two apples, putting one in front of Grace. "So are you going to live in a nice apartment or a dump?"

"A nice one, of course," Grace said.

"That's going to run you at least six hundred. We'll assume you're not going to live in a high cost of living area like Boston or New York." Carey took a bite out of her apple. "I've watched you eat. Figure three fifty for food and household things."

"That much?" Grace asked with surprise.

"Easily," Carey said. "And don't forget about your utilities."

"Included with rent?"

"Not a chance," Carey said. "Electric and heat will run you at least a hundred a month if you live in a temperate climate. More if you live in the north."

"A hundred for utilities," Grace said, scribbling the number down on the paper.

"Phone and cable?"

"Sure," Grace said. "That's what, fifty?"

"More like fifty each," Carey said. "So what do you have?"

Grace added up the numbers. "One thousand fifty."

Carey gave her a humorless smile. "That's with no going out to eat, no new clothes, no car or bus fare, no Internet, and no extras. Now there's 4.3 weeks in a month, so how much do you need to earn each week to make ends meet?"

Grace looked at the paper. "So I divide 1050 by 4.3 to get the weekly amount." Carey flashed her the rare smile. "Let's see...so I move the decimal point...that's a two...and that's four...$244.18."

"Let's make it easy," Carey said. "Let's say you need to make $250.00."

"So if I need to make $250.00 a week and there's forty hours in a work week," Grace began writing out the equation. "So it would be X times forty equals $250.00."

"So forty X equals $250.00. Figure it out," Carey encouraged.

"6.25," Grace said cautiously, looking to the older woman for confirmation.

"So you think a job paying six and a quarter an hour is enough for you to live on?" Carey asked.

Grace rechecked her figures, then nodded. "Yeah. So if I got a job paying seven bucks an hour, I'd have enough for extras."

"You think so?" Carey took the pencil and paper. "Every week when you get paid, you'll get a pay stub. 34% of my pay goes to either federal or state taxes. Another 6% goes into my retirement fund and twenty bucks a week is deducted for my insurance." She wrote out an equation. "Now taking that into account, how much do you need to make?"

Grace did the math. "Over 375 or...9.375 dollars an hour."

"Let's round up to ten," Carey said. "And again, that's without many of the extras."

"Wow," Grace said, surprised by the figure.

"Are you qualified for a job that pays ten dollars an hour?" Carey asked. "I'd like to see you find one without a college degree."

THREE MONTHS

"All right, settle down," Carey said as the girls entered the classroom. "Open your books, get those pens out and plug your brains in." Sitting on her desk, she waited for silence. "I've decided to make life easy on you." She noted the smiles on her charges, then continued. "You're still having your test next class, but I've made half of the answers multiple choice." Twenty teen faces drooped. "Now that I've made your day, let's talk about chapter twelve. What's the point of case history number six, the college student and the party?" She looked around, deciding who would be her first victim. "Bowen?"

"She took a chance and lost, ma'am."

"Well, that's one way to put it," Carey said. "Waters."

"She had unprotected sex just once, ma'am."

"Just once and she contracted HIV," Carey said. "What was her reasoning behind having sex without a condom, let's see...Jones."

"He said he didn't have one, ma'am."

"Think that's a good enough reason?"

"No, ma'am," several girls answered.

"Why not? Campbell."

"She could have carried some with her if she was planning on getting laid, ma'am."

"She could," Carey agreed. "What was her other reason? Rosetti."

"He didn't look like someone who would have any diseases, ma'am."

"That's right, if someone is carrying HIV, it's obvious, right?"

"No, ma'am."

"So because she was horny and he looked good, she played Russian Roulette with her life and lost," Carey said. "All for the cost of a condom. At least then she would have had a fighting chance. Campbell, since you think it's all right to have sex with strangers as long as you carry condoms, would using a condom have made her completely safe?"

"Mostly, ma'am."

"Believing that a condom will protect you is like believing that an umbrella is going to protect you from the rain," Carey said. "It tears, it rolls off, certain lubricants can weaken or even dissolve the latex, and of course the best is Prince Charming takes it off before entry because he doesn't like the way it feels. So what's the answer?" She looked around, noticing every girl found great interest in the floor or wall with the hopes that she would not call upon them. "Bowen, why don't you enliven us with one of your witty answers?"

"Stock up on batteries, ma'am?"

Carey waited for the giggling to die down. "That's actually one of your better answers," she said. "Certainly in hindsight Jane would have chosen masturbation over anonymous sex."

"Kinda hard with thirty-three other people in the room," Rosetti said.

"Not that it stops you," Jan said.

"Eew," Latisha said. "That's disgusting."

"All right," Carey said. "Cut the cross talk. Jones, it's perfectly natural to masturbate, though there are appropriate times and places."

Grace looked down at her textbook, knowing that was one of the benefits of not living in the barracks. She was lucky the couch did not have metal springs that could squeak and give her away on the rare occasions when the need had arisen. It certainly made things easier for her despite the fear of being discovered.

"And as far as Bowen's answer is concerned," Carey continued. "Remember that rechargeable batteries or plug-in models are better for the environment." Several girls giggled and a few made buzzing sounds until she held her hands up for them to settle down. "It's safer than exposing yourself to someone else's sex life."

When the question formed in her mind as it so naturally would, Grace found she could not look at Carey's face, embarrassed to even think of it. *She doesn't. She can't. She goes right to sleep, every night. Could she? With me in the next room? No way.*

"Waters."

"Yes, ma'am," she said, looking at the instructor's hair and not her face for fear she would blush and give her thoughts away.

"Back to the original question, if condoms alone cannot protect you from a sexually transmitted disease, what can you do to protect yourself?"

"Know your partner's sexual history, ma'am?"

"You need more than that," Carey said. "You'd need to know the history of everyone your partner has had sex with and who they've had sex with and on and on. Try again."

"Um...I can't think of anything except being with a virgin, ma'am," Grace said.

"Like you'll find a guy who is," Rosetti said.

"And even if you did, who'd want him?" Campbell added. "He wouldn't know what to do."

"They don't know what to do no matter how much experience they have," Jan said.

"Before this gets out of hand," Carey said. "The only way to truly protect yourself is to have both of you take a physical as well as blood tests to check for HIV or other diseases, then stay abstinent during the required period thereafter to take a second test."

"Like any guy is going to wait," Mo said.

"It's your choice to take chances with your life," Carey said. "If you're planning on spending a life with him, a few weeks shouldn't make a difference and if he respects you, he'll wait." She shrugged. "If he doesn't...well, what does that say about him?"

"What?"

"I didn't say anything," Grace said, making sure she looked down at the book in her lap.

"Grace, you've been looking over here at me every ten seconds for the last five minutes," Carey said, closing her book and removing her reading glasses. "Now either you want to talk to me about something or I've grown horns out of the top of my head. Which is it?"

Caught, Grace tried to think of a tactful way to ask her question. "I was just thinking about something you said in class today," she said. "It's not important."

"If it wasn't important, you wouldn't be fidgeting like you have ants in your pants," Carey said.

"I don't know how to say it," Grace admitted, feeling the blush creeping up her neck. "It's...embarrassing."

"Ah, I take it your question has something to do with Sexual Responsibility and not Self-Defense." Carey leaned forward in her seat. "What's your question, Grace?"

"Well..." *Just say it.* "You were talking about—about masturbation," she said, blushing hotly. "And well...I was wondering..." Grace found she could not look the instructor in the eyes and focused her gaze on the coffee table. "You said it was natural and there's nothing wrong with it."

"I'm glad you were paying attention," Carey said. "It's perfectly normal to masturbate. My grandmother used to say, now mind you she was a product of the thirties and forties, but she used to say better to get a little sauce on the hand than a bun in the oven."

"You mean pregnant," Grace said, receiving a clarifying nod. "So everyone does it?"

Carey shrugged. "I don't know about everyone, but I bet most people do from time to time."

"Do you?" It was the question that insisted on coming out and once it did, Grace would have given anything to take it back. "I'm sorry, I shouldn't ask that."

Carey put her hands on the armrests and pushed back, forcing the foot of the recliner to rise. "I think that's rather personal, don't you?"

Grace shook her head. "Forget I said anything. I'm sorry."

"Grace, look at me." Carey's face was understanding and kind with no trace of censure. "I don't want you to be embarrassed about sex, but your question did catch me off guard. I don't think anyone has ever asked me that before. But for your information only, and I don't want to hear about it in the teenage grapevine, yes." Grace remained silent, prompting Carey to ask, "Was that all you wanted to know?"

"Um, yeah, I guess so."

Grace adjusted the pressure and temperature, then stepped into the shower stall. The water pressure in Carey's cabin was higher than in the barracks, a fact that Grace was sure only she could appreciate. Of course, she could only appreciate it when Carey had evening duty, lest the instructor question why she was spending so long in the shower. Leaning against the wall, she set her left foot on the corner seat, exposing herself to the pulsing water. *Oh Carey, you should try this,* she thought, adjusting herself to get just the right angle for the pulsing bursts of water. *Then again, maybe you already do.* Closing her eyes, Grace conjured up her faceless woman, always ready and willing to do her bidding. The sensation was different from her fingers, making it easy for her to imagine her faceless lover kneeling between her legs and pleasuring her. *That's it, lick it,* she silently bade her fantasy woman. *Oh, this feels so good.* A low groan escaped her throat as she held herself open to the pulsing water. Eyes shut tight, she envisioned a dark head just beyond her fingers, her pleasure giver suddenly becoming less of a blur. Flashes of Carey playing around with her in the lake, holding her on the rappelling wall, on top of her in Self-Defense, and just hanging around in the cabin all flashed through her mind as the sensation became too intense and she tumbled over the edge. "Oh God," she gasped, sliding down along the shower wall until she was sitting. Water pelted her face and hair while she gave herself time to recover. *Carey? The woman that loves to drop me for ten every chance she can get?* Grace shook her head. *Oh no. I cannot think of her like that. I have to live with her. I can't be thinking about what she looks like naked.* She thought back to the day at the lake. *I bet she's got nice ones, nice and big and suckable. No no no, absolutely not.* Still she could not deny the erotic thrill that shot through her veins at the thought of Carey kneeling between her legs.

"Name please?" Instructor Donaldson asked, pen and clipboard ready.

"Richard Waters," the large burly man said, looking up from his compact rental car. "I understand my daughter Graceful is here."

"I'm sorry, sir, but you're not on the approved list," she said. "You're her father?"

"Yes. I'm allowed visitation. I have a copy of the custody order." He held out a paper, worn along the folds. The blonde woman took the paper, looking it over before handing it back.

"Please wait here," she said, waving at the dark-haired woman to come over. He rubbed his short beard while the two women talked. The blonde woman returned. "Pull over to that building. Instructor Carey will meet you there."

"Thank you," he said, putting the car in gear. He pulled into the lot and parked his car, getting out when the dark haired woman approached. "Hello, I'm Richard Waters," he said, holding out his hand.

"Instructor Joanna Carey," she said. "Come inside please." She opened the door but he refused to move.

"Ladies first," he said. Carey gave a slight nod, then led him to her office.

"Please have a seat," she said, setting her hat on the hook and running her fingers through her short black hair. "I'm afraid we had no notice of your arrival," she said. "Usually all visitations are pre-approved."

"I wasn't sure I'd make it and no one told me about having to get permission first," he said. "Can you at least tell me if she's all right?"

"She's fine," Carey said. "I'm Grace's mentor as well as head instructor here. I understand you haven't seen her in many years."

He looked down. "That's true," he admitted, scratching the short blond beard. "It's been just about ten years now." He looked up. "But that's still a valid visitation order."

"I'm going to check on that," Carey said, opening the bottom drawer and pulling out Grace's folder. "Do you have identification, by the way?"

"Oh sure," he said, pulling a thick wallet from his back pocket. "Do you want my phone number there, too?"

"I think that would be a good idea," she said, pushing a piece of paper and pen across the desk.

"Here's my driver's license," he said, holding the fat wallet open. Carey glanced at the identification but what caught her attention was the thick fanfold strip of photos.

"Are these all Grace?" she asked, the top picture showing a young girl sitting on the steps, her blonde hair shining in the sun.

"That's her," he said, taking the wallet back. "And this one..." He tapped the next photo. "She always looked so pretty in that dress."

"She looks about six or seven," Carey said.

"Ayup," he said. "She would have been six and a half when I took that picture." He scratched his beard and closed his wallet. "The last time I saw her she had pigtails and scabbed knees."

"That was a long time ago," she said, closing the folder.

"I know," he said. "Listen, here's my calling card number too, in case she needs to call me for anything." He wrote a long series of numbers on the paper.

"If I can ask, why now?"

"I didn't know where she was before this," he said. "I received a notice from the court that my support payments were being diverted to the state and so I called to find out why. They just told me she was here and that the third Sunday of the month was the only time for visits so I hopped on the first plane I could find and headed out."

"How could you not know?"

"I have a vindictive ex-wife," he said, leaning back in his seat, his bulky frame filling the whole seat. "She kept moving and not letting me know, and when I complained she went back to court and made up lies to get a restraining order. That allowed her to get her address sealed from me. It didn't help that I lived on the other side of the country."

Carey looked over the court document, verifying the visitation order had not been superseded by the state's custody order. "You're right," she said. "Living so far away probably didn't help. Everything is in order here. I'll take you to one of the rooms and have Grace brought to you."

"Miss Carey? Can you tell me something about her?" He looked away. "I mean, is this place going to help her?"

Carey stood up, causing him to rise as well. "Mr. Waters, Grace is an intelligent young woman who needs discipline, guidance, and a great deal of love and support. Everything else I think you can ask her about."

He rubbed his hands together. "What if she doesn't want to see me?"

Carey walked to the door. "Unfortunately, that's a chance you're just going to have to take. As I said, she needs a great deal of love. I don't think she'll turn away an opportunity to get that love."

Grace entered the rec room, spotting Jan sitting near the window. "Bowen, you up for ping pong?"

"Sure," Jan said, rising from the chair and joining her at the table. "No visitors either, huh?"

Grace shook her head. "No. I didn't figure she'd come back after last time." She handed the other teen a paddle. "You serve."

"My dad's given up on me, I think," Jan said as she took her side. "Zero serving zero."

Grace snorted, then returned the serve. "Mine gave up a long time ago," she said. "I haven't seen him since I was...damn." Picking the ball up off the floor, she tossed it over the small net. "Lucky shot."

"Luck nothing, Waters. One serving zero."

"Anyway, I haven't seen him since I was a kid. Aha!"

"Now that was luck," Jan said, tossing the ball to her. "I wish I hadn't seen mine since I was a kid. He's a real prick. Thinks I'm going to have an eight o'clock curfew. I'm seventeen, for Christ's sake."

"One serving one. The problem is they can't remember what it was like when they were our age." They volleyed several times before Grace failed to make the cross shot. "Shit. That's the problem, you know. They forget what it's like."

There was a knock on the wall. "Waters." Instructor Donaldson stood in the doorway. "You have a visitor."

"I don't want to see her, ma'am," Grace said, motioning for Jan to throw her the ping pong ball.

"Funny, I don't remember asking," the tall blonde said. "Move it, Waters."

Grace set the paddle and ball on the table. "Yes, ma'am. See you later, Jan."

"Good luck," Jan replied.

Grace expected to see her mother waiting for her when she entered the room. "Excuse me, I must have the wrong room," she said when she saw the man sitting at the instructor's desk.

"Graceful?" He had aged, his hair no longer the thick blonde that she remembered but now thin and receding. Still, there was no mistaking the blue eyes looking back at her so much like her own.

"Daddy? H-how?" Shocked, she allowed herself to be engulfed in his lumberjack arms. The short beard that tickled her cheek and the smell of his cologne resurrected memories long ago forgotten.

"My little pumpkin," he said, his deep baritone voice still the same as she remembered. "Let me take a look at you." He held her at arm's length, his smile as wide as it could be. "Look how pretty you've become."

"How did you know where I was?" she asked, thinking he used to seem so much taller than he did now. Of course, she was much shorter then. "Did you talk to Ma?"

"No," he said. "I got a notice from the state saying they were taking your child support so I called to find out why. I have to tell you I damn near fell out of my chair when I found out." He squeezed her shoulders. "Are you doing okay here?"

"I'm surviving," Grace said, backing away from him and sliding into the nearest desk chair. "Ma told me she had no idea where to look for you except that she thought you might have been in Alaska."

"She knew where your grandparents lived," he said. "They knew where I was. The courts knew where I was because they sure enough took child support from me." He shook his head. "That's neither here nor there now."

Now that the shock was wearing off, question after question formed in her mind. "Why didn't you ever come see me?"

He pulled the teacher's chair out from behind the desk and sat down next to her. "I don't have a good answer for that, pumpkin. Your mother and me were fighting so hard and every time I came to see you we'd get into a fight and after a while it was just easier to stay away. Then I got the job in Anchorage and even though it was far away, the higher pay was enough for me to live on and still pay my child support." He took his hand in hers, his callused fingers rubbing over her knuckles. "I thought I'd do it for just a few years and save up enough money to afford to come back but—I'm sorry, Grace. I love you very much and I never meant to hurt you."

"You didn't try hard enough," Grace said, the little girl's pain flaring inside. "All I know is one day you were gone and you never came back. You didn't come back for my birthday, you didn't come back for Christmas, you just disappeared and forgot all about me."

"I never forgot about you," he said. "You know what?" He reached back and pulled out a thick leather wallet from his rear pocket. "Look." Opening it up, he showed her the photo section filled with various pictures of her as a little girl. "I carried these with me because they were all I had of you."

"Why didn't you take me with you?"

"It wasn't for lack of trying," he said. "I went to court against your mother half a dozen times and she kept coming up with lies to keep me from getting anything more than minimal visitation."

Grace stared at their intertwined hands, remembering the poison her mother used to spew about her father when they were going through their divorce. "I wish you had won," she said sadly. "Ma got involved with a lot of assholes after you left."

"I'm sorry, pumpkin," he said. "I know I should have been there." He looked around the room. "Maybe then you wouldn't be here."

Grace pulled her hand back. "Did they tell you what happened?"

"I came home from logging and found the letter from the state. It just told me about the support." He took her hand again. "All I could think of was something terrible had happened to you. I called and they told me you were here."

"Did they say why?" she asked. Her father shook his head. "I threw a chair at a teacher," she said, wondering what his reaction would be. *So much for being his perfect little daughter,* she thought to herself. *Bet you wished you stayed in Alaska.*

"Well..." He gave a quick squeeze. "Sounds like you inherited the Waters temper."

"Big disappointment, huh?"

"I'm not happy to hear that you did something like that but you're not a disappointment to me, Graceful. It happened, it's in the past, you move on and do better the next time."

"People call me Grace," she said.

"Grace, hmm?" Letting go of her hand, he reached out and cupped her cheek. "You'll always be my Graceful little girl."

"Whose idea was that anyway?" she asked. "Do you have any idea what it's like going through life with a name like Graceful Lake Waters?"

He chuckled and sat back. "It was both," he said. "Your maternal grandmother's maiden name was Lake and I came up with Graceful."

"The last two years have been anything but graceful," she said. "Obviously, I'm here."

"But it's in the past and tomorrow's another day," he said. "You move on from here." Leaning his elbows on his knees, he clasped his hands together. "Graceful, you can be anything you want to be if you try hard enough. I know I haven't been there the last ten years but I can still remember the little girl who wanted to ride a bike without training wheels more than anything. It didn't matter how many times you fell, you just kept getting back up and had me give you another push."

"And I used to cry because you made me stop when it got dark out," she said, sharing the memory. "I remember when you came home with that bicycle."

"I have a picture of you on that bike," he said, gesturing at the wallet. "I had it blown up and it sits on the mantel in my house."

"I still can't believe you're here," she said. "I can't believe you still came to see me after finding out where I was."

"It doesn't matter," he said. "Once I knew how to find you, nothing else mattered. You're my daughter. If you came and told me you wanted to tattoo your entire body and marry a rock star, I'd ask you if you've seen a psychiatrist and then I would ask if you were happy. If you were, I'd give you my blessing."

"What if I wanted to be the rock star?"

"As long as you didn't inherit the Waters tin ear, if it made you happy and you could earn a living at it, why not?" He took her hand again. "I don't want you becoming a drug dealer or a porn star or anything like that," he said. "But who am I to deny you something that makes you happy?"

"I'm an adult now," she said. "I can do what I want."

"For the most part," he said. "But you'll always be my little girl and I'm always going to want what's best for you."

135

"Why Alaska? That's so far away."

"That's where the money was, pumpkin. I earned almost twice as much as I was making here. There aren't that many trees left in this state. In my line of work, Alaska was the only place where I could make a decent living." He let go of her hand and stood up. "I'm sorry, Graceful. In hindsight I should never have gone." Turning his back to her, he leaned forward and put his meaty hands on the desk. "I suppose in a way this is my fault too for not being there for you."

Silence reigned as Grace worked through her feelings. First there was the seven-year-old who cried for her father night after night until it was clear he never would return. There was the thirteen-year-old who cursed him for leaving her, for not acknowledging birthdays and special events. Finally there was the seventeen-year-old, struggling to reconcile the past with the gentle man before her, admitting his mistakes and wanting to do better. The decision was hers, keep the hurt and push him away or forgive him and try to repair the frayed bond between them. "But...it's in the past now, right?"

The blond man nodded and turned to face her. "Tomorrow is another day," he said.

"Is this a one-time thing or will I see you again?"

"I gave my phone number and address to one of the ladies in charge here," he said. "I spend a lot of time up at the logging camps but I'm usually home once or twice a month. Cell phones and pagers don't work too well up there. Towers can't get the feed into those remote areas. If you want to see me, just send word and I'll make sure either you can get to me or I will get to you. You're a senior this year, right?"

"I was," she said. "I'll be taking my GED test soon."

"Are you going to college?"

"I can't afford college even if one would let me in with my grades," she said.

"I suppose you know your old man never made it out of eleventh grade," he said. "Always thought my girl would go to college."

"So you want me to go college?"

"It's what you want that's important," he said. "What is it you want?"

"I don't know," she said. "Part of me wants to because I want to get a degree and make good money but another part doesn't want to spend four more years in school even if I could afford it."

"So if there was a way you could afford to go, would you?"

"Maybe. What do you want?" she asked.

"I want my daughter to be happy," he said. "If you want to go to college, we'll figure out a way to make it happen. I'll love you no matter what."

Carey found Grace sitting at the kitchen table, her notebook open. "How did your visit go?"

"Hi." The teen looked up, smiling. "It was great," she said. "He stayed until visitation was over."

"I know. I saw you walk him to his car."

"He said he'd come back next month," Grace said.

"That's good," Carey said. "I'm glad you had a nice visit."

"I did. I was surprised to see him but he's great. He looks older but he's still Dad. I told him what I did to end up here and he was really understanding about it."

"And you're all right with seeing him again after all these years?" Carey asked. "You're not angry with him?"

Grace shrugged. "A little. I told him so but like he said, we can't change the past."

"This from a girl who threw a chair at a teacher because he told her she wasn't living up to her potential," Carey said, ruffling the short blonde hair as she passed. "I'm really glad you had a nice visit with your father."

"He said he's coming back next month."

"I know, you told me already." Carey smiled and opened the refrigerator. "It only takes a little effort on each side to repair that bond you two once had."

"He doesn't seem as tall as he did then."

"That's because you've grown since you saw him and he hasn't," Carey said, taking a can of soda out of the refrigerator.

Grace giggled. "Yes he has," she said, holding her arms out in front of her stomach.

"He is a big man," Carey said, opening her soda. "He's a lumberjack, right?"

"Right."

"Certainly looks the part." She took a sip. "So you told him everything you did?"

Grace looked down. "Not everything," she admitted. "I told him the big thing I did and he didn't seem worried about the rest of it."

"Did you talk to him about what's going on with you and your mother?"

"No."

Carey leaned back in her chair. "Your father mentioned he and your mother had an acrimonious relationship after the divorce."

"If that means they hated each other's guts, yeah," Grace said.

"Your definition is pretty close. Did they fight in front of you?"

"If they were in the same house, they fought," Grace said. "Dad would tell you that it started the minute he came through the door but she'd be badmouthing him to me before he'd get home." She returned to the table. "How can two people who got married end up hating each other so much?"

"Unfortunately it happens," Carey said. "That's why it's so important to get to know the man you're with before you tie the knot and make babies."

"I'm not planning on getting married or having kids anytime soon," Grace said.

Carey silently watched as the young woman scribbled across a piece of paper, tore it out of her notebook, then started writing on a fresh sheet only to repeat the process seconds later. "Time for a break," she said, opening the refrigerator and pulling out a second can of soda. "What are you working on, anyway?"

"What else," Grace said. "Goal setting for PF."

Carey held out the can. "And I know how much you love setting goals. Let's go into the living room and talk about it, then you can come back and try again."

"Okay," Grace said, following her out of the kitchen.

Carey sat in her recliner and put the footrest up, then turned on the lamp next to her. It was one of her favorite times of the day, when she would relax in her chair and help Grace with homework or just listen to the teen sort out the complex issues of life. "So you need to set some goals. Here's the million-dollar question. What do you want your life to be, Grace?"

"I don't know," the teen said. "I know I want to own my own house and a nice car and money and all the things everyone else has."

"That's quite a bit," Carey said. "So start with the first one. A house. Why a house, why not a condo or rent an apartment?"

"Renting sucks," Grace said. "You pay all that money every month to someone else and you don't get anything for it."

"And with a mortgage you know that every month you're paying toward owning it outright," Carey said. "So one of your goals is to own your own house."

"I can't just put a simple answer down," Grace said. "Gage wants not only the goal but the means to get the goal."

"So think about what kind of house you want, where it would be, how much it would cost. Where you live makes a difference too. In Iroquois County, the tax rate is higher than up north in Seneca County."

"So if I buy in an area with a lower tax, it'll be cheaper for me to live," Grace said.

"It should, but keep in mind that there are other factors. If not, everyone would live in counties with lower tax brackets and turn the bigger ones into ghost towns. Let's take Seneca County. Many of the properties up there are on the lakes or up in the mountains, not near any supermarkets, schools, or even emergency services. I have a cottage on

Lake Bragg and going to the store requires getting in the truck and driving around the lake if I want to use the little market in Packard. There's no grocery store on every other corner. If I want to go to a supermarket, that's a good hour drive."

"You could use up the savings just in gas," Grace said.

"Actually with planning the trips would be minimal, so there is a savings," Carey said.

"So you own a house?"

"It's a cottage," Carey said. "Want to see a picture?"

"Sure," Grace said enthusiastically, moving to the near end of the couch.

Carey opened the lamp-table drawer and pulled out a photo album. She found the right page and handed the album over.

"Big cabin," Grace said. "It's on the lake?"

Carey nodded. "North side. Biggest bass I've ever seen."

Grace flipped the page. "Is this your boat?"

"Yes. You can't see it in the picture but there's an outboard motor on the end. I built the fishing seats myself."

"Wow," Grace said, turning the page. "If I had a place like this, I'd never leave it."

Carey chuckled, knowing that feeling well. "Someday I'll retire and when I do, that's where I'm going. I love it up there."

"So why not live there now?" Grace asked.

"My goals," Carey said. "I want to retire when I'm forty-five. In order to do that, I have to have enough money saved up to be able to live comfortably. The cottage and lake are ideal for tourists and hunters, so I rent out the cabin and put that money away."

"And you'll be able to quit working then?"

Carey shrugged. "Maybe. I might have to wait until I'm fifty. Depends on how my investments are doing."

"Wow, you're lucky," Grace said.

"Not luck, Grace, planning." Carey took a sip of soda, then set the can on the coaster. "When my father passed away, most of his estate went to my mother, but he left me some money. I bought the cottage even though I was still on active duty so I'd have a place to go when I was discharged. I rent it out to vacationers and hunters."

"Active duty. You mean when you were in the Coast Guard?"

Carey nodded.

"So you went from the Coast Guard to Sapling Hill?"

"I thought we were supposed to be talking about you and your goals," she said, taking another sip. "I served six years in the Guard, then came here. It'll be four years this August."

"So you get money from the renting and your paycheck here. You must be rolling in it."

Carey chuckled again. "I wouldn't say that, Grace, but I'm careful with my spending. I have monthly expenses living here like my phone and electricity. I have insurance on the truck and I pay a management company to oversee the rentals. I put money into my retirement and money market accounts, and I'm paying extra on my mortgage each month. It'll be paid off by the time I'm thirty-five. Again, what I have is because I planned long ago for what I wanted in the future."

"Uh-huh," Grace said. "Your cottage sounds really nice. I bet it's beautiful inside."

"It is," Carey said. "But when I retire I'm going to put an addition on the east side for a home office. I'm tired of doing my paperwork on that tiny little desk in the bedroom."

"So why not get a bigger desk for here?"

Carey held her arms out. "And where would I put it? Economy of space was the key when they designed this cabin. So, back to goals. Sometimes a sacrifice is required to make the goal a reality. And I think break time is over, young lady." She jutted her chin in the direction of the kitchen. "Back to work."

"All right," Grace sighed, rising from the couch. "I really like that cottage. Do you have more pictures?"

"Some, but I want to see some homework done and I want to see more practice questions for the GED test finished before I even think about showing them to you."

"Grace, it's five thirty."

The teen groaned and rolled over. "Okay, I'm up."

"Are you sure?" came the lightly teasing voice. "I don't hear any movement."

"I'm moving, just real slow," Grace said, sitting up and rubbing her eyes. "I'm not sure which I want more, the coffee or the bathroom."

"You're not making a puddle on my kitchen floor," Carey said. "Go. I'll make your coffee."

When Grace returned, a fresh mug of coffee was waiting for her on the counter. "You think you're ready?"

"As ready as I'm gonna be," Grace said, taking the mug and enjoying the first sip. "Either I know it or I don't."

"The GED isn't as hard as the SAT," Carey said. "You'll do just fine."

"What if I tank it?"

A reassuring hand squeezed Grace's shoulder. "You won't. I have faith in you."

"That makes one of us," Grace said, taking a sip. "So who's giving the test?"

"Instructor Donaldson," Carey said. "You'll be taking it in her classroom." She walked to the kitchen sink and rinsed her mug. "Look on the bright side, either way you're getting out of PT today."

"I'm not sure which is worse," Grace said. "I hate these kind of tests."

"I've got to go. You might want to break out the iron before you go to formation," Carey said. "Those creases looked a little weak yesterday."

FOUR MONTHS

"Ten hut!" Carey shouted. "All right, girls, it's pretty hot today, isn't it?"

"Yes, ma'am!"

"I bet you'd love it if we didn't have a run today, right?"

"Yes, ma'am!"

"We have a surprise for you girls today," she said, waving her hand to signal the other instructors. "For those of you who think only in terms of Schedule A and Schedule B, today is the fourth of July. For some reason the state doesn't think giving us a box of explosives is such a good idea, but hopefully what we have planned will make up for the lack of fireworks." Donaldson, Gage and Mitchell wheeled out large canvas bins, parking one in front of each of their squads, then headed back behind the building, returning a minute later with the last bin which they put in front of Bravo Squad. Carey made a show of wiping her brow. "Boy, it's really hot. Think we should do calisthenics?"

"No, ma'am!"

"But we need to get your PT in somehow," she said. "Well, I guess we'll have to do something different. Alpha and Bravo Squads, line up at opposite ends of the formation area facing each other. Charlie and Delta Squads, I suggest you move back...way back."

The girls took position and Instructor Gage stood between them. "Here's the rules. When the whistle blows, get your ammunition and fire. Direct hit and you're out. Ready?" Gage backed up out of range, then blew her whistle. "Go!" The girls ran for the bins, squealing with delight when they saw what their ammunition was. Red and blue water balloons went flying. The instructors scrambled to avoid being hit while calling out those who were soaked enough to be called out. They were only partially successful since a few were "accidentally" thrown at them. "Campbell, Rosetti, you're out," Carey called just before a balloon exploded against her back. Turning to see who the culprit was, she found a horrified Grace looking back at her.

"It was an accident, ma'am," Grace said, dodging a red balloon aimed at her.

"It's all right, Waters," she said as the teen started heading back to the bin to get more balloons. "We have a little surprise for you later."

Bravo Squad won the first round while Delta defeated Charlie in their battle. Instructors Donaldson and Mitchell wheeled out two new bins, this time filled with large water balloons. "First one to empty their bin wins," Gage said, blowing her whistle. Since it was hard to reach the bottom of the bin, Bravo Squad took the rules to the letter and hoisted Latisha into the bin. What balloons she didn't break with her feet were handed to the others to throw at Delta Squad, allowing Bravo to handily defeat their opponents.

"All right," Jan said, giving Grace a high five. Together they helped Latisha out of the bin. "Girl, you are soaked."

"You think I am? Take a look at Scary."

"Damn, talk about the high beams being on," Jan said, causing Grace to turn her head and look across the formation area to where the instructors were standing. Carey's top was completely soaked, her sport bra and nipples visible even from the distance.

"Earth to Grace."

"Huh?"

"What planet are you on?" Jan asked, wringing the bottom of her shirt then tucking it back into her shorts. "Come on, Charlie still has some balloons left."

"Uh, yeah sure," Grace said, tearing her eyes away from Carey, or rather, Carey's bosom. *Please let there be more water games later.* She took two steps before she was pelted in the side of the head with one of the small water bombs. "Damn!" There was nothing gentle about the toss and she only had to turn her head to see the culprit standing less than ten feet away. "You are such an asshole, Grenner."

"What's the matter, Scary's bitch can't take a little water?"

"Walk away," Latisha said, grabbing Grace's arm.

"Come on, Grace," Jan said. "Don't let her ruin our fun."

Grace allowed herself to be led away but not before giving Lauren Grenner a murderous look. "Someone should slap that bitch silly," she grumbled.

"Yeah but not you," Jan said, putting her hands on Grace's shoulders and pushing her away from the possible confrontation. "Come on, it seems like it's gonna be an easy day today. I don't want anything to screw it up."

Since Bravo Squad won, they got to sit back while the losing squads collected all the broken balloon bits and put them in the trash. "Don't split those shorts, Dawson," Jan said.

"Obviously she decided to skip the undies today," Grace said.

"Damn," Latisha chimed in. "Can she get it any deeper in the crack?"

"Gonna take her an hour to dig them out," Grace said, hugging her arms around her knees and enjoying the summer sun. "Look how tan I'm getting."

"Never get as tan as me," Latisha said, holding her dark brown arm against Grace's. "So what do you think is next?"

"No idea," Grace said. "Oh, look. There goes Viking and Mitchell."

"Think it's another balloon fight?" Campbell asked from behind Grace.

"Doubt it," Jan said. "Hey, what's that?"

"Sounds like an engine," Grace said. "Like a tractor."

"Bravo Squad," Carey called as she approached. The girls rose to their feet. "Bowen, Campbell, go man the hose." As she spoke, the tractor they had heard appeared, towing behind it a wooden dunking booth. "Jones, Rosetti, go to the supply shed and get the bucket of softballs just inside the door." She tossed a large piece of colored chalk at Grace. "Waters, once the booth is in place, count off twenty paces and draw a thick line. Bowen, no goofing around with that hose. You put it in the tank and you fill it, nothing else."

"Yes, ma'am," Jan said as she and Campbell headed for the side of the building where the hose was located. The hose was powerful but it still took a while to fill the tank, during which the sun helped dry most of the girls' shirts and shorts, though the sneakers continued to squish as the girls ran around.

"All right, squad formation facing the booth," Carey said. "Yes, I think you can all figure out what that is. Now here's how it's going to work. Your squad's instructor will go up and each member of the squad will get two chances to dunk her." Cheers went up through the group. "You think it's that easy?" Her lips curled into a devilish grin that Grace recognized immediately. "You'll be read one trivia question. You get it right, you get a shot. Get it wrong, you're the one that gets wet. All right, since Bravo Squad won the balloon fight, they go first." Carey took off her hat and mirrored sunglasses, handing them to Instructor Gage as she passed. "Bravo Squad, line up and take your best shot." Carey removed her sneakers and socks, then climbed up the ladder and swung herself onto the short bench above the tank.

"Oh let me go first," Grace said to the others as they huddled near the chalk mark.

"No way," Hathaway said. "I got three hits from her this week. I'm going first." She grabbed a softball from the basket, then walked up to the chalk line.

Instructor Donaldson stood near the booth, holding several index cards. "Name the capital of Maine."

Hathaway wiggled her glasses and assumed a pitcher's stance. "Augusta, ma'am."

"Fire away," Donaldson said.

"Come on, Mo. Dunk her," Jan said as she and the others clapped in encouragement. Hathaway took aim, then threw the softball.

Unfortunately it was high, missing the target and bouncing harmlessly against the wooden frame. Before the teen could react, Instructor Mitchell was there with a bucket of cold water, her aim much better than Mo's.

"Oh! Oh, that's cold!" Hathaway sputtered, pushing her drenched hair out of her face.

"That's what you get for throwing like a girl," Carey taunted from her perch.

"Please let me go next," Grace said. "I made JV softball as a freshman. I know I can hit her."

"Let her go before she has a frigging heart attack," Jan said. Grace ran up to the mark.

"Waters," Donaldson said. "Capital of California."

"Um...Los Angeles, ma'am."

"Sacramento," Donaldson said as Grace was soaked by Mitchell.

"That should cool you off," Carey said, waving her legs and smiling broadly.

"Hey, Grace, your village called. Their idiot is missing," Campbell said.

"Yeah yeah," Grace said, handing the softball to Latisha. "And there's a ventriloquist missing his dummy."

"Jones, alphabetically, which state capital comes first?"

"Boston, ma'am."

"Albany." Mitchell's aim was true, drenching Latisha. Some got their answers right but their aim failed to hit the center of the bull's-eye. Campbell came closest, her ball pinging off the edge of the metal target. Carey continued to tease and taunt her squad while sitting high and dry on the bench.

"Did you plug your brain in this time, Waters?"

"Yes, ma'am," Grace said, bouncing the softball in her hand.

"Waters, name..." Donaldson stopped and looked at Carey. "She's gonna get this one," she said. "Waters, which state boasts the highest latitude?"

Grace looked directly at Carey. "Alaska, ma'am," she said, causing Instructor Mitchell to pause with the bucket.

"I knew you'd get one right sooner or later," Carey said. "Now let's see how good your aim is."

Grace tossed the ball back and forth between her hands. "Oh, I have very good aim, Instructor Carey." She focused on the red bull's-eye, took her position, and fired. The metal target moved back, causing the bench to collapse and Carey to fall into the tank while the girls cheered. Grinning from ear to ear, Grace turned and bowed at her friends. "Thank you, thank you," she said, looking back to see Carey standing up and wiping her face. "I told you I had good aim, ma'am."

Carey reached up and reset the bench. "Yes you did, Waters." She climbed the ladder, water running from the back of her shorts. "Don't you worry, we get our revenge later."

Grace stood to the side as the others took their remaining shots, her eyes focused on the soaked woman. *Guess that's why guys like wet tee shirt contests,* she thought, wishing Carey hadn't worn her sports bra.

The dunking booth kept the group busy until lunch, when the girls were happy to be told that they could attend in their PT clothes instead of changing into their dress uniforms.

"All right, this should be a snap for all you big mouths," Carey said, holding a bushel of apples on her shoulder. "You have sixty seconds to get an apple for your squad. Did I mention just to make things a little more interesting, you'll be blindfolded. Now be careful, we don't want any of you to drown." Once Gage had the bucket filled with water, Carey leaned over and dumped the apples. "Alpha Squad, line up."

"Well, look who's going first," Grace muttered to Jan as Lauren Grenner knelt down in front of the bucket.

"Figures," Jan said. "Talk about big mouths."

"Look at her go," Grace said. "What's she gonna do? Drink all the water?"

"Naw." Jan bumped her. "She's just trying to get her weekly bath in."

"And time," Instructor Gage said, tapping Grenner on the shoulder. "Next."

"Dumb ass couldn't even get an apple," Grace said.

"The trick is to suck against it, then bite," Jan said. "If you just try to bite it, it'll move out of the way. Look, that toadie Dawson is trying now."

"No way," Grace said. Being careful not to be overheard by the instructors, they passed the time picking on and gossiping about the girls of Alpha Squad.

"All right, that's five apples for Alpha Squad," Carey said. "Bravo Squad, line up."

"I'm going first," Jan said, moving to the front of the line. She knelt down, waited to be blindfolded, then dunked down and snared an apple on the first try. Grace and the others cheered and clapped, hoping their turns went as well. "Next."

"Go on, Grace," Latisha said, giving her friend a shove.

"Come on, who's next?" Carey asked.

"I guess I am, ma'am," Grace said, walking over to the bucket and kneeling down.

"Good luck," Carey whispered as she tied the blindfold. "Ready?"

Only three of the six members of Bravo Squad that had gone before her were able to secure apples and Grace felt pressure not to let Alpha Squad get the best of them. When the whistle blew, she dove in head first, careful to keep her arms out of the water per the rules. She tried to sink her teeth into the apple but it moved, forcing her to quickly find another. *Come on, come on. Time's running out.* She picked her head up, took a deep breath, then plunged in again, not stopping until she had an apple pinned against the bottom of the bucket. Grace bit down, made sure she had a firm grip, then stood up quickly, proudly showing off the apple in her mouth.

"Thanks a lot," Carey said as she wiped the water off her face.

Grace let the apple drop into her hand and tried not to smirk as she saw just how much water had been splashed on the instructor. She dared to take a quick glance. *Yup, got them too.* "Sorry about that, ma'am," she said, not meaning it a bit.

"That's four apples so far for Bravo Squad," Carey said, running her fingers through her short black hair and flicking off the excess water. "Next."

"Great job," Jan said, pulling Grace away from the instructor. "Good job nailing Scary too," she added in a whisper. "You should have seen the look on her face when you came up and soaked her."

Grace now allowed herself to chuckle. "Yeah," she said. "Carey looked like a drowned rat."

"Yeah, you got her good," Jan said. "Hey, it's Mo's turn."

Grace took a bite of her apple, peeking over the top of it to watch Carey bend over and add more apples to the bucket. *Nice ass.*

"Earth to Grace."

"Huh, what?"

Jan shook her head. "You spaced out there for a sec."

"Sorry, got lost in thought," Grace said. She turned so she could no longer see Carey. "What'd you say?"

"I said if Mo gets this then we're tied with Alpha Squad." They heard the whistle and saw a soaked and disappointed Mo stand up. "That's it," Jan said. "Rosetti's our last chance to tie." She prodded Grace with her elbow. "Of course if anyone knows about sucking, it'd be her."

"Yeah," Grace said, daring to pivot and gaze at Carey again. *Damn, she's nice to look at.*

The whistle blew and seconds later Rosetti pulled her head back, proudly displaying a large red apple between her lips. "Told ya," Jan said.

"Uh-huh."

"Now we just have to hope that Charlie and Delta don't get more than five."

"Uh-huh."

"If it's a tie, we'll probably have some kind of sudden death thing."

"Uh-huh."

"Your ass is on fire."

"Uh-huh."

Jan nudged her hard. "What are you looking at?"

"What? Oh, nothing." She put her back to Carey. "Yeah, we're tied with Alpha Squad."

"Did you get water in your ears or something?" Jan asked. "If you did, I think it leaked into your brain."

"It's the heat," Grace said, wiping her brow for emphasis. *Yeah, it's heat all right.* "Maybe they'll let us take the shortcut to the lake and go swimming." That thought generated more images of Carey soaking wet, only adding to the emotions heightened by teenage hormones. *I hope she's working the late tour tonight. I need some time alone.*

"Maybe they will," Jan said, oblivious to her friend's plight. "I love playing Tarzan with that rope."

"You love hitting the water like a cannonball and splashing everybody," Grace said, tossing her apple core in the nearby trash can.

"Not everybody," Jan said. "I didn't mean to soak Viking. She took that chance when she decided to sun herself on that rock."

"You're the one that had to do the pushups," Grace pointed out. "Not her." They bantered back and forth until Delta Squad managed to pull seven apples from the bucket, winning the event. Then it was time to line up for the next activity, which, much to Grace's joy, was a trip to the lake. She began heading up the hill with the others when a firm voice made her stop.

"Waters, ten hut."

Grace stood still, watching the other girls walking past her, curious looks on their faces. *What did I do?* she wondered while waiting nervously for Carey to reach her.

"Did I tell you earlier that I would get my revenge later?" the instructor said from just behind her. "Guess what?" Grace felt the neck of her shirt being pulled back. "It's later." An extremely cold water balloon slid between her shirt and skin.

"Oh! Oh that's cold," she yelped but before she could pull her shirt free from her shorts, a well-aimed smack caused the balloon to burst. "Hey!"

"Watch your mouth," Carey warned through her laughter as Grace danced around in a futile attempt to escape the cold water. "Pretty cold, hmm?"

Grace glared at her and pulled her shirt free, wringing as much water as she could. "Yes, ma'am."

"It should be," Carey said as they continued up the hill. "I put it in the freezer to help get just the right chill."

"That is so mean, ma'am."

"And you absolutely deserve it," Carey said. "Don't forget who soaked whom in the apple-dunking contest."

149

Grace grinned broadly. "I got you good too, but it was an accident, ma'am."

"It may have been an accident but I saw the look on your face when you realized what happened." They crested the hill, meeting the main trail near the three-mile marker. "Besides, you look like you needed cooling off."

"But we're going to the lake," Grace said. "Ma'am."

"I don't think the lake is as cold as that water balloon," Carey said. "And it was much more satisfying than tossing you in the lake would have been."

Carey had been right about the lake. Except in the shadiest of places, the water was warm from the sun. Grace chose to head for a shady area, away from the noise and splashing of others. There, floating on her back with her eyes closed, Grace allowed the gently rocking water to lull her into a light doze. She had no idea how much time passed as she enjoyed the lazy summer day, and would have basked longer under the warm summer sun if a sudden splash of water had not woken her up. Opening her eyes, she found herself face to face with a grinning Carey. "This isn't nap time, Grace."

After a quick look to make sure no one was watching, the teen returned a splash to Carey. "Sure felt like it. I was dozing nicely until someone decided to bother me." She tapped her chin with her finger. "Gee, I wonder who that could be."

"You looked too peaceful," Carey said as she treaded water. "Besides, you were starting to float away and I didn't want you to wake up on the north end of the lake and have to swim back."

Grace looked around, surprised by how far she had drifted from where she first closed her eyes. "Must have been the Z-burger at lunch."

Carey pointed toward the shore and the two began swimming. "I'd buy that if you actually had a Z-burger for lunch, but I saw you inhale three hot dogs, not to mention several handfuls of potato chips. I'm surprised you didn't sink to the bottom."

"I'm a growing teenager," Grace said. "I've probably burned all that off by now."

"You think so?" Carey paused long enough to send a friendly splash Grace's way. "Try eating like that when you're twenty. It'll go right to your hips."

Putting a little more distance between them, Grace readied herself. "Oh, is that what happened to you?"

"What? Why you little..." Carey pounced, catching the backpedaling teen easily.

"Kidding, I was kidding," Grace protested through her laughter as she found herself hoisted out of the water, then sent backward into the shallow depths. She took in water but before she could orient herself, she was pulled back up to the surface.

"Easy now," Carey said, holding her upright as Grace coughed out the lake water. "You're supposed to keep your mouth shut when you go underwater."

"I do when I know I'm going under," Grace said, very aware of the warm body pressed against her own. *Oh, dunk me anytime if it means I get this afterward.* "I didn't think you'd catch me."

"You all right now?"

"Yeah," Grace said reluctantly, moving away from Carey but not before she managed to brush her calf against the outside of the older woman's thigh. *Soft.* The water lapped at her breastbone as she stood up and ran her fingers through her short blonde hair.

"I can't believe you thought you could outrun me," Carey said.

"You got lucky," Grace taunted, slapping a little water at her mentor. "Bet you couldn't do it again." *Please, do it again.*

"Oh no?" Carey approached with comical menace, arms raised and fingers curled like talons. "Get ready to kiss the fishies, Waters."

Closer, closer. Grace dipped her hands under the water and waited until Carey was almost on top of her before scooping up a wave right into the older woman's face. "Hah! Gotcha," she said as she made a halfhearted attempt to escape. Carey caught her easily, sending Grace underwater. This time the teen was prepared, moving quickly to plant her feet and hook her arms around Carey's leg. *Oh yes, very soft.* One good tug sent the instructor off balance, then a retaliatory move put Grace in the same position. When they surfaced, it was only to start a flurry of splashes at each other that continued until Grace held up her hands and surrendered. "I give up," she said, putting up with several more spatters of water before Carey stopped and grinned victoriously.

"Wuss," Carey said. "I was just getting warmed up." She wiped the water from her face, then combed her hair with her fingers. "Try not to float off anywhere. It'll be time to go back soon."

"Are you getting out now?"

Carey nodded. "I want to dry out a bit."

"Yeah, it's a good time to head in," Grace agreed and together they sloshed through the water toward the shore. "So what's next?"

"It's getting close to dinner time so we'll be letting everyone go get dried off and changed," Carey said. "Then it's free time until lights out."

"What do you want me to do with my wet clothes?" Grace asked. "I can hang them in the shower or over the porch rail to dry."

"I don't want you to do that," Carey said. "I suppose you'll never get near the dryers with all the other girls trying to take care of their clothes. Use my dryer."

"Yes, ma'am," Grace said, realizing they were now within earshot of others.

"And clean the lint trap."

"Yes, ma'am."

"Run your clothes through the washer first."

"Yes, ma'am." Grace looked straight ahead to keep from rolling her eyes.

"And don't use too much detergent."

"I won't, ma'am."

"Make sure you balance the load or the washer will shake."

Yes, Mother Hen. "Yes, ma'am. I'll do everything right, ma'am."

"All right," Carey said. "I'll trust you." They had almost reached the shore when Instructor Donaldson approached.

"Instructor Carey, may I speak with you for a minute?"

"Sure," Carey said.

Grace took the cue. "Um, I have to get my sneakers, ma'am."

"Make sure you wear them," Carey said. "I don't want you getting any splinters."

"Yes, ma'am." Grace quickly walked away, hoping to avoid another list of dos and don'ts. Her mild annoyance was rapidly replaced by quite a different feeling. *She played with me.* Unable to contain it, the teen smiled happily as she sat down and pulled on her sneakers. *I bet she didn't spend time like that with anyone else.* The smile remained with her throughout the walk back to the cabin.

"Your favorite time of the day," Carey said as she unlocked her office. "So what should we talk about for forty-five minutes?"

"I aced my paper for English, ma'am," Grace said.

"Good," Carey said as she tossed her cap on the hook and took her usual seat behind the desk. "I knew you would. Let's see, that took ten seconds. What else do you want to talk about?"

Grace shrugged. "I don't know, ma'am."

Carey leaned back in her chair. "One of these days you're going to surprise me and actually want to talk about something," she said. "I just hope I don't have a heart attack from the shock." She picked up an envelope from the top of her desk. "Here. You have mail," she said, handing Grace the envelope. "I thought you would want to open it."

"Is it my test scores?" Grace asked, tearing it open at the perforation.

"I would think so," Carey said, ignoring the slip. "Come on, let's see how you did."

Once the three sides of the envelope were torn off, Grace hesitated. "What if I didn't do good, ma'am?"

"Do well," Carey corrected. "I've told you before, as long as you do your best, that's all that matters. You can always take it again." She rose from her seat and walked around the desk, leaning against it so she was facing the teen. "Open it."

Grace looked at the scores. "Seven twenty on the verbal, seven sixty on the math, ma'am."

"You're kidding," Carey said, taking the paper to look at it. "A fourteen eighty combined? That's fantastic."

"Is it, ma'am?"

Carey smiled and handed back the paper. "Yes," she said. "That and your GED will get you into college."

"If I passed the GED," Grace said. "Ma'am."

"You passed it," Carey said confidently, pushing off the desk to return to her chair. "You're too smart not to, and you told me yourself that it was an easy test. Right now it's just a matter of waiting for the diploma to arrive."

"Diploma?"

"Three, two..."

"Ma'am."

Carey smiled. "Yes, Grace. A diploma. It is called the General Equivalency Diploma, after all." She took a piece of paper and folded it in half, using it as an example. "The top half is the score and your certificate number and the bottom half is your official diploma from the state." She scribbled a quick note to herself on the paper. "You really didn't know that?"

Grace shook her head. "I didn't think about it. I figured I'd get something like this." She held up the SAT scores. "Does it look like a real diploma?"

"A little smaller, but yes, it looks like a real diploma because it is one," Carey said. "I'll tell your father what size frame to get." She circled the note she had made. "You should be proud of yourself for those SAT scores, Grace. By the way, what happened to ma'am?" She chuckled at the panicked look in the teen's blue eyes. "I suppose getting a fourteen eighty on the SAT earns you a free pass today. Relax." Opening the bottom drawer of her desk, she pulled out Grace's folder. "I need to make a copy of those scores before you can keep them," she said. "I want to put it in your record."

Grace set the paper on the desk. "Thanks. So it's really a good score?"

"Yes," Carey said. "You can thump your chest all you want." She leaned back, resting her left ankle on her right knee. "Are you going to tell your mother about the SAT?" She watched as the light left Grace's face, replaced with the stony tough-girl look the teen got whenever she was trying to protect herself from some inner pain.

"Why bother? She doesn't care."

"I don't think that's true, Grace," she said. "You're her only child."

"So?" The teen crossed her arms. "I'm almost eighteen. I will be by the time I get out of Crestwood. I'm never going back there." Blue eyes focused hard on the paperweight. "Never."

"You don't have to but, for better or worse, she is your mother," Carey said. "You only get one of them." She found herself in the unenviable position of defending a woman she personally disliked. "Grace, I know she's made mistakes."

The teen snorted. "Just a few."

"I don't see a halo over your head," Carey said. "How many times did she have to come pick you up from school because you managed to get yourself suspended? How about the police station?"

"So I'm a lousy daughter," Grace said, still staring at the glass egg. "She should be happy to get rid of me then, right?"

Those walls go up so fast, don't they? "If she was happy to get rid of you she wouldn't have shown up here on the first visitation day," Carey said. "She loves you, Grace. It may be hard to see sometimes but she does." She waited for a response but none came. "Uncross your arms and look at me. You think I don't remember how excited your were that day when you were waiting for her to come? It may be hard to admit it but under all that pain you love her, Grace. Don't look away." She waited for the teen to focus on her again. "You do."

"You want her to get a copy of the scores? Fine, I don't care."

"Watch that tone with me," Carey warned. "I'm not the one you're mad at." *Actually at the moment you're probably pretty pissed at me,* she thought, seeing the teen glaring at the paperweight. "The decision is yours, Grace. I know you're hurt and angry with her now, but that doesn't mean you have to cut her out of your life."

"I'm not ready to forgive her."

"I know, but someday you will," Carey said. "It's a lot easier to fix a bridge if you don't burn it first." She reached out and took away the paperweight. "Up here, Grace."

There was a long silence before Grace spoke. "I suppose if I saw her I could be civil," she said. "But not if he's with her."

"He won't be," Carey said. "Not here, anyway. But once you're out in the real world that's a problem you're going to have to face."

"No I won't," Grace said. "I'll just tell her if she wants to see me that she has to leave that jerk somewhere."

"So you're willing to work at fixing your relationship with your mother?"

Grace shrugged. "If she wants to."

"I didn't ask that," Carey said. "I asked if you were willing." *Look at those gears turn,* she thought as she waited for Grace to answer.

"Yeah, I guess so."

"So you'll send your mother a copy of the SAT scores along with a note telling her she can come visit?"

"Just her," Grace said.

"Just her," Carey repeated. "You know, if your mother and father both came for visitation, it would be an excellent time for a family conference."

"You mean put my mother and father in the same room together?" Grace shook her head vehemently. "No way."

"Why?"

"Because they'd fight. They can't stand the sight of each other. I don't want to listen to them yelling. I'd rather visit with her for a little while and then spend the rest of the time with Dad."

"Don't rule the idea out completely," Carey said. "A family conference could be very beneficial." There was a quick rapping, then the door swung open.

"We've got a problem," Instructor Gage said from the doorway.

Carey knew from her friend's look that it was serious. "Waters, we'll talk later."

"Yes, ma'am."

Waving Sue in, Carey closed Grace's folder as the teen left. "What's going on?"

"Our little saboteur struck again. Broke into the shed and punctured every ball."

Carey sighed and reached for her cap. "And I was hoping it would be a quiet day."

With Carey working late and her homework done, Grace decided to go to the rec room and hang out for a while. She was pleasantly surprised to see Jan playing solitaire at the table. "Hey."

"Hey there," Jan said. "Thought maybe you forgot this place existed."

"I get bored with jigsaw puzzles and checkers," Grace said. "So have you heard anything?"

"Nothing more than the usual," Jan said. "Most think Grenner and her toadie did it, but no one saw them."

"So those bitches get away with it again, right?" Grace picked up a paddle. "You serve."

"Looks like it," Jan said as she retrieved the ping pong ball and the other paddle. "And we suffer with no more basketball, soccer or volleyball."

Grace spun the paddle in her hand. "So what are we supposed to do for PT? Run every day?"

"Unless Scary and Short Shit decide to set up more obstacle courses," Jan said. "Ready? Zero serving zero."

"Oh please no," Grace said as she returned the serve. "Anything but obstacle courses."

Jan hit the ball hard, grinning when Grace missed it. "My point. Hey, walking piles of shit coming in."

Grace, who had been kneeling down in search of the ping pong ball, glanced at the doorway. Lauren Grenner and Sally Dawson entered while several girls decided the barracks would be a better place to hang out and left. *There's gonna be trouble,* Grace thought as she tossed the ball to Jan.

"Well look who's here," Grenner said. "If it isn't Scary's bitch."

"Go away, Grenner," Grace said. "Jan, serve."

"Scary must be working night tour tonight," Lauren Grenner continued. "Why else would her little slut have time to hang out here?" Three more girls left the room. "What's the matter, Waters? You deaf or something?"

Carey will be pissed if I get in a fight. It was that thought that kept Grace from snapping back at Grenner. "Come on, Jan. Let's go," she said, tossing the paddle on the table.

"Hey, bitch, she's talking to you," Dawson said.

"You got something to say, Toadie?" Jan said, moving between Grace and the other two girls. "I'll kick your ass from here to Mohawk and back."

"Stay out of it, Bowen," Grenner said. "Don't you have to give Gage her nightly licking or something?"

"Ignore her," Grace said to Jan. "She's just trying to get us into trouble." She looked to see a handful of girls still in the rec room. *They're hoping for a fight,* she thought. "Come on, Jan."

"Yeah, these two assholes aren't worth it," Jan said, making a false lunge at Dawson, then smirking when the smaller teen ran behind Grenner for protection. "That's right, Toadie. Hide behind your mistress like a good little fraidy cat."

This isn't going to stop, Grace thought as she walked to the door.

"Oh look," Grenner said. "Scary's little slut is leaving."

"What the hell's your problem?" Grace snapped, turning around and glaring at her adversary. "Why do you always have to start trouble?"

"Ignore her, remember?" Jan whispered as she ushered Grace out the door and down the steps.

"Fucking bitch," Grace hissed, kicking at one of the loose stones lying on the asphalt. "Can't even play a damn game of ping pong without her causing trouble." She heard the rec room door open. "Ah damn."

"Where you going?" Grenner taunted as she and the others came outside. "Gotta hurry back home and get ready for Mistress Scary?"

"Go to hell, Grenner," Grace said, stopping halfway across the paved lot.

Grenner laughed. "Go to hell, Grenner," she mimicked. "Make me, bitch."

Grace heard the doors of the barracks open and knew others were coming to see what they hoped would be a fight. "Naw, you're not worth the effort," she said, glancing around for any sign of an instructor.

"No, come on, you big-mouthed bitch," Grenner said. "You think you can beat me?"

Grace shook her head dismissively and started walking away, trusting Jan to watch her back. "I'm not going to fight you."

"Fucking coward," Grenner snarled. "You don't want to fight me because you know I'll kick your ass."

"I don't want to fight you because you're not worth getting in trouble for," Grace said. "Come on, Jan."

"Yeah, just a fucking coward."

"Ten hut," Instructor Donaldson said as she came around the corner. "Waters and Bowen, get back here. Someone want to tell me what all the shouting is about?"

"They started it," Dawson said, pointing at Grace and Jan. "We didn't do nothing, ma'am."

The blonde instructor shook her head. "I believe that as much as I believe little green men live on Mars. Jones, what happened?"

"I don't know, ma'am," Latisha said. "I was in the barracks."

"Bowen?"

"Grace and I were playing ping pong when those two came in and started making trouble," Jan said. "We left to avoid a fight and they followed us out, ma'am."

"Waters?"

"Yes, ma'am," Grace said. "Just like Jan said, ma'am."

Donaldson looked at Grenner and Dawson. "And if I asked you two I'd get a completely different version, right?"

"We just went in to play a game and they started harassing us, ma'am," Grenner said, doing her best to look innocent.

"And so when they left the situation you just had to come out after them, right?" the blonde instructor asked. "You two are on restriction until Sunday. Bowen and Waters, you two were headed somewhere so get going. As for the rest of you, I think twenty pushups should help remind you that proper young ladies don't cluster around like a bunch of hooligans hoping for a fight. Now drop!"

Together Jan and Grace walked toward the trail that led to the cabins. "How the hell did we get away without having to do pushups?" Jan asked.

"Guess Viking decided we were telling the truth," Grace said. "And we were walking away rather than getting ready to fight."

"Yeah, there's a switch, eh?" Jan shook her head and gave a little laugh. "This place is getting to me, Grace. Next thing you know I'll be taking tests and trying to get into college too." They stopped, looked at each other, and began laughing. "Not," they said in unison.

"But it is good not to be in trouble," Grace said. "We could be back there doing pushups or even stuck on restriction."

"Short Shit will drop dead of shock," Jan said. "Bet I can get an extra hour of TV out of this."

They stopped where the trail split apart. "Lucky you," Grace said. "Carey's working late tonight but I bet tomorrow I can talk her into playing cards."

"Ooh, fun city," Jan said, taking the left side of the fork. "Night."

"See you tomorrow," Grace said, going to the right and heading for the cabin. It was starting to get dark, the trees becoming nothing more than silhouettes on either side of the trail. *How does Carey find her way at night without a flashlight?* The cabin came into view, the motion detector turning on the outside light once she was close enough. *Wonder how long it'll take Viking to tell Carey what happened.* Kneeling down next to the steps, she felt around for the false rock, then retrieved the key hidden within.

Once inside, Grace went to the refrigerator in search of the leftover pork chop Carey had told her earlier she could have. She had just put the plate in the microwave when the phone rang. "Guess it didn't take long," she said as she walked over to the phone. On the fourth ring the answering machine picked up.

"Grace, pick up the phone."

She put the receiver to her ear. "I didn't start it."

"So I've heard."

"I didn't fight," Grace said, leaning against the counter. "I walked away."

"I heard that too. You did good, Grace. I'm proud of you for keeping your cool."

Hearing the approval in Carey's voice, Grace smiled. "Thanks."

"So what are you doing right now?"

"Waiting for the pork chop to heat up. Can I have a soda?"

"May I have a soda, and yes."

Grace made a beeline to the refrigerator. "Thanks."

"Only one, and make sure there's grape left for me."

"You have two left. I'm taking a root beer."

"All right. I'll be home around nine thirty. Try to leave some food in my fridge."

"I will," Grace said, pressing the cancel button just as the microwave started to beep. "So you're proud of me?"

"Yes, Grace. You saw a situation starting and walked away. You wouldn't have done that a month ago. You acted like a mature young lady instead of a juvenile delinquent."

"Are you very proud of me?"

She heard the chuckle on the other end of the line. "Don't push it. What do you want?"

"Well there are five ice cream bars in the freezer..."

"And I wonder why my grocery bill's jumped twenty bucks a week. One, and you'd better wipe out the microwave this time. I know you didn't put a paper towel over your plate to keep the splatter down."

"Whoops. I forgot."

"Just like you forgot to replace the roll of toilet paper after you used up the last sheet."

"I said I was sorry about that."

"That didn't help me when I was sitting there with nothing to dry myself with. Go eat and I'll see you when I get home." They said their good-byes and Grace hung up the phone.

"I knew you'd be proud of me," she said aloud to herself as she took the plate from the microwave. While it bothered her that Grenner had gotten away with calling her a coward in front of the others, Grace took a certain amount of satisfaction in not being the one on restriction. "Besides," she added with a smirk as she began cutting up her meat. "I'm the one getting soda and ice cream."

The morning sun beat down on the group while Instructor Gage paced back and forth in front of the two squads. "Last chance, girls."

Grace looked around, knowing full well that no one would admit to vandalizing the equipment. She spotted Grenner and Dawson sharing knowing smirks. *You want to know who stabbed the basketballs, ask them.*

"Fine, if that's the way you want it," Gage said. "Everyone drop for twenty."

Oh great, Grace thought as she hit the ground. *Gage woke up on the wrong side of the bed this morning, didn't she?* She glanced over at Jan, who mouthed the letters PMS. *Figures. Not bad enough she's pissed about the balls. She's gonna work our asses off and make today suck.*

"When you finish those, you can do twenty sit-ups, then stretch and get ready for your morning run," the petite instructor said. "And for those of you that think you can just jog along at a leisurely pace, I'm going to be running at the back of the pack and I expect to see some hustle today." She clapped her hands impatiently. "Let's go, girls. We don't have all day."

"No, just four hours for you to squeeze as much hell in as you can," Grenner said under her breath.

"Did I ask for a commentary, Grenner?" Gage yelled.

"No, ma'am."

"So why did I hear your mouth?"

"Sorry, ma'am."

"You're always sorry, Grenner. Four months and you don't know enough to keep your mouth shut."

Grace smirked as the instructor continued to berate Grenner. *Maybe today won't be so bad after all.*

Grace was sitting on the couch happily munching on a cookie when Carey entered the cabin. "Hi," the teen said around a mouthful of cookie.

"Hi, Grace," Carey said, kneeling down to unlace her boots. "How many of those have you had?"

"Just two."

"Two or two dozen?"

Grace smiled. "Just two. I'm saving the others for later."

"Others? I said you could have three cookies, so where do you get others?"

"Well...you usually let me have more than three," Grace said hopefully. "And it is a new box."

"There was a time when a box lasted me all week," Carey said, putting her boots neatly next to Grace's sneakers on the newspaper near the door. "You sure you're not related to Cookie Monster?"

Grace pretended to check her skin tone. "Nope, not turning blue yet."

"Could have fooled me," Carey said. "What are you doing there?"

"Working on my goals list."

"Revising?"

Grace nodded. "Wanna see?"

Carey walked over to the couch. "Move over," she said, settling down on the cushion next to the teen. "You crossed off the question mark next to college."

"Yeah," Grace said. "If I passed the GED, Dad says I should be able to go to a community college." She circled the dollar signs next to the word *college*. "The only problem is gonna be money."

"You would be surprised how much money is out there for college if you want it," Carey said, patting Grace's shoulder. "Good move. Now you have to decide on your major."

"I have no idea," Grace said. "I'm good at math and figuring things out, but I can't imagine what kind of job I want to do for the rest of my life."

"So that's something you need to look at," Carey said. "I'll see if I can get hold of a college catalog. That will show you what careers are available and what courses are needed to get that degree. It might help."

"It would at least give me ideas," Grace said, closing her notebook. "I can't think anymore."

"You've had a big surprise today," Carey said. "Oh, speaking of surprises, I have one for you."

"You do?" Grace's eyes lit up. "What?"

"You clean up this mess," she said, pointing at the paper napkin covered with cookie crumbs. "I'll go get it. Don't get too excited. It's not as wonderful as you think." Carey went into the bedroom and retrieved the package that had arrived the day before. "You remember Mrs. Hamlin?"

"My math teacher?"

"That's the one," Carey said, entering the living room. "Since you've done as much as you can with the math books we have, she sent this for you."

Grace opened the brown paper wrapper. "She sent me a math book?"

"Trigonometry," Carey said. "Give you a head start for college. After all, we can't have you doing nothing during math period."

"I can think of a few things to do," Grace grumped good-naturedly. "Thanks."

"A letter thanking Mrs. Hamlin would be good too," Carey said.

"I'll write it tomorrow," Grace said just as the phone started to ring.

Carey looked at the clock on the wall. "I wonder who that could be?" She stepped into the kitchen and picked up the receiver. "Hello?" Grace flipped the pages of her new math book, trying not to listen to the phone call. Unfortunately, she was curious and it was too easy to hear each word. "...thought you two were happy together." Whoever it was, Carey didn't seem to be too pleased as the older woman began pacing in the kitchen. "That's not really any of your business." Grace made sure to keep her eyes on her book. "Now isn't a good time. Because we're in session, that's why and even if we weren't, I don't think it would be a good idea." Grace heard the refrigerator open, then slam shut. "Eve, I'm not interested. No. No. I don't care." There was a silence on Carey's end while the other woman spoke, then the instructor exploded. "Well if I'm so damn controlling, then why are you calling me after all this time?" Grace winced when she heard something come down hard on the counter, guessing it to be the angry woman's fist. "I know, I know, it's all my fault. The fact that you came home pregnant had nothing to do with it, right?"

Oh, I should not hear any more. Grace grabbed her sneakers. As she headed out the front door, she heard Carey say "...and you want to talk about fair?" Grace closed the door and sat down on the wooden steps. It was clearly a private conversation that she should not have been listening to, but still she could not stop from replaying the snippets of the conversation. It took little to add up the pieces, especially when she added in the way her mentor reacted to Eve's call. Even from outside she could hear the force in which Carey hung up the phone. *She is so pissed. I'm waiting right here until she cools off.*

Several minutes later, the door opened. "You can come back in now," Carey said, leaving the door open and walking to her recliner. Grace went in and sat on the couch, unsure what to say, or if she should say anything at all. Even with the shadows cast by the lamp, she could see the hint of red rimming Carey's eyes. *She made you cry? I didn't think anything would make you cry.* Carey put the footrest up and rubbed her temple. "How much did you hear?"

"I tried not to," Grace said. "I left when you said something about being fair."

"Wonderful," Carey said, letting out a long breath of air. "Well, too late to do anything about it now." She pinched the bridge of her nose. "Any questions?"

Grace thought carefully before answering. "Are you okay?"

Carey's head popped up, brown eyes locking with hers. "That's not what I thought you'd ask," she said.

"The other stuff doesn't matter," Grace said. "You seemed pretty upset."

"It was an unexpected call," Carey said, leaning her head back against the cushion. "If I had realized who it was, I would have let the machine get it."

"I won't say anything," Grace said. "I swear."

"About what?" Carey asked, her lip turning up in a half smile. "About the phone call, or what you learned about me?"

"Both," Grace said. "It'll be like I didn't hear anything."

Carey smiled. "I doubt that, Grace. You heard, whether I like it or not." She rubbed her forehead again. "What the hell, I guess. You girls probably figure I am anyway."

"Actually everyone thinks Viking, I mean Instructor Donaldson, is," Grace said, her eyes widening when she realized what she'd said.

Carey smiled. "Viking, huh? Fits. She's straight, though."

"You, we weren't sure about," Grace said. "Some think you are and some think you aren't."

"We don't keep you girls busy enough, do we?" Carey said. "I don't even want to know how much of your day is spent trying to figure out the sex lives of your instructors. It's probably better than talking about going to kennels looking for dates." Grace colored and looked down.

"It was just talk," the teen said.

"I know what it was," Carey said. "And I know how easy it is to let loose a juicy piece of gossip."

Grace looked up quickly. "No," she said. "It's your business, not theirs." She looked down. "Not mine, either. I'm sorry I didn't leave as soon as I realized it was a personal call."

"And just when was that?"

"When you began pacing and slammed the fridge," Grace admitted. "You don't usually do that, no matter how mad you get. Instructor Gage is the pacer."

"Everyone has buttons," Carey said, resting her elbows on the armrests and lacing her fingers together. "So did you think I was or wasn't?"

"I wasn't sure," Grace said. "I thought maybe, but it's not like I could just come out and ask if you were..."

"A lesbian?" Carey offered. "It's okay to say the word, Grace. It doesn't make you one."

"I know that," Grace said hotly. "And how do you know I'm not?"

"I don't," Carey said, pushing the footrest down. "Sex is a subject you manage to avoid quite nicely, even in SR class. You can dance around an answer better than anyone I know, and you remember what happened the last time I pushed you about it." She rose to her feet. "I'm not in the mood to dodge any chairs."

Grace grimaced at the reminder. "I said I was sorry about that."

"You can be sorry all you want," Carey said. "The trick is to learn from your mistakes and not repeat them."

"I promise." She looked at Carey expectantly.

"What?"

"Can I ask you another question?"

"May I, not can I," Carey said. "I won't promise that I'll answer it, but go ahead."

"I don't know who else to ask," Grace said nervously. "You're the only one I know."

"One what?"

"Um...lesbian."

"You haven't been listening to the teenage grapevine," Carey said, settling back down on the recliner.

"I heard," Grace said. "But that's just talk because they went off on that walk together for so long."

"What's your question?"

Grace rubbed her hands together, her eyes focusing on her notebook. "When did you know? That you were?"

"That's not an easy question to answer, Grace," Carey said. "May I ask why you want to know?"

"You don't have to answer," Grace said. "Forget it."

"There has to be a reason," Carey said. "I always knew I felt different but I didn't accept being gay until I was in my early twenties."

"You didn't want to be?"

"It wasn't a question of wanting to be or not wanting to be," Carey said. "It was more a question of accepting who and what I was."

"I don't understand."

Carey put the footrest down and leaned forward. "It wasn't a choice between being gay and being straight. I'm a lesbian and nothing is going to change that. The hard part for me was acknowledging that fact and dealing with it. Now, why are you asking?"

Grace stared at the coffee table. "You said you felt different...like from the other girls?"

"You're answering a question with a question," Carey pointed out. "When I was a teen the latest boy bands didn't send me swooning. My walls were covered with female rockers. I didn't have too many friends over to see my room."

The grains of the table blurred as Grace let her mind drift back. "The first time I saw a naked woman was in a magazine one of my mother's boyfriends left behind." Her heart began pounding. "I kept it hidden in my room and looked at it all the time. It was my little secret. I...I thought there was something wrong with me." She took a deep breath, then let it out slowly. "When I think about sex...I think about it with women."

"How long have you felt this way?"

"Since I was thirteen or so," Grace said. "When I found the magazine and started reading the stories and seeing the pictures." She rubbed her hands together. "When other girls were talking about kissing boys, I was thinking about kissing them."

"Have you had sex with a woman?"

Grace shook her head. "No. My cousin and I showed ourselves to each other once but there wasn't any touching."

"Have you had sex with a man?"

The question caught Grace by surprise, causing her to look up at her mentor. "Uh..."

"Be honest with me," Carey said.

"Yes."

"Intercourse?"

Grace looked down, feeling completely ashamed. "Yes." She heard Carey move from the chair and braced herself. *Please don't ask me about it tonight.* "Um, I have homework."

"The homework can wait," Carey said, sitting on the cushion next to her. "Do you want to talk about it?"

"No."

"You can talk to me about anything," Carey said.

"I know."

"Grace, how old were you?"

"I don't want to talk about it."

"Sixteen? Fifteen? Younger?"

Grace stared at the coffee table. "Fifteen."

"What happened?"

The teen shrugged her shoulders. "Nothing important."

"It affected you," Carey said, her voice understanding and gentle. "It is important."

"Please."

Several seconds passed before she heard Carey let out a deep breath. "All right, Grace. I told you I'm not in the mood to dodge chairs tonight. I'm here if you want to talk."

"Can...may I ask you another question?"

"What?" Carey asked softly.

"Do you think...if I told my dad how I feel..." Grace closed her eyes. "Do you think he'd still love me?" She felt a hand rest gently on her shoulder.

"I think any man that carries that many pictures of his daughter in his wallet will love her no matter what," Carey said. "What do you think?"

Grace swallowed hard. "He told me he'd love me no matter what but he didn't want me to become a porn star or anything like that."

Carey gave a soft snort. "I wouldn't want you to become one either," she said, giving the teen's shoulder a quick squeeze before withdrawing her hand. "He loves you, Grace. I know that."

"Maybe I'll talk to him about it when he comes to visit."

"You should," Carey said. "Your father seems to be a very understanding man. Now, any more questions?"

Grace shook her head. "No, I guess not."

"All right." Carey went back to the recliner.

"Well, not really."

"Grace..." Carey pinched the bridge of her nose and closed her eyes. "I've had a really hard day."

"I'm sorry. I just..." She looked up at Carey. "Well, I just wondered if you needed to talk."

"Probably," Carey said. "But it would be entirely inappropriate to do it with you. You know that."

"I know," Grace said. "If you wanted to call someone or something, I could go to the rec room for a while. I'd just need a flashlight to see my way back."

Carey shook her head. "You have homework to do."

Grace rose to her feet. "My homework's done and I don't mind, really."

"Promise you'll stay out of trouble?" Carey asked.

"I swear," Grace said.

Carey rubbed her face and nodded. "There's a flashlight in the junk drawer."

"Okay." Grace walked into the kitchen. "Do you want the phone?"

"I can get it."

"It's okay. I'm out here already." Grace picked up the phone, noting how loose the base was on the wall. "Um, I think you pulled out the screws."

"I'm sure I did," Carey said. "I'll fix it tomorrow."

Taking the flashlight from the drawer, Grace returned to the living room and handed the phone to Carey, their fingers briefly touching. "Here you go," she said. "I'll be back by lights out."

"You don't have to stay away that long," Carey said as she began pressing buttons on the phone.

"I don't mind." Grace looked at the empty spot on the mat, realizing only then that she was still wearing her sneakers. *Glad she didn't notice,* she thought.

"I'd rather you weren't out that late by yourself. No more than—oh, hi, Mom, hold on." Carey looked at her. "No more than an hour."

"Okay." Grace opened the door and stepped outside, causing the motion sensor to turn on the outside light. She could hear Carey talking on the phone but was unable to make out the words. *At least you have someone you can talk to, even if it isn't me. Your mom, huh?* She shook her head and turned on the flashlight. *Last person I'd talk to about my problems is my mother.* She began walking down the path, the light just enough for her to see where she was going. *So Carey's a lesbian.* She smiled broadly at the thought. *I know what I'll be doing after lights out tonight. Then again, why wait? I'm all alone out here. Nah, with my luck I'd get poison ivy on my ass or something.* She grinned devilishly at the thought of lying over Carey's lap while calamine lotion was applied. *Oh, it'd be worth it. Then again, she'd probably just send me to the nurse instead and I don't want those cold hands on my ass.* She kept walking, toying with the fantasy in her mind until she reached the rec room.

"No, I promised Instructor Carey I'd be back in an hour," Grace said apologetically. "We both have first period free tomorrow. We can have a rematch then."

"You're on, girlfriend," Latisha said, walking with Grace as far as the barracks. "I'll see ya tomorrow."

"Bright and early," Grace said. "You know Gage is doing PT tomorrow."

"She'd better be in a better mood than yesterday," Latisha said. "She needs a Midol sandwich."

Grace chuckled and began walking away. She had barely cleared the asphalt and entered the trail when she heard the crack of a twig. Pretending not to notice, she turned on the flashlight and began walking, listening carefully to the sounds around her. When the person behind her rushed at her, Grace was ready, ducking to the side and tripping her assailant. *Grenner.* Shining the flashlight in the larger girl's eyes, Grace darted around her and ran up the trail.

"That's right, run you fucking coward!" Grenner's voice echoed in the darkness. "You know I'll kick your ass if I catch you."

Shutting off the flashlight, Grace stood still and listened for any sound of pursuit. *You're out of your mind if you think I'm going to get into a fight with you tonight. Carey has enough on her mind.* Confident she was alone, she turned the light back on and made her way to the cabin.

When she entered the cabin Grace was surprised not to see Carey in either the living room or kitchen. "Carey?"

"Be out in a minute," the older woman said from the bedroom.

"Okay." Grace took off her sneakers and set them by the door, then went to her footlocker and pulled out her sleeping shorts and shirt. Tossing the clothes on the couch, she unbuttoned her shirt and was just removing it when the bedroom door opened and Carey stepped out.

"Did you have fun?"

Grace held her hand out and wiggled it. "Ah, I beat Latisha in ping pong but other than that it was pretty boring."

"What happened to your shirt?"

"Huh?"

Carey took the shirt from Grace's hand and showed her the stain near the left shoulder, brushing off some of the loose dirt. "What happened?"

"I tripped?"

Sighing, Carey pointed at the floor. "Drop."

Damn. Walking over to the empty space between the living room and kitchen, Grace lowered herself to the floor and began doing pushups. As she did, she watched Carey take the soiled shirt into the kitchen. "How many?"

"Ten, then you can come here and tell me the truth," her mentor said. "You know you're very hard on your clothes?"

"I don't mean to be." Doing the last two pushups, she stood up. "Oh, I can take care of it," she said when she saw Carey pre-treating the dirt stain.

"You can finish getting changed," Carey said. "Right after you tell me what really happened."

"I was coming back from the rec room and Grenner jumped me," she said. "I tripped her and ran away. That's all."

"That's all? Did you two exchange blows?"

"No. She tried to get me from behind and I tripped her. Once she was on the ground I took off." Seeing that Carey had her back to her, Grace quickly peeled off her undershirt and bra, replacing them with the white tee shirt used for sleeping. "Please don't say anything."

"She attacked you and you don't want me to do anything about it?" Carey asked as she put the shirt in the washer.

"If you do then she'll know I told you," Grace said.

"And you don't want to be a snitch, right?" Carey shook her head. "You sure you're not hurt?"

"I'm fine," she said as she unbuckled her belt and reached for the zipper. "Can I put the rest of these in too since you're doing that one?"

Carey turned around, realized what Grace was doing, and turned away again. "I wish you'd change in the bathroom or at least warn me."

"You told me to get changed," Grace said. "Besides, you were doing that."

"Just hurry up and get finished," Carey said, keeping her back to the teen while retrieving a soda from the refrigerator. Grace quickly stripped and put on her shorts, then brought her dirty clothes into the kitchen.

"So is it okay to put these in too?" she asked.

"Of course," Carey said, settling down at the kitchen table. "So if it wasn't your fault, why did you try to hide what happened?"

Grace shrugged and put the clothes in the washer. "I didn't want to upset you. You had enough on your mind."

Carey took a sip of soda, then nodded. "I appreciate that, but you still should have just come out and told me."

"Sorry."

"You're the one that had to the do the pushups," Carey said.

"It's okay, I haven't had to do them in a while." Grace flexed her arms. "I can handle ten easy now." She started the washer, then joined Carey at the table. "Please don't do anything about it."

"I hate the idea of her getting away with it," Carey said. "You promise me you won't do anything to try and get revenge on her. You want me to let it go, you have to let it go as well."

"I promise," Grace said.

Carey rubbed her face. "What a day."

"Is there anything I can do?" Grace asked.

"You already did," Carey said. "My mother says I don't call her often enough." She had some more of her soda, then wiggled the can. "You can have one."

"Thanks," Grace said.

Carey rose from her seat. "Relax, I'll get it." As she passed, she reached out and patted Grace's shoulder. "Thank you, by the way, for earlier. I really needed that time. Cola or orange?"

"Orange. So your mom knows about you and she's okay with it?"

Carey removed the can from the refrigerator and handed it to Grace. "Yes. She's always been supportive of me, no matter what I did."

"Must be nice," Grace said as she opened the can. "I wish I had a mom like that."

"My mother's not perfect," Carey said as she sat down. "No mother is. We just have to make the best with what we have."

"Easy for you to say."

"Your mother really does love you, Grace. It's just that some people have a hard time showing it."

"She wants me to be perfect and I've disappointed her. I think if I told her about this it would be the last straw."

Carey reached over and squeezed her shoulder. "She might surprise you if you give her a chance."

"You don't understand. I gave her a chance. I told her something really important and she didn't believe me. I love her, but when I needed her..." Grace shook her head. "Never mind. It doesn't matter anyway."

"I think it matters more than you want to let on."

Grace shrugged her shoulders. "I'm just not ready to forgive her yet, and I don't want to talk about it anymore."

Carey gave her shoulder a final squeeze. "Just remember I'm here if you ever want to talk."

"Hey," Grace said when she felt Jan bump casually against her.

"Feel like cards?"

"No," Grace said, her eyes still on the entrance to Sapling Hill. "I bet he gets here early."

"Your dad?"

Grace nodded. "I'm gonna show him the A I got on that English paper and my SAT scores." Her eyes lit up at the sight of the red rental car. "There he is. See ya later." She ran out of the rec room and raced for the administration building, determined to be waiting at the door for him. When the car stopped, however, Grace could no longer contain herself and ran across the parking lot, meeting him just as he was stepping from the car. "I knew you'd come," she said as she hugged him.

"I told you I would," he said. "I brought the photos like you asked."

"That's great," she said as they started to head toward the administration building. "I can't wait to..." She left her sentence unfinished as a familiar figure walked through the front gate. "I didn't think she'd come."

"Your mother's changed a bit, hasn't she?" he said, seeing his ex-wife for the first time in over a decade.

"Yeah," Grace said. "In the ass."

"Graceful, that's not nice," he admonished. "I've put on a few pounds over the years too."

"I don't want to see her."

"Then tell her that," he said. "You can't just not see her."

"Promise you'll wait?" Grace asked.

"Of course, pumpkin," he said. "Spend some time with your mother if you want or if she wants the three of us to talk, we can do that too."

"Be right back," Grace said, running across the parking lot to where her mother had walked in from the road. "I didn't think you were coming," she said.

Her mother stared in the direction Grace had come from. "Is that...?"

Grace nodded happily. "He came last month too."

"So you've decided to go with your father instead of me?"

Grace crossed her arms. "If that asshole's going to be living with you, yes."

"Have you forgotten that he left us? I'm the one with custody and you'll be coming home to me, not him. And don't talk about Bob that way. He loves us. He wants to make a home for us. Both of us. When you come home, you'll see."

"I'll talk about him any way I want to," Grace said. "Don't defend him to me, Ma."

"He drove me up here," her mother said. "He's parked just down the road waiting for me. Now would he do a thing like that for me if he didn't care about you?"

"Ma! Stop it!" Grace spun away, her anger rising. "I don't want to know where he is, what he's doing, and I sure as hell don't wanna hear about how he feels about me."

"Grace, please don't start a fight," her mother said.

"Why can't you just listen to me?" Grace asked angrily, turning around to face her. "You never listen to me."

"I do listen to you," the older woman said.

"Bullshit!" Grace shouted. "I told you." She clenched her hands into fists. "I told you and you didn't believe me."

"Please don't bring that up again," her mother said. "You know how it upsets me."

"Upsets you?" Grace yelped. "If it upsets you, you wouldn't be with him." She angrily kicked at a stone. "You're not upset about what he did, you get upset because I won't just pretend it didn't happen like you want me to." She stormed toward her mother, causing the older woman to back up and unbeknownst to her, Instructor Donaldson to come running toward them. "Well, it happened, Ma! That son of a bitch came into my room and raped me and you let him get away with it. Are you listening to me now?"

"Waters," the blonde instructor said as she approached.

Grace felt a firm hand land on her shoulder but jerked free. "You want to be with him? Then go." She pointed at the gate. "Be with a son of a bitch that has a thing for little girls. I hope you're real fucking happy."

"Grace, please don't be like this," her mother said, dabbing her eyes.

"Like what?" Grace shouted, taking yet another step toward her mother. "Like someone who won't go back to that hellhole?" Her eyes narrowed. "Never! Do you hear me? Never!"

"Waters!" Donaldson's sharp bark snapped Grace back to the moment. Looking down at her clenched fists, she realized just how close she had come to losing control. Forcing her hands to relax, she saw the crescent red marks where her nails had bitten into her palm.

"Don't come back," she said, glaring at her mother with all the anger and outrage she felt inside. "You had a choice and you chose him. As long as you're with him, you don't have a daughter."

"Grace—"

"No!" She turned away, feeling her throat tighten. "You were supposed to believe me, to..." Her eyes stinging, she closed them and shook her head. "Don't come back." She began walking toward her father, ignoring her mother's repeated calls to her. *Never. I'll live with Dad or I'll get a place of my own or I'll be homeless, but I'll never go back there. I can't.* She blinked rapidly as tears threatened to spill out. *I'll kill myself first.* Seeing her father holding his arms out, she ran the remaining distance.

"Come here," he said. The tenuous hold she had on her emotions broke as soon as she was in her father's arms. She began crying, scalding hot tears soaking into his flannel shirt. "Tell Daddy what happened," he said, stroking her head like he did when she was young.

All Grace could do was shake her head and cry, taking comfort in his strong arms.

"Okay, pumpkin, okay. Daddy's got you," he said over her sobs. "Shh, Daddy's got you."

"Mr. Waters, if you'd like to take her inside." It was Carey's voice, though Grace had not heard her approach.

"Do you want to go inside?" he asked. Grace sniffled and shook her head, clinging tighter to his shirt.

"There's a lake up that path," Carey said. "She knows the way."

This time Grace nodded. "O-okay." She felt a hand much smaller than her father's gently rub her shoulder.

"Grace," Carey said, giving a gentle squeeze. "I hope you have a good talk," she said before stepping back. "Take all the time you need."

Wiping her eyes with her sleeve, Grace pointed at the path. "It's this way," she said, keeping one arm around her father's side. His arm went around her shoulders and they quietly began walking up the dirt path, gradually becoming surrounded on either side by trees with only the sounds of birds and crickets to keep them company.

"I love you, pumpkin," he said. "Whatever it is, you can tell me."

"Daddy..." It felt so strange to her to say that word after so many years. "Dad. I've done things...I mean..." She looked down the path, unable to make eye contact. "I...I'm not a virgin."

"I suppose I'm too late for the father-daughter chat, hmm?" he said, gently squeezing her against him. "I hope you used protection and that you cared for him."

"You'll love me no matter what?" she asked, feeling her throat tighten as the lake came into view.

"No matter what," he said.

Grace disengaged herself and sat down on a fallen log. She rested her elbows on her knees and stared at the ground. "I don't know if I can tell you this."

He sat down next to her. "I suppose you're too old to sit on my lap?"

She nodded. "At least six years," she said. "But..." She lifted his arm and he shifted closer, allowing her to rest her head against his chest. "You always wore flannel," she said, inhaling the scent of her father's cologne and smiling at the memories it evoked.

"That's what you get for having a lumberjack for a father," he said. "But you graduate from college and I'll buy whatever suit you want me to wear. Come here." He pulled her closer, then kissed the top of her head. "You want to talk about it?"

She shook her head. "Not now," she said, snuggling against his chest. "But sometime, maybe."

"Whenever you're ready," he said, stroking her hair. "Anything you want to tell me."

"Anything?"

"Anything," he repeated, giving her a gentle squeeze. "So, any boyfriends?"

Grace smiled and rubbed her cheek against the soft flannel. "No."

"Girlfriends?"

Her head shot up. "Why would you say that?"

He chuckled and pulled her back against his chest. "You said no to a boyfriend so there's really only one other option unless you plan on going into the nunnery."

"I don't have a girlfriend either," she said. "Would it bother you if I did?"

"I told you," he said, rubbing her upper arm. "If you're happy, that's what matters."

Grace was quiet for several moments before gathering up the courage to speak. "Dad? What if I told you I think I'm gay?"

"Are you asking me or telling me?" He gently rubbed her shoulder. "I love you, Grace. You can't help who you love and if being a lesbian feels right to you then that's just the way it is," he said, kissing the top of her head. "You're old enough to know how you feel about that."

Taking a deep breath, she brushed her cheek against the red flannel of her father's shirt. "It does feel right," she said.

"So tell me," he said softly.

"I'm...I'm a lesbian, Dad."

"And you're still my little girl and I love you," he said, his blond beard scratching her forehead. He released her from his embrace and swung his leg over the log so he was facing her. Using his thumb, he wiped away the moisture on Grace's cheek. "Of course no one will ever be good enough for you in my eyes," he said, causing her to smile. "Does your mother know?"

Grace shook her head. "No."

"Why?"

She straddled the log, then began picking at the bark. "We don't talk about things like that." A sliver of bark went flying. "Ever." Another piece. "Even when..." The pain, still so close to the surface, threatened to bubble over. "Even when I told her, she wouldn't believe me," she said, her fist coming down hard on the log. "I told her and she fucking didn't believe me."

"I'll believe you," her father said, covering her fist with his hands. "You can tell me."

"I can't." Despite her earlier words to the contrary, she climbed onto his lap, feeling his strong arms holding her safe. "I love you, Dad," she said, burying herself against him. "Please don't make me go back and live with them. Please."

"Your mother?"

Grace nodded and sniffed. "And her asshole boyfriend." She gripped handfuls of flannel. "He...he..." She shook her head. "I can't go back there."

Richard let out a deep breath and hugged her tightly. "Will you answer a question for Daddy? Pumpkin, did he touch you?" She let out a strangled cry and burst into tears, her control breaking. "Okay," he said, rocking his sobbing daughter. "You don't have to go back there. We'll work it out. Shh. Daddy's got you."

"Don't make me go back."

"I won't," he said.

She sniffled and gripped his shirt tighter. "I can't. He's too strong. I...I..."

"Okay," he said tenderly. "Shh. You're not going back there. I promise." His gentle words and comforting embrace gave Grace the cocoon of safety she needed to let out the tears if not the words.

Carey rolled over and opened her eyes, realizing the sound she was hearing was not part of a dream. It took a few more seconds for her to wake up enough to determine the cause of the keening cry. *Grace.* Hopping out of bed, she moved to the living room. "Grace," she said softly, reaching for the lamp. The light showed the teen twisted in the blankets, her face wet with tears. "Grace," she said louder, kneeling down next to the couch. "Come on, you're having a bad dream." Without thought she reached out and stroked the young woman's hair. "It's all right, Grace." The cries became more desperate and Carey had to back up when the teen's arms began thrashing about. "Grace. Grace, wake up now."

"No...help, help! No!" Grace shot up into a sitting position, eyes wild.

"Shh, Grace it's just a bad dream," Carey said, putting her hand on her shoulder. Slowly the blue eyes focused on her. "Easy now, just a bad dream."

"Oh God," Grace whispered, burying her face in her hands. "It seemed so real." Carey remained quiet, giving her time to form her thoughts. "It felt like I was right there." Grace took a shuddering breath, then another. "It was so real. I just..."

"Keep going," Carey urged, gently rubbing the upset young woman's shoulder. "It won't stop until you let it out."

The teen shook her head, tears leaking out between her fingers. "I can't."

"Yes you can," Carey said.

Grace fought to control herself, then laid back down, her tears glistening in the lamplight. "I'll be okay," she sniffed. "Sorry I woke you."

"It's all right you woke me," Carey said, pulling the covers up over the teen. "But as for being okay..." She tucked the blanket around Grace's shoulder. "That won't happen until you stop giving him control over you and talk about it. Grace, did you tell your father what happened?"

Fresh tears leaked from upset blue eyes as the teen nodded. "A little. I couldn't tell him all of it, I just..." She closed her eyes and shook her head. "It hurts."

"I know it does," Carey said, using the corner of the sheet to wipe the tears from Grace's face. "And the more you fight it the more it's going to hurt until you get it out. You deserve to get past this," she said, giving Grace's shoulder one last squeeze before standing up. "You really do." She walked over to the lamp, turning the knob and sending the room into darkness. "Try to get some rest," she said, fighting the urge to sit in the recliner until Grace fell asleep.

"Thanks, um...ma'am."

Carey smiled in the darkness. "Instructor Carey doesn't fit any better at a time like this, does it?"

"No," Grace said. "Joanna doesn't seem right either."

Moving to the archway, Carey leaned against the wall. "My friends just call me Carey. Between us and only in private," she said.

"Of course."

"Now go to sleep."

"Good night...Carey."

"Night, Grace."

Grace showed up at formation seconds before Instructor Gage called Attention, saving her from having to speak to Latisha or Jan. The words being said might as well have been in Hungarian for all the meaning they had to her, empty sounds fluttering through the air. Unfortunately for her, there was no way to avoid conversation at breakfast. She mumbled hellos to those that greeted her but kept her eyes down and on her tray as she moved through the line.

"Hey girlfriend," Latisha said when Grace arrived at the table, tray in hand.

"Hey," Grace said without enthusiasm.

"What's the matter, Scary on your case again?" Jan asked.

"Just tired," Grace said, keeping her eyes on her tray and not on her friends.

"Too bad," Jan said. "So what do you think, is Short Shit going to have us run five miles today?"

"Who cares," Grace said. "Pass the syrup."

"Who put the boot up your ass?" Jan asked as she handed Grace the squeeze bottle.

"I told you, I'm tired," Grace said, putting the bottle on the table with more force than necessary. "Could they water the syrup down just a little more?" she said, stabbing at the waffle. "Of course they wouldn't need to if they'd make the food at least partially edible," she said, her voice rising. "What the hell is it with the damn waffles?" She let the fork drop. "They're not that fucking difficult to make."

"Oh yeah," Latisha said, making a circle with her forefinger and thumb. "Sure, Grace. Just tired. What did Scary do to you this morning?"

"Nothing," Grace said, pushing her tray away. "Just drop it, okay?"

"Damn, get the girl some coffee," Campbell said.

"You want coffee?" Jan asked.

"Do I look like I want coffee?" Grace pushed her tray away. "Oh, forget it. I'm not hungry anyway."

"Is there a problem here, ladies?"

175

"No, Instructor Donaldson," Grace said, rising from her seat. "I'm just leaving, ma'am."

"You haven't touched your food," Donaldson said, pressing down on her shoulder. "Sit."

"Yes, ma'am," Grace said in a resigned tone, giving her friends a dirty look as she sat down. The table was silent until Donaldson left.

"Whatever," Jan said, looking to make sure no instructors were watching them, then taking one of Grace's waffles. "You're entitled to a bad day."

"If you need to talk," Latisha offered.

Grace waved her hand. "Thanks but I'll be fine. Just something I need to work through myself." She pushed the other waffle onto Jan's plate. "See ya later." After taking a quick look to make sure Donaldson was otherwise occupied, she left her tray on the table and ran out of the mess hall. She was halfway across the parking lot when she heard Jan calling her name. "I don't want to talk about it," she said when her friend caught up with her.

"Come on, what's got you so wigged out?" Jan asked. "You were so excited yesterday about your dad coming to visit."

"But she had to come too and ruin everything."

"Your mom?"

"Yeah."

"What did she do?"

"She came up here with that asshole husband of hers. She knows I hate him, but she doesn't care. She still thinks she can get me to come live with them, but I'd kill myself if she tries to make me go back there. I swear I would."

Jan took her arm. "You can't mean that, Grace."

"I mean it all right." Grace pulled her arm away and walked off.

Jan just stood and watched her go. There was something about the way Grace had looked at her when she said it that made her believe her. *Damn. What do I do now?*

"Instructor Carey, can I talk to you?"

Carey stopped in front of the door to her office. "Don't you have class right now?"

"I have study period, ma'am," Jan said, nervously looking up and down the hall.

Opening the door, Carey held her hand out. "After you." They went inside. "What can I help you with, Bowen?" she asked as she put her cap on the hook.

"I shouldn't say anything because I don't want her to think I'm a snitch or that I'm narcing her out, but I'm worried about Grace, ma'am."

"Shut the door," Carey said. "What about her?"

"She's probably just having a rough day but I've never seen her so...I dunno, depressed, I guess," Jan said. "She's not gonna have to go back and live with her mother again, right, ma'am?"

Carey sat down in her chair. "I'm not going to comment on her situation with you," she said. "Why are you asking?"

"She said something that..." Jan shrugged. "She just said something, ma'am. That's all."

"About her home life?"

The teen nodded. "About what she'd do if she had to go back there, ma'am."

Carey leaned forward. "What did she say?"

"She probably didn't mean it, ma'am," Jan said. "But she just seemed so upset."

"Bowen, I'm not going to ask you again," Carey said. "What did she say that has you so concerned you came to see me?"

"I caught her after she left the mess hall and talked to her a little bit," Jan said. "She said she'd never go back there, to live with her mother, I mean." The teen shook her head. "I don't think she really meant it, ma'am."

Carey stood up, her fists on the desk. "Meant what?" she asked. "Stop stalling."

"She said she'd kill herself before she'd ever go back there," Jan said. "But she wasn't talking like she was thinking about suicide, ma'am. I swear."

Carey swallowed and sat down. "What do you call it when someone threatens to kill themselves?"

"I'm just worried about her, ma'am. I don't really think she'd kill herself, I really don't, but she seemed so down. I got to thinking about a neighbor lady of ours who had a sister that killed herself. Mrs. Connor said that her sister had talked about it but she didn't do anything because she didn't think she would really do it." Jan cleared her throat and fidgeted in her seat. "Grace is my friend and I couldn't live with myself if I didn't tell someone and then something happened to her."

"You did the right thing, Bowen. Grace is lucky to have a friend like you."

"Thank you, ma'am." Jan got to her feet. "If you don't mind, ma'am, I'd better get back. I have a test I need to study for."

Carey nodded her head and got up to walk her to the door. She had been worried about Grace too, especially after that nightmare last night. Now she was more convinced than ever that she needed to get Grace to open up. *But how do I do it?*

Jan opened the door, then paused and looked back at Carey. "Please don't tell her I said anything."

"I won't. I promise."

Jan nodded her head and walked out the door.

"It's time for your mentoring session, is it?" Carey said when Grace entered her office.

"Yes, ma'am."

"So what would you like to talk about?" Carey asked, resting her elbows on the armrests and lacing her fingers. "Or rather, what do you not want to talk about?"

"I don't want to talk about that," Grace said, her gaze going to the glass paperweight. "I'm sorry I woke you up, ma'am."

"You said that last night," Carey said. "That secret is trying so hard to get out, Grace. Why do you keep fighting it?"

Grace blinked several times. "I'm not ready, ma'am."

"Whether you like it or not, you're more than ready," Carey said, leaning forward and taking the egg-shaped paperweight. "Now look at me. You were quiet this morning and you've been walking around all day with a face that tells me exactly what you've been thinking about."

Grace looked at her hands. "I can't stop thinking about it."

"At me, Grace," Carey said, waiting until the teen's eyes were upon her. "Would you feel more comfortable talking to Instructor Gage or Donaldson?"

"No, ma'am."

"Then why are you so afraid?"

"Why does it matter if I talk about it or not?" Grace asked, looking down at her hands. "It's not going to change what happened."

"No, but it will change how you react to it," Carey said. "Grace, look what it's doing to you today." The teen continued to look downward. "It wasn't your fault. You need to know that, Grace. No matter what happened, it wasn't your fault." Her eyes raised at the soft snort. "Look at me. What did I just say?"

"It wasn't my fault," Grace said without emotion.

"Now if only I could get you to believe that," Carey said. "You were the victim, Grace, not the abuser. Why do you keep protecting him?"

"I'm not protecting him!" Grace snapped, blue eyes flashing anger, instead of the melancholy look Carey had seen all day. "Why do you say things like that?"

"Because you are," Carey said.

"Protect him from what?" Grace asked in the same angry tone. "From the cops? Bullshit. They won't do anything and you know that. It doesn't matter what I say or do, nothing changes." The teen shifted in her chair, leaning her right elbow on the armrest and rubbing her chin. "I don't want to talk anymore...ma'am."

"I gave up counting how many times you forgot, long ago," Carey said. "You're right that the lack of evidence would make prosecuting him difficult if not impossible, but I don't care about that right now. Grace, I'm telling you for the last time, look at me. I care about you and what this is doing to you."

"I'm fine."

"No, you're not," Carey said, rising from her seat. "You keep your eyes on me," she said, moving around the desk. "You're holding on right now by a thread and it's about to break...soon."

"So?"

It was almost enough to make Carey lose her temper. "If you don't know..." She turned her back to the teen and slowly counted to ten. "So maybe I don't want to find you hanging by a rope or lying next to a bottle of pills," she said, turning around and locking eyes with Grace. "You're too special to be another statistic." She leaned on her desk, inches away from the chair where Grace sat. "I'm not kidding here. I'm really worried about you."

"I'm not going to do anything," Grace said.

Carey sighed and pinched the bridge of her nose. "Let's stop tiptoeing around this," she said, watching as the girl clenched her jaw. "Grace, you were sexually abused whether you want to admit it or not." Blue eyes flickered away from her. "You're also seventeen and clearly miserable. Any idea what that spells a recipe for?"

"I hate feeling like this," Grace said.

"Then change it," Carey said. "Change it by opening up and letting that secret out. Talk about what happened to you, how you feel about it, anything but just talk before this destroys you."

"Let's take a seat, girls," Instructor Gage said as she entered the room and put her hat on the hook by the door. "You've been learning a great deal about yourselves and each other over the last four months. Now that those chips have been knocked off your shoulders and you're acting like civilized young ladies, it's time to take a deeper look at why things went so wrong at home." Gage took the remaining seat in the circle chairs. "Who wants to start? Waters."

"I don't have anything to say, ma'am," Grace said, her eyes focused on the carpet.

"You seem to be having a rough day," Gage said. "What's going on?"

"Nothing, ma'am."

"So answer the topic. Why do you think things went wrong at home?"

"What's the point?" Grace asked. "Nothing's gonna change. They're not going to change, ma'am."

"We can't change other people," Gage said. "The only thing we can do is change ourselves and change the way we react to those around us."

"Bullshit," Grace said, clenching her hands into fists. "Nothing's gonna change, ma'am. That's why I won't go back there."

"Why, what's happening at home?" Gage asked, her gentle voice a stark contrast to her usual tone.

Tears stung Grace's eyes. "He's there," she said, sniffling. "He's there and if I went home he'd be waiting for me." She closed her eyes as the tears began to spill out. "I hate him so much, ma'am."

"This is a safe place," Gage said. "No one can hurt you here." The words, eerily reminiscent of Carey's, caused Grace's heart to pound, her body to tremble. "Waters?"

"What, ma'am?"

"What did he do?"

"Doesn't matter, ma'am."

"You know you can't get away with that kind of answer in here," Gage said. "What did he do to you?"

"He...he..." Grace jumped from her chair, pushing it back so she could escape the circle. "I'm sorry, I can't, I..." Feeling the sob in her throat, she threw open the door and ran down the hall, ignoring the instructor calling her name. Grace ran, though the side door and outside, unsure of where to go but knowing she needed to get away.

There was a sharp rap on the door before it opened and Sue Gage entered. "You got a problem," she said, slumping into the chair in front of Carey's desk.

"What?"

"Waters," Gage said. "She ran out of Anger Management like a bat out of hell."

Carey was instantly on her feet. "Grace? Where did she go?"

"Took off running," Sue said. "I started to go after her but she ran off into the woods and I thought you might want to talk to her."

"Damn," Carey said.

"I'm sure she didn't go far," the petite woman said. "Probably just needed a quiet place to go and have herself a good cry."

"What happened?"

"I almost got her to talk about her mother's boyfriend," Gage said. "First time I've seen her cry."

Carey rubbed her face. "I knew it was coming," she said. "Marilyn tell you what she heard Grace say to her mother yesterday?" Gage shook her head. "She said Boyfriend has a thing for little girls."

"No question about it now," Gage said. "Not that there was much doubt."

Carey nodded. "I wish it wasn't true," she said, rapping her knuckles on the desk. "She's a good kid deep inside." She reached for her cap. "I'll go after her. You said she headed into the woods?"

"Toward the ball field," Gage said. "I'll cover you for mess hall duty."

"Thanks, I have a feeling this is going to take a while."

Carey found her sitting at a picnic table near the ball field. "Ten hut!" Grace jumped off the bench and stood at attention, allowing the older woman to see the red-rimmed and puffy eyes. *I'm sorry, Grace, but this can't go on any longer.* "You drop and give me twenty, NOW!" She waited until Grace had finished that task and returned to attention. "Did you have permission to leave class?" she asked, her voice was firm and commanding.

"No, ma'am."

Carey moved to stand by Grace's right shoulder. "Did you tell Instructor Gage where you were going?"

"No, ma'am."

"Did Instructor Gage tell you to return to class?"

"Yes, ma'am."

"And you chose to leave anyway, right?"

"Yes, ma'am," Grace said, using her sleeve to wipe the tears off her face.

"Did I tell you to move?" she asked, raising her voice.

"No, ma'am."

"Rule one, Grace, when you're at attention, You Don't Move!" Seeing renewed tears streaming down her face, Carey found herself tempted to back off and be gentle but she knew this time, a hard push was needed. "Why did you leave?"

"I...I don't know, ma'am."

"You know," Carey said. "What's his name?" Grace hesitated. "His Name!" the concerned instructor yelled.

"B-Bob, ma'am."

Good girl, Carey thought to herself. "What did Bob do to you?"

"He...he..." Grace shook her head.

"WHAT DID HE DO?" Carey shouted. "SAY IT!"

"He...he...r-ra..." Grace's bottom lip quivered. "He...he..."

"He raped you," Carey said, finding the words hard to say herself. "Say it, Grace."

"H-he raped me," Grace cried, her shoulders slumping as sobs racked her body. "He raped me. He raped me. He came into my room and he...he held me down and...and..." She covered her face with her hands.

"Come here," Carey said softly, taking the teen into her arms. "I know, Grace," she whispered. "Let it out."

"He...he told me she wouldn't believe me," Grace sobbed. "An...and she didn't."

Carey took a deep breath, then released it slowly. "I believe you, Grace," she said, gently rubbing the teen's shaking back. "I believe you."

"I-I told him no," Grace cried, her voice muffled against Carey's shirt. "But he...h-he..." her voice trailed off into helpless sobs.

"I know," Carey said, rocking the teen in her arms. "You're doing great, Grace. Take your time, the words will come."

Carey looked up from the manual she was reading when Grace entered the cabin. "Did you find Instructor Gage?"

"Yes, ma'am," Grace said. "We...talked."

"Good." Carey said, gesturing at the couch. "Did you make it over to the mess hall?"

Grace sat down on the couch. "Yes, ma'am."

Carey waved her hand dismissively. "You're inside now, Grace. Did you eat anything?"

Grace shook her head. "I didn't feel like eating."

Carey left her chair and sat down on the cushion next to Grace. "If you get hungry, there's a plate in the fridge for you."

"Thanks."

"Talk to me," Carey urged gently.

Grace rested her elbows on her knees, leaning forward and staring at the coffee table. "I don't know what to say."

"What's going on in that head of yours?"

"I feel like someone took a blender and mixed everything up inside," Grace said. "I want to cry, I want to smash things, I want to just run away and hole up someplace where the pain can't get to me." She took a shaky breath. "It's like...something broke inside and all this pain is there and I don't know what to do."

"Something did break," Carey said softly, putting her hand on Grace's back and rubbing in slow, gentle circles. "That shell of attitude and anger that you hide behind finally broke and all the hurt you kept locked away so long wants to come out."

"It hurts," Grace said, a tear rolling down her cheek. "It hurts and I don't know what to do and I feel so damn alone." Her shoulders shook as the tears increased. "I need...I...I just need..."

"What?" Carey asked gently. "What do you need?" She was pushed back against the couch by the teen throwing herself into her arms. "I guess you need this," she said, putting her arms around Grace and continuing the comforting rubbing as tears soaked her shirt. "It's going to be all right. Go ahead and let it out. I've got you." She stroked the short blonde hair as the teen sobbed helplessly against her. "Let it out."

"Looks like it's time for lights out," Carey said, closing her book and setting it next to the table lamp. "It's going to be a busy day tomorrow."

"I feel like I could sleep for a week," Grace said.

"Long day for you," Carey said, walking over to the footlocker. "Do you want me to let you sleep in tomorrow?"

"No," Grace said. "I like getting up in the morning with you."

Her back to the teen, Carey smiled. *I like our time in the morning too.* "I think you just like being able to have coffee that doesn't come from a huge vat," she said, picking up the pillow and bed linens. "Don't think I didn't see you take a third cup this morning."

"You make good coffee," Grace said as she took the sheet. "Besides, you have half-and-half instead of that powdered junk."

"The luxuries of life," Carey said, tossing the pillow on the couch. "Don't let me get my coffee in the morning and you'll really see Instructor Scary." She laughed at the wide-eyed look. "You think I don't know what you girls call me?"

"I never say that," Grace said.

"I don't suppose you do," Carey said, pushing the blanket into her arms. "But I have heard bitch come out of that sweet little mouth of yours more than once."

"Not about you," Grace said. "Well, not for a while, anyway."

Warmed by her words, Carey reached out and put her hand on Grace's shoulder. "I'm glad to hear it. I guess I won't have to lock my bedroom door in fear that you'll lynch me during the night, hmm?" Using her free hand, Carey cupped Grace's chin. "I know you've had a rough day and everything feels pretty raw right now. I care about you, Grace. Know that. I'm right in the next room if it gets too bad and you need to talk, okay?"

"Okay."

Carey patted her shoulder, then stepped back. "Now hit the sack. Five thirty will get here soon enough." She turned and started to her room.

"Carey?"

Carey stopped and faced her, surprised by the nervous tone in Grace's voice. "Yes?"

"Would it be all right to ask for a hug?"

Carey held her arms out. "Come here." Wrapping her arms around the smaller form, she pressed her cheek against the golden hair. "You're going to be all right, Grace. I know it."

"Hey," Jan said, bumping against her. "You doing better today?"

"I guess so," Grace said.

"Grace, we're friends, right?"

She nodded. "Right."

"So if you need to talk about something," Jan said. "I'm here. I know there's some things that you just don't want the Goon Squad to know about."

"Thanks," Grace said. "But I'll be okay."

Jan tugged on her elbow. "Come here." They walked to the side of the mess hall.

"Jan, we need to get in there."

"They won't notice we're missing for at least five or ten minutes," Jan said. "Christine told Latisha that you ran out of AM yesterday and at dinner you went through the line and left without coming anywhere near the table."

Grace shrugged. "Wasn't hungry."

"Yeah, I bet," Jan said, leaning against the building. "Sucks, doesn't it?"

"Sure does."

"Scary spouts a lot in SR about abstinence but she doesn't understand it's not like we really had a choice." Jan looked off at the trees. "Right?"

Grace squatted down and picked up a stone. "She understands," she said, sending the stone skittering across the pavement. "How'd you know?"

"I guess when you've been through it, it's easy to pick out others," Jan said.

"I never thought that about you," Grace said. "Christine yes, but not you."

"It's easy with her," Jan said. "No one hates their father that much otherwise."

"Think others know? About me, I mean."

Jan shook her head. "No. You keep it pretty cool." She sank down until she was sitting on the ground, using the side of the building as a backrest. "Even if they did, who cares? Does it really matter to either of us about Christine?"

"No," Grace said. "She's okay."

"See? And after we're outta here, it's not like we'll ever see those people again. Why worry about it?" Jan picked up a stone and threw it. "I don't care if people know about my step-father. Wasn't my fault."

Grace pulled her knees to her chest and wrapped her arms around them. "Did you ever feel like it was?"

"You know how many counselors have asked me that?" Jan said. "I knew it was his fault, no question." She threw another stone. "I was thirteen. Sure as hell wasn't my idea."

"Hmm," Grace said. "I guess at thirteen it's pretty easy to see. Harder at fifteen."

"Is it?" Jan asked quietly, both teens looking at the trees and not each other.

"Yeah." More pebbles flew as Grace found the need to do something with her hands. "Hey, we'd better get in there."

"I suppose," Jan said, making no effort to move. "I remember when I was fifteen." She let the remaining stones in her hand drop to the ground. "Thought I had control over everything and everyone around me." She shook her head and gave a rueful smile. "Just goes to show how much I didn't know back then."

Grace rose to her feet. "Yeah, well...we'd better head in."

"Hey." Jan stood up and bumped her. "I don't think it was your fault."

"Um...thanks."

"I mean it," Jan said, holding Grace's arm to keep her from walking away. "Remember what you said yesterday? About what you would do if you had to go back to live with your mother?"

"I remember," Grace said. "I'm never going back there."

"But even if something happens and you find yourself there, promise me you won't do it. We'll stay friends once we're out of here. If things ever get too rough for you, you can always come stay with me."

Grace looked at her. "I won't," she said. "I know I said that but I was just upset and everything. Besides, I'm getting out of here, out of Crestwood, then I'm going to go to college and get a degree. I'll never have to worry about living with my mother again."

"Grace? About that." Jan let go of her friend's arm. "I have to tell you something. I was worried about you yesterday and well...I told Scary what you said."

"You what?"

"I was worried," Jan said. "I didn't want you to do anything, you know, stupid."

"Carey didn't say anything to me about it," Grace said. "When did you tell her?"

"First period. Are you mad at me?"

Grace thought about it. "No. You weren't trying to get me in trouble."

"I wasn't," Jan agreed. "I was just worried, that's all."

"I guess if you came to me and said you were thinking about suicide, I'd probably tell someone too."

"Friends?"

"Friends," Grace said.

"Okay, enough of this serious shit," Jan said, giving a nudge with her elbow. "Let's go eat."

Feeling better than she had before, Grace nodded and looked up at the sky. *Looks like it's going to be a nice day.* "I hope we're having pancakes."

They headed for the mess hall, unaware of the dark-haired woman standing around the side of the building who had heard nearly every word of their conversation.

FIVE MONTHS

Grace was surprised to see a very muddy Carey open the door. "Get newspapers and make a path to the kitchen for me, please," the instructor said.

"What happened?" Grace asked, taking the neatly folded paper from the coffee table and protecting the section of carpet between the door and the kitchen. "You look like you fell into the swamp."

"I smell like it too," Carey said, following the newspaper trail into the kitchen. "The swing rope broke." The once white, but now slimy brown, shirt was peeled off and tossed to the floor next to the washing machine. "Oh, that stinks."

"Is there anything I can do to help?" Grace asked.

"No," Carey answered, pushing her shorts down, then sitting on the floor to unlace her boots. "Actually yes, get me a large bath towel, please."

"Sure." Grace went to the bathroom and returned with the towel. "Here you go."

Carey stood up, her sport bra and panties stained from the swamp. "Turn around." Grace did so, allowing the instructor to finish stripping off the rest of her clothes and cover herself with the towel. "All right, I'm going to take a shower," Carey said, moving past Grace. "I'll take care of the mess when I get done."

"Okay," Grace said, watching the towel-clad woman retreat to the bathroom. Once she heard the water running, the teen gathered up the muddy clothes and put them in the washing machine. Unsure what to do with the boots, she used paper towels to wipe off the muck and clean them up as best she could, then set them on the front steps to dry out. "What a mess," she said aloud when she got a good look at the kitchen floor. Reaching under the sink, she found the bucket.

"There, that's better," Carey said when she entered the living room. "I washed my hair three times and I swear I still smell that swamp." She stopped at the entrance to the kitchen. "Where's my clothes?"

"I put them in the washer," Grace said. "I didn't know how to clean your boots so I put them on the steps to dry."

"You didn't have to do that," Carey said, then gave the teen a smile. "Thank you."

"You're welcome," Grace said. "It didn't make sense for you to get all cleaned up and then touch those filthy clothes."

"I appreciate it," Carey said, opening the washer and adding detergent. "I see you did the floor too."

Grace shrugged. "Only took a few minutes. I didn't want you to have to do it."

"Thanks."

"You're welcome," Grace said, her heart rate rising at the smile given to her. "I'm glad I could help."

Carey rubbed the back of her neck. "I think I pulled something."

"Would you like me to rub it for you?" Grace offered, trying hard to hold back her excitement at the possibility of touching the older woman's skin.

"Ah, no." Carey grimaced. "I don't think it would look good to have you sitting here rubbing my neck. I'll put some deep heating rub on it."

"I don't mind," Grace said, feeling her chance slipping away.

"No," Carey said, unknowingly crushing the teen's hopes. "Thanks for the offer, though."

"Um, you know the pulsating head on the shower might help," Grace said, looking at the washing machine instead of the object of her lust. "It'd be like a massage."

"I never thought of that," Carey said. "Is that what you've been using it for?"

"Huh?" Grace froze, unable to think. *How did she know?*

"I've gone in a couple of times and found it set on the pulsing one," Carey said.

"Oh, yeah. I um...well, my back sometimes from PT." *Oh, please buy that.*

Carey rubbed her neck again. "Maybe I'll give that a try first," she said.

"I'll get it," Carey said, rising from the recliner to answer the door. "What's up?"

Instructor Gage stood in the doorway holding the two broken ends of rope. "Take a look."

From her vantage Grace could not see but whatever Carey saw, it made the dark-haired woman bright red with anger. "Waters, take your books and report to the barracks until I come get you," Carey said without looking at her.

"Yes, ma'am," Grace said, quickly gathering her papers. The instructors were silent as she left.

"Hey, girl," Latisha said as Grace entered the barracks. "What are you doing here?"

"Carey and Gage wanted to talk about something so I got booted," Grace said, flopping down on her friend's cot.

"Hey, Waters."

"Hey, Jennings," Grace said, motioning the girl to join them. "You did great on the obstacle course yesterday."

"Thanks. You know I lost another five pounds?"

"I thought you looked thinner," Grace said.

"Yeah, now we don't have to strap 'wide load' to her ass anymore," Latisha teased, then dodged a playful swat from Jennings.

"Keep it up and I'll use those dreadlocks to mop the floor," Jennings bantered. "I'm still bigger than you."

"Not by much," Grace joined in. "Your ass is going to need a sign soon."

"Oh no, you didn't say anything about my ass, girlfriend," Latisha said, giving Grace a light shove.

"Well look who's here," Grenner said as she and Dawson approached the trio. "If it isn't Scary's little bitch."

"Go to hell, Lauren," Grace said, aware of how quiet the barracks suddenly became.

"You gonna make me or are you going to sic your pet Scary on me instead?"

"Fuck you."

"Naw," Grenner said. "I wouldn't want to make Scary jealous."

"Ignore her," Christine said. "She's just trying to cause trouble."

"Stay out of it, fat ass."

"Leave her alone," Grace said. "You got a problem with me, deal with me. You got a problem with Instructor Carey, take it up with her."

Grenner hopped up on her toes and pretended to tinkle a pair of bells. "Oh, it's Instructor Carey, is it? Is that what she makes you call her when you're down on your knees in front of her?"

"She probably calls her Mistress Carey," Dawson chimed in.

"You got something to say, Shorty?" Jan said as she entered the barracks, moving between the pair and Grace.

"Leave her alone, Bowen," Grenner said.

"Make me," Jan said.

"Ten hut!" The girls scrambled to positions, Grace moving to the foot of her old cot frame as Instructor Donaldson entered the barracks. "Formation. Now!"

"What's going on?" Grace asked in a low whisper after standing there for ten minutes with no sign of an instructor.

189

"Don't know, but Scary Carey is pissed as hell," one of the girls behind her answered. "I saw her and Gage a few minutes ago heading for—uh-oh. Here they come."

The group immediately silenced as Gage and Carey entered the formation area. Grace noted that Carey was wearing the mirrored sunglasses, making it impossible for her to see the instructor's eyes. Still, even with the distance between them, Grace could see the tightness in Carey's jaw. "She's really pissed," she whispered, catching Latisha's slight nod with her peripheral vision.

"Obviously we, as your instructors, have failed," Carey said, throwing the two pieces of swing rope on the ground in front of the group. "We have spent over four months teaching you about responsibility and consideration for your fellow human beings. But you haven't learned a damn thing, have you?" She picked up the short end of the rope and held it up in the air. "I was on this when it broke." Grace saw that while there were a few strands that appeared frayed, the rest appeared to be neatly cut. "Someone deliberately rigged this rope to break," Carey continued. "I want that person front and center right now." Grace looked around, seeing others also wondering who the culprit was. "Fine," Carey said after a few seconds. "You are a team, the actions of one affect the whole. Since no one wants to come forward and take responsibility, everyone will pay."

"You think we've been rough on you so far?" Gage added. "You're going to be crying for your mommas by the time we're through. Now drop for forty!"

"They're trying to kill us," Grace said, bringing her elbows up to touch her knees.

"Stop the chatter, Waters," Gage said as she passed. "This isn't social hour."

"Yes, ma'am," Grace said, exchanging a look with Latisha.

"Carey, I think these girls could use a good long run, don't you?" Gage asked.

"Give them time to think about what it means to respect other people's property," Carey said. "Ten hut." The girls all jumped to attention, though not as fast as usual, fatigue slowing them down. "Are you having fun yet?"

"No, ma'am," came a chorus of teenage voices.

"Do you like that one of you is making the rest of you suffer?"

"No, ma'am."

"If you don't like it now, let's see how you feel after a nice five-mile run. Move it!"

"Just kill me and get it over with," Grace said as she collapsed on the grass, joining the half-dozen others that had finished the run.

"I would but I'm too tired," Jan said from her prone position. "You tell me who fucked with that rope though and I'll find the energy."

"Make that two," one of the other girls chimed in.

"Wha...what do you think they're gonna do to us next?" Grace asked.

"Call ambulances to haul our lifeless bodies away," someone said as she joined the group. "It's gotta be after eleven."

"They'll let us go to bed soon, I bet," Grace said. "They can't keep us up much longer."

"I heard some of the other girls talking," Latisha said. "They think Dawson did it."

"Why?"

"She took a hit from Scary yesterday during barracks inspection, snuck some food back from the mess hall."

"Yeah but everyone's been caught at some point doing that," Grace said. "Carey could have really been hurt in that fall. Personally, I bet Grenner had something to do with it. I still say she's the one that sliced up the bunks."

"Can't prove it," Latisha said. "I can't tell you how many times her bunk's been ripped apart. If she has a knife, she's got it hid real good."

"Please tell me you're letting us sleep in tomorrow," Grace said as she trudged up the steps to the cabin.

"You can sleep in," Carey said, opening the door. "I'll get you up before I leave. You'll still have half an hour before formation."

Grace sat down on the couch and grabbed her pant leg to pull her left foot up over her right knee. "But it's almost one thirty," she said, tugging at her boot lace, which stubbornly refused to come free. "I'll never make it on four and a half hours' sleep."

"You wouldn't have to if one of your buddies came forward and told the truth," Carey said, removing her own boots and setting them by the door. "Here, let me help you with that."

"But why punish all of us?" Grace asked, moving her tired hands out of the way so Carey could undo the laces. "You know I didn't do it."

Carey smiled and tugged the boot free. "I never thought you did," she said. "Give me your other foot. Grace, I'm not doing this to be mean. This is more than just finding out who did it. What if I didn't do a test run first? What if it was one of you girls on that rope?"

"I think Grenner did it," she said, closing her eyes as the other boot was removed.

"You think or you know?"

"Think."

"I can't punish her for what you think," Carey said. "Lie down."

Grace waved her hand. "I'll get it."

"Down," Carey said, rising and getting the linens. "You care about the sheet?"

"No."

Carey unfolded the blanket and tossed it over her. "Lift your head."

"Too tired," Grace mumbled.

"Uh-huh," Carey said, squeezing her hand between Grace's head and the cushion, then lifting and shoving the pillow in place. "Good night."

Blue eyes opened. "Wait. Don't I get a hug good night?" She held her arms out expectantly.

"I think you're taking advantage of this hug thing," Carey said, though she knelt down and accepted a short hug. "Now go to sleep."

"Good night, Carey."

"Night, Grace."

"Hey," Latisha said as Grace entered the formation area. "You won't believe what happened last night."

"What?"

"A bunch of girls started in on Hathaway, saying she's the one that screwed with the rope," Latisha said.

"Did she admit it?" Grace asked.

"Hell no," Latisha said. "But Grenner said she saw Mo near the tool shed yesterday."

Knowing there were a few minutes before the instructors arrived, Grace walked over to where Hathaway and several other girls were standing. "Mo."

"I didn't do it so go fuck off, Waters," Mo said. "I don't give a shit what Grenner says. I was nowhere near the damn tool shed yesterday."

"So why would she say you were?" Grace asked.

"Because she's a ho with nothing better to do," she said, pushing her glasses up on her nose. "Besides, what the fuck was she doing near the shed to see me in the first place?"

"You think I want to spend all day doing PT?" one of the other girls said. "If I thought Hathaway did it, I'd turn her ass in myself."

"No you wouldn't," Rosetti said. "Then you'd be a snitch and I'd have to jump you. I can't stand snitches."

"Fuck that," Mo said. "I'm sick of getting punished for something someone else did. I'd tell Scary and Gage in a second."

"Ten hut."

Everyone fell into formation, apprehensive of what the day would bring.

"Another day, another chance to do the right thing," Gage said, beginning her usual pacing in front of the group. "Are you tired?"

"Yes, ma'am," the group said.

"You think you deserve a break today?"

"Yes, ma'am."

"Well this isn't McDonald's!" the short woman yelled. "And yesterday is going to look like a trip to Disneyland compared to today if I don't get some answers, and I mean right now!" She took two more paces, then said, "All right, I hear who did it and you can all go back to the barracks until lunch. You want to protect your friend, your buddy, the one who's got your back, then you can have a five-mile run followed by two trips through the obstacle course and then another run before lunch. How's that sound? A nice relaxing Sunday or a day of hell?"

Oh please, someone narc Grenner out, Grace thought.

"Must be a day of hell you want then," Gage said. "Now move."

Grace set her tray down and dropped into her seat. "Heard anything?"

"Nothing," Latisha said. "Everyone thinks Grenner or Hathaway did it."

Dipping her French fry into a dollop of ketchup, Grace shook her head. "My money's on Grenner."

"I bet Dawson knows," Latisha said.

"No doubt," Grace said. "But she's not talking either. I can't believe that bitch is smart enough to hide that knife all this time. They've searched the barracks I don't know how many times, and there's no sign of it?"

"It can't be in the barracks," Latisha said. "They've done everything but flip over our uniform lockers."

Grace popped another French fry into her mouth. "Yeah, but they've searched the lockers, right?"

Latisha nodded, then used her fork to swipe two fries from Grace's plate. "Maybe she hid it in a tree somewhere."

"It's gotta be in the barracks," Grace said, pushing her chair back. "I'm gonna take a look."

"I'll go with you," Latisha said.

As Grace and Latisha were leaving, they ran into Jan and Mo. "You're going in the wrong direction," Jan said. "Lunch is that way."

"We're gonna check the barracks," Grace said.

"Don't waste your time," Mo said. "Viking and Scary checked while we were running our asses off."

"That knife has to be somewhere," Grace said. "Come on, Latisha."

"Hang on, I'll go with you," Jan said.

"What the hell," Mo said, wiggling her glasses. "I'm not really in the mood for Z-burgers anyway."

The group entered the barracks, Latisha staying by the door to stand guard. "Start with the bunk?" Jan asked.

"The locker," Grace said, opening the metal doors.

"I'm taller, I'll check the shelf," Jan said while Grace knelt down and peered at the base.

"You know there's about two or three inches between the bottom and the floor?" she said, banging her knuckles on the metal.

"Unless she made a trap door there's no way to get to it," Mo said. "Those things are too heavy to move."

"No," Grace said, disappointed. "There's no sign of that."

"Nothing here," Jan said. "Maybe Dawson's hiding it?"

"You think Lauren would trust Sally to do that?" Mo asked.

"Well, let's check her bunk too," Jan said.

"Might as well," Grace said, rising to her feet. "How heavy is this anyway?"

"Let's see," Jan said, moving to the side of the locker and pushing on it. "Oh shit, what did they make this out of, lead?"

"Here, I'll help," Mo said. Together they were able to tilt it sideways.

"Hang on," Grace said, dropping to her belly. "I'll look beneath. Can you lift it a little more?"

"It's not like I have anything to hold onto here," Jan said. "Be quick, will ya?"

"It's too dark," Grace said when it was lifted another inch. She reached in, hoping to feel the elusive weapon.

"Look out," Jan said as she lost her grip.

"Ah, damn. Get it off, get it off!" Grace yelped.

"What happened?" Latisha asked as she came running over.

Grace pulled her hand free and sat up. "Fuck. Oh damn, that hurt."

"I'm sorry," Jan said. "It slipped and I didn't know your hand was under there."

There was an indentation across the back of Grace's hand where the metal had pressed into her skin. She slowly flexed her fingers, then made a fist. *Damn!* She stood up and shoved Grenner's bunk out of the way. "Screw it," she said, grabbing hold of the opposite side of the locker. "Let's tip it."

The heavy metal locker crashed to the floor, the noise echoing throughout the barracks. There on the floor previously hidden by the locker was the sharpened butter knife. "I knew it," Jan said.

"I'll kill her," Grace said angrily.

"Oh shit," Latisha said a split second before the barracks door opened.

"What the fuck are you doing?" Grenner shouted, racing toward her bunk.

"You bitch," Grace said, diving at the larger teen and slamming her shoulder into Grenner's midsection. The force sent them both crashing to the concrete floor. "You could have killed her!" She took a punch in the side, returning it with a solid hit of her own.

"Fuck you!" Grenner spat as she pulled Grace's hair. "Scary's...slut. Oof."

Grace raked her fingers across the other teen's face, forcing Grenner to release the hold on her hair. She heard the sound of bunks moving but could not turn to see what was going on as hands gripped her shirt and jerked her off balance. She tried to roll out of the way but Grenner's boot caught her in the solar plexus, knocking the wind out of her and forcing Grace to curl up in a defensive position as she fought to regain her breath. Helpless to protect herself, she suffered a painful shot to the back before she heard Jan shout and tackle Grenner. "Ohh," she groaned, slowly rolling to a sitting position. She saw Latisha and Mo keeping Dawson pinned face down on the floor while Jan continued to trade blows with Grenner. Grace pushed herself to her feet, then charged at her enemy. "Bitch!" she yelled, hooking her arm around Grenner's neck. Together with Jan she managed to get the larger teen down to the floor. "Not so tough without your damn knife, are you?" she said, ignoring the shouts and voices behind her. "You have a good laugh when she fell? That give you a fucking thrill?" Grenner reached for her arm, trying to break her grasp, but Grace was too angry to let go. "Huh? You're not laughing now, are you?"

"Let...go."

"Not so funny now, huh?" Grace asked through gritted teeth, tightening her hold.

"Grace, let go," Jan said, tugging on her arm. It took both hands but she finally separated them, Grenner rolling away and gasping for air while Grace held her midsection and trembled with anger.

"They're coming," Rosetti said. When the doors opened, Mo and Latisha released Dawson.

"The knife is right here, ma'am," Mo said, pointing by the fallen locker, when Carey and Instructor Donaldson entered. Gage followed, taking several girls aside to find out what happened.

"I don't know anything about it, ma'am." Grenner said as she got to her feet. "They must have planted it there."

"No we didn't," Jan said as Grace got to her knees, then used the bunk to stand up. "We tipped the locker over and it was there, ma'am."

Carey walked over and picked up the knife. Even from the distance Grace could see the tightening in her mentor's jaw. "Instructor Donaldson, take Grenner to my office and keep her there."

"Let's go," the blonde instructor said, grabbing the teen by the arm.

"It's a setup," Grenner protested. "Waters and Bowen, they put it there."

"Just get moving," Donaldson said, pushing Grenner toward the door. Mitchell arrived, stopping at the entrance to get updated by the other instructor.

"Dawson!"

"Yes, ma'am?"

"Where did the knife come from?"

"No idea, ma'am."

"You had your chance," Carey said, putting the knife in her back pocket and reaching for the teen. "Let's go. Instructor Gage, take those two." She pointed at Grace and Jan.

"The rest of you get this place cleaned up," Instructor Mitchell said.

"We're in trouble," Jan whispered.

"Not a word," Gage said. "Not a sound from either of you until I ask you a question, got it?"

"Yes, ma'am," they said.

"All right," Gage said after Jan and Grace gave their versions of what happened. "Bowen, go back to the barracks and help the others clean up the mess you helped make."

"Yes, ma'am."

Great, Grace thought as Jan left the room. *I am in so much trouble.*

"I can only assume there's a clone of you that sits in my Anger Management class," Gage said.

"She tried to kill Instructor Carey, ma'am," Grace said.

"First of all, I don't think a fall into a swamp is going to kill anyone," Gage said. "And that still doesn't give you the right to put your hands on someone else, no matter how mad you get. You know that."

"I know, ma'am," Grace said.

"You may think that we don't know what's going on outside the classrooms," Gage said. "But I know a great deal more than you think. I know you've been labeled by Lauren and her friends as Scary's bitch."

Grace nodded. "It's just talk, ma'am."

"Does it bother you?"

"No, ma'am, they're just trying to get a rise out of me."

"Looks like it worked," Gage said. "You could have seriously hurt her when you choked her."

"She shouldn't have cut that rope, ma'am."

"Would you be this upset if someone else had been on the rope when it broke?" Gage asked.

"I...I don't know, ma'am," Grace said. "I guess it would depend on who it was."

Gage stopped pacing and sat down on the folding chair. "Instructor Carey doesn't need you to fight her battles."

"I know, ma'am. It's just that..." Grace put her elbows on her thighs and buried her face in her hands. "I can't explain it. You wouldn't understand, ma'am."

"It really must be a clone that goes to AM if you don't think that I'm capable of listening and understanding. What's going on, Grace?"

"I can't talk to you about it, ma'am."

"Then talk to Instructor Carey."

Grace snorted. "I definitely can't talk to her about it."

"Is the problem with her?"

With her? It is her. "It's my problem to deal with, ma'am. You can't help me."

"Grace, if you need to talk, I'm here," Gage said.

"Do you have to tell her what we talk about?"

Gage reached out and pulled Grace's hands away, forcing her to look at her. "If it involved hurting yourself or someone else, yes I would."

I'm already hurting. Every time I look at her. "I like Instructor Carey." Taking a chance, she looked up at Gage. "I mean I really like her."

"I see," Gage said. "Have you talked to her about this?"

Grace shook her head. "No way. She'd kick me to the infirmary until graduation." She rubbed her hands together. "Please don't say anything to her."

"What are you going to do?"

Grace shrugged. "What can I do? She'd never be interested in me."

"Probably not," Gage said. "You can't change that."

"So what do I do?"

"My first suggestion is to talk to Instructor Carey about this."

Grace shook her head. "I can't do that," she said. "It's my problem."

"Then you need to learn to accept the things you cannot change," Gage said. "You can't make her love you." She put her hand on the teen's shoulder.

"Yes, ma'am. I know that."

Gage shook her head. "Okay, Waters, I'll let Instructor Carey decide what your punishment will be for fighting. Now go on."

"Yes, ma'am."

Grace slowly walked to the cabin, unsure of what mood Carey would be in after the fight. Opening the door, she spotted the dark-haired woman sitting in the recliner. "Hello, ma'am," she said, hesitating by the door.

"Think I'm about to drop you for a hundred pushups, don't you?"

Grace nodded and closed the door. "At least."

"I should," Carey said, rising from her chair. "You had no business fighting." She stopped in front of Grace and cupped her chin. "I will tell you that I'm very disappointed in you for that." She ran her finger along the length of the scratch on Grace's face. "You're on restriction until graduation. Now go in the bathroom and put some antiseptic on that cut so it doesn't get infected."

"Carey?" Grace lowered her eyes. "I'm sorry."

"And you'll never do it again, right?"

"Right."

Carey sighed. "What am I going to do with you? Go wash up. I'm going to make a pot of coffee."

"Okay." Grace walked into the bathroom, shutting the door and the world out behind her. *God, what a day.* Closing her eyes, she put her hands on the vanity and let out a deep breath. *Gage said she wouldn't say anything, but she's Carey's buddy. What if she does? Oh, I'd never be able to face Carey if she did that. She's mad at me enough for fighting.* She turned on the cold water and let it run for several seconds before splashing some on her face. *Now I have to go face her and explain why I lost it with Grenner. How am I going to explain that? Sorry, Carey, the thought of you getting hurt bothered me so much I put someone in a choke hold?* She shook her head. *That'd go over like a lead balloon.* Shutting the water off, she opened the medicine cabinet and found the tube of antiseptic cream. She finished applying the cream, then put the tube away and stared at herself in the mirror. "You screwed up good this time," she said to her reflection. Taking advantage of the privacy, she lifted her shirt and hissed at the discoloration on her lower ribcage. She twisted but could not see the bruise she knew was forming on her back. *If Gage saw these she'd send me to the infirmary for sure.* Tucking the shirt into her pants, she took one last look at herself. *Time to go out there and face her,* she thought, certain Carey was not finished reprimanding her about the fight.

"I thought you fell asleep in there," Carey said when Grace entered the kitchen.

"Sorry."

Carey pointed at the table. "Sit. The coffee's almost done."

Grace did as she was told. *Here it comes,* she thought when her mentor took the chair next to her.

"You're very lucky, you know," Carey said. "In case you didn't see anyone on your way back here and hear it from the teenage grapevine,

Sally Dawson admitted she helped Lauren hide the knife and played lookout while the bunks were destroyed as well as cutting the rope."

"That's good."

"I'm not finished," Carey said. "By all accounts, you went after Lauren and started the fight."

Grace looked down at her hands. "Yes, I did."

"You're still that upset about your bunk being ruined?"

It was then that Grace realized her mentor had no idea what the fight was really about. Maybe she could pull it off after all. "She's done more than that," Grace said. "She let everyone be punished for something she did."

"You still should have kept that temper of yours under control," Carey said. "You've been doing so well lately."

The sound of disappointment in her mentor's voice bothered Grace more than any amount of yelling could ever do. "I'm sorry."

"People are going to do things to upset, annoy, or even hurt you. That doesn't allow you to resort to violence. I thought you wanted to go to college, not end up in Irwin serving time for assault."

"I do," Grace said.

"Then make a decision," Carey said. "College, or a life of answering to guards and working in the prison laundry."

"College."

"So stop doing things that could take that choice away from you," Carey said, taking the mugs out of the cupboard. "And start thinking about your major. While you're at it, come get your coffee."

"I think computers would be interesting," Grace said, reaching for the coffeepot. "Web design or something like that."

"It's a growing field," Carey said. "Certainly computer skills are in demand."

"That's what I was thinking," Grace said, setting her mug down and opening the refrigerator. "Plus it's good money. Where's the half-and-half?" she asked.

"Oh, I think it's behind the orange juice," Carey said, leaning over Grace and reaching into the refrigerator. As she did so, her hand inadvertently pressed against the teen's back.

"Ah, damn." Grace dropped to her knees, pain lancing through her back.

"What is it?"

"Ow, nothing," Grace said, moving out of the way and slowly standing up. "Grenner got a good kick in, that's all."

"What did Instructor Gage say about it?"

"Um, she didn't see it," Grace said. "I didn't tell her. It's just a little bruise."

"Uh-huh," Carey said, putting her hands on Grace's shoulders and turning her around. "Let me see." She lifted the cotton tee and let out a low whistle. "That's more than a little bruise, Grace."

"I don't want to make a big deal out of it," Grace said. "It's not like anything's broken."

"What did she hit you with? A two-by-four?"

"Her boot, I think," Grace said, leaning her hands against the counter. Carey's fingers began moving along her back, gently checking the injury. "Does that hurt?"

"No," Grace said, her eyes fluttering shut. *Oh God, that feels so good.*

"How about there?"

"A...a little." Grace stifled a moan as Carey's fingers lightly touched her skin.

"You might want to sleep on your stomach tonight."

"She punched me there too," Grace said, her heart racing at the thought of Carey checking that injury as well. "It...it knocked the wind out of me." *Please don't stop.* The tender touch became too much and a low moan escaped from her throat.

"Grace?"

"Mm?" Her eyes opened when Carey's hands left her body.

"I think we need to talk."

Grace lowered her head and closed her eyes, knowing she had finally given herself away. "I don't want to talk about it."

"We have to," Carey said, moving away to sit at the kitchen table.

"It's not some phase or a stupid crush," Grace said, refusing to turn around. It was painful enough without having to look at her. "I know how I feel."

"I didn't say it was," Carey said softly. "Come sit down."

"Why?" Grace asked, feeling the tightness in her throat. "So you can tell me how someone like you would never be interested in a juvenile delinquent?"

"Aside from the fact that it's illegal and morally reprehensible?" Carey asked. "Grace, I'm twenty-nine years old. You're seventeen."

"I'm going to be eighteen next month." She stared at her now lukewarm cup of coffee. "That doesn't make a difference, does it?"

"It's not that easy," Carey said. "You've been placed in my care by the state. I'm responsible to take care of you."

"You don't believe me," Grace said, her heart breaking. "You think I'm so screwed up that I don't know how I feel."

"That's not true, Grace," Carey said. "Please, come sit down."

Grace shook her head, knowing she was dangerously close to tears and seeing Carey would send her over the edge. "I never understood, you know? I tried but boys just never...and then I thought it was because of what happened, that it somehow turned me off, but it wasn't." She took a deep breath, letting it out slowly. "I didn't understand until I met you. God, this hurts." She heard the scraping of the chair on the floor, then felt Carey's presence behind her.

"I know it hurts," Carey said softly. "Grace, I care about you, very much."

Grace wiped away a tear. "But not that way, right?"

"But not that way," Carey repeated.

"Just a stupid kid."

"No," Carey said. "You're not stupid, Grace. You're a smart, sweet, caring young woman who has the whole world before you. If circumstance were different, if you were older, if I wasn't in charge of teenage girls..."

Grace took her mug and moved to the sink, keeping her back to Carey. "And if the moon and sun lined up in perfect harmony, then I might have a shot, right?" She dumped the coffee into the sink. "I don't want to talk about it anymore."

"Don't shut me out," Carey said.

Grace turned the water on and rinsed her mug. "Nothing to talk about." She set the mug haphazardly in the drainer, then shut the faucet off. "You've made it clear how you feel."

"Grace—"

"Instructor Carey, may I be excused to do my homework?" Grace blinked rapidly, taking deep breaths and fighting with all her might not to break down and cry.

"Don't do this."

"Instructor Carey, may I please be excused to do my homework?"

Several seconds passed before she heard the older woman let out a breath. "Go ahead," Carey said.

Keeping her back to Carey, Grace went to the living room and sat down on the couch. Staring at her closed textbook through glistening eyes, she listened to the sound of footsteps going into the bedroom. Now that she was alone, the tears began to run. *Damn. How stupid can I be? If I had just stayed quiet she never would have known.* Fearing Carey would come out and see her crying, Grace ran into the bathroom, sliding down the door until she was sitting on the tiled floor.

Grace struggled to calm herself down when she heard the bedroom door open. She listened as Carey walked into the living room, then came back and stood outside the bathroom for several seconds before knocking. "Grace?"

Grace sniffled and wiped her face with wadded-up tissue. "I'm fine. I'll be out in a minute." She looked up to see the doorknob turn. *She's checking to see if I locked the door,* she thought as the knob returned to its original position.

"I wish you would," Carey said softly.

"I don't want to talk about it," Grace said. "Can't we just forget it?"

"You can't just forget your feelings."

"I can't help them either but that doesn't matter, does it?" She stood up and walked to the sink, met by red-rimmed eyes looking back at her from the mirror. *And you were worried she'd be mad about the fight. Try getting a hug out of her now.*

"Grace?"

"I'll be out in a minute." She watched in the mirror as the knob was tested again. *Don't worry, the razors are safe.* Soaking her washcloth with cold water, she pressed it against her face. *How am I gonna face her? I can't go out and just sit there and pretend nothing happened, and I can't talk about it.* She soaked the cloth again. *I'll tell her I'm tired and go to bed early. No, she'd know I was lying. What am I gonna do?* "Fucked up big time," she whispered as she wrung out the washcloth and draped it over the sink. "No way to fix this one." She looked at her reflection one last time. *Be tough. Don't cry. Don't let her see how much it hurts.* "Ready?" She took a deep breath, then let it out slowly. *Be tough.*

Opening the door, she looked down at the carpet and waited for Carey to move out of the way before going into the living room and taking her usual position on the couch. She opened her textbook and pretended to be finding the correct page as Carey claimed the recliner. *Please just let it go tonight,* she silently begged, watching from the corner of her eye as the dark-haired woman opened the drawer and donned the black-rimmed reading glasses. *Good. Grade papers or something. Don't bring it up.* She looked down quickly when Carey glanced in her direction. *Please don't say anything,* she thought, relieved when Carey picked up the paperback sitting on the corner of the table. Grace tried to pay attention to her textbook but the words made no sense, her mind refusing to let her escape from the feelings welling inside. "I'm going to bed," she blurted. Carey closed the novel. "If that's what you want to do," she said, turning off the lamp.

I want to crawl into a hole and disappear, Grace thought to herself as she collected the bedding. Deliberately keeping her back to Carey, she laid out the blanket and sheet, then crawled between them and faced the rear of the couch. She heard footsteps as Carey moved, then a creak as the older woman sat down on the edge of the coffee table.

"I wish I knew the right words to say," Carey said softly.

Grace sniffled, wiping her eyes with the pillow. "Just something I have to work out myself."

"If you want to talk about it..."

"I know." She pulled the blanket tighter.

"I'm sorry, Grace. It can't be any different."

Grace kept her back turned to Carey, but she nodded her acceptance. "It was stupid of me to think that someone like you would ever be interested in a screw-up like me anyway."

Carey reached over and grabbed her shoulder, pulling her over onto her back. "I'm not going to listen to you put yourself down like that. You've changed so much since you arrived here. You've learned to set goals, and work to achieve them. And until tonight, you've been able to keep that temper of yours under control. That's something that you couldn't do a few months ago." Carey released Grace's shoulder, a thoughtful look on her face.

"I'm so proud of you, Grace. I hope you know that. And you know we can remain friends when you leave here."

Grace smiled for the first time that evening. "I'd like that, Carey."

Carey smiled back. "Good. Now I'm going to get out of here and let you get some sleep." Reaching over she tugged the blanket that had fallen away when she pulled Grace over, and tucked it back up around the young girl. "Sweet dreams, Grace," she said as she stood to leave.

"You too." Grace watched her leave. *Wow. She's proud of me.* Those words warmed her from the inside as she let herself believe them. Smiling, she rolled over on her side and closed her eyes, the pain of the last hour easing. And the fist that had been gripping her insides slowly releasing its hold. Things were not the way she wanted them, but Carey was proud of her. That was enough for now.

Try as she might, Grace just could not pay attention to her homework, her eyes flitting up to catch a glimpse of the woman sitting in the recliner. Carey had been quiet these last two days since she had found out about how she felt, and Grace couldn't help wondering if her being there was making her uncomfortable. When Carey caught her looking again, she quickly looked back down at the book in her lap.

"What?"

"Nothing."

"Grace, I'm too tired to play this game tonight."

"Sorry." The teen looked down at her notebook. "I guess it's been really hard for you having me underfoot."

"I miss my closet but other than that it hasn't been too bad," Carey said. "Was that the question?"

"No," Grace said. "Do you want me to trade places with Jan?"

Carey removed her reading glasses. "You mean you stay with Instructor Gage and Bowen comes here?" She shook her head. "Why change things now?"

"Because of me," Grace said. "I don't want to make you uncomfortable."

"And you think sticking me with Jan would make me comfortable?"
Grace looked down. "No."

"Look at me. Do you want to trade places?"

"No."

"Is it going to be too hard for you to stay here?"

Grace thought about it. No matter how much it hurt, she could not deprive herself of even one minute more with Carey. "It might be," she admitted. "But I want to stay." She wiped at a tear. "Please."

Carey nodded. "I'm not the one that brought it up," she said, leaning forward in her seat. "Grace, I know it hurts, and what I had to say was hard for you to hear, but I need you to know that I do care about you. If you need to talk, I'm here."

"It does hurt," Grace said, swiping at another tear. "I feel like there's something wrong with me."

"Not wrong," Carey said. "Incomplete. A whole new life is going to begin for you soon and you have to give yourself time to live that life before you can even think of giving yourself to another person. You have to take that lump of clay that is your future and mold it into something, make yourself into someone. The someone you want to be."

"What then?"

"What do you mean?"

Grace looked down. "What if I do that? Get my degree, start a career, achieve those goals I've been making for the last five months. Would you consider me...you know...that way?"

"I don't know," Carey said. "And I can't allow myself to even think about the future in those terms because of the way things are today. I want to be your friend, Grace. I'm your mentor now and that's not going to end after graduation. In many ways, I feel like a big sister to you. As for anything else, I can't, and I know that while it hurts now, someday you'll understand why."

If circumstances were different. The words echoed through Grace's mind long after she had closed her eyes for a sleep that refused to come. *Goal number one, Carey. So how do I get that goal? Become what she wants in a lover. Succeed at college. Get a degree so she'll see me as an adult and not a screwed-up kid. Can't do anything about the age but wait.* She sighed and laced her hands behind her head. *What else? Get a job, save money, get good credit to show her I'm responsible. Stay out of trouble, there's one of the biggies. No way in hell she'd choose me if I got myself into a mess.* Sitting up, she listened carefully for several seconds, then quietly went over and turned on the lamp. *You're always telling me to make a plan for the future,* she thought as she opened her notebook. She wrote Carey's name at the top of the paper. *Now, steps to achieve goal.*

"Thank you for coming, Mr. Waters," Carey said, gesturing at the chair. "Please have a seat. I'd like to speak to you for a few minutes before we bring Grace in."

"Fine," he said. "How's she doing?"

"She's had a few rough spots, but overall she's done a complete turnaround from the first day she arrived here," Carey said. "You should be proud of her, I know we are."

"I am," he said. "And if there's anything I can do for her, just tell me."

"She told you she passed her GED test?"

"Yes," he said. "I told her I'm going to take down my trophy fish to make room for her diploma."

"I'm sure that made her happy," Carey said. "Mr. Waters, Grace doesn't know this yet, but after tomorrow, she's going to be released from state custody."

"That's wonderful," he said.

"At that point, she has to be released to her legal guardian."

"Her mother," he said.

"She's seventeen," Carey said. "She can choose which parent she wants to live with. But," she cautioned, seeing the hopeful look in his eyes. "Her early release is conditioned on her staying in Iroquois County for six months." She watched him work through the problem.

"I can't get it done by tomorrow but I can move here if I have to," he said.

"She can live on her own once she turns eighteen," Carey said. "The problem is the next month."

"It would really hurt but I could probably swing a hotel for that long," he said. "I have some savings bonds I've been holding onto." He rubbed his beard. "Then I'd have to get her set up in an apartment. Help her find a job or get into school. Can she?"

"I've done some research, Mr. Waters," she said. "If she goes to Iroquois Community College, and if she takes a student loan, there are enough grants and programs to help her cover tuition. A part-time job would cover her living expenses but I'm not sure if she'll be able to handle rent, especially in a college town."

"What can I do to help?" he asked.

205

SIX MONTHS

"Am I ever going to see you again?"

"Grace, I can't answer that question," Carey said. "Neither of us knows what the future will bring."

"I hate this," the teen said, wiping her eyes. "I don't want to leave you."

"You knew this was coming," Carey said, wishing she knew the magic words to ease Grace's pain. "It's time for you to make those goals a reality."

"I love you," Grace said, wrapping her arms around Carey's waist and resting her head on the older woman's upper chest.

"I know," Carey said softly. "And I care about you, very much. It can't happen, Grace. I know you understand why."

"I do." Grace said. "But I still don't like it."

Carey smiled, gave Grace a quick hug, then stepped back. "I have something for you. Stay here." She went to the bedroom and returned a moment later with a brightly wrapped box. "Happy graduation." Her smile grew when she saw the wide-eyed look in the teen's blue eyes. "Careful, it's got some weight to it."

"What is it?"

"Set it on the table," Carey said. "It's actually a few presents. Take the lid off." Grace did. "Open the manila envelope first. Careful, there's a bunch of papers in there." Carey watched excitedly as Grace pulled out various forms and applications along with an Iroquois Community College catalog. "You'd still have to get a student loan and a part-time job to make ends meet, but those are the application forms for all the tuition programs and grants that I could find that you qualify for. It's enough to cover your tuition and probably your books too."

"That's great, but I can't go," Grace said, setting the papers on the table. "I still have to serve another month at Crestwood, and classes start in two weeks."

"Uh-huh," Carey bit her cheek to keep from smiling too much and giving everything away. "Open that second envelope." She bit harder as the teen pulled out the legal papers.

"Modification...probation..." Grace looked at her. "I'm free?"

Now Carey could not keep the smile in check. "Signed by Judge Grimm himself. He's the one that sentenced you here, wasn't he?"

Grace nodded. "Bald, no sense of humor. Gets angry easily."

"Uh-huh, I bet having a clown-haired teenager mouthing off at him had something to do with it, don't you think?"

Grace colored and nodded. "A bit, I guess. How did you get him to do this?"

"What makes you think I had anything to do with it?" Carey waited a beat. "Actually all I did was send some letters to the judge along with a copy of your record here and mentioned that forcing you to serve that month at Crestwood would keep you from being able to attend ICC."

"Some letters?"

"Instructors Gage and Donaldson had something to say about you as well," Carey said. "Now that just means that the judge has agreed to release you on probation provided that you stay in the county and attend school. You have to meet with a probation officer weekly and submit to random urine tests. That's not going to be a problem though, is it?"

Grace shook her head vigorously. "No, not a chance," she said, the realization sinking in. "I can go to college."

"Registration is next week and classes start the week after that," Carey said. "Not much time to get everything ready but I know you can do it."

Grace set the judge's order down and touched the stack of aid forms. "And I really can afford this?"

"I believe so," Carey said. "We'll sit down later and go over the figures, but I checked them out a few weeks ago and I came up with enough to cover the major expenses with some left over for the unexpected." She tapped the box. "Next. Now be careful, don't drop it," she said as Grace reached in. The teen ripped through the tissue paper that Carey had so carefully wrapped around it the night before.

"A computer?" Grace pressed the button, opening the laptop. "Oh my God, it's a computer."

"Let me explain," Carey said. "It's not new. My friend Leslie gets a new one every two years for work and this is her old one. It's missing whatever you need to get on the Internet, and there's no printer, but she said something about using the disks and the school printer."

"Sure," Grace said, her eyes wide as she looked over the black laptop. "You put what you want to print on a disk, then use the school's computer and printer to print it out." She closed the laptop, her fingers delicately brushing the surface. "I can't believe you got me a computer." Setting the computer on the table, she surprised Carey by leaning over and giving her a big hug. "Thank you so much."

"You're welcome, Grace. I don't know much about computers," Carey said. "But Leslie said it's more than enough for school. She said it has a word processing program and some other programs you'd find useful."

"This is great," Grace said, sitting up and touching the laptop again. "It's got a CD/DVD drive built in." She grinned at her mentor. "Now I really am ready for college."

"Not quite," Carey said. "Come on, there's more in the box."

"More?"

"Just a little bit," Carey said. "I hope you like blue." She watched as Grace pulled out a blue backpack. "For carrying your books to class."

"Oh, it's great," Grace said, "It even has wheels." She opened the hook and loop sections. "It's got a place for pens and other stuff. Hey, it's even got a mirror."

"Yeah, well, worry more about having a pen that works than your makeup," Carey said. "Your last present is inside the pack. You should have seen me standing at the computer store trying to pick it out."

Grace's eyes lit up more, if that was possible. At least it seemed so to Carey. "An encyclopedia. Two CD set. Oh, this is the really good one." She flipped the case over and glanced at the back. "Yeah, this is the one with the built-in detailed atlases and world timelines. Oh look, it can do footnotes."

"So it's a good one, right?" Carey asked, not certain until that moment that she had bought the best one. The smile on Grace's face answered her question. "I'm glad you like it. All of it."

"Go ahead, open it."

"Thank you," Grace said, giving her father a hug before tearing open the envelope. "A credit card?"

"Debit card," he said. "I asked the man at the bank what the best way was to help you out and he suggested this. You use it like a credit card but it comes out of a special account I set up just for you."

"We learned about them in Personal Finance," Grace said, excited to see her name in raised silver lettering.

"It's easier than sending you checks each month," he said. "Since you're turning eighteen and my child support will end, I suddenly have this extra money each week and I can't think of a better way to spend it than to help my girl get the education she deserves." He put his arm around her and pulled her close. "And once you say your good-byes I'm going to take you to Mohawk and we're going to get you some clothes and whatever else you need. Then we'll find you an apartment."

"B-but how?" she asked. "Dad, you don't have that kind of money."

"I can't buy you a car and make it so you don't have to work while you're in school, but I can take care of most if not all of the rent and give you a little something for spending money."

"But do you know how much clothes cost?"

"Graceful, you're my only daughter and if I want to spend my money on you, then I will. Consider it early birthday and Christmas presents if you want."

Grace's father closed the trunk but her attention was on Carey approaching them. "Dad, do you have any film left?"

"There's three pictures left," he said.

"Hang on," she said, jogging up to meet the dark-haired woman. "Can I have a picture?" she asked, not bothering to mention she had used up half the roll snapping shots of her during the day.

Carey smiled. "Sure. You're all set to go?"

Together they headed toward the rental car. "Everything's packed," Grace said, the pain of separation weighing heavily upon her. "This is hard. I don't want to leave you."

Carey stopped and put her hands on Grace's shoulders. "I know," she said softly. "I'm going to miss you too, but it's time for you to go out on your own and make your own life. I'm only a phone call away." Her smile eased the pain in Grace's heart.

"I'll call," the teen said. "You know I will."

"You'd better," Carey said. "I want to know what's going on with you. I care, Grace." She gave Grace's shoulders a quick squeeze. "Now let's get that picture taken so your dad can take you shopping."

"Dad, take the picture," Grace said, slipping an arm around the older woman's waist, pleased when Carey didn't make her move it. As soon as the camera clicked, she tightened her hold. "Wait, just a couple more, please? Just in case he didn't get that one right."

"One more," Carey gave in.

"Okay, Dad," Grace said happily. "Take another one."

"Satisfied?"

"Wait, there's only one picture left on the roll," Grace said. "It'd be a waste not to use it."

"Do you have any of you and your father yet?" Carey asked.

"No."

"Go stand by him," Carey said, walking the teen over to the lumberjack. "Mr. Waters, would you like a picture of you and your daughter?"

"Ayup, I'd love it," he said, putting his arm around Grace's shoulders and handing Carey the camera. "Just aim and shoot."

Carey looked through the viewfinder until she felt she had the best picture of the two of them, then clicked the shutter button. There was a click, then a whirling sound as the camera automatically rewound the film. "Here you go," she said, handing the camera back to him. "Mr. Waters, you do understand that you're taking a seventeen-year-old girl to the mall, don't you?"

"Sure," he said. "What's wrong with that?"

Carey tried to suppress a smile. "Have you ever taken a seventeen-year-old shopping?"

"No. Can't say as I have."

She put her hand on his arm. "You have my utmost sympathies," she said. "I'd rather take thirty-six girls on a five-mile run than one to the mall."

"Pshaw," he said, waving his hand dismissively.

"There's an ice cream place on the way if you want to stop," Richard said.

"If you want," Grace said, looking out at the endless fields and trees.

"Nope," he said. "This is your day. I just thought you might like a nice double scoop of mint chocolate chip to get your energy for the mall."

Grace's eyes lit up. "You remembered," she said looking at him.

"Ayup, can't forget my daughter's favorite flavor," he said. "So it's settled. We'll get some ice cream, then you can tell me why you're so glum about leaving that place."

"I'm not glum," she said. "I'm happy to be free."

"Partially free," he said. "You have to stay in Iroquois County for the next six months and you have to see your probation officer once a week."

"Yeah, but, Dad," she said, shutting off the radio. "If I want to walk down the street I can do it without having to ask permission, and worry about leg chains or having someone watching me. We're going to the mall. You know how long it's been since I've been to the mall?"

"That woman warned me about taking you to a mall," he said. "You're not going to run your poor father ragged, are you?"

"Oh no, we'll do it the easy way," she said. "We'll start at one end and work our way down. What did Carey say to you?"

"She gave me her sympathies and said she'd rather take a bunch of girls on a run than to take one to the mall."

Grace smiled. "She's not the mall type," she said. "When Carey wants to buy something, she hits the catalogs and mail order places. Did I tell you she bought me an encyclopedia for the computer?"

Richard smiled. "Twice."

"She went to the mall to find it for me," she said. "Hey Dad? I bet there's a photo place at the mall. Can we drop the film off there to be developed?"

"If you want," he said. "I want a copy of the one of us together."

"They usually have those free double sets," she said. "If we get those, I can send a copy of the ones of me and Carey together to her. Did I tell you that she said I could call her each week?" She looked out the window. "Not the same as seeing her every day, though."

"Well, I reckon I know why you're so glum," he said. "Better stock up on those prepaid calling cards."

"I planned on it," Grace said, looking back at him. "I gotta get stamps and envelopes too so I can send her letters."

"She's really special to you, isn't she?"

"Very," Grace said.

"This is the mall?" Grace asked skeptically when her father pulled the car into the large parking lot.

"This is it," he said.

"It's only got one floor."

"Ayup, how many do you need?" He pulled into a spot halfway down the parking aisle and shut the engine off. "Now before we go and spend some money, let's get some rules down." He reached into his front pocket and pulled out a thick wad of bills. "I'm not a rich man, Grace, but I want to do this for you. Here's forty bucks for your own pocket. I'm not buying you anything I think is foolish or too expensive."

"Okay, Dad," she said. "Thanks. I won't waste it on junk, I promise."

"Graceful, Graceful, please wait up."

Grace turned around to see her father lumbering toward her, his hands full of bags. "Oh, I'm sorry, Dad," she said, walking back to meet him.

"I think it's time for another trip to the car," he said, setting the bags down and collapsing onto a bench. "That Miss Carey wasn't kidding. Where do you get the energy?"

"I don't know," Grace said. "Shopping is fun." She looked down at her new watch. "Hey, Dad, it's been an hour. Can we go back to the photo place?"

"But...but that's at the other end of the mall," he protested, looking back at the seemingly endless aisle of stores. "Pumpkin, can't we stop on the way back?"

Grace reached down and took a handful of bags. "You said we had to drop these off at the car anyway."

Richard reached into his pocket and pulled out several bills. "I'll make you a deal. You take those out to the car and get the photos. I'll wait here and regret every cheeseburger I've ever had."

"Okay," Grace said, taking the money, then giving her father a hug. "I'll be back in a few minutes." Gathering up the bags, she began walking briskly to the photo booth. *The pictures are supposed to be ready. They said one hour and it's been one hour and five minutes. They'd better be ready.* Reaching the kiosk, Grace excitedly pulled out her stub and handed it to the clerk. "Are they ready yet?"

"I'll check," the pimply-faced boy said, pulling open a drawer full of photo envelopes. "Here they are," he said. "Just finished these a few minutes ago."

"Great," Grace said, taking the envelope and handing him a twenty-dollar bill. There was no way she could wait to look at the pictures. Shuffling quickly through them she found the ones she had taken of Carey. "This is the one," she said.

"Pardon, miss?"

Grace held up a picture of her and Carey standing together, her arm wrapped around Carey's waist. "I'd like this one enlarged to eight by ten."

"Oh, sure. We can do that for you." He reached over and took the envelope from her, checking the negatives until he found the right one. "Enlargements take longer than an hour, though. You'll have to pick it up tomorrow."

"Okay, I'll be back tomorrow."

"Okay, here we are," he said, signaling to turn into the motel parking lot. "Graceful...I'm sorry, Grace. This isn't the best motel in town but it's better than the one that rents by the hour."

"This is nice," Grace said, looking at the brightly colored sign and well-lit parking lot. "They're all over the country, aren't they?"

"Ayup," he said, pulling in and shutting off the engine. "I want to talk to you about the room or rooms." He tapped the steering wheel with his fingertips. "Do you want your own room or would it be all right to get one with two beds?"

"Isn't it cheaper to get one room?" she asked.

"Ayup." He nodded. "But I want you to be comfortable, Grace." Reaching out, he gave her hand a squeeze. "I'm not very good at this, I'm afraid." He returned his hand to the steering wheel and gripped tightly. "I look at you and I still see that little girl with the blonde ponytails who wasn't afraid to bait her own hook." Grace watched his knuckles turn white from the exertion. "I'm worried you think all men are like that bastard," he said.

Grace leaned her head against his oversized upper arm. "I know not all men are like him," she said, brushing her cheek against the flannel shirt. "I thought we were gonna stay up and watch TV and I could show you everything I bought."

"You mean everything I bought," he said. "Are you still hungry? I can order a pizza."

Grace sat up and smiled. "With mushrooms?"

"If you like," he said. "So, one room or two?"

"One," she said. "I figured that's what we were gonna do anyway."

"If you change your mind, you tell me," he said, letting go of the steering wheel and flexing his fingers. "I want you to be comfortable."

"Dad?" she said, stopping him from opening the door. "I don't think of you like I think of him." She looked out the windshield. "I know you wouldn't do that to me."

"Never," he said firmly. "And if I ever get my hands on that son of a bitch, I'll feed his ass through a wood chipper after I break every bone in his worthless body."

Grace smiled, feeling warmed by her father's words. "Grizzly bear," she said, remembering the name she called him when she was a little girl. "Always protecting me. Remember when I was in first grade and that big boy hit me? You went and scared the hell out of his father and they both came over to apologize."

Richard chuckled. "I don't think that little man in glasses knew what to say when I showed up in his dooryard screaming about his boy hurting my little girl."

"Greg something or other," Grace said. "He never came near me again until I got to high school."

"He bothered you again in high school?" he asked.

Grace shook her head and laughed. "He didn't hit me again," she said. "He hit on me. Wanted to take me out."

Her father laughed. "That be how it goes sometime," he said. "And now your grizzly bear is hungry. Come on, we'll rent a movie on pay per view and you can show me everything."

Richard Waters carried his daughter's suitcase into the room that was to be hers for the foreseeable future. It had taken some looking, but they had managed to find a room to rent in the home of a widowed woman who had decided to rent out her spare bedroom to supplement her income. It was far less expensive than an apartment, and it included meals. Besides, he felt better knowing that Grace was not alone. They had both liked Estelle Somers right off, and now that Grace was eighteen and could legally live on her own, it was time for him to return home.

"Don't you worry about a thing, Mr. Waters, she'll be fine."

"I know," he said, turning to Grace and opening his arms for a good-bye hug.

"You call me if you need anything, pumpkin."

"I will," Grace said. He kissed the top of her head, then turned to leave. She watched him walk down the hall with mixed emotions. It was hard to watch him go, yet at the same time exciting. She was finally on her own and it felt good. She picked up her suitcase and carried it to the bed. She unzipped the large case and began to organize her room, as her stomach reacted to the wonderful smells that were coming from the kitchen.

Carey smiled and put on her reading glasses when she spotted the yellow envelope in the stack of mail. Using her letter opener, she slit the envelope and opened the letter.

Dear Carey,

It seems like ages since I've talked to you and it's only been two weeks. I'm having a great time here. I can't believe all the homework and studying I have to do. I owe Instructor Gage a million bucks for teaching me how to study and take notes. Would you believe girls who graduated from high school are coming up and asking to borrow my notes?

Thought you'd want to know that I got A's on both of my tests and I'm sure I passed my English paper too. The computer classes are the most interesting and Mr. Reilly said I have an aptitude for it.

I don't miss Sapling Hill, but I miss you. Mrs. Somers is nice but it's not the same. The laptop is working great and I really love the encyclopedia. Of course, here I have my own room instead of a couch, but I'd take your couch over a room of my own any day.

I promised myself I wouldn't write you long, boring letters. I'm always thinking of you and hope we can see each other soon.

Love,
Grace

Carey was rereading the letter when Instructor Gage stopped by. "Come on in," she said to the knock.

"You have a mentoring session now?"

"No," Carey said, setting the letter down. "Amazingly enough, I'm free."

"Nice smiley face," Gage said, tapping her fingernail on the yellow envelope.

"Letter from Grace," Carey said. "She thanks you for teaching her how to study."

"Does she? And what does she thank you for, Carey?"

"You know better, Sue," Carey said. "I'm just being supportive to her while she gets settled in."

"I've never seen you be this supportive before," Gage said.

"She has a good shot at making something of herself," Carey said. "I'm just helping her out by being a pen pal. It's just her and her father now that she's cut her mother out of her life. She doesn't have any female role models."

"Grace, Grace, wait up."

She stopped on the concrete path and waited for the young man to catch up. "Hi, Tom."

"Hi," he answered, slightly out of breath from running. "I need to ask a favor."

"What?" Grace asked, thinking the man who sat next to her in Computer Programming needed help with their latest project.

"My parents' best friends are in town and want to take me and my girlfriend out," he said, wiping his hands on his pants. "I don't have a girlfriend."

"I uh...Tom, you're really a nice guy but—"

"I have a boyfriend, Grace," he said. "My family doesn't know. They think Stuart and I are just roommates."

"Oh."

"Grace, I don't know who else to ask," he said. "And well, you do carry a picture of a woman taped to the inside of your notebook." He shrugged his shoulders. "My gaydar goes off every time you walk into class."

"Gaydar?"

"Yeah, like radar," he said.

"Oh."

"Look, do you have a class now?"

"No," she said. "I was going to head to the Dungeon to get some coffee and look over my Trig homework."

"Let's go to the Coffee Bean," he said. "It's cleaner, quieter, and my treat."

"You don't have to do that," Grace said, knowing coffee there was three times or more the cost of the school's lunchroom.

"I may be gay but I'm still a gentleman," Tom said. "Please."

Grace hesitated, then nodded. "Sure, I've been wanting to try a cappuccino."

"Great." Tom smiled broadly.

"So," Tom said as he sat down at the small table. "I'm right about you, aren't I?"

Grace moved the plastic stirrer through the frothy drink. "Yeah," she said. "But she's not my girlfriend."

Tom smiled broadly. "But you want her to be, don't you?"

Grace nodded. "Very much. She thinks I'm too young for her."

"Her loss," Tom said. "So why don't you ever go to the Last Straw? A lot of baby dykes hang out there."

"Not interested," Grace said, tapping her notebook. "That's who I want."

"Well if you change your mind, Stuart and I would be happy to take you out to the juice bar," he said. "So, back to my question. Will you be my fake girlfriend and go with me? I'll return the favor if you ever need it."

Being able to say she was seeing someone would put an end to the stream of men who asked her out, and Grace found she could not come up with any good reason to say no. "Sure," she said. "But I don't have the clothes to go anywhere fancy," she warned.

"What you have on now is fine," Tom assured her. "We're going to the Lobster House so you'll end up with a bib anyway."

"Hello?"

"Hello, Mrs. Somers. This is Carey, is Grace around?"

"Oh, hello, dear. No, she has a date tonight."

"A date?"

"Yes, with a very nice young man. Tim or Tom or something like that."

"Oh," Carey said, her mind imagining different scenarios, all bad. "Did she say when she would get in?"

"No, but I imagine it will be late. She seemed pretty excited. I'll tell her you called."

"Thanks. Bye."

"Good-bye, dear."

Carey hung up the phone. "It's a school night, Grace. What are you doing out?" she said to the empty room. She picked up the phone again and dialed.

"Hello?"

"Sue, it's Carey."

"Didn't I just see you an hour ago at dinner duty? What's up?"

"Are you busy or do you feel like coming over and playing cards?"

"I could be tempted but it's going to cost you."

Carey smiled and walked to the refrigerator. "Let me guess, you haven't eaten yet."

"Well I'm staring at a microwave dinner that promises to be low on fat and high on taste but I could be tempted."

"How does leftover stuffed peppers and beer sound?"

"Sounds like a cribbage game is about to happen."

"Thanks a lot, Grace," Tom said as he walked her to the door. "I owe you big time."

217

"It was fun," she said. "The lobster was great."

"I didn't know you never had it before," he said, smiling broadly. "You should have seen the look on your face when they brought them out."

"I didn't know they came in their shells," Grace said, sharing the smile. "I'm glad the restaurant gives bibs."

"It's standard with lobster," Tom said. "Listen, why don't you come over for dinner tomorrow night? Stuart's an excellent cook and I know he'd just love to meet you."

"Should I bring something?"

"Just yourself," he said. "Stuart always complains I never bring my friends home to meet him so this will be great. I'll see you in class tomorrow."

"Good night, Tom."

"Night, Grace, thanks again. It really means a lot to me."

Entering the house, she was not surprised to see Mrs. Somers waiting for her. "Hi."

"Hello, dear," the older woman said, scooping up the cards she was playing solitaire with. "How was your date?"

"It was fun," she said, removing her jacket and hanging it on the hook near the door. "I had lobster."

"Messy," the landlady said. "I'm from Maine originally, don't you know, and there is nothing to compare to a fresh lobstah. Oh, your friend called twice."

"Carey?"

Mrs. Somers nodded. "Seemed a bit upset."

Grace was instantly concerned. "I'd better call her."

"You can use the phone in my room if you want some privacy."

"Thanks."

"What bug is up your ass tonight?" Gage asked. "You invite me over to play cards and all you're doing is sitting there shuffling them."

"Grace is out on a date," Carey said, passing the deck to her. "It's a school night, Sue. What's she doing out?"

"She is eighteen now," Gage said. "Going out on dates is part of college life."

"I called at nine and she wasn't home yet."

"Should we call the state police?"

"It's not funny, Sue."

"You're jealous."

"I am not," Carey protested. "I'm just...concerned. How much does she know about this guy?"

"Deny all you want," Gage said. "You're jealous because she's out having a good time instead of staying home and pining over you. Give her a break, Carey."

"She's over that," Carey said. "Just a phase she was going through because we were so close."

"And you believe that?" Gage shook her head. "I don't think so."

"She's too young for me and I'm too old for her. She'll realize that sooner or later," Carey said, the very thought paining her. "Looks like she realized it now."

"Those brown eyes are definitely turning green," Gage said.

"I'm not—" Carey said as the phone rang. "That's her." She moved quickly, catching it before the end of the second ring. "Grace?"

"Hi. Mrs. Somers said you called twice. Is everything okay?"

"Are you just now getting home?"

"Yes, but my first class tomorrow isn't until nine."

"What were you doing out until after ten?" Carey asked, ignoring the smug look on Gage's face.

"Well, we went out to dinner but then Mr. Crenshaw wanted to go out for dessert."

"Who is Mr. Crenshaw?"

"Oh, he and his wife are friends of Tom's parents."

"And who is Tom? The guy you went out with?"

"Yes. He sits next to me in programming class. Is something wrong?"

"Wrong? What should be wrong? You're supposed to be studying, not out gallivanting around with God knows who."

"What are you upset about? Nothing happened."

"Only because you're lucky. Were you alone with him?"

"He picked me up and we met the Crenshaws at the restaurant. After the ice cream place they went back to their hotel and he drove me home. Nothing happened and he was the perfect gentleman. I didn't do anything wrong."

"You've never mentioned him before," Carey said. "How serious is this?"

"Oh, Carey, you sound like an overprotective father," Gage said from the kitchen.

"It's not serious. He needed a date for dinner with his folks' friends. That's all."

"So you're not going out with him again, right?"

"I'm going over to his apartment for dinner tomorrow." There was a pause. "He wants me to meet his boyfriend Stuart."

"Boyfriend? He has a boyfriend?" Carey glared at Gage as the diminutive woman began laughing hysterically. "Why didn't you tell me that before?"

"First, I didn't think it was important. Second, I didn't know I had to get approval from you to go out with someone, and third, you know how I feel." Carey heard the hurt in Grace's voice and felt guilty about upsetting her. "I'm not looking for anyone and I'm sorry if you were worried."

"I'm sorry, Grace," Carey said. "It's just that I called and she said you were out on a date and..." She leaned her forehead against the wall. "And I jumped to conclusions."

"It's nice to know you care."

"You know I care," Carey said. "I worry about you."

"I'm fine. Now, what are you doing up so late?"

"I'm um...Sue needed help grading essays," she said, earning a snort from Gage.

"Well, I won't keep you. When Mrs. Somers said you called twice I wanted to make sure everything was okay."

"Everything's fine, Grace. I'm glad you had fun tonight."

"I did. I'll write you all about it."

"Please do. I'll talk to you soon."

"Okay, good night, Carey."

"Night." Carey hung up the phone. "Don't say it," she warned.

"Say what?" Gage asked. "That you're acting like a jealous lover instead of a mentor?"

"He's gay. The guy she went out with. She was just covering for him with his parents' friends," Carey said. "She's not interested in him and he's got a lover."

"And you drove yourself nuts all evening for nothing," Gage said.

"I did not," Carey said. "She's only eighteen, Sue."

"Legal in every state."

"That's not the point," she said. "I don't date teenagers."

"So what's the magic age for you?" Gage asked. "You'd better let Grace know so she has an idea how long she has to wait."

"That's not funny," Carey said.

"It wasn't meant to be. You're telling her you're not interested and then you freak out when she goes on a date. You're sending mixed messages, Carey."

"I didn't freak out," Carey said. "I'm her mentor, her friend. I'm allowed to worry about her."

"Keep telling yourself that," Gage said.

TWELVE MONTHS

Grace could not have been more excited. Spring break brought not only a week off from school but a promise from Carey that she could come visit since Sapling Hill was between sessions. Everything was packed and she was now waiting on the porch for the truck that would come, and more importantly, the woman driving it. "Come on, Carey, hurry up," she muttered, growing more anxious by the minute.

The second she saw the blue truck turn the corner she was on her feet and dragging her suitcase down the steps. "I thought you'd never get here," she said as Carey pulled the truck to a stop.

"Hello to you too." Carey unbuckled her seat belt and stepped out. "I told you I was coming," she said as she walked around the front of the truck. "You just have no patience."

"Hi," Grace said, a shy smile coming to her lips. "Can I get a hug?" At Carey's hesitation she added, "Friends hug, you know."

"I know," Carey said. "All right, a quick one and then let's go."

Grace paid no attention to anything said after she was given the go-ahead, wrapping her arms around Carey's waist and sighing happily.

"I've missed you so much," she said against the thick winter jacket.

"Going through another growth spurt?" Carey said, giving Grace a quick squeeze, then backing up and reaching for the suitcase.

"I think so," Grace said. *Did you miss me too?* "Either that or my jeans are getting shorter." She picked up her backpack and hoisted it into the bed of the truck, letting it fall with a loud thump.

"Don't dent my truck," Carey said, opening the passenger door and stashing the suitcase behind the seat.

Grace found her to be too close to resist and moved in for another hug. "I really missed you."

"I missed you too," Carey said, gently but firmly moving Grace back after a few seconds so she could get out from between the truck and the passenger door. "And that's enough hugs right now."

Grace looked down. "I'm sorry." Gentle fingers lifted her chin, bringing her face to face with soft brown eyes.

"I'm sorry too," Carey said. "I don't want to hurt you, but I don't want to feel uncomfortable either."

"I'll be good, I promise," Grace said. She forced a smile to her face. "Well, okay, let's go."

"My God, Grace," Carey said as she hefted the backpack. "What is in this?"

"Books," the teen said. "Economics, Accounting, both computer courses and my English Comp. You don't think the professors would give us a week off without piling on the homework, do you?"

"Ugh," Carey said. "Just don't ask me to help you with it. It's all over my head." She carried the backpack in and set it next to the closet. "Are you hungry?"

"Starved."

"I'll get dinner started while you get settled," Carey said, kicking off her sneakers.

"Want help?"

"I'll get it," Carey said. "You relax."

"Carey?"

"Hmm?"

"You wouldn't be in the mood for some of that great coffee you make so well, would you?" Grace asked, batting her eyes.

"You think that's going to convince me?" Carey leaned against the archway to the kitchen and crossed her arms.

Grace smiled. "I'll...clean the oven."

Carey shook her head. "It's self-cleaning. Try again."

"Um...I'll mop the kitchen floor?"

"Already mopped."

A devilish thought popped into the teen's head. "I'll be your slave for life." The words had the desired effect, wiping the smile from Carey's face.

"I was thinking more along the lines of doing the dishes," Carey said, turning away from Grace and going into the kitchen. "Behave."

"Mmm," Grace said as she took a sip. "I've missed your coffee."

Carey smiled. "Did you?"

"The closest I've found is a blend at the Coffee Bean, but it's almost two dollars a cup," Grace said. "Oh this is good."

"Two dollars? You spend two dollars on a cup of coffee?"

Grace took another swallow before answering. "It's one of my few extras," she said. "Only once or twice a week."

"I'll have to send you home with some," Carey said. "Do you have a coffeemaker?"

Grace nodded. "Dad sent me one. I don't have that many outlets so if I want to make coffee I have to unplug the laptop. Mrs. Somers doesn't allow extension cords or power strips."

"Are you ready for another cup?"

"I'll get it," Grace said, rising to her feet and reaching for Carey's mug. "Cream, no sugar, right?"

"Right, thanks."

"My pleasure," Grace said as she headed for the kitchen. Her back to Carey, she smiled as she filled the two mugs, taking enjoyment from being able to do even the littlest thing for the woman she cared about so deeply. "It must be nice to have a break from work," she said.

"It is," Carey said. "Five months with only every other Sunday off is hard. We deserve this month off, even if half of it is spent doing paperwork and getting ready for the next session."

"Was the last group better or worse than mine?" Grace asked, smiling at all the papers stuck to the refrigerator with ICC magnets.

"A slightly different mix, but about the same," Carey said. "The usual characters, the usual situations."

"I got a letter from Jan Bowen," Grace said as she returned to the living room. "She's working at the mall in Mohawk. Management trainee."

"Good for her," Carey said as she took her mug. "How are things going for you at the diner?"

"It's okay," Grace said. "I hate being on my feet so long and having to bus the tables, but the tips are decent and dinner is free." She sat down on the couch and tucked her left leg beneath her. "The customers can really suck sometimes, though."

"Decided to let your hair grow out?"

"Too busy to get it cut," Grace said. "Do you like it?"

"As long as it's all one color," Carey said.

"I don't do that anymore," Grace said. "But did you like it shorter?"

Carey smiled. "Grace, what I like or don't like doesn't matter. It's your hair. Wear it the way you want to."

"But—"

"Shorter," Carey said.

Grace smiled. "You like short hair?"

Carey nodded. "I'm partial to short hair," she admitted.

"Did Eve have short hair?"

Carey looked at her for moment before answering. "Yes. At least she did then. I wouldn't know now."

"Were the two of you together long?"

Carey took a deep breath, then let it out. "You won't be happy until I tell you, will you?" Grace shook her head. "All right. Eve and I met when we were both in the Coast Guard. We were together for almost two years before we broke up."

"When she called that day," Grace said. "You said something to her about not being the one who came home pregnant."

"She had a boyfriend on the side," Carey said. "I don't tolerate cheating, especially like that."

"Like that?"

"With a man," Carey said. "Without protection. I thought we were a monogamous couple." She clenched her jaw, then slowly relaxed. "I had no idea. The whole thing still disgusts me."

Grace moved from the couch to the corner of the coffee table, her knees inches from the footrest. "I would never do that to you," she said.

Carey gave her a small smile. "We're not a couple," she reminded gently. "I'm sure someone will come along to turn your eye."

"They haven't yet," Grace said. "And it's not like I haven't been offered." She touched Carey's sock. "I know who I want."

"Grace..."

"I know how you feel," she said, patting Carey's foot, then sitting back. "I'm not pushing. I just want you to know I'm not off getting laid by every girl in school."

"I never thought that," Carey said. "But I don't want you giving up a chance at true happiness waiting for me."

"It doesn't make sense to get involved with someone my age," Grace said. "I know these women. One week they're madly in love, the next week they're living together and six months down the road they break up. I don't want that." She gave Carey a sly smile. "I bet they don't use dental dams either." Carey smiled and looked away. "What?" Grace asked, smiling at the older woman's blush. "Oh, please tell me."

"I shouldn't," Carey said.

Grace scooted closer. "Come on, I'm sure I've heard worse."

"No. I don't want to give you any ideas."

"Michelle says using a dental dam is like trying to lick an ice cream through plastic wrap," Grace said. "No point if you can't taste it."

Carey looked at her in surprise. "What are they teaching you at that school?"

"Michelle is a friend that I met through the gay and lesbian student union," Grace said. "I know lots of great lesbian jokes."

"Your friend has a point," Carey said.

"I wouldn't know," Grace lamented with an exaggerated sigh.

"Behave," Carey said.

"You gonna tell me what you were thinking?" Grace asked. "It had to be good the way you turned red."

"It was just a joke I heard once," Carey said. "I can't tell you."

"Oh you have to," Grace pleaded.

Carey covered her face with her hands. "All right, why do lesbians like whales so much?"

"Why?"

"Because they have a really long tongue and an air hole on the top of their heads."

Grace started laughing. "That's bad."

"I told you so," Carey said, peeking through her fingers, then uncovering her face.

"Okay," Grace said, sitting up. "What's this?" She stuck her tongue out.

"What?"

"A lesbian with a hard-on."

Carey chuckled and slowly shook her head. "We need to change the subject."

Grace frowned. "Okay."

"I'm going to get dinner started," Carey said, standing up and walking toward the kitchen. As she did, she stopped behind the couch and leaned over. "As for your joke, if that was the case your tongue would never be in your mouth."

"Hey," Grace said, trying to sound offended. "Not all the time."

"Oh right," Carey said, continuing into the kitchen. "You do sleep from time to time."

"I've been good," Grace protested. "I haven't tried to get a hug from you in at least an hour."

"I should stop them," Carey said. "It's almost the equivalent to you being able to cop a feel."

"Don't, please," Grace said, turning around and kneeling up on the cushion to look at her. "It's all I can get. Don't take it away."

"I feel like I'm leading you on," Carey said. "It's not fair to you, Grace."

"So what?" Grace asked, leaving the couch to walk over to Carey's side.

"So I don't want to see you hurt by this," Carey said.

"And you don't think it'll hurt for you to not give me a hug anymore?" She reached for Carey's arm, then pulled back.

"Perhaps it'll hurt less in the long run," Carey said. "Grace, six months ago you were under my care. It makes me very uncomfortable to hug you and know you're thinking about me as a potential lover and not just a friend."

It hurt to hear those words and Grace turned away, knowing that was exactly what she was doing with her "friendly" hugs. "I have homework to do," she said.

"Wait," Carey said. Grace felt the touch of the older woman's hands on her shoulders. "I'm not trying to upset you."

"I know," Grace said. "And you're right...about the hugs. It's just that..." She closed her eyes and let her head fall forward. "A hug is the only way I get to touch you, and sometimes it's so hard not to." She reached up and touched Carey's hand for emphasis. "It's not like you. You get to touch me any time you want to."

"I'm sorry," Carey said, pulling her hands back. "I don't even notice when I do it."

"I don't mind," Grace said unnecessarily, turning to see Carey smiling at her quick response. "It makes me feel special. I just wish I could do it sometimes."

"Let's make a compromise," Carey said. "Friendly touches once in a while, ease up on the hugs, all right?"

Grace smiled happily. "Yes." Testing her new liberty, she reached out and briefly touched Carey's hand. "See? I can be good."

"When you want to," Carey said. "Grace? How long have I been doing that?"

"What? Touching me?" Grace thought about it. "You mean other than when you were making me do pushups or clobbering me in SD?"

"You know what I mean," Carey said.

"I think the first time I remember is when I was in the infirmary after that asshole hit me and I got the bump over my eye." She touched the spot over her left eyebrow. "You brought me a clean shirt."

"I remember," Carey said. "I remember how angry I was that he dared to lay his hands on you here and that your mother tried to minimize it."

"It really hurt that she wouldn't stand up to him for me. That she always took his side. You know?"

"I know."

Grace brightened up. "But that's in the past. I try not to dwell on it anymore. Life's too short to dwell on things I can't change. My life is good now."

Carey smiled. "I'm glad."

"So what are you doing now?" Carey asked, sitting down next to her.

"I was just going to get some more programming done," Grace said. "See? I've got the flow chart done but it's a chore putting the code together."

"I hate to tell you but this makes no sense to me."

Grace smiled and turned on the laptop. "The hardest part is not figuring out how to do something, but how to make the subroutines work without causing endless loops."

"And in English that means?"

Taking a chance, Grace gently bumped the older woman with her shoulder. "It means I'm a computer geek and I love knowing something you don't." The startup screen changed to her desktop, causing her to blush and immediately close the laptop. "Um, let me change something here."

"Let me see," Carey said, lifting the screen. She smiled. "How did you do that?"

"Um..." Grace tapped the touch pad, bringing up a menu. "Tom has a scanner."

"Please tell me I'm not all over the Internet," Carey said, recognizing the picture as being taken on Grace's last day at Sapling Hill.

"No," Grace said. "I only have access at school and we just scanned the picture and put it on disk so I could transfer it to my laptop." She tapped the pad a few more times and the background changed from a picture of Carey to a bluish green color. "Do you want me to delete it?"

Carey patted her shoulder. "You can keep it," she said, thinking of the picture she had on her desk. "Besides, how would I know if you didn't?"

"Because if you told me to delete it, I would," Grace said.

"Sheets in the closet?"

Carey smiled. "Yes. You can change in the bathroom."

Grace gave her a devilish grin. "Or I could change out here."

"Behave," Carey said. "Or I'll make you sleep in the truck."

"I'll behave," Grace said. "Do I at least get a hug good night?"

Carey hesitated. "I'm not sure I should," she said, dropping the pillow on the couch. "Grace, I don't want to lead you on."

"I know," the teen said, stepping into Carey's personal space. "You're not."

Carey put her arms around Grace and pulled her close, very much aware of the sigh that escaped the young woman's lips. "I care about you," she whispered into golden blonde hair. "I don't want to see you hurt, especially because of me."

"I can't help how I feel," Grace said, giving a squeeze before she stepped back. "Any more than you can, I guess." She reached for her suitcase. "I'll be back in a minute."

"I hope you have homework to do," Carey said as she carried the box of file folders in. "It's going to take me hours to do this."

"What is it?" Grace asked, moving her books to make room on the coffee table for the box.

227

"The spring/summer session," Carey said. "Two weeks before the girls arrive, we get the files from the courts. I have to review them and prepare care sheets."

"So you knew about me before I arrived?"

Carey nodded. "Only the base facts from the court reports and from Crestwood." She set the box down and gave the teen a smile. "I knew you'd be a hard nut for me to crack."

"But you did eventually," Grace said.

Carey shook her head. "Not me. I could have used a sledgehammer and I wouldn't have gotten through. It was you pecking away from the inside that broke the shell."

"I still think it was you," Grace said, pressing her finger to Carey's lips to stop her from disagreeing. "And you'll never convince me otherwise." She pulled her hand back. "Now, are you going to sit out here or use the desk?"

Carey looked at the recliner. "I can do it out here," she said.

"I'm not tuning you out but I'm going to put a CD on, okay?" Grace asked. "I'll use my headset."

"Fine with me," Carey said. "Don't turn it up so loud it hurts your ears."

"Yes, ma'am," Grace said, smiling and shaking her head. "You can't drop me for ten anymore, you know."

Carey looked at her and slowly gave her a wicked smile. "Don't tempt me."

"I'll keep it to a reasonable level," Grace said, reaching for her soft-sided suitcase.

"What kind of music do you listen to?" Carey asked, watching the teen unzip a CD organizer and flip through the discs.

"Mostly lesbian singers," Grace said, pulling a CD from its sleeve. "I have some older stuff like Bread, Journey, Hall and Oates, that kind of stuff." She touched a button on the front of the laptop, causing the CD tray to zip open. "I have speakers built in if you want to listen to something. I have some of Cris Williamson's vintage CDs."

"Whoever that is," Carey said.

"The goddess of lesbian music, that's who," Grace said, shaking her head. "I'll use the earphones."

Carey chuckled and opened the first folder. *The goddess of lesbian music. I'm not even going to ask how she managed to find music like that. There's not exactly a lesbian section in the record store that I've ever seen.* Reaching for her coffee, she took advantage of Grace's preoccupation with whatever was on the computer screen to observe her. The blonde hair was longer but there were other changes as well. Six months had made quite a difference in Grace's face. Cheeks once rounded by a hint of baby fat were more angular, accented by the subtlest amount of blush. *No wonder the girls are chasing you,* she thought, peeking over the rim of the mug. Several moments passed before Carey realized she was staring and turned her attention to the paperwork in front of her. Grace started humming to the music, tapping her fingers against the sides of the laptop. "Grace."

"Oh, sorry," she said, stilling her fingers. Seconds later the humming started again. *"So dream on, little teen queen. Angels on horseback will carry your dream..."*

"Grace," Carey said again. "Try playing one that doesn't move you to song."

"Sorry," Grace said, pulling the headphones down. "I'll find another one." She flipped through the plastic sleeves, then put a different CD into the tray. "I guess I'm used to being alone in my room."

"At least you can carry a tune," Carey said.

"You can't sing?" Grace asked, her eyes widening.

Carey chuckled. "I can see that pedestal you have me on dropping a few inches," she said. "Hate to disappoint you but singing is not something I do. Yelling I'm good at." She smiled broadly. "Want to hear me yell?"

Grace smiled. "I'm quite familiar with your yell, thank you," she said. "I still can't hear out of my right ear." She wiggled her ear for emphasis, a light blue stud in the center of the lobe.

"If you had listened in the first place, I wouldn't have had to yell," Carey said. "Get back to your homework."

"You're the one that interrupted me," Grace pointed out.

"You were singing."

"But I sing good."

"Sing well," Carey corrected. "And yes you do, but I can't concentrate on this..." She tapped the folder. "When you're singing."

"I'll be quiet," Grace said, smiling as she pushed the CD tray in. "Sorry you get distracted by me."

"It's all right," Carey said, looking down at the paperwork in front of her, then realizing what the young woman said. *I'm not distracted by you,* she thought to herself, her eyes flicking to see Grace still smiling as she typed. *I have got to watch what I say around you.* Reluctantly, she turned her attention back to the work in her lap. Within minutes Grace was humming again. *I knew you couldn't last.*

"I know the angel, I feel heaven in your wings. You are an an-gel, I can surely hear you sing. Because you ta-ake me so-o light-ly, I know...I know that I can fly..." Grace resumed her humming, apparently oblivious to having burst out in song. Carey shook her head and gave up, accepting the occasional breaks in concentration without comment.

"I hate leaving you," Grace said. "Especially when I won't see you again until next summer." She let her suitcase drop on the floor.

"Won't see me again?" Carey looked at the framed photo of herself next to the bed, taped to the window, and the one tacked to the corkboard. "You have a whole roll of film in there," she said, tapping the suitcase with her foot. "We talk on the phone every week and you know you can always call any other time if you need to." She opened her arms. "Come here." Grace moved quickly. "I care about you, Grace. I really do."

"You didn't have to do this," Grace said as Tom stepped back and waved her inside. "It's not really something to celebrate."

"Are you kidding?" he said as they made their way into the kitchen where Stuart was busily slaving over the stove. "Stuart, Miss Thing here doesn't think getting off probation is worth having a party."

Stuart wiped his hands on the apron and reached for his drink. "Any excuse will do," he said. "I'm surprised he didn't throw one for Butterfly Recognition Day."

"When's that?" Tom asked, feigning excitement. "We could hang butterflies from the ceiling and have a guess the species contest."

"I don't know why I put up with him," Stuart said.

"Because I'm so good in bed," Tom said, patting his older lover on the rear as he headed for the refrigerator. "Beer, Grace?"

"I'm under twenty-one," she reminded him.

"So am I," Tom answered, pulling out two bottles of beer. "You driving?"

"You know I don't have a license or a car," she said, taking the offered bottle. "I just don't want to do anything to get Stuart in trouble."

"It's my house," Stuart said. "What I allow to go on here is my business. Speaking of which, no more probation means no more drug tests, right?"

"Right," she said, taking a sip of beer. *Just one...maybe two. I won't get drunk.* "No more peeing into a cup while someone watches." She shuddered. "God, I hated that."

"I made sure to have something special here for you," Tom said. "Let me go get it." He ran up the stairs, returning a few seconds later with a tall red acrylic waterpipe. "I've been waiting how many months now to share a hit with you?"

"Oh, I don't know about that," she said, though she was sorely tempted to take him up on the offer. "I'd better not."

"Come on," Tom said. "You told me you used to get stoned. I thought that'd be the first thing you'd want once you were free."

"Yeah, well, I don't think Carey would like it."

"We didn't invite her," Stuart said. "We won't say anything but it's up to you. Tom, don't push her."

"Maybe later," she said, surprised the bottle in her hand was half empty already. "So who else did you invite?"

"Oh, just a few friends," Tom said. "Michelle, Susan, Mary, Jimmy..."

"You didn't invite him, did you?" Stuart asked. "You know I don't care for him."

"He's bringing a date, so he won't bother you," Tom said, setting the bong on the counter. "Grace, it's here if you want some."

"Okay."

"Ready for another?" he asked, pointing at her beer.

"No, I'm good for now," she said.

"I almost ordered a keg," Stuart said. "But I decided bottles would be easier. There's plenty of beer, though; help yourself."

"I'm not planning on having too many," she said. "I promised Carey I wouldn't get drunk at a party."

"You need to get a girlfriend who's not such a prude," Tom said.

"She's not a prude," Grace said. "Well, maybe a little, but do you know how many women are raped at college parties each year?"

"The only guys here are gay," Stuart said. "You're safe."

"Uh-huh." She tipped the bottle again, taking several swallows. "You said you invited Susan. You know she's always coming on to me."

"Does she?" Tom said, turning to Stuart and giving him a sly wink.

"Don't give me that 'does she' bullshit. You know she does."

"Lighten up, Miss Thing. It's not like I set you up on a blind date or anything. There'll be plenty of people around to protect you from her." He put a hand on her shoulder. "Besides, she's nice. Why not have a little fun until Miss Iceberg thaws out enough to give you a chance." He looked over his shoulder at Stuart and added. "If she ever does."

"She will."

"For your sake, I hope she does, sweet cake. But there's no law against having a little fun, is there? I mean it's just a party. No one expects you to go to bed with her, so relax. It'll be a blast." A song came on that Tom liked and he grabbed her hands and started dancing around the kitchen with her. Grace couldn't help but laugh and join in the fun.

"Hey, Grace, wait up."

"Hi, Tom."

"You have any more finals?"

"No, that was my last one. I can't believe it's finally summer. My brain could use a break."

"You taking any summer classes?"

231

"No," Grace said. "I've got a chance to work at the Waterhouse full time."

"Oh, nice tips."

"I hope so," she said. "They're raising tuition next year, you know."

"Too bad for my parents," he said.

"You're so lucky you don't have to worry about money for school."

"Don't I know it."

"Well, I do get a week with Carey before my new shift starts. She's going to her cottage for a fishing trip, and I convinced her to take me with her," Grace said. "Just us and a lake full of fish. I can't wait."

"Playing with smelly fish is not my idea of fun, sweet thing," he said, wrinkling his noise.

"I've never been fishing, but Carey loves it. I really don't care what she wants to do, as long as she lets me tag along."

"Hey, come out with us tonight. It's eighties night at the Straw. It'll be a blast."

"I shouldn't," she said. "You know I have to watch every penny."

"Let us treat."

"I can't do that," she said. "How much do you think it's going to cost?"

"No more than twenty bucks, and if it does, Stuart and I will cover it. Come on, Grace. It'll be fun. A real blast." He batted his eyes at her. "Please?"

"Oh, all right," Grace said, laughing at his puppy-dog antics. "Where is it?"

"We'll pick you up. Do you have a tie?"

"Now why would I have a tie?"

"Because it's eighties night, silly," he said. "You have to wear a thin leather tie and a button-down shirt, preferably white. That was the style back then."

"I don't have anything like that."

"We do," he said proudly. "We'll swing by around seven thirty."

"I feel silly," Grace said as she stepped out of the car. "Are you sure I need the hat?"

"Oh you are one sexy dyke tonight," Tom said. "The girls are going to just fall all over you."

"I don't want the girls to fall all over me," she said. "You promised to show me how to play pool."

"I did," he said. "But don't be surprised when they start asking you to dance. Very déclassé to refuse." He nudged her shoulder. "See?"

Grace turned to see and colored instantly when the two women smiled at her. "Oh God. Tom, I can't do this."

"Oh yes you can," Stuart said, hooking his arm through hers. "You're going to die. It's absolutely fabulous in here."

Fabulous was not the word Grace would have used to describe the Last Straw. Dim, smoky, seedy, and loud were the terms that came to her mind. Once through the door, they had to navigate past the bar and what Tom explained was the "meat rack," a rail that ran along the wall opposite the bar where people looking for a companion would stand. Beyond the bar was the largest area, half decorated with neon lights and mirrors where everyone danced and the other half done in a combination of license plates and hubcaps where the pool table sat. The back section was the pinball machines and small tables that were used more for a place to put drinks down than to sit at. "I've got the first game," Tom said, walking over to the chalkboard and adding their names to the list.

"I'll get the first round," Stuart said. "What can I get you, Grace?"

"Do they have coffee?"

"In ten different flavors," he said. "I know what he wants, a virgin piña colada. Wait here, I'll be right back. I'll get you the mocha hazelnut, you'll love it."

Grace kept an eye on Tom as he stopped to talk to someone, unaware that she was being watched until she felt the warmth of another body pressing against her right side. "Hello," the soft voice purred. "I haven't seen you here before." The woman held her hand out. "Rachel."

Oh, easy on the makeup, Grace thought as she shook hands. "Grace."

"Would you care to dance, Grace?"

"No, thank you," she said. "Besides, how do you dance to this?"

"The DJ takes requests," the older woman said, her cigarette breath too close for Grace's comfort.

"Excuse me," Grace said, walking away and over to Tom. "Don't leave me alone again," she said. "That Rocky Horror reject just tried to pick me up."

"Rachel?" Tom laughed. "I'm sorry, I didn't warn you about her. She's here every night. She likes the young ones."

"Apparently," she said. "What is that?" she asked, pointing at the television mounted high on the wall, the angle of which made it impossible for her to see it before. "Oh no, are they? They are. Tom, they're—"

"I know," he said with a grin. "We can't rent them in the video stores but we can come here and watch them for free. Guess that's not your cup of tea, huh?"

Grace looked away from the television. "Seeing two guys going at it is not my idea of fun," she said.

"Hang around," he said. "They show the girls around midnight."

233

Stuart arrived with the drinks, setting them on the wide rail that ran along the wall. "Isn't the music great?" he said. "I can't believe they're playing *Puttin' On The Ritz.*"

"He loves the era of glam rock and video music infancy," Tom said. "Ah, she sank the eight ball. I'm next. I'll win the table and then I'll show you how to play." Tom walked over to the cue rack and selected the one he wanted, then introduced himself to the woman who currently ran the table. Grace watched, wondering what was taking so long. Then Tom and the woman approached. "She wants to play doubles."

"Oh," Grace said, looking at Stuart. "Go ahead. I'll watch."

"No," Tom said. "You and me against the two of them."

Grace smiled and shook her head. "I don't know how to play."

"That's okay," the beefy teen with straight black hair and gothic makeup said. "Mary doesn't know how to play either." She held out her hand, pale white in stark contrast to the black fingernails. "I'm Cassie."

"Grace."

"Nice to meet you, Grace. You guys rack."

"I'll do it," Tom said, reaching above the light for the triangle.

"They get to break," Stuart explained. "Then you and Tom alternate shots. You'll either be going for the high balls or the low balls based on what they end up getting. The low balls are solids and the high balls are stripes."

Grace nodded, taking a sip of her flavored coffee while Tom set the balls on the table, then stepped back. Cassie made the break well, scattering the balls all over the table. "Stripes."

"So you two have solids," Stuart said. "Now watch how Tom's holding the cue stick. See the fingers? Nice and smooth, just line up your shot and let it go." Tom sank two, then missed. Mary took her shot, sending the cue ball into the pocket. "Your turn," Stuart said.

Grace took the offered cue from Mary, then walked over to Tom. "Now what do I do?"

Tom took the cue ball and set it on the table, lining up an easy shot at the two ball into the corner. "Okay, come over here, lean over, and just hit it straight on." He positioned her fingers. "Not too hard and not too soft."

"And I'm supposed to know what's too hard and what's too soft, right?" she asked, giving him a bump with her hip.

"Just hit the cue ball hard enough to send it into the two ball."

"The white ball into the blue, right?"

"Right."

Grace looked down the line of the cue stick, the tip of her tongue sticking out between her lips. Pulling the cue back, she sent it forward with what she thought was a good medium force. The cue ball smacked into the two ball, then bounced off the table.

"Scratch," Cassie said.

"Shit," Grace said, handing the stick back to Mary.

"A little softer next time," Tom said, handing her drink to her. Grace brought the mug to her lips just as Cassie moved close and whispered in her ear.

"Hey, sexy, there's some smoke going on out on the deck."

"Thanks, but I'm fine here," Grace said.

"Open invitation," Cassie said, moving to the other side of the table to make her shot.

"Having fun?" Tom asked.

"Sure," Grace said. "I've been propositioned by a Rocky Horror reject, seen a gay porn video, and had a joint offered to me."

"Oh good, and Stuart was worried you wouldn't have any fun," Tom said. "Your shot."

"Okay," Grace said, looking at the half dozen balls on the table. "What should I go for?"

Tom frowned. "You don't really have any decent shots," he said. "It's a long shot but you could try for the four in the far corner."

Grace tried to position herself. "It's too far away."

"Lean over the table," he said. "Just don't move any of the other balls."

Grace looked at the shot again. "All right, but don't yell at me when I miss." Carefully she leaned over the table, then situated the cue stick where she wanted it. *Don't miss. Don't miss.* Nervously she sent the cue forward, connecting with the white ball and sending the four ball into the pocket. When she straightened up, it was to the sound of a wolf whistle and clapping from behind.

"Thank you," Mary said when Grace turned around.

Embarrassed by the blatant action, Grace nodded and quickly walked over to Tom and Stuart. "I can't believe you didn't warn me she was standing there," she said, lightly punching Tom's arm.

"That's Mary Barracuda," Tom said. "She goes after all the ladies. Come four o'clock if she's still here she'll go after Rachel."

Grace shuddered. "Ugh. I wouldn't touch her if she was the last woman on earth."

"Enough to send you straight, eh?" Stuart joked.

"No way," she said. "I'd just stock up on batteries."

"And rent a lot of adult movies," Tom added.

"I don't have a VCR," she said. "Just the thirteen-inch TV my Dad got me." She smirked. "Maybe I should ask for a VCR for my birthday." She turned at the light touch on her shoulder.

"Would you care to dance?" Mary asked.

"Actually, I—"

"One dance," the redhead said, tugging Grace's arm. Grace reluctantly followed the redhead to the dance floor just as the music changed. *No, not a slow song,* she groaned mentally as a Marvin Gaye classic began to play. Hands went around her waist, pulling her close enough that their bodies touched.

"You're very pretty," Mary said, her hands moving to Grace's hips. "I'd love to go out with you sometime."

"Thanks, but I'm interested in someone," Grace said, taking a step back to put some distance between them, her hands barely reaching the redhead's shoulders.

"In the meantime, you're here, I'm here, why not have a good time?" Mary said, her roaming hands moving up Grace's sides.

"No," Grace said. "I told you. I'm interested in someone."

"Lucky her," Mary said, her fingers tracing the waistband of Grace's jeans. "So there's no chance?"

"It's look, don't touch," Grace said, politely but firmly removing the redhead's hands. "I'm taken."

"Close your eyes," Carey said, and Grace complied without asking why. The sun was setting and Carey could see the color spreading across the sky. She knew the lake would be breathtaking with a sky like that reflected in all its glory in the shimmering waters. They emerged from the woodland and Carey pulled the truck to the side of the road. Below she could see the small community of Packard, and she smiled. "Keep them closed. I'm going to come around and get you."

Grace couldn't help but giggle and wonder what her mentor was up to. The truck door opened and Carey took her hand and helped her out, then led her to the perfect spot to view the panorama below them.

"Okay, you can open them now."

"Wow," was all Grace could say. This had to be about the most beautiful sight the city girl had ever seen. The timing could not have been better, the lake and the sky merging into one in glorious array of color.

"I love this view," Carey said, taking a deep breath and letting it out slowly. She pointed to the left where a few buildings could be seen in the distance. "Over there is the town proper. Population is about 1,800 year-round residents."

"Why don't more people live in a beautiful place like this?" Grace asked.

"Most people like the conveniences of city life. Packard has the bare necessities. If you wanted to go to a mall you'd have to be willing to drive an hour to get there." Carey walked over to a large rock and sat down. "In the summer the population swells to about 2,000. I only get up here a couple of weeks a year." She looked over at Grace and smiled. "But like I said before, I intend to move here when I retire."

"Where's your cottage?" Grace asked as she walked over to stand by her friend.

"See the little island at the north side of the lake?"

Grace squinted and shook her head. "No, I don't...oh, wait, I see it. That tiny little speck is an island? Don't tell me you have a cottage on that little bit of ground?"

Carey laughed. "It's bigger than it looks from here, but, no, that's just my landmark. I'm east of the island tucked back against that stand of trees." She stood up and brushed off her pants. "Come on. I'm gonna buy you dinner at Martha Jane's Diner. She serves the best chicken fried steak you ever tasted."

"Mm, can't wait," Grace said as she followed Carey back to the truck.

"Wake up, sleepyhead," Carey called through the door.

"Let me sleep a little longer," Grace said, as she buried her head under her pillow. She started to drift off again when suddenly her covers were yanked off and Carey grabbed her ankles and pulled her to the bottom of the bed.

"What?" Grace said, blinking rapidly.

"I've got the coffee on and the batter for pancakes ready. Now get up. We need to get out there while the fish are biting."

Grace looked at the window. "But it's still dark out."

"Won't be by the time we get out there." Carey reached out and grabbed her hands, pulling her to her feet. "You hit the bathroom and I'll start cooking."

Grace laughed as Carey turned and marched from the room. "A little anxious, aren't we?"

"Hey," Carey called from the other room. "I don't get up here much and I don't intend to waste a moment."

Grace shook her head and padded to the bathroom.

"How will I know when I get one?"

Carey grinned. "Don't worry, you'll know."

"But how?"

"When you feel a tug on the line, you've got one. Or when you see the bobber go under, you've got one." Carey handed Grace a pole. "When that happens you give a quick jerk to set the hook."

Grace nodded. "It doesn't sound so hard."

"It's not, once you get the hang of it." Carey glanced back at her boat and shook her head. She had wanted to take it out on the lake, but one of her renters failed to tell her that they had damaged it. *Shouldn't take too long to repair*, she thought. *We'll take it out tomorrow.*

Grace looked at the bucket of thawed-out shrimp that Carey had brought along for bait. "I thought you were supposed to use worms for bait?"

"You can use lots of things for bait. Worms, crickets, chicken liver, cheese. Any number of things, really."

"They all sound pretty disgusting to me. Well, all except the cheese."

Carey laughed. "If you're going to be a first-class fisherwoman, you'll try them all." She walked to the edge of the dock. "The water's pretty shallow around the dock, so you're going to have to cast your hook out to the deeper water. I want you to practice a few casts before you bait your hook. Watch me."

Grace watched everything the older woman did and it looked pretty easy to her.

"Piece of cake," she said, taking her rod and flipping it back over her shoulder, then screaming out as the fishhook embedded itself in her backside. She dropped her pole and grabbed Carey's arm. "Get it out!"

"Turn around and let me see," Carey said, trying her best not to laugh at the whimpering young woman.

Grace turned around, but she flinched every time Carey tried to touch her.

"You're going to have to be still, Grace."

"Okay, just get it out...please." Grace bent over and squeezed her eyes shut. She held her breath and tried to be as still as possible.

"Got it."

"Ouch!" Grace stood up, rubbing her backside.

"Come on," Carey said. "Lets go back to the cottage and clean you up. We don't want that pretty little ass of yours getting infected." She couldn't hold back the laughter any longer, tears running down her cheeks as she watched Grace stomp back toward the house.

Carey retrieved her first aid kit from the truck and joined Grace in the cottage. The sight that greeted her when she opened the door caused her to stop dead in her tracks, her breath catching. Grace was standing with her jeans and panties down around her ankles, trying to look over her shoulder at her injured butt.

"Does it look bad?"

Carey didn't need an invitation to stare at the beautiful young woman. She couldn't help herself. "Not too bad," she finally answered, pulling herself out of her daze. "Go lie down on the couch and I'll be right there."

Grace didn't miss the look of desire that flashed in Carey's eyes. *Hmm,* she thought. *That hook hurt like hell, but it just might have been worth it.* Grace kicked off her jeans and walked to the couch, aware that the older woman's eyes never left her.

Carey knelt down next to the couch and opened up her kit. She dabbed at the wound with a cotton ball that had been saturated with hydrogen peroxide. She felt the young woman tremble, heard a small gasp.

"Did I hurt you?"

"No, it feels wonderful."

"Behave," Carey said, sticking a bandage over the hook bite, then giving a small slap to the other cheek. "Now are we going to do some fishing or what?"

Grace put her suitcase on her bed and turned to say good-bye to Carey. The week at the cottage had gone too fast, and it seemed that every time they had to part it was harder to say good-bye. "I had a great time, even if I did rip a hole in my ass."

"I had fun too. I'm glad you came."

"Can I have a hug?"

Carey smiled and opened up her arms. "Come here."

Grace rushed over and wrapped her arms around her. "I wish you could stay longer."

"I wish I could too, but I'll call you."

"Remember that I'm working until closing at the Waterhouse now, so I'm not sure when you should call."

"Are you sure you should be working that late? How are you getting home?"

"It's only five blocks."

"Grace, I don't like the idea of you walking home at that hour by yourself."

"It's a well-lit street. What else am I supposed to do? I can't waste the money on a cab and I certainly can't afford a car."

Carey's first thought was to offer to loan her truck but realized that would not be appropriate. "I still don't like it. Are you sure you'll be safe?"

"As sure as I can be. If I get worried, I'll see if someone can escort me home or give me a ride, okay?"

"It'll have to be," Carey said. "It's a nice restaurant, right? Not some cheap diner."

"People make reservations."

Carey still did not like it but there was little she could do. "Just promise me you'll be safe and not take chances."

"I promise."

"Good. If you do something stupid, I'll—"

"You'll make me do twenty, right?"

"At least," Carey said.

"I'll miss you."

"But we talk every week."

"It's not the same."

"I know."

Grace undid the top two buttons, finding the juice bar to be abnormally hot. She ordered a tall soda instead of her usual coffee, then headed back to the pinball machines to use up the quarters weighing down her pocket. She no sooner put a quarter in the machine than she was bumped from the side.

"Hey, good looking, what's up?"

It took only a second to recognize her friend. "Jan!" She gave Jan a hug. "It's great to see you."

"You too. How've you been?"

"Great, how about you?" The pinball game forgotten, Grace leaned against the machine. "You still working up at the mall?"

"Yeah," Jan said. "But I might get a promotion to the new store they're building out at the strip mall near the airport."

"Wow, that's great, I hope you get it."

Jan smiled. "You really look great," she said as her eyes swept over Grace's body. "But then I always thought you were hot. You have no idea how many times I came close to kissing you when we were alone."

"Jan, that was a long time ago."

Jan shrugged. "I know. I've got a girlfriend now and she gets really pissed when I screw around on her, so I'll behave. You got someone?"

Grace reached for her drink. "I'm working on it," she said. "You up for a game?" she asked, gesturing at the pinball machine.

"Sure."

Grace tossed another quarter in and hit the start button. "You can go first." She stepped out of the way.

"So how come I haven't seen you in here before?" Jan asked, her eyes on the silver ball pinging off the bumpers.

"I don't come here much," Grace said. "I just needed to get out tonight."

"I try to get out two or three times a week," Jan said. "Sondra and I fight if we're around each other too much." She smacked the machine as the ball went down the side. "Damn."

As Grace moved to take her turn, she felt Jan brush firmly against her backside. "So are you going to school, or just working?" she asked, hoping Jan would get the hint if she ignored the touch.

"Just working," Jan said, standing just behind Grace's left shoulder. "I make enough money. I don't need school. How about you?"

"Still at ICC," Grace said. "Working at the Waterhouse right now." She smiled as the lights began flashing. "Ha! Multi-ball."

"Lucky you," Jan said. "So you see anyone from the hill?"

Grace tapped the flippers repeatedly, fighting to keep all three balls in play. "No, not really," she said. "I talk to Carey a lot, but none of the other girls that were there. I heard Latisha was moving to New York City to live with one of her aunts."

"You still talk to Scary Carey?"

"Come on, Jan. She wasn't that bad. She's really a nice person once you get to know her."

"And how well did you get to know her?" Jan asked.

"Not like that," Grace said, though she did allow herself a smile at the thought. "But not for a lack of trying."

"You were interested in Scary? The same woman you told me you wished would get run over by a bus?"

"That was when I first got there," Grace said. "You know we were getting along really well by graduation."

"Yeah, but Scary?"

"Don't call her that," Grace said. "I really care about her. She's the one for me."

"Grace, don't waste your time," Jan said. "She's not right for you."

"How do you know?"

"Oh come on, you mean you're gonna be able to light up a joint in front of her or have a few beers? Sc-Carey's so straightlaced she'd never allow that."

"Once I turn twenty-one she has no say in whether I drink or not, and I'd rather have her than pot."

Jan shook her head. "Don't say I didn't warn you. You're only asking for heartbreak going after that one."

"It's my heart to break," Grace said.

"So, did you hear about that bitch Grenner?"

One of the balls slipped past the flippers. "Shit. No, what'd she do?"

"Tried to knock off a convenience store over in Iroquois. She was still on probation and just turned eighteen so they threw the book at her. She's serving a nickel at Irwin."

In quick succession Grace lost the other two balls, ending her turn. "Guess Sapling Hill didn't help her at all, did it?" She moved out of the way, careful not to brush up against Jan.

"Not a damn bit," Jan said as she pulled back the plunger. "Look at your score. I'll never catch up."

"Good thing we didn't bet on it, hmm?"

Jan gave her a rakish look. "Depends on the bet."

Grace smiled and shook her head. "What would Sondra say?"

Jan turned and leaned on the machine, ignoring the ball as it rolled down the center and between the flippers. "She'd say she's leaving me...again." She shrugged. "No biggie. I get a two-day vacation and then she's back."

"My turn," Grace said. "Doesn't sound like you two are very happy."

"Ah, we do okay," Jan said, draining her glass. "Buy you a drink?"

Holding the plunger to keep the ball from going into play, Grace jutted her chin in the direction of her drink. "I'm good for now."

"I know the bouncer at Kitty's. Twenty bucks and I can get you in."

Grace tapped the flippers. "And get caught underage in a bar? I'm happy being off probation."

"You wouldn't get caught unless the cops raided the place," Jan said.

"I'm not taking the chance," Grace said. "I'd hate for my dad to come down from Alaska just to bail me out of jail."

Jan shrugged. "Suit yourself. Wanna go out on the deck?"

"I don't have anything," Grace said, losing one of the balls down the side.

"I do."

"Maybe later. Hah! Sixty million."

"Twenty more and you get a free game," Jan said.

"I've done it a couple of times," Grace said. "Get a hundred million and Joey gives a free drink." She lost another ball. "Christian doesn't, so I'm glad he's not working the bar tonight." She smacked the flippers repeatedly, saving the last ball by sheer luck. "Whew, that was close. Hey, you up for a game of pool after this?"

"I'd rather dance," Jan said.

"You gonna behave?"

"Do I have to?" Jan asked as Grace finally ended her turn.

"Yes," Grace said. "I told you, I want Carey and I don't want to do anything to screw it up."

"She doesn't have to know," Jan said, pulling the plunger, then walking away from the game. "There, you won."

Grace reached for her drink. "Jan, I'm not interested."

"All right, I get the picture. She must be pretty special for you to turn down a chance to get laid."

"She is," Grace said.

"So do I get a dance or not?"

"Behave?"

Jan gave an exaggerated bow. "I'll be a perfect gentledyke."

"You busy?"

Carey looked up from her paperwork. "Come on in, Sue. What's up?"

"Just checking on you. You almost took Kosnowski's head off."

"She shouldn't have tied McCafferty's laces together," Carey said.

"It wouldn't have anything to do with Grace going to Alaska for two weeks to go fishing with her father, would it?"

"I think it's great she's spending time with her father," Carey said. "She wants to show off her new fishing skills. She really was pretty good once she got the hang of it."

"But she won't be anywhere near a phone. How are you going to survive?"

"Don't start, Sue," Carey said. "I can survive two weeks without talking to Grace."

"Are you sure?" Gage asked. "You haven't had to do it since she left."

"She said if she saw a pay phone that she'd give me a call," Carey said.

"Why don't you just admit you have something for her?"

"We've talked about this before," Carey said. "It would never work out."

"And what crystal ball did you get that information from?"

"I don't need this today, Sue."

"Because you miss Grace," the petite woman said. "Admit it." She set her hip on the corner of the desk. "You have to dig through the photo album to show me a picture of your mother but..." She tapped the framed photo of Carey and Grace on graduation day. "Do you want me to start on your refrigerator?"

"She's too young."

"Joanna Carey, you are a great big coward," Sue said. "You'll use any excuse in the book to avoid admitting what's right under your nose."

Carey sighed and pinched the bridge of her nose. "Sue, she's going to wake up one day and realize that I'm not right for her."

"Better to keep her at a distance no matter what you feel so she doesn't break your heart, right?" Sue shook her head. "You're not doing a good job. Weekly phone calls, letters, visits, presents." She tapped the photo again. "Mixed messages, Carey."

"So what'd you think of that COBOL final?"

"Hey, Michelle," Grace said. "I think Professor Smith is a sadist. A hundred questions and write code?" She shook her head. "I'm glad I'm done with that. What are you up to?"

"June and I were going to head over to the Coffee Bean for a little while. You wanna tag along?"

Grace looked at her watch. "I have Spirmaker's final first thing tomorrow morning. I'd better go home and study."

"Grace Waters, you never take a break, do you?" Michelle made a clucking sound with her tongue. "I can get Linda to come along." She elbowed Grace. "You know she's dying to go out with you."

"I know and I'm not interested," Grace said. "I'd love to get a cappuccino but I can't be late getting back. I need to get a few more hours of studying in for Spirmaker's final."

"Look, it's not even five yet," Michelle said. "We'll head to the Bean, then maybe grab a bite to eat afterwards. Come on, it'll be a blast."

Grace debated for a few seconds. "All right, but no Linda," she said. "She looks at me like I'm dinner."

"Deal," Michelle said. "Come on, June's waiting for me at the car."

As they approached the beat-up hatchback, Grace saw June sitting on the hood, cigarette in mouth and a soda bottle with the label torn off in her hand.

"Hey, sexy," June said when she saw her.

"Hi, June," Grace said. "This thing runs?"

"Sure does," June said, patting the hood. "I had the engine souped up a bit. Purrs like a kitten or Michelle after a good night."

Always has to bring up sex, Grace thought. "I wouldn't know."

"I would," June said with a grin. She pulled the lever, flipping the driver's seat forward. "Climb in."

Grace looked at Michelle but seeing no concern on her face, squeezed into the small back seat. She reached between the seat bottom and back for the belt. "Where's the seat belt?"

"I don't know," Michelle said as she shut the passenger door.

"Don't worry about it," June said, starting the engine, then pressing the accelerator down several times. "I'm an excellent driver." She took the corner sharply, barely missing a cyclist. "Hey, after the Bean we can go over to the Brew and Beef. They've got the best steaks around."

"Don't you have to be twenty-one to get in there?" Grace asked. "I'm only nineteen."

June took her eyes off the road and looked at her lover. "She worries too much, doesn't she?"

"You only have to be twenty-one if you're at the bar," Michelle said. "If we sit in the back, we can usually get someone to bring us a few drinks."

"Watch the road," Grace said as they flew under the light just as it turned red. "The Bean is fine but I'll pass on the Brew and Beef." She was nervous enough about June's driving without having to worry about her being intoxicated behind the wheel.

"Suit yourself," June said, taking another corner with enough speed to send Grace hard against the door. "Hey, Grace, you ever been to Gary's Go-Karts?"

"Oh we have to go," Michelle said. "You'll love it. They've got the greatest go-karts around and they just got a new foosball game in the arcade."

Carey rolled over and fumbled for the phone, finding it before the third ring. "Hello?"

"Miss Carey? This is Richard Waters."

The tone of his voice was enough to bring Carey to full wakefulness. "What's wrong?"

"I'm sorry to call so late." She heard a shuddering breath before he continued. "The hospital called...she's been in an accident."

"Oh God," Carey said. "How bad?"

"I don't know." The pain and fear in his voice matched her own. "She was brought in by ambulance and the woman said...she said they were working on her."

"Mr. Waters, which hospital? The medical center?"

"Yes. The nurse said I need to get there b-but the airport's snowed in."

"Don't worry," Carey said as she stripped off her pajamas. "I'll get there as fast as I can and call you as soon I find out anything."

"I don't know her mother's number."

"Maybe the school had it on file for her," Carey said, pulling her jeans on. "If not we might have it here in the old records."

"I can't get there," he said just before there was a click on the line. "This could be the hospital. Hold on."

"Of course," she said, then heard a click as he switched over to pick up the call waiting. She took advantage to set the phone down and put her bra and shirt on, then put the receiver to her ear and sat down on the bed to put her socks on. Her mind raced with horrific images as she feared the worst. *Please be all right, Grace.*

"Miss Carey?"

"Yes, I'm here," she said.

"That was Dr. Ma—I can't remember his name." There was another shuddering breath. "He's treating my daughter and I can't remember his name."

"It's all right," she said. "What did he say?"

"They're taking her for surgery."

"Surgery?" She fumbled with the laces on her sneakers.

She heard him move the phone away and sniffle. "She's bleeding inside."

Carey covered her eyes and took a deep breath. "I'll call you as soon as I get there," she said.

"You have the number?"

"Yes," she said, shoving a small address book into her back pocket. "Grace gave it to me a while ago." She pulled her jacket off the hook and pushed one arm through the sleeve. "Mr. Waters, I'm sure she's going to be fine," she said, trying her best to sound convincing. "I'm leaving now."

"Okay. When you see her, you give her a big hug for me."

"I will," she said. "Good-bye." Hitting the button, she waited briefly for the dial tone, then with a trembling finger dialed another number. "Come on, come on, answer," she said as she heard ring after ring.

"Hello?"

"Sue, it's Carey. I need you to cover morning formation and PT."

"Carey? It's...almost two in the morning."

"Grace was in an accident. I've got to go. Cover me in the morning." She hung up the phone, snatched her keys from the hook and headed out the door.

Carey moved quickly through the automatic doors of the emergency room and headed for the first nurse she saw. "Excuse me, they brought a friend of mine in. Grace Waters."

"Are you family?"

"A friend of the family. Her father's stuck in Alaska. He called me to come down."

"Just a moment," the nurse said, turning and typing some information into the computer. "She's still in recovery," she said. "You can wait over there. I'll let the doctor know someone is here for her."

"Hey there," Carey said, when she saw Grace's eyes flutter open. "It's about time you woke up. You gave us quite a scare." She reached down and used her fingers to brush Grace's hair back. "Your dad's snowed in."

"It hurts," Grace said, wincing as she shifted.

"Easy," Carey said. "You just had major surgery."

"I'm glad you're here."

"Think I'd let you go through this all alone?"

"I was scared," she said, blue eyes locking with brown. "I've never been in an ambulance before."

Realizing what she was doing with her hands, Carey stopped playing with the short blonde locks and gripped the bed rails. "You needed one."

"What happened?"

"You were in a car accident," Carey said. "The doctor said you must not have been wearing a seat belt."

"Car?" She shook her head. "I don't remember."

"You were with two girls," Carey said. "Michelle something..."

"Michelle Blake?"

"That's it," Carey said. "I don't remember the other girl's name."

"June?"

"Could be. I really wasn't paying attention to that part," Carey said. "I was more worried about you."

"Are they okay?"

Carey reached down and took the teen's hand in hers, careful of the tubing. "Their injuries were minor compared to yours," she said. "They've already been released."

"I can't remember any of it," Grace said, holding her hand up to look at the IV tube sticking out of it, but refusing to release Carey's fingers. "I really did it this time, didn't I?"

"You're alive," Carey said. "That's what matters. Grace, you were thrown around pretty good. You broke two ribs and ruptured your spleen." She took comfort in feeling Grace's hand squeezing hers after hours of being still while she waited for Grace to regain consciousness. "You were in shock by the time they got you here."

"Ruptured?" She licked her lips. "Doesn't sound good. Can I have some water?"

"I don't know," Carey said, reaching for the nurse button. "It's not good, but it could have been much worse. They had to remove it."

Grace closed her eyes. "That really doesn't sound good. What does the spleen do?"

"Helps fight infections and clean the blood," Carey said. "They're giving you antibiotics through the IV." She pointed at the small bag piggybacked to the larger bag of fluids.

"Carey?" Her voice sounded small and scared, making Carey want to take the young woman in her arms and protect her from harm. "Can I live without a spleen?"

"Yes," Carey said, rubbing her thumb over the back of Grace's hand. "The doctor said you'd be more susceptible to infections but after a while your other organs will compensate and that problem will be minimal." She reluctantly released Grace's hand and moved out of the way as the nurse came in. "She wants some water."

"I'll check her chart," the nurse said, glancing at the monitor mounted on the wall. "Miss Waters, how are you feeling?"

"Tired," Grace said. "Everything hurts."

"I'll check to see what pain medicines you're allowed," the nurse said, picking up the clipboard hooked to the foot of the bed. "I'll let the doctor know you're awake as well."

"Shh, easy now," Carey said, gently touching Grace's forehead.

"Hurts," the teen groaned, her face contorted with pain.

"I know," Carey said. "They said the pain would come and go for a little while."

"Tell it to go."

"Do you want me to leave?"

"No!" Grace opened her eyes and tried to sit up.

"Easy," Carey said, pressing on Grace's shoulder to get her to lie back down. "Relax. I'll stay for a while longer."

"Promise?"

"I promise." She turned her head at the sound of people entering the room.

"You'll do anything to get out of one of Spirmaker's tests, won't you?" a thin blond man said, setting a small basket of flowers on the tray. He stopped when he saw Carey, his eyes widening. "Ohmigod! It's you!" He reached out and took Carey's hand in both of his, shaking it rapidly. "I am so pleased to finally meet you. I'm sorry, I'm Tom and this is my boyfriend, Stuart." He turned to the older man standing next to him. "Stuart, this is the one and only Carey."

Carey looked at Grace, who was blushing furiously. "What did you tell them about me?"

"Nothing, nothing at all," Grace said, trying to sound innocent and failing miserably. "Tom, don't you say a word."

"You finally let me meet her and you expect me to not speak to her?" He made a tsking sound. "Forgive her," he said. "I try, but you know these young dykes. You just can't tell them a thing about manners."

"Stuart Masterson," the older man said, holding out his hand. Carey guessed him to be in his early forties, gray dominating what was left of his short curly hair.

"Hi," she said as they shook hands.

"So, Carey, did she show you her stitches yet?" Tom asked, earning a smack on the arm from his lover. "Ow. Don't hit me. I didn't ask if she showed her the tattoo, did I?" His eyes widened. "Oops."

"Tattoo?" Carey gave Grace a stern look. "Don't give me the deer in the headlights look," she said. "Where is it, what is it, and does your father know about it?"

Grace looked around her to Tom. "You know when I get out of here I'm going to kill you, right?"

"Don't worry," Stuart said, slapping his hand on the young man's shoulder. "I'll kill him for you."

"Grace," Carey tapped her nails on the bed rail. "I'm waiting."

"Um...it's a heart with a double woman's symbol in the middle," Grace said, looking down at her gown. "Do you know how many stitches I got, or if they were staples?"

"I didn't ask," Carey said. "And you didn't answer the rest of my question."

"Oh, Tommy boy, you are in big trouble," Stuart said.

"It's um..." Grace blushed all the more and crooked her finger. Carey leaned closer. "Let's just say I'd love to show it to you but the boys would have to leave the room first," she whispered.

Carey swallowed as her mind raced with possibilities. "I think we'll let this one drop for now."

"Good idea," Grace said. "The pain is coming back."

"I think you're giving me an excuse," Carey said.

"If you really want to see it," Grace offered, reaching for the neck of her gown.

"No, no, that's quite all right," Carey said, giving the teen a look for teasing her. "You behave," she whispered so the men would not hear.

"I'll be good, I promise."

"I've heard that one before," Carey said, though she settled back down in the chair.

"So," Tom said, deciding it was safe to approach his bedridden friend. "Spirmaker said you can do a make-up after you get out."

"Thanks," Grace said. "I'm still going to kill you, though." She reached for Carey's hand, intertwining their fingers. "Can you stay a while?" she asked.

"A little while longer," Carey said, rubbing her thumb absently over the back of Grace's hand. *I'm going to owe Sue big time for this.* "Do you want some water?"

Grace swallowed and licked her lips. "Please."

Carey went to reach for the pitcher. "Um, Grace? You have to let go." She wiggled their linked hands.

"Oh yeah, like that will happen," Tom said.

"I don't want to," Grace said as she let go and tried to sit up.

"Stay," Carey said. "I'll help you." She poured a small amount of water into the plastic cup, then added a bendable straw. "Do you want me to raise the bed or help you sit up a little bit?"

"Help," Grace and Tom said at the same time.

"Thomas Michael, stop it," Stuart reprimanded. "You're embarrassing Grace."

Carey gave Grace a soft smile. "Nice and slow, all right?" she said, putting her right hand behind the blonde head. "That's it, easy." She waited until Grace had drunk her fill, then helped her settle back down.

"Thanks."

Carey indulged herself, taking a moment to smooth Grace's ruffled hair and ignoring the smirk on Tom's face. She watched as her young friend's eyes closed for a moment, then slowly opened again. "You need your rest."

Grace nodded. "I am getting tired, but I'm afraid if I go to sleep, you'll be gone when I wake up."

Carey leaned over and kissed her forehead. "I'll be here, I promise. Now close your eyes."

"Yes, sweet thing, you close those eyes. Stuart and I will be back tomorrow. We don't want to tire you out." He turned to Carey. "And you really don't know how glad I am to meet you. I was beginning to wonder if you were just a figment of her imagination."

"Tom..."

"Okay, okay. We're leaving before I put my foot in my mouth again." He blew Grace a kiss, then grabbed his lover's hand and dragged him out the door.

"Your friends are nice."

"Yeah, they are. I'm glad you got to meet them." Grace's eyes closed for a moment. "I'm glad you're here," she said as her eyelids fluttered. She forced them open in a desperate attempt to stay awake.

Carey reached over with the tips of her fingers and gently closed her eyes. "Sleep."

A tired smile curled Grace's lip. "Yes, ma'am."

Carey sat and watched as Grace's breathing slowed and sleep claimed her. This scare had really shaken her. It forced her to accept how important the young woman was to her. *I don't know what I would have done if I'd lost you, Grace.* She closed her eyes and sighed. A smile came to her face as she thought of Tom's reaction when he met her.

"What have you been telling them about me, young lady?" she whispered softly as she reached over and stroked Grace's cheek.

TWO YEARS

Grace closed her suitcase and looked around to see if she had forgotten anything. It had seemed to take forever for spring break to arrive. It was hard to believe that it was less than two months until graduation.

"Grace, dear, your friend is here to pick you up."

"Thanks, Mrs. Somers," Grace said, as she practically ran down the stairs, suitcase and laptop in hand. "I'm ready."

"Relax," Carey said, smiling at the young woman's exuberance. "I would have waited." She held out her hand to take the suitcase, noting Grace had grown even more beautiful in the last few months. The only visible reminder of the accident was a tiny scar on the edge of her chin. "Turn around and let me get a better look at the new haircut."

"You like?" Grace said, handing her the suitcase and spinning around in a circle.

"It looks great."

Grace decided she could wait no longer and wrapped her arms around the older woman's waist, mindful not to drop the laptop. "I've missed you so much," she said, inhaling deeply.

Carey opened the oven, then bent over to check the potatoes. A soft hand rested on the small of her back. "Few more minutes," she said, expecting Grace to remove her hand.

"Smells wonderful," Grace said.

Carey stood up, finding herself enveloped in the young woman's arms. "Grace."

"I've missed you so much," Grace said, resting her head on Carey's chest. "You said we had a few minutes."

"You can't behave for a few minutes," Carey said, though she let her arms hang loosely around Grace's shoulders. "I'm surprised you've lasted this long." She glanced at her watch. "Must be at least, oh, ten or fifteen minutes since you got a hug."

"It's been over an hour," Grace said. "Be nice and I'll show you my tattoo."

"You still haven't told me where it is," Carey said.

"Where do you think it is?"

"I have no idea," Carey said, refusing to guess and mention any body parts.

"You have ideas," Grace said. "You just don't want to say them."

"You're right," Carey said. "Stop teasing me."

Grace hugged tightly, then stepped back. "Okay, since you don't wanna guess, I'll have to show you." She walked over to the table and pulled out a chair.

"I don't think this is a good idea," Carey protested.

"Instead of calling you Scary, they should have called you Scaredy, as in scaredy cat." She removed her right sock and put her foot on the chair, turning so Carey could see her ankle. "I didn't find out until afterwards that it hurts more when you have it done near the bone. Next time I'll get it done on my ass, there's enough padding there."

Carey knelt down to get a better look at the tattoo. "Pretty," she said, tempted to trace the heart with her finger. "What prompted you to get this?"

"Pure spur of the moment kinda stuff," Grace said, sitting down and putting her sock back on. "Tom, Stuart, and I were walking back from a bistro when we saw the tattoo parlor. One thing led to another and I got this."

"And you want more?"

"Maybe," Grace said. "Would it bother you if I did?"

"I think tattoos are nice...on other people," Carey said. "It's your body, but remember, once you get one, it's there for life."

"You didn't answer my question," Grace said. "I know you were surprised, but I can't tell if it bothers you or not."

"How I feel about it shouldn't matter."

Grace growled in frustration and went into the living room. "Forget it."

Carey looked at the clock, frowning at the time. Sleep absolutely refused to come to her. She thought about reading but her glasses were in the other room. Just knowing that Grace was out there asleep on her couch was driving her crazy. Not wanting to get up and admit total defeat, she turned on the lamp and opened the nightstand drawer. There, on top of other letters, was the most recent one from Grace. She reached into the envelope and pulled out the snapshot that had been sent with the letter. *Her hair definitely looks better short,* she thought to herself as she looked at the picture. It had been taken at a party in someone's back yard; arms and backs of other people caught on the outer edges of the photo. Grace was laying on a chaise lounge, her eyes closed and her nipples showing prominently through the sheer material of the bright blue bathing suit. *You are such a tease,* Carey thought, setting the photo on the nightstand. "Oh, Grace, what am I going to do with you?" *Lay her down and make a woman out of her,* the voice inside said. *I can't do that,* she answered herself. *She's nineteen. I'm thirty-one.* Still, there was no denying the attraction, the desire that existed when she thought of what was beneath that bathing suit. *Damn it, Grace. Why do you do this to me?* Closing her eyes, Carey reached into her pajama bottoms, knowing sleep would come no other way.

"Where do you want it?"

"Just drop it anywhere," Grace said, setting her laptop down on the desk. "I'll try one last time. Stay for a little while?"

"I can't," Carey said. "I have a meeting this afternoon."

"One more hug?"

"You are incorrigible," Carey said, stepping toward her. Grace snuggled against her chest and made that happy sound in her throat that Carey secretly loved. Unable to resist, she nuzzled the blonde hair. "I'll miss you," she said, holding Grace tight.

"Promise you'll come to graduation?"

"I promise."

"I love you."

Carey pressed her lips against Grace's head. "I'm sorry," she said, brushing the young woman's hair with her lips. "I care so much about you."

Grace hugged tighter. "Like a sister, I know."

Taking a deep breath, Carey smiled and shook her head. "Trust me when I tell you my thoughts of you have been far from sisterly," she said, kissing the blonde head again. "You've made sure of that."

Grace lifted her head. "Then why do you keep holding back?"

"You're still in school," Carey said. "I'm over an hour away. It wouldn't be fair to either of us."

"But it feels so right," Grace said, resting her head on Carey's chest again.

"If it's right now then it'll be right later," Carey said, rubbing Grace's back. She debated for only a second before cupping Grace's cheeks and tilting the young woman's face up. "I will miss you," she said, her lips moving closer to Grace's mouth. "You're not the only one who hates saying good-bye." Grace's whimper when their lips met was almost enough to break Carey's resolve, but with great effort she ended the kiss after a few seconds. "I'll see you at graduation and I'll call you Friday night."

It was easy for Carey to spot Richard Waters amongst the crowd, the lumberjack being larger than most of the men there. "Hello," she said when she reached him.

"Miss Carey, mighty nice to see you again," he said. "Grace said you were coming."

"Have you seen her yet?"

"This morning," he said. "I think she was more worried about you getting here in time to see her walk across the stage than on actually graduating."

"It took some serious maneuvering to get a Saturday off but I did promise her I'd get here," she said. "I had to work until noon and then push the speed limits to get here."

"I'm glad you did," he said, slapping her on the back. "I wouldn't want to face my daughter if you hadn't shown up."

Carey gave a sociable laugh, wondering what exactly Grace had told her father about the two of them. Her thoughts were interrupted when she spotted another familiar face, or rather, a pair of faces. "Why don't we go find a seat?" she suggested as the couple unknowingly came closer to them.

He patted his camcorder. "I want to make sure I get a good view of her," he said. "I got a zoom lens last week just to be—"

"I think it's quicker this way," she said, knowing exactly who Richard had seen.

"I doubt Grace knew she was coming," he said.

"She didn't say anything to me about it," Carey said, her eyes narrowing as she got a clear view of Bob Garvey.

"Answer me a question, Miss Carey."

"If I can."

He turned to her and looked at her in all seriousness. "Is that the man that hurt my little girl?"

Carey met his gaze, blue eyes so much like Grace's, begging her to answer. "Yes," she said.

"Would you excuse me for a minute?" he said.

"Of course," Carey said, clapping with everyone else as the dean approached the podium. He bored her quickly, droning on about futures and endless rainbows of opportunity. Looking around, she spotted Grace's mother sitting on the opposite side of the arena, the seat next to her empty. *He wouldn't.* Dropping the program on her seat, Carey went off in search of Richard.

When she found him, it was too late. Richard's meaty fist had connected solidly with Bob Garvey's face, sending the smaller man to the ground with blood spurting from his nose. The angry father went to swing again but Carey stepped in front of him. "Mr. Waters, don't." She looked quickly to see Garvey's look of surprise at her identification of the man who had slugged him. "He's not worth it." As tall and strong as she was, Carey knew she would be no match for Richard if he chose to go after the man who had raped his daughter. "Don't ruin Grace's day."

"You son of a bitch," he snarled, scaring the smaller man into staying right where he was on the ground. "You go near my daughter and I'll kill you."

"I didn't do anything," the bleeding man said. "She's lying."

"Shut up," Carey said. "Or I won't stop him." She knelt down, letting every bit of her outrage and anger show on her face. "Your lying bullshit won't work on us, so don't bother trying. You're a pathetic excuse for a man. Why Grace's mother can't see it is beyond me." She stood up and took Richard's hand. "Let's get back. We want to be there when Grace receives her diploma."

It was so hard for Richard to turn and walk away, but he did. Carey was right. That bastard had hurt Grace enough. He couldn't let this escalate into something that would spoil graduation for her, too. She had worked too damn hard for it.

Carey knew there was no way to refuse when Grace ran at her with open arms. "Congratulations," she said when the younger woman embraced her. "I'm so proud of you."

"God it's good to see you," Grace said, her voice muffled against Carey's shoulder. "I've missed you so much."

"I missed you too," Carey said, her nose brushing Grace's short blonde hair. "Look at you. All grown up." Her breath caught in her throat when she felt a soft kiss on her neck. "Grace..."

"It's about time you noticed," Grace said, stepping back and taking Carey's hands in her own. "Dad wants to take me to dinner. Come with us?"

"Oh, no, you go have dinner with your father," Carey said, her skin alive where soft lips had kissed it. "I should head back anyway."

"No!" Grace gripped the older woman's hands. "You can't leave yet. Please." She moved closer, her black robe brushing against Carey. "I really want to spend some time with you," she said. "If it's a choice between you or Daddy, I'm going to spend all summer with him. I only have today with you."

"But it's your graduation day," Carey said. "Your father paid good money to get you to this point. He deserves to spend it with you." Pleading blue eyes did her in. "If your father doesn't mind."

"He won't mind," Grace said, squeezing Carey's hand.

"I get the feeling he won't have a choice," Carey said.

"He won't," Grace said, stealing a quick kiss before going off in search of her father.

You're getting too bold, Carey thought to herself.

"I'll be right back," Grace said, setting her napkin on the table and standing up. She left in the direction of the ladies room, leaving her father alone with Carey.

"You must be very proud of her," Carey said, reaching for her water glass.

"I am," he said. "3.6 average. And what about you, Miss Carey?" His eyes, so much like Grace's, pinned her. "Are you proud of her?"

"Of course," she said. "I told her so."

He smiled, his lips disappearing under his full beard. "I'm glad to hear it. A kind word from you lights up her day."

Carey looked down at her plate. "I don't know about that, Mr. Waters."

"Yes you do," he said. "You've had my daughter's heart for over two years now."

Carey rubbed her finger along the stem of the water glass. "Did she tell you that?"

"Graceful speaks about two things when she calls me. You and school, and guess which one comes first?" He rubbed his blond beard. "I've heard about every present you've given her and I see them all each time I visit. That young lady is ass over teakettle for you."

"I know," Carey said, daring to look at him. "I want you to know I've never—"

He raised his hand. "I know," he said. "Trust me, I know." His smile grew wider. "I believe you were the reason she gave for a thirty-five dollar purchase on her debit card from Happy Adult Products." He patted her hand. "Or the lack of you, as the case may be."

Carey blushed and picked up her water glass again. "Please don't tell me that's why she wanted rechargeable batteries and a charger for her birthday last year."

"Okay, I won't," he said, smiling broadly. "Grace is very open with me."

"Apparently," Carey said, draining her glass and wishing Grace would hurry back.

"I also know that you could easily break my little girl's heart," he said. "She worships the ground you walk on."

"I'm not trying to hurt her," Carey said. "Mr. Waters, don't you think thirty-one is a little old for her?"

He shrugged his shoulders. "It's not for me to say. It's up to Graceful who she loves, and she's chosen you. And after two years I think it's time you started calling me Richard." He looked up. "Ah, here she is."

"I hope you were talking nice about me," Grace said, waving her father down when he started to stand. Her soft blue eyes locked on Carey. "Were you?"

You don't want to know, Carey thought, nodding dumbly.

"Good," Grace said, scooting her chair closer as she sat down. "So what were you saying?"

"I um..." Carey looked to Richard for help.

"We were just talking about your presents," he said, winking at the dark-haired woman. "I hope that's the right kind of computer."

"It's perfect," Grace said, casually shifting in her seat. "Tom's got a program I can use to upload all my programs and data from the laptop into it and there's at least ten programs my friends can give me that I can't use on the old one."

As the happy graduate was talking, Carey was very much aware of the knee pressing against hers. *Oh, please don't tease me in front of your father,* she prayed as Grace continued to talk about computers, seemingly unaware of their bodies touching. As subtly as possible, Carey shifted her leg away, then reached for her drink. She had just taken a mouthful when a firm hand gripped her knee, pulling her leg back where it was before. Grace continued to chat away, acting completely innocent. *Fine, you want my knee that bad, keep it.* The food quickly lost priority when the mischievous hand began rubbing up and down her thigh. As casually as possible, she reached under the table and captured Grace's hand, putting it on the teen's thigh instead of hers. She picked up her fork and barely put it through a piece of chicken before the impish hand returned.

"Grace, did you tell your father that your final program worked perfectly?" Carey asked, giving the graduate a warning look. *Behave, please.*

"I told him," Grace said, her fingers still wandering over Carey's thigh and her blue eyes twinkling with danger.

You're not going to behave, are you? Carey discreetly reached under the table and stilled Grace's hand. "Have you thought about where you want to work?"

"There's a web design firm in town that offered me an entry level job, but I'm not sure if I want to take it."

"Why not?" Carey asked, feeling the heat of Grace's hand through the jeans.

"I still haven't decided if I'm going to transfer to a four-year school and continue my education. I have options; depends on how things go."

Carey felt her thigh squeezed by the hand trapped beneath hers. "Well um, I hope everything works out for you." *Wrong answer,* she thought when Grace looked at her with devilish blue eyes.

"I hope so too."

What do I say that you can't turn around on me? "So, you're spending the summer in Alaska?"

"Yes, Dad has the whole summer mapped out for us."

Grace used her foot to close the door as her hands went around Carey's neck. "I've been waiting all day to be alone with you," she said, her fingers sinking into the older woman's hair.

"Grace..." It would be so easy to just give in and take the kiss being offered. But then what? "Let's sit down."

"Sure," Grace said, guiding her to the bed. "We can sit here."

"Oh sure, that's much better," Carey said sarcastically, sitting down on the soft mattress. "I don't know if this is a good idea."

"Why?" Grace asked, rising to her knees and straddling Carey's thighs. "Do you have any idea how hard it was to sit there at dinner and not touch you?"

"You did touch me," Carey said, putting her arms around Grace's back, supposedly to keep the younger woman from losing her balance. "I'm sure that wasn't your father's hand on my leg. I'm surprised you didn't play footsie."

"You ignored me," Grace said, her arms going around Carey's neck. "If my dad wasn't there I would have made sure I got your attention."

"You had my attention," Carey said. "You know damn well I was aware of each time you touched me."

"Were you?" Grace smiled, sliding her knees out to sit on Carey's lap. "I love touching you." She drew a finger along the older woman's cheek. "I need to touch you." The delicate finger caressed Carey's lip. "And kiss you...now."

"We shouldn't," Carey weakly protested, only dimly realizing her hands were roaming over the young woman's back.

"One kiss," Grace said, cupping Carey's cheeks with her hands. "If nothing else, I have to have just one more kiss."

"Grace, I—" She was silenced by the young woman's fingers on her lips

"No. Whatever it is, let me have this first."

Soft lips brushed against her own, and Carey was helpless to stop them. *Oh that's nice.* Absorbed in the kiss, Carey was only vaguely aware that they were moving. She sank into the thick comforter, the welcome weight of Grace's body atop hers. The happy moans and hums drove Carey's senses wild as Grace thoroughly enjoyed herself, their lips parting and passion taking over.

"I've wanted you for so long," Grace murmured, her lips moving down Carey's chin to her throat. "Mmm, so nice."

"Grace," Carey groaned as soft lips found the sensitive spot on her neck. "We...we need to stop."

"I don't want to," Grace said, sighing as she undid the buttons on Carey's shirt. "Mmm, I want to kiss every inch of you."

"Oh, Grace..." Carey tried to think of her list of reasons why Grace should stop but the soft kisses on her breastbone were rapidly driving away all rational thought. Instead of her hands pushing the young woman away, her fingers sank into the soft blonde hair. The sport bra was pushed up out of the way, exposing her breasts to Grace's hungry gaze.

"Beautiful," Grace said, kissing the underside of each breast, then extending her arm and licking her lips. "So beautiful."

Carey could not stop herself from pressing down on the back of Grace's head, guiding her, though no guidance was necessary. She inhaled sharply when she felt soft lips close around her nipple, gently suckling while erotic moans of happiness reached her ears. "Grace...oh...a little harder...more...oh yes..." She arched into Grace's mouth, enjoying a feeling that her fingers could never duplicate. Reaching down, she found Grace's hand and brought it to her other breast, squeezing the young woman's hand beneath her own. "That's it...you won't hurt me." Her breathing increased and her hips pressed up against Grace's. "I want you," she said, jeans becoming a barrier she could no longer tolerate. "Lift up." The tight jeans refused to budge. "Grace..."

"Mmm," was the answer she received.

Carey arched up when Grace switched breasts, the cool air causing her nipple to harden even more. "Please." The delicious suction on her breast stopped when Grace lifted her head. "Take these off," Carey said, tugging at the jeans.

"You have no idea how many times I dreamed about you saying that," Grace said, kneeling up and bringing Carey's hands to her zipper. "Help me." Carey was frozen as Grace's fingers went to the bottom button of her shirt. "You want this off too, right?"

Carey swallowed hard. "Yes."

The next button was undone. "I love your breasts," Grace said. "I could worship them all day." Carey groaned as more skin was revealed, knowing she was falling under an erotic spell woven by Grace's words. "I wore this special," Grace said, letting the shirt slip off her shoulders, revealing a lacy bra with the closure in front. "Just for you." She leaned forward, bracing herself with her arms so her breasts were only inches away from Carey's face. "Do it," she whispered. "Please...touch me."

Carey watched, mesmerized as her own fingers moved to the small clasp between the cups, touching the soft skin and drawing an erotic moan from Grace. The cups fell away, revealing to her what she had dared not imagine for so long. "Oh Grace..." Lifting up, she kissed one dusty pink nipple, then the other, smiling when she heard Grace whimper. "Come here." Taking Grace in her arms, she positioned their bodies so they were lying side by side. "Just for me, hmm?" she said, hooking the strap with her finger. "Very pretty." She pushed the bra off Grace's arm, then ran her finger down the young woman's cheek. "Just like you."

Carey rolled over; lost somewhere between sleep and wakefulness. Her naked body pressed up against warm softness that moaned happily at the contact. "You awake?" she asked in a low whisper, not wanting to wake the young woman.

"Sorta," Grace said, reaching back and pulling Carey's arm over her. "I'm enjoying this too much to get up."

"We have to get up sometime," Carey said, opening her eyes and kissing the bare shoulder that was too close to resist.

"But if we get up then the day will start and you'll have to leave," Grace said.

"The day has already started," Carey said, lifting her head to look at the clock. "And we have less than an hour before I have to go."

Grace rolled over, pinning Carey beneath her. "Any suggestions on how to pass the time?" she asked, lowering her lips to kiss Carey's neck.

"You can't start this," Carey said, though her hands began roaming over Grace's sides. "We need to get up." The lips that had sent her to heaven and back the previous night claimed hers, the kiss going from gentle to hot in seconds. Carey brought her hands between their bodies and began gently rubbing Grace's erect nipples.

"Ohh," Grace moaned, her head dropping and her eyes closing. "Oh, Carey, that...mmm, that feels so good."

Carey smiled, remembering how easily she sent Grace over the edge the night before. "You want me to stop?" she asked with feigned innocence.

Grace shook her head vehemently. "Don't...oh yes, keep doing that. Oh that's nice."

"I keep that up and you won't last long," Carey said, lightly rubbing her fingertips over the undersides of Grace's breasts and smiling when the young woman frantically moved to get her attention back on the sensitive nipples.

"Don't tease," Grace said, groaning when Carey lightly pinched the erect points. "You're going to kill me."

Carey stilled her fingers. "I don't want to do that," she said.

"Argh...Carey!"

Laughing lightly, Carey resumed caressing Grace's breasts. "For someone so new to this, you certainly don't hesitate when it comes to letting me know what you want in bed," she said, raising her right leg squarely between Grace's legs. "I knew you wouldn't last long," she said in answer to the low groan and immediate rocking motion.

"Carey...I-I can't...feels so good...oh, Carey."

"Yes?" she asked innocently, flexing her leg muscles. "Are you going to do it again?"

Grace nodded vigorously. "I can't help it," she gasped, her hips moving purposefully against Carey's thigh. "Oh...Carey."

Carey was no less amazed than she was the first time. Grace's eyes were tightly closed, unintelligible sounds coming from her parted lips as her rocking increased to a frantic rhythm. "I'm right here," Carey said, rubbing her knuckles against the erect nipples.

"Mmm, it...oh...oh Carey it feels so good...oh...don't stop."

"I won't," she promised, using her thumbs and forefingers to pinch lightly.

"Oh God...Carey...Carey...mmm...I...I..." Grace threw her head back, teeth gritted as her body trembled. She gave a soft cry as waves of pleasure buffeted through her.

Carey rolled over, capturing Grace's mouth with her own. "I have to go," she said apologetically.

"I know," Grace said, gently guiding Carey onto her back and snuggling up against her.

"What are you thinking about?" Carey asked.

Grace kissed Carey's shoulder. "I was just thinking I'm happy I waited."

Carey smiled and pulled her closer. "You think so, huh?"

"You're a wonderful lover," Grace said softly. "You were so gentle and...and..." She kissed the bare skin again. "I don't know how to explain it." She sighed happily. "Better than I imagined it would be."

Carey kissed the top of her head. "Sweet talker."

"Carey?"

"Hmm?"

"Was I...I mean...did I do okay? Really?"

"Oh, Grace," Carey said. "You..." She rolled them over so the young woman was beneath her. "...were terrific." She touched Grace's lips with her finger. "Everything I could ask for...and then some," she added with a smile.

"Know what?"

"What?"

"Now I understand why lesbians don't use dental dams," she said, wiggling her eyebrows.

Carey smiled and groaned. "Don't get me thinking about that," she said, giving Grace a quick kiss before getting out of bed. "Sue's gonna kill me. I should have been on the road by now," she said, grabbing her clothes and quickly pulling them on.

Grace crawled to the edge of the bed and watched her dress. "I wish you didn't have to go."

"I wish I didn't have to either." She walked to the dresser mirror and quickly ran a comb through her hair. "Well, I guess I'm ready."

"Are you going to miss me?" Grace asked, a little pout forming on her face.

Carey walked to the nude woman perched on the edge of the bed. "I'm going to miss you desperately." She opened her arms. "Come here."

Grace fairly flew off the bed and into her arms. "It's not fair that I had to wait so long, and now you're leaving."

"I know, baby. But I have responsibilities. I have to go."

"Why did I have to fall in love with someone who's so...responsible?"

"I haven't a clue," Carey said, brushing her lips against Grace's. "But I'm awfully glad you did."

Grace wrapped her arms around Carey as she deepened the kiss.

"Believe me when I tell you that it's just as hard for me to leave you as it is for you to watch me go," Carey said when they finally came up for air. "I'd give anything if I didn't have to leave you right now." She leaned over for one last kiss, and then she was gone.

"It's about time you got here," Carey heard as she reached the mess hall.

"Sorry, traffic was murder," she said to Gage. "Any problems?"

"Not at this end. How was graduation?"

"Nice," Carey said. "Her father gave her a new computer for a graduation gift."

"Did she like your present?"

"Um...yes," Carey said, coloring at the thought.

"Uh-huh. Joanna Carey, tell me you didn't."

"How did PT go?" she asked, knowing full well her friend could read the answer on her face.

"You did," Gage said, moving closer so they wouldn't be overheard. "You slept with her?" she whispered.

"Let's talk about it later," Carey said.

"Oh no," Gage said, guiding her away from the noisy teens and over near the door. "So now what?"

"I don't know," Carey said. "Grace is going to visit her father in Alaska for the summer and then decide if she's going to go on to a four-year college or get a job."

"And what about the two of you?"

Carey shook her head. "I'm not moving to Alaska, so I guess it's up to her."

"Are you going to move her into the cabin if she comes back?"

"You're assuming she wants something more with me," Carey said, keeping her eye on the roomful of girls. "Maybe what happened will change things for her. You know, you try so hard to get something and once you've got it, you don't want it. Maybe she'll meet someone in Alaska."

"Uh-huh," Gage said. "And maybe I'll wake up and be six feet tall."

"It's possible, Sue," Carey said. "She's had the experience now. The thrill is gone, as they say."

A truly devilish look came over Sue's face. "I didn't know you were that lousy."

"I'm not," Carey said, giving withering glares to the girls who looked their way. "That's not what I meant." An image of Grace leaning over her, naked and on the verge of orgasm, flashed through her mind. "Far from it," she said with a rakish grin.

"Well I'm glad she enjoyed it," Gage said. "She certainly waited long enough."

Carey smiled when she heard the car pull up. "I knew you'd be early," she said, rising from the recliner and going to the door. When she opened it, an excited Grace ran into her arms. "Hi."

"Hi yourself," Grace said, brushing her lips over Carey's. "I've missed you so much."

"I've missed you too," Carey said, pulling her inside and closing the door. There was no hesitation as she leaned forward, trapping Grace against the door, kissing her with all the pent-up feelings that two months without her brought. "Mmm, so much."

"I need to get my suitcase."

"Later," Carey said, as she took her hand and led her into the bedroom. "I have to have you now."

"Absence really does make the heart grow fonder," Grace said as Carey started to unbutton her shirt. "What happened to the woman that ran from me for two years?"

Carey pushed the shirt over her shoulders, then leaned forward for another kiss. "She was seduced by a beautiful blonde vixen, and then spent two months alone dreaming about it."

"Did she, now?"

"Yes, she did. Now shut up and kiss me."

Grace wrapped her arms around Carey's neck, happy to oblige.

Carey rolled onto her side and pulled Grace into her arms. "That was so worth the wait."

"Oh, yeah," Grace said, leaning over for another kiss.

"I thought I was gonna go crazy from wanting you." Carey's hand slid down Grace's back and stopped to caress her lovely backside. "I just don't seem to be able to get enough of you. I love to touch you."

"Sweetheart, two months is nothing. You don't know what going crazy from wanting is until you spend two years waiting and hoping."

"It felt like forever."

"I know."

They held each other in comfortable silence, happy that the waiting was finally over.

"Carey?"

"Hmm?"

"I decided to take the job in Mohawk," Grace said.

"Did you?"

Grace snuggled closer. "Mmm." She kissed Carey's neck. "I couldn't bear the thought of being away from you for two more years."

Carey smiled. "I'm glad. I don't think I could bear it either."

"So what happens tomorrow?"

"What do you mean?"

Grace sat up and looked down at her prone lover. "Do I start looking for an apartment?"

Carey rolled onto her side and propped her head up with her hand. "When do you start your job?"

"Next Monday," Grace said.

Carey took several breaths before speaking. "You know it's an hour each way to Mohawk."

"It's a pretty ride."

"Not in the winter."

"Carey?"

"Hmm?"

"Do you want me to find an apartment?"

"What do you want?"

"You should know what I want by now," Grace said, gently rubbing Carey's belly. "I want to be with you."

"You sure? Two hours a day might not seem too much at first, but day in and day out might be a strain."

"Ah, but I forgot to tell you that I'll be working from home on my computer. I only have to drive into the office once a week, but I wouldn't care if it was ten hours away, I'd drive it happily to be with you each night." She leaned down and kissed Carey's shoulder. "But I'll never sleep on the couch again."

Carey smiled. "I didn't think you would," she said. "You worked too hard to get into the bedroom." She let her fingers play idly with the short blonde hair. "I miss you when you're not here. Sue can tell you what a bear I've been."

"I want to stay," Grace said.

"I can't make any promises, Grace."

"I know."

Carey looked at her for several seconds before answering. "I should say no."

"If it's a snowy night, I'll stay in Mohawk," Grace offered. "I can stay with Tom and Stuart or I can get a motel." She kissed Carey.

Slowly nodding, Carey gave in. "We can give it a try." She looked deeply into crystal blue eyes. "I care about you so much. I don't want to see you hurt, especially by me."

"I'm not seventeen anymore," Grace said softly. "I know what I'm getting into. I'm willing to take the chance." She lightly stroked the side of Carey's breast. "I want to be here with you."

"Grace, why are you taking these?" Carey asked, holding up a green and white pill case.

"Well not for what you're thinking," Grace said, taking the birth control pills from the older woman's hand. "I was getting bad cramps and the doctor said these would help." She set them on the counter with the rest of the things designated for the bathroom. "Do you want me to finish the unpacking by myself?"

"No, I said I'd help." Carey reached for another box. "Stuff. What room does 'stuff' go in?"

"Depends on what it is," Grace said, opening another box. "See? This stuff box is kitchen stuff."

"Grace?"

"What?"

"Are these what I think they are?"

Grace turned and blushed. "Um...they look like movies to me."

"I can see that," Carey said. "Interesting titles."

"Interesting movies," Grace said, wiggling her eyebrows. "Wanna see them?"

"I don't think so," Carey said, putting the videotapes back into the box. "I can't believe you own porno movies."

"Lesbian porno movies," Grace said without looking at her. "I had to have something to keep me occupied and out of trouble on those cold winter nights."

"Grace?"

"What?"

"Why do you have roach clips?"

Grace took a quick glance, then went back to the box she was working on. "They're not roach clips. They're nipple clamps."

"Nipple clamps? What are you doing with nipple clamps?"

"Not what you think," Grace said. "They were a gag gift from Tom."

"And what did you get him?"

"You sure you want to know?"

Carey shook her head and tossed the clamps back in the box. "No."

"You probably don't," Grace said.

"Um, Grace?"

"Hmm?"

"I know I'm going to hate asking, but what's this?"

"What?" Turning around, Grace saw what Carey was holding and smiled. "That's Little Carey. A poor substitute for the real thing."

"You know, your dad told me you bought something and hinted that's the reason you needed rechargeable batteries," Carey said, looking at the purple toy. "What's this piece for?"

Grace joined her. "It vibrates," she said, kissing Carey's chin. "Variable speed right on the—"

"I get the idea," Carey said, visions forming in her head. "And you..." She pointed at the longer end. "You actually used this?"

"Well," Grace said, wrapping her arms around Carey's waist and kissing the corner of her mouth. "You weren't there to do it for me." She moaned softly, then licked the older woman's earlobe. "Though I used to imagine you were."

"You imagined me..." Carey's voice dropped a level, reacting to the erotic thought and Grace's overtures. "Using this on you?"

"Oh yeah," Grace whispered huskily. "Every time I used it."

Carey swallowed hard. "I think I'll put this in the bedroom."

"Good idea," Grace said before she claimed Carey's lips with her own. "Want me to show you how to use it?"

Carey groaned, then disengaged herself. "Do that and we'll never get your stuff unpacked."

Grace wrapped her arms around Carey from behind. "You like that idea, don't you?" Carey nodded, her breath quickening. "Which part?" Grace lowered her voice to a husky tone. "The idea of using Little Carey on me or the idea that I think of you when I touch myself?" She cupped Carey's breasts, loving the way they felt in her hands. "Tell me," she whispered.

"Both."

"You have no idea how many nights I lay on that couch imagining that it was you touching me instead of my own fingers," Grace said. "How many nights I dreamed about you taking me..." She stepped up on her tiptoes and kissed the back of Carey's ear. "...touching me...going inside...nice and deep..." Carey groaned, covering Grace's hands with her own and squeezing hard. "You like that idea, don't you?" Grace asked, tracing Carey's ear with the tip of her tongue. "To have me lying there beneath you...around your fingers...mmm..." She ground her pelvis against Carey's hip. "Are you sure we need to finish unpacking right now?"

"You're incorrigible."

"No," Grace said, releasing Carey's breasts and reaching down to unbutton the jeans that were in her way. "I'm horny."

"You're always horny."

Grace lowered the zipper, then slipped her hand inside. "Only when I'm around you," she said, pressing against Carey's mound through the panties. "And right now I really, really need to make love with you." She smiled at the dampness her fingers found. "Then again," she said, pulling her hand free. "If you'd rather I behaved myself and made a pot of coffee..." She took two steps away before a strong arm pulled her back.

"I want something, but it isn't coffee," Carey said, her voice husky with desire. "You have no idea what you do to me."

"Show me," Grace said, sliding her hand under Carey's shirt and pinching the nipple she found.

"You want me to show you?" Carey asked, pulling Grace back against her. "I want you...right now, right here," she said, using her right arm to hold Grace still while her left rubbed the young woman's breasts.

"Oh yes," Grace hissed, reaching up to lock her fingers behind Carey's head and giving the older woman total access to anything she wanted. "Touch me."

"Mmm, Grace..." She nibbled the young woman's neck, groaning at the soft moans it produced. "I don't know how you do it," she said huskily, slipping her left hand under Grace's top. "No one has ever made me feel like this." She let go long enough to send the cotton shirt flying, then resumed holding Grace tightly against her. "You make the sexiest noises," she said when her lover sighed.

"Carey...I want..."

"Hmm?" Carey rubbed her fingertips over Grace's nipples. "What do you want?"

"I want...take me."

"I want to ask you something."

"Go ahead," Carey said, kissing the top of Grace's head.

"Earlier, you said no one ever made you feel like I do," she said, lifting her head to look at Carey. "What about Eve?"

"I don't like the idea of comparing the two of you," Carey said. "You're the one I'm with, not her. That should tell you something." She kissed the young woman's forehead. "And there is no comparison in the bedroom. Even if I wanted to use dental dams, they never would have been needed with her."

"But you like it," Grace said, snuggling into Carey's neck. "And I love doing it."

"I know you do," Carey said. "And trust me, I enjoy it, very much." She gave another kiss to Grace's forehead. "Very much."

"So if you like it, why didn't she do it?"

Carey shrugged. "She said she didn't like doing it. Our sex life was one of our bigger problems."

"It won't be one of ours," Grace said confidently. "I love making love with you."

Carey hugged her. "You are a sex addict and you're turning me into one. And I love making love with you, too."

Grace settled down, putting her head on Carey's chest. "I can tell," she said, closing her eyes and smiling happily.

Carey smiled, kissing Grace's forehead. "You can't go to sleep there."

"Not sleeping," Grace said, rubbing Carey's belly. "Just cuddling."

"Grace?"

"Hmm?"

Carey gave the young woman a soft, gentle kiss. "I love you," she said solemnly. "I should have realized it long ago."

Grace buried her face into the crook of Carey's shoulder. "It doesn't matter," she said, her voice cracking. "I love you too."

"Hey," Carey said softly, feeling the young woman's shoulders shake. "I didn't mean to make you cry."

Grace sniffled and hugged her tightly. "Happy tears," she said. "It's all your fault. I never used to cry before I met you."

Carey kissed the top of the blonde head. "I love you," she said, the words seeming as natural as breathing. Tipping Grace's face up, she kissed away a tear. "I love you."

Carey reached up and placed her grandmother's angel at the top of the Christmas tree. It was the first time it had been out of the box since Gram had died, eight years ago. She looked over at Grace, who was painstakingly placing one strand of tinsel at a time on each and every branch on the tree. She smiled at the look of sheer contentment on the younger woman's face.

Grace finished her choir and stepped back to admire her handiwork. "It's gorgeous," she said, turning and wrapping her arms around Carey and squeezing tightly. "Don't you think so?"

"Most definitely," Carey said, returning the embrace. "I haven't put up a tree in so long that I forgot how much fun it can be." She looked at the angel at the top. "And it's nice to finally be able to use Gram's angel. Eve liked a star at the top of the tree, and I didn't think it was worth arguing about."

"I love having her on the tree," Grace said. "She's so elegant."

Carey pulled Grace tightly against her. "These past four months with you here with me have been the happiest of my life." She leaned over and placed a quick kiss on Grace's upturned mouth. "Thank you for not giving up on us."

"Never." Grace took her hand and turned for the bedroom. "Come on, love. Five a.m. comes early, let's get some sleep."

Carey followed along like a lovesick puppy. Sleep was definitely not what she had in mind. Stripping out of her clothes quickly, she lay down and opened her arms, sighing when Grace snuggled in close.

"Comfortable?" Carey asked, gently stroking her hair.

"Mmm, very," Grace said, turning her head to kiss Carey's breast. "Nice soft warm pillow."

"You have a pillow. Right up here."

"I like this one better," Grace said, lifting her hand and cupping the soft mound. "Nice and fluffy."

"Just don't treat it like you do your regular pillows," Carey said. "You have no idea how many times I came out in the morning and found your pillow on the floor."

"Oh no," Grace said, running her fingertips over the soft skin. "I worked too damn hard to get this pillow. I'm not about to let it go." She shifted and when she did, the flats of her fingers pressed down on the outer edge of Carey's breast. "What's that?"

"What?"

Grace pressed down again, this time moving her fingers in a slow circular motion. "Right there. What's that?" She rubbed over the bump again, then moved to the other breast to see if it felt the same. She remembered the doctor had told her to always check the other breast if she felt something she wasn't sure of. If it was on the other breast too, then it was normal. She frowned as her fingers worked their way over the other breast and found no matching lump.

"It's probably just a milk gland or something." Carey wrinkled her brow. "Is that what you call them?"

"I don't know what you call them, but if that's what it is there should be one on the other breast too, and there's not." Grace brought her hand back to Carey's right breast, pressing her fingers into the flesh. "Here." She took Carey's hand and placed where her fingers had been. "Feel it?"

"I feel it," Carey said. "I don't know what it is. I never noticed it before."

"You don't check?"

Carey shifted, covering Grace's body with her own. "I don't check, but that doesn't mean it's cancer." She kissed the young woman's lips, hoping to erase the concerned look in the blue eyes. "I'll call tomorrow and make an appointment." She braced herself with her arms and waited patiently as Grace continued to examine her breasts for any other irregularities. "I promise I'll have it checked."

"I love you," Grace said.

"I love you too," Carey said, giving her lover another soft kiss. "Please don't worry."

Grace blinked several times. "I can't help worrying."

"Sweetheart, I'm too young to worry about breast cancer, and besides, cancer doesn't run in my family." She kissed Grace again. Her heart ached at the pain and worry in the blue eyes. "I love you, Grace."

"Joanna?" The woman in a white lab coat entered the room. "I'm Dr. Sapiel."

"Hello," Carey said.

"I understand you've found a lump on your breast?"

"It's probably nothing," Carey said. "But I promised someone I'd come and have it checked."

"Well, we'll just take a look," the doctor said. "Lie back, Joanna. That's it. That was the right breast?" she asked, checking the notes her nurse had written in Carey's file.

"Yes," Carey said. "It's on the outer edge."

The doctor nodded. "Put your right arm up behind your head."

"It can't be cancer," Carey said, closing her eyes to avoid the glare of the overhead lights. "Cancer doesn't run in my family."

"It could be any number of things," the doctor said, opening Carey's gown to expose her breasts. "About 80% of the lumps we find turn out to be benign, but we take any irregularity very seriously until we determine exactly what it is. Family history is something we look at, but 70% of women who develop breast cancer have no history of cancer in their family."

Carey felt the doctor's fingers exploring her breast, pausing when they found the lump.

"This is very small, Joanna. Most women don't notice lumps until they're larger than this. You must be very diligent with your self examinations."

"Actually, I didn't find it. My partner did."

The doctor nodded and moved to Carey's left breast. "That's not uncommon. Probably close to half the lumps that are discovered are found by a partner. You're very lucky. At your age we don't do yearly mammograms, so it's important that your breasts are checked regularly."

"How do we find out what it is?"

"I'm going to order a needle biopsy. That will tell us exactly what we're dealing with here. Let's not worry until we have to. I meant it when I said that most of these lumps turn out to be benign." She closed Carey's gown and picked up her file, scribbling a few notes before she spoke again. "I also want to do a mammogram to make sure there are no other smaller lumps hiding in either breast."

"Is that likely?"

"Not really, but I prefer to be cautious. Someone will be in touch to schedule the biopsy, and my nurse will check to see if they can get you in for the mammogram today."

"So what'd they say?" was the first thing Grace said when Carey returned.

"I have to go back tomorrow for a mammogram and she referred me for something called a needle biopsy to have the lump checked." Carey pulled Grace into her arms. "Don't look so worried, love. The doctor told me most lumps that are found are not cancer."

Grace buried her face in Carey's chest. "Is that supposed to make me feel better?"

Carey kissed the top of the blonde head leaning into her. "Yes, it is. So let's take the doctor's advice and not worry until we need to."

Grace sighed and squeezed tighter. "That does make me feel a little better," she said, "but I love you so much, I can't help being a little scared."

"I love you too."

"Joanna Carey," the nurse said, and Carey froze. She wanted to bolt out the door. Standing, she followed the plump woman down the hall to Doctor Sapiel's office. She had been dreading this moment ever since the needle biopsy proved that the lump was not a fluid-filled cyst. She had been told that this was the most common type of benign lump. The lump had been solid, which meant the chances that it was cancer had increased some.

"Have a seat, Miss Carey. The doctor will be right in."

Carey nodded her head and sat down, her hands gripping tightly to the arms of the chair. "Thank you." She watched the nurse leave and tried to still her racing heart. The next few minutes would determine the rest of her life, and she was not sure she was ready for what she might find out. The week of waiting for the results of the biopsy had been the longest week of Carey's life, and now that the waiting was almost over she wasn't sure she wanted to know. If they didn't tell her, it wouldn't be real.

The door opened and Doctor Sapiel walked in with Carey's chart in her hands. She glanced quickly through it then looked up. "Well, we do have a malignancy."

God, she really said it! Cancer! Carey's fingers were going numb from clutching the chair so tightly. It took a moment before she could speak. "I want this out of my body." It was all she could think of to say.

Doctor Sapiel nodded. "The growth is small and we have a good chance that it has not spread to surrounding tissue, but we have to be sure. I want to remove the lump, the tissue surrounding it, and two lymph nodes. We'll biopsy the nodes, and if they're clear, then we'll start radiation therapy about six weeks after the surgery."

"And if the lymph nodes aren't clear?"

"We'll go back and remove all the nodes and you'll start a course of chemo and radiation therapy."

Carey scheduled the surgery, then walked to her car in a daze. *This can't be happening.* Opening the door, she climbed in and picked up her cell phone. Why had she insisted that Grace stay home? She needed to talk to Grace, hear her voice. Needed something to ground her. She listened to the phone as it rang, emotions building with each ring.

"Hello?"

Carey heard the beloved voice and couldn't speak. She was almost choking trying to hold back the sobs. Breaking the connection, she dropped the phone on the seat beside her as the tears began to fall. Leaning over the steering wheel, her head dropped to her arms and sobs wracked her body. Helpless to stop them, she let the tears run their course.

Grace heard the truck pull up, and she was on her feet in an instant. She knew the news was not good when she saw Carey's eyes. They were red and puffy, it was clear she had been crying. As much as she wanted to break down and cry too, she held herself together. Carey was in enough pain right now without her adding to it by breaking down. There would be time for that later when she was alone. Right now Carey needed her to be strong.

"I guess the news wasn't good."

Carey shook her head. "I scheduled the surgery for week after next. I just want this damn thing out of my body." She tossed her keys on the table and walked over to Grace. "You know, I was thinking about something on the way home. We're pretty new, you and I. Perhaps it would be better if we ended this now. I'll be here when this is all over, if you're still interested."

Grace wrapped her arms around Carey and pulled her close. "Don't be silly."

Carey stiffened and pushed her away. "I'm serious about this, Grace. I want you to leave." She turned abruptly and walked to the window, unfocused eyes gazing out at nothing.

"You want? What about what I want?" Grace was angry now. "How dare you dismiss me as if this was just an affair. We made a commitment to each other." She walked over and took Carey's arm, pulling her around to face her. "I love you. I'm not going anywhere. Now drop and give me ten."

Carey's mouth dropped open, then a smile crept onto her face, and she dropped to the floor. "Yes, ma'am."

Carey finished her push-ups, then rolled over onto her back. "I'm sorry, Grace. I should have known better. It's just..."

Grace dropped to the floor beside Carey. "How could you think I would let you send me away?"

"Things are uncertain for me right now and I just wanted to give you an out. I didn't want you to feel stuck."

"Well, my dear, I am stuck...on you. They would have to pull me kicking and screaming from your side. We're in this together, love." She reached out and stroked Carey's cheek. "Got that?"

Carey turned and pressed a kiss into Grace's palm. "I love you." She pulled her down into a tight embrace. "I don't know what I did to deserve your love, but whatever it was, I'm awfully glad I did it." Tears began again and her grip tightened. "I'm scared."

"I'm scared too, but we're gonna get through this," Grace said. She held Carey in her arms until the tears subsided, then she pulled off her shirt and wiped Carey's tear-stained face. "Together we're invincible. This isn't going to beat us. You have to believe that, because I do."

Carey nodded and sat up, pulling her knees to her chest, hugging them to her. "If you can believe, then I can too."

"That's my girl," Grace said as she stood and reached down, pulling Carey to her feet.

"I like the sound of that."

"What?"

"Your girl. I like that. Although your woman might be more appropriate." Carey reached over and cupped her cheek. "And for what it's worth, I am yours, Grace. Heart, body and soul."

Tears started down Grace's face. "It's worth a lot." She pulled Carey in for a hug. "It's worth everything."

"I'll be here when you come back," Grace said, doing her best not to lose it as the nurse opened the flow on the IV.

"I'll be fine," Carey said. "Don't worry." She jutted her chin at the door. "Your dad's here."

Grace turned her head. "Hi Dad."

"Hi pumpkin," he said, moving closer and putting his arm around her shoulders. "Getting some good drugs there, Carey?"

The dark-haired woman nodded. "You keep an eye on her for me."

"Don't worry," he said.

The gray-haired woman exited the elevator and walked to the nurse's station. "Excuse me, I'm looking for my daughter, Joanna Carey? She was admitted this morning."

"Mrs. Carey?" Grace said, walking up behind her.

The woman turned and looked at her. "Yes, I'm Barbara Carey."

"I'm Grace Waters."

"It's nice to finally meet you, Grace," Barbara said, removing her gloves.

"You too, Mrs. Carey." Grace extended her hand. "I'm so glad you got here. She wasn't sure you were going to make it."

"Logan was snowed in until late last night."

"Well, you got here. That's the important part." Grace looked past her to the nurse's station. "Any word yet?"

"Miss Carey is still in recovery," the nurse said. "She'll be brought up soon."

Grace turned away from the nurse. "She's probably getting tired of me asking that." She led Carey's mom back to the waiting room where her father was nodding off in a chair. Hearing footsteps, he started awake to see Grace and a woman he assumed to be Carey's mother walking his way.

"Oh," he said, standing and wiping his hand on his pants.

"Dad, this is Carey's mom, Barbara."

"Richard Waters." He clasped her hand in both of his. "You've had a long trip. Would you like something to eat or drink?"

"Oh you don't—"

"Please," he said, releasing her hand. "It would be my pleasure and I'm sure Grace could use some coffee."

"Yeah," Grace said, reaching into her pocket for change.

"It's okay," he said, "my treat. What can I get for you, Mrs. Carey?"

"A cup of coffee would be great. And please, call me Barbara."

"Only if you call me Richard," he said. "Do you have luggage?"

"I had it sent to the hotel."

"I'll be right back then, ladies."

"Remember it's down on the second floor," Grace said. She patted the cushion her father had just vacated. "Please sit down, Mrs. Carey. You must be tired from the trip."

"It's more tiring trying to find my way around this hospital," she said. "And I'd like it if you'd call me Barbara." She smiled at Grace. "After all, we are practically family."

"Barbara," Grace said, returning the smile. "Carey said she told you what the doctors said they were going to do."

"She did," Barbara said. "In her own 'don't worry, Mother' way." She reached out and cupped Grace's chin in a manner reminiscent of her daughter. "How are you doing?"

"Scared," Grace said. "She tells me things in her own 'don't worry, Grace' way too."

"She loves you."

Grace smiled. "I know. I love her very much."

"Have you seen her?"

Grace nodded. "Yes. They let me in the recovery room with her for a few minutes, but she didn't know I was there. She never woke up. The surgeon told me she did just fine and not to worry, but she looked so pale. They told me it's the anesthesia, and she'll look much better when the effects wear off. I came up here a little while ago to let my dad know she was okay." Grace stood and started pacing. "I just wish they'd bring her up here to her room. I'll feel much better when she's awake and I can talk to her."

Carey opened her eyes and smiled. "You're here."

"Of course I'm here," Grace said softly, absently playing with Carey's hair. She cupped Carey's cheek with her hand. "How are you feeling?"

"Like I've been hit by a truck," Carey said. "What's it look like?"

"Like a bunch of bandages," Grace said. "The surgeon said everything went well." She traced Carey's lips, smiling when she felt the soft kiss on her fingers. "I love you."

"I love you too," Carey said, letting her head loll to the side. "I'm so tired."

"Then sleep," Grace said, leaning forward to kiss Carey's forehead. "Your mother is here."

Carey's eyes opened, albeit slowly. "She made it?"

"Yep. Got here a little while ago. Logan was snowed in and she had to take a later flight. I promised I'd tell her when you woke up. Dad's keeping her company. I'll go get her so she can see you before you fall asleep again."

Carey nodded, her eyes fluttering closed. "Better hurry, I'm not gonna last long."

Grace walked up to the couple seated next to each other in the waiting room. She smiled and shook her head. No one looking at them would believe that they just met. Barbara was laughing at something her dad had said, and they just seemed so comfortable with each other that Grace had to smile.

They noticed Grace at the same time, and both turned searching eyes her way. Barbara stood.

"How is she?"

"Tired, groggy. They're going to let her sleep off the anesthesia, then give her a bit of Jell-O. If she keeps it down, we get to take her home." She looked at Barbara. "She said to tell you to hurry. She's having a hard time staying awake."

"Hi, baby," Barbara said as she leaned over and kissed Carey on the forehead.

Carey's eyes opened and she smiled. "Hi, Mom."

Barbara reached over and took her hand, squeezing gently. "Does it hurt much?"

"Not too bad."

"Grace said you may be released today."

Carey smiled at the sound of her partner's name. "You met Grace."

"Yes, I did. Haven't had much time with her, but I like her very much."

"I knew you'd like her." Carey's eyes closed, but the smile stayed. "I know she's young, Mom, but I love her so damn much."

"From what I can tell, the feeling is mutual. I'm so glad you found someone that makes you happy."

"She does, Mom. I thank God every day that I didn't blow it. I tried so hard to discourage her, but she never gave up on us." Carey's eyes opened briefly, then fluttered closed again. "She never gave up." This time her eyes stayed closed as sleep claimed her.

Barbara reached out and stroked her daughter's cheek. "Sleep well, baby."

"She's sleeping," Barbara said as she joined Grace and her father in the waiting room. Looks like she's going to be out of it for a while."

"No sense sitting around here watching her sleep," Richard said as he got to his feet. "It's way past lunchtime. Barbara, would you care to join us for a bite to eat?"

"I'd love to, if you're sure it's no trouble."

"Trouble? Pshaw." He waved his hand dismissively. "I'm lucky enough to have two beautiful women at my side. No trouble a'tall."

"Your accent, are you from Maine?"

Richard smiled bashfully. "Ayup."

"Maine is such a pretty state."

"I live in Alaska now," he said.

"Really?" Carey's mother smiled. "I'd love to hear all about it."

"Dad, would you mind going without me? I'm not really hungry, and I'd kinda like to be here if Carey wakes up."

"Of course not, pumpkin. We won't be gone long."

Sleep had worked its magic, and a more alert Carey sat looking dejectedly at a bowl of green Jell-O. She was tired and hurting, her mind still clouded from the drugs she had been given.

"I don't feel like eating," she said, letting her head fall back against her pillow. Just holding her head upright was a chore that she simply didn't have the energy for at the moment.

Barbara reached over and picked up the spoon. She scooped up one square of the green substance, offering it to her daughter. "Just try one bite, baby. You don't need to eat it all."

Carey reluctantly opened her mouth and accepted the bite. Her mother offered a second bite and Carey frowned. "I thought I only had to eat one?"

"Just one more. Please?"

Carey sighed. "Okay, but this is the last one." She took the bite, then closed her eyes and let it melt in her mouth, not having the energy to chew.

"That's my girl," Barbara said.

Grace, who had been standing on the other side of the bed, reached over and squeezed her hand. "See, that wasn't so hard." She looked up at Barbara and silently mouthed, "thank you." She had been trying to coax Carey into eating with no luck at all.

Barbara just winked at her and smiled. "I know I'm leaving you in good hands, so I'm going to go to the hotel now and get some rest. I didn't really sleep at all last night and I'm beat." She leaned over and kissed Carey on the forehead. "I'll see you tomorrow, baby. Richard and I are going to meet for breakfast, then drive out to your place together."

"Thanks, Mom."

Barbara walked around to Grace and surprised her by pulling her in for a hug. "You take good care of my little girl, now."

"Don't worry. I will."

Grace watched the older woman leave the room. "I really like her." She turned back to Carey. "You're so lucky to have a mother like that."

Carey smiled. "I know."

Grace's stomach growled and she looked at the Jell-O sitting on Carey's hospital table. "Are you sure you don't want to eat a little more of that?" she said, pointing to the green squares.

"I'm sure. The doctor said I had to be able to keep something down, he didn't say I had to eat it all."

Grace reached over and picked the dish up. "Good, I'm starving." She spooned a bite into her mouth. "I like orange best, but beggars can't be choosers."

Carey shook her head and managed a small laugh. Then her eyes rested on something behind Grace. "Uh-oh."

Grace turned to see what she was looking at and found a nurse standing there with her arms crossed. She looked down at the empty dish in her hand and smiled sheepishly. "She ate all she wanted, honest."

The nurse walked over to Carey and picked up her wrist to take her pulse. "Any nausea?"

"No," Carey said. "When do I get to go home?"

"The doctor will be in to see you shortly. If everything looks good, you should be released to go home." The nurse checked her blood pressure, then walked to the end of the bed and made a note on her chart.

"I'm going to give you a quick lesson on how to take care of the drain," she said as she walked back up and pulled the cover back. "Don't worry, it's not difficult," she added when she saw Carey cringe.

Grace watched as the nurse pulled back the covers and picked up a bulb that was attached to a slender drainage tube that disappeared into the bandages under Carey's armpit. The bulb was clear, and Grace could see liquid in it.

"You'll need to empty this several times a day," the nurse said to Carey.

Carey frowned and looked over to Grace. "This is going to be fun." She looked back at the nurse. "Just kidding."

"It's very important that you keep the liquid drawing, or your arm will swell up like a balloon." Removing the bulb, the nurse emptied it out. "Now this is the important part. It's easier for the liquid to collect in your arm than to run into this tube, so we need to create suction." The nurse squeezed all the air out and folded the bulb in half so it could not re-inflate itself. She then reached for the tube to re-attach the bulb. "This creates a vacuum that will help siphon out the fluids that would otherwise build up in your arm." She opened her hand and allowed the bulb to open up and begin drawing liquid.

"How often does it need to be emptied?" Grace asked.

"That's hard to say. When it gets full, empty it."

Grace nodded and sat on the bedside chair. She reached out and took Carey's hand, squeezing gently. "Piece a cake."

"You think so?" Carey said. "Then you get to empty it."

"Do you need anything?" Grace asked for the tenth time that morning.

"I'm fine, hon. You don't need to hover over me."

"You didn't sleep well last night. You woke up before dawn and you didn't eat much, are you sure I can't get you something?"

"Grace, sit down." Carey patted the empty spot on the couch beside her.

Grace sat down and Carey reached over and grabbed her hand, squeezing it gently. "Sweetheart, I'm okay. Really, I am." She lifted the hand and pressed it to her lips. "If I need anything, I promise I'll let you know. Okay?"

"Okay, but remember, you promised. I'm gonna wait on you hand and foot. I don't want you lifting a finger. You got that?"

Carey smiled. "I got it."

The phone rang and Grace jumped up to get it. "Hello? Oh, hi, Dad. I didn't expect to hear from you this early. What? I don't know, hang on." She held the phone to her chest. "Carey, is your mother allergic to flowers?"

"No, she loves flowers," Carey said. "Why?"

"I don't know," Grace said, turning her attention back to the phone. "Carey says she likes them...I didn't ask that." She sighed and took the phone away from her ear again. "He wants to know what her favorite flower is."

"I have no idea."

"She said she has no idea. No...no...I don't know...try carnations or something." She sat back down on the couch next to Carey. "That sounds fine, Dad...uh-huh...yes, that's very nice...uh-huh...no idea, Dad...hold on, I'll ask."

"What?"

"He wants to know what her favorite color is," Grace said, making a circle motion at her head, then pointing at the phone.

"Blue," Carey said, shrugging her shoulders. "I don't know."

Grace put the phone to her ear. "Blue...well, if they don't come in blue then buy them in whatever color they do come in. Dad...Dad...hey Dad, Carey needs my help. I've gotta go...yes, Dad...uh-huh...I'll ask her...okay, Dad...yes, Dad...okay...Dad, what do you want? A biography? Okay, Dad, hold on." She covered the receiver and turned to Carey.

"What does he want to know?"

"He wants to know if your mother likes chocolate," Grace said, holding out one finger. "And if so what kind." A second finger joined the first. "And if you knew what topics she liked to talk about." She held out a third digit. "And what her favorite type of restaurant is."

"Your father and my mother?"

Grace chuckled. "Yeah. Can you believe it?"

Carey shook her head and smiled, then held out her hand for the phone.

"Hi, Richard, this is Carey. My mom loves chocolate. Any kind. She especially loves See's nuts and chews." She thought a moment. "And you can't go wrong with Chinese. She loves Chinese food. You're welcome. I'll see you in a while...bye." She looked up at Grace and grinned. "Your dad is so darn cute. He sounds like a teenager with his first crush."

Grace plopped herself down on the couch next to Carey and snuggled close. "I guess it runs in the family."

"Good night," Carey said as she watched Grace's father open the door and stand aside so that her mother could go through first.

"Good night, kids," Barbara said, linking her arm with Richard's. "I'll see you tomorrow."

"He held her chair for her," Grace whispered.

"And she's giggling like a schoolgirl," Carey whispered back. "I think she's flirting with him."

"Think?" Grace nudged her. "She's looking at Dad like he's the last single man on Earth."

"Your father was the one who asked her why some lucky man hadn't snatched her up," Carey said.

"But that was after your mother said he was 'positively charming,'" Grace said, mimicking Barbara's inflections.

"How many men do you know nowadays that hold a chair for a woman?"

"Dad's just old fashioned," Grace said.

"Well, I think it's cute. You know my mom was only going to stay a week, and it's not me that caused her to change her plans, because I'm doing fine."

Grace nodded. "You think this is going to turn into something serious?"

Carey shrugged. "Your guess is as good as mine. But I think they make a great couple."

Grace reached out and closed the front door. "Come on, hon, let me take a look at the drain. It's been quite a while since we checked it." She took Carey's hand and led her to the bathroom. "Hardly anything in there," she said as she removed the bulb and inspected it.

"You take such good care of me," Carey said as she watched her lover tuck it back into her waistband." I'll be so glad when they take that damn thing out tomorrow." She motioned at the bandages. "All of it."

Grace jumped up as Carey came through the door. "Well?"

"The doctor said everything looks good and I'm healing up nicely." Carey smiled. "God, it's good not to have that drain hanging out of my armpit anymore. Now that it's gone, and the staples are out, are you going to stop treating me like an invalid?"

"I didn't mind. I like taking care of you."

"I know. And I loved it. Really I did. But we need to put this behind us. Get some normalcy back into our lives."

"Back up a minute," Grace said. "Did I hear you say staples?"

"Yes, you did."

"They really put staples in you?"

"Yep."

"Did it hurt when they took them out?"

Carey nodded her head. "They said it wouldn't hurt. But they lied." She saw the distressed look on Grace's face and started laughing. "It wasn't that bad. I was kidding." She glanced at her watch. "As much as I like hanging around doctors' offices, it's almost time to meet the folks for lunch. Come on, let's go home and get changed. I can't wait to have a real shower again."

"I'll help."

"That's okay," Carey said. "I don't need help."

"Carey, are you afraid to let me see?" Grace asked, putting her arms around the older woman's waist.

"A little, I guess," she said. "They said the scarring would fade with time, but it looks pretty red and ugly right now. And I have a dimple."

Grace smiled. "Isn't it lucky that I just love a woman with dimples. And a little scar is certainly not going to change how I feel about you." She leaned over for a quick kiss. "I love you, Joanna Carey. A scar or dimple isn't going to make a difference to me."

Carey opened the door and walked inside the cabin and glanced around. "I'm home," she said as she deposited a canvas shopping bag on the half wall that divided the living room from the kitchen.

It had been five weeks since the surgery, and she had spent the day at the cancer center, meeting with the radiologist and getting everything ready to begin radiation treatment the following week.

She started walking toward the bedroom when the bathroom door opened and she was greeted by Grace's smiling face.

"Whatcha got?" Grace asked as she walked over and peeked in the bag.

"Did you know that most deodorants have aluminum in them?" Carey asked.

"What?"

"Really, they do." Carey reached into the bag and pulled out a package of deodorant. "They sent me to the health food store to pick this up. Apparently the regular deodorant makes the radiation cause burns because of the trace amounts of aluminum in it." She pulled Grace into her arms and leaned over for a kiss. "And I'll have you know that you're not the only tattooed lady around here any more."

"My, my, you're getting daring, my love," Grace said. She stepped back and placed her hands on her hips. "Well, what are you waiting for? I want to see it."

Carey pulled her shirt over her head, then unhooked her bra, revealing a series of dots tattooed on her breast. "You think they'll be able to hit the target?"

Grace crossed her arms over her chest. "You brat. I thought you meant a real tattoo."

Carey looked down at her breast. "These are real." She pulled Grace back into her arms. "What? You thought I had your name tattooed on my ass?"

Grace smiled. "I wouldn't complain if you got my name tattooed on your ass. In fact, I rather like the idea."

Carey threw off the covers for the second time that night and sighed in frustration. She hated the hot flashes that had begun shortly after she started taking the estrogen suppressant her oncologist had prescribed.

The six weeks of radiation treatments had been uneventful, and the only side effect Carey had suffered was fatigue. She seemed to be tired all the time. But at least the radiation treatments were behind her now, and the doctor had assured her that her energy would return.

She turned her pillow over to find the cool side, then snuggled down to try to get back to sleep. Of course she knew she would be wakened again to pull the covers back when the heat left her body. Grace yawned and rolled over onto her back. "What's the matter, honey, another hot flash?"

"Yeah," Carey said, lightly touching her lover's hair. "I didn't mean to wake you up."

Grace propped herself up on one elbow, her naked breasts visible in the moonlight. "Something's bothering you," she said. "I can feel it."

Carey reached out and traced Grace's lips with her fingertips. "I love your lips. Have I told you that?"

"No changing the subject, Carey. I need to know what's been bothering you."

"I want to go fishing."

"Now?"

"No, not now," Carey said. "I mean I want to be able to wake up and go fishing."

"At your cottage? But you can't do that and be here."

"I know," Carey said. "And I can't afford to be there."

"Maybe you can't," Grace said. "But can we?"

"I don't know."

"We should figure it out," Grace said. "Two can live cheaper than one and I'm making good money. At least as good as I can get with an associates degree and a telecommuting job."

"Would you make more if you went to the office every day?"

"I like having to go to town only one day a week," Grace said. "I love making my own schedule and I have one of the highest productivity ratios in the office." She leaned down and rested her head on Carey's chest. "I can work from home wherever home is," she said, kissing the soft skin near her lips. "I love you."

"And I love you, but it's not that easy," Carey said. "Right now we're not worrying about paying the mortgage, and it's almost an hour more each way for you to commute from the cottage to Mohawk." She hugged Grace close. "That beat-up wreck of yours would never make it."

"Your truck would," Grace said. "Or I could buy a better car. I've been saving money, you know."

"I hoped you were," Carey said. "But your finances are your business."

"I wanted to talk to you about that," Grace said. "I don't hide my pay stubs and I'd be happy to show you how to use my banking program." She propped herself up again, looking down at Carey. "I don't want it to be my finances, I want it to be ours. We're a couple. Why do we keep the money separate?"

"You know how to bring up the big subjects, don't you?" Carey said, turning on the lamp. "What happens if we break up?"

Grace brushed her lips over Carey's. "I hate when you say things like that," she said. "I'm not planning on going anywhere so don't quote me statistics about lesbian relationships not lasting. We're going to sit down and look at everything and see if together we can afford to move to the cottage." She settled down and cuddled against Carey's side. "Now go to sleep."

"And that's it, hmm?" Carey said, kissing the top of Grace's head. "No discussion?"

"Give me a good reason, other than you being afraid of commitment, and we can discuss it," Grace said, pulling the blanket up over them. "Good night, my love."

"Are you serious?"

"Of course I am," Richard said.

"But Dad, you live in Alaska, she lives in Massachusetts."

"I'll move."

"But that will make her my step-mother." Grace followed the logic. "And Carey would be my step-sister."

"I love her, Grace."

Grace hesitated. "Are you sure about this?"

"Very."

"If she makes you happy, Dad." She covered the receiver with her hand when Carey walked in. "They're getting married."

"Who's getting married?"

"Your mom and my dad."

"Is that your dad?" Carey asked, pointing at the phone.

Grace nodded.

Carey snatched the phone out of Grace's hand. "It's about time you made an honest woman of her, you old reprobate. I was beginning to wonder if I was going to have to get my shotgun out." She heard laughing on the other end of the line. "Seriously, congratulations. I can't think of anyone that I'd rather have as a step-dad. My mother has very good taste."

"I guess good taste runs in your family."

Carey looked over at Grace and smiled. "No doubt about it."

"I'm planning on making the move to Boston, but I'm keeping my house here. We plan to spend part of the summers here."

Carey laughed. "You'll make a country gal out of her yet. So, have you two set a date?"

"This weekend, actually," Richard said. "We don't want a big affair. We've both been through that once, and once was enough. We thought we'd just fly off somewhere, just the two of us. Make it a combination wedding, honeymoon trip. We just need to settle on the destination. I think it's going to be Hawaii."

"Sounds romantic."

"I've got another call coming in, Carey, so I'll say good-bye now. Say good-bye to Grace for me."

"Will do, Rich—Dad. See you soon." She hung up the phone and turned to Grace. "He told me I have good taste." Carey stroked Grace's cheek. "I have to agree."

Grace leaned over and put her head on Carey's shoulder, snuggling against her. "It's kinda strange thinking about our parents getting married."

"Why is that?"

"Well, technically that will make you my sister." Grace lifted her head and looked at Carey. "Doesn't that seem a little strange?"

"Well, it is unusual, but I don't think of it as strange."

"I guess," Grace said. "The important thing is that they're happy."

Carey pulled her close. "Yep. That's all that matters." She kissed the top of Grace's head. "I've been doing some thinking about what we talked about the other night. You know, moving up to the cottage."

"And?"

"I think we can swing it. I'm sure I'll be able to find some kind of a job. It won't pay as much as I make here, but it should pay the mortgage. And we only have two more years to pay on it. Then it's ours, free and clear."

Carey walked into the mess hall, her eyes scanning the room. Finally she spotted who she was looking for and walked over to Gage, who was chatting with a couple of the girls with Instructor Donaldson. She walked up behind them and tapped Gage on the shoulder. "Can I talk to you for a minute, Sue?"

Gage followed her over to an empty table and sat down across from her friend. "What's up?"

"I've been doing a lot of thinking lately about what's important in my life. I guess finding out you have cancer can make you look at your priorities in a different light."

Gage nodded. "I guess it can."

"I've turned in my notice, Sue. I'm leaving Sapling Hill at the end of session. I recommended you as my replacement, so if you want the job, it's yours."

Gage was stunned. She had noticed that her friend had been kind of introspective lately, but never expected this. "I don't know what to say."

"Nothing to say, really. My mind's made up. It's done."

"I'll have to think about it. Taking over running this place is a big responsibility. I'm not sure I'm up to it."

"I wouldn't have recommended you if I didn't think you were up to it, but I don't want you to think I'm pushing you."

"I don't, I'm just...I'm just surprised, that's all."

"You'll have the whole summer to find a replacement for yourself so there shouldn't be too much pressure. And you know if you have any problems, all you have to do is call and I'm here."

"Are you sure about this?"

The conversation came to an abrupt halt when Carey suddenly sprang to her feet and ran across the room to break up a fight that had started between two girls. One of them was howling because she had been stabbed in the hand with the other girl's fork.

"You're gonna pay for this, you fucking bitch!" The girl balled her hand into a fist and caught the other girl in the nose.

"All right, break it up," Carey said as she grabbed the girl with the bloody nose and pulled her away before she could return the punch.

"She started it!" the girl with the bloody hand shouted.

"I did not, you—"

"I don't care who started it. Both of you drop and give me twenty." The girls just stood there glaring at each other. "Now!"

The girls dropped and started their push-ups and Carey motioned for Donaldson to come over. "Take care of this for me, will ya? When they finish get them over to the infirmary to check on those injuries."

Carey walked back to the table and dropped into her seat. "I just don't need this kind of stress in my life anymore, ya know?"

"I know."

"It used to be a challenge that I enjoyed, now I just want to be able to spend more time with Grace."

"What are your plans?"

"We're moving to the cottage. I'm sure I'll be able to find some kind of job that will allow us a more normal life." She looked around the room. "Because this isn't it."

Gage reached over and covered Carey's hand with her own. "I wish all the best for you, my friend. But I'm sure gonna miss you."

"I'll miss you too."

Carey put her book down when she heard a car pull up. A storm had rolled in the day before and she had insisted that Grace stay in Mohawk with Tom until it blew over. She met her at the door and helped her off with her coat. "I missed you," she said, as she pulled her into her arms.

Grace wrapped her arms around Carey and returned the hug. "Did you?"

"Desperately." Carey released her hold and led her to the couch. "I told Sue that I'm leaving Sapling Hill today." She sat down and pulled Grace with her.

"How did she take it?"

"She was shocked, but I think she was happy about the promotion."

"I'm glad they accepted your recommendation," Grace said. "I think she'll do great."

Carey nodded. "I do too. Oh, I almost forgot to tell you, we got a postcard from the folks. They're having a wonderful time in Hawaii."

She got up and walked into the kitchen to retrieve the card. "Look," she said, holding the card out as she returned. "They had it custom made with their wedding picture on it."

"I can't remember when I've seen my dad look this happy," Grace said, her eyes misting over with tears. It was a nice shot of the two of them. They were standing at the altar, facing each other, and Richard was slipping a ring on Barbara's finger. She wiped a stray tear away with the back of her hand, and looked up at Carey. "I don't believe this." She glanced at the postmark on the card. "They got married on Monday, and Tuesday they already had postcards to commemorate the event in the mail."

"I guess they were anxious to share their wedding with us, and with digital cameras and computers, they probably had the postcards in hand before they left the chapel." Carey laughed. "It was probably part of the wedding package."

Grace sniffled and leaned into Carey, the postcard clutched to her chest. "Can you imagine what it would be like to stand at the altar like that and pledge yourself to the one you love?"

"To tell you the truth, I've never given it much thought," Carey said.

"I think it would be wonderful." Grace looked at the picture and smiled. "They look so happy."

"So what is it?" Gage said as she unwrapped her sub.

"What's what? I can't invite my friend to my office for lunch?"

"Uh-huh," Gage said. "I only get free lunch from you when you want to talk about something...usually Grace."

Carey leaned back in her chair and smiled. "You know me too well."

"That I do, my friend." Gage picked up her soda and took a sip. "So out with it. What's on your mind?"

"Well, it is about Grace," Carey said. "We got a postcard from our parents yesterday. It was their wedding picture, and Grace got all sentimental and misty-eyed."

"What'd she do, ask you to marry her?" Gage joked, then took a bite of her sub.

"No," Carey said. "She just mentioned how happy they looked, and that she could imagine us standing at the altar."

"Earth to Carey, in the real world that's called a hint," Gage said.

Carey nodded. "That's kinda what I was thinking."

"Better get those two months' pay saved up."

"Two months' pay? For what?"

Gage shook her head. "A ring, oh dense one. You are going to give her a ring, aren't you? Standard rule of thumb is two months' pay on an engagement ring."

"That's outrageous," Carey said. "You know how much money that is?"

"It's a small price to make your wife happy," Gage said. "Or do you call her something else?"

"I have no idea," Carey said, still in shock. "Two months' pay?"

Gage nodded. "That's what I hear. I wouldn't know from personal experience though." She took another bite of her sandwich and watched Carey sit and fiddle with the wrapper on hers. "Do you think you'll ask her?"

"I can't imagine life without her anymore, Sue. It took me some time to get it through my thick head that she really is the one, ya know?" She smiled sheepishly and shook her head. "I can be really dense sometimes."

Gage laughed. "That's the understatement of the year."

Carey relaxed a little and laughed too. Finally she picked up her sub and took a bite, chewing thoughtfully. "I'm going to ask Reverend Pellegrino if he would be willing to marry us. You think he will?"

Sue shrugged. "Only one way to find out."

Carey spotted the jewelry store. "You know I've never gone past this place without there being a sale going on?"

Grace smiled and walked over to the large display window. "Different sales," she said. "One week it's a gold sale, the next it's a diamond sale. This week it's engagement rings and wedding sets." She pointed at the sign showing a bride and groom exchanging rings. "Some of these are so gaudy."

"Which ones?" Carey asked casually, hoping to pick up clues as to what kind of ring Grace would like.

"Well, like that one," Grace said, pointing at a large solitaire. "That's a 'no glove' ring. The diamond's so big you can't wear a glove with it."

"So you don't like large stones?"

Grace shook her head. "Not that kind. Now this one is nice." She pointed at a ring with two bands of small diamonds. "That's pretty."

"You like that one?"

"Well, it's nice, but not for me," Grace said. "First of all I could never afford it, and secondly I like white gold, not yellow."

White, not yellow. Got it. "But you like that style?"

"It's nice," Grace said, then pointed at a similar one. "But see how that one has a larger diamond in the middle of the band? That's nicer, I think."

Carey looked closer. "But it is pretty."

Grace pointed to one of the wedding and engagement ring sets on display. "I think it's silly to wear two rings when one will do. I mean, why spend all that money on an engagement ring and then get a band for the actual wedding. Of course, I wouldn't spend that kind of money on a ring." She looked at Carey's bare left hand. "At least, not for myself. What kind of rings do you like?"

"I don't have a jewelry box for a reason," Carey said. "I'm not really one to wear rings."

"Did Eve give you a ring?"

"We were in the Coast Guard," Carey said. "It wouldn't have looked good for us to be wearing matching rings."

Grace smiled. "I guess not. Come on; let's go to the food court. I'm starving."

Jan took a bite of her pizza, then froze in mid chew. She had noticed a couple of women holding hands in line at Pizza Express. But when they got their food and turned to find a table, she recognized her friend Grace and Scary Carey. *She did it. She actually did it.* "I'll be right back," she said to her friends at the table. "I think I see someone I know." She walked over and tapped Grace on the shoulder. "Hi there, stranger, long time no see."

Grace stood up and gave her friend a quick hug. "Carey, you remember Jan."

"How could I forget." Carey smiled and pointed to an empty seat. "Good to see you, Bowen. Would you like to join us?"

"No thanks, ma'am. I've got friends waiting for me. I just wanted to say hi."

Grace laughed. "Ma'am? Jan, we're not at Sapling Hill any more. You can call her Carey."

"Or Scary, if you prefer," Carey said.

Jan's face reddened and she looked at Grace. "You told her?"

Carey burst out laughing. "No, she didn't tell me. She didn't have to."

"I...I'm sorry, ma'am."

"Just Carey. Okay?"

"Yes, ma'am." Her face reddened even more. She shrugged her shoulders. "It's a hard habit to break." She turned to Grace. "Call me and let me know what's been going on with you." She glanced at Carey, then leaned a little closer. "And I do mean everything."

"Come to my office," Carey said, tugging on Sue's arm.

"Why?"

"I want to show you something." She unlocked the door and stepped inside. "You can't say anything to Grace," she said, crossing to her desk and opening the top drawer.

"You didn't," Sue said, smiling when she saw the black velvet box. "Let me see."

Carey opened the box, showing the white gold ring with two bands of small diamonds and a larger square stone in the center. "Think she'll like it?"

"If she doesn't, I'll marry you," Sue said, taking the ring and examining it from different angles. "Very nice. Must be at least two carats."

"Two and a quarter," Carey said, taking the ring back. "I can't believe I'm doing this."

"It's not a real marriage," Sue said. "It's a ceremony."

"It's real enough," Carey said. "I saw my lawyer while I was in town." She reached into the open drawer. "I had my will changed, drew up a power of attorney, and started the paperwork to make her joint owner of the cottage." She dropped the legal papers on the desk. "I'm not sure what was harder, getting the ring or doing this." Closing the velvet box, she leaned against the desk and let out a deep breath. "After Eve, I never thought I'd give my heart to anyone again." Shaking her head, she let out a small snort. "Certainly not a twenty-year-old."

"That's the problem with commitment," Sue said. "You have to give something of yourself. That's why I'm happily single."

"I love her," Carey said, staring at the box. "I can't imagine not being with her."

"So you said. Now stop being so nervous and go give her the ring."

"I can't just ask her," Carey said. "Don't you know you're supposed to ask the father for permission first?"

Sue laughed. "That is so archaic. Go ask her."

Carey shook her head. "If I'm going to do this, I'm going to do it right. The folks are in town and they're coming for dinner tonight." She closed her hand around the velvet box. "I'll talk to her father, then I'll..." She took a deep breath. "Pop the question."

"I don't know what you're worried about," Sue said. "You know she'll say yes."

"She loves me," Carey said softly. "She'll say yes...I hope."

"Joanna, what do you think?"

"Huh?"

Her mother tsked. "I said we're thinking of selling the house and buying an RV and I asked you what you thought."

"Oh. Fine."

"Joanna."

"I'm sorry, what?"

"Where is your head today?" Barbara asked, reaching up and feeling Carey's forehead. "You're not running a fever. Are you feeling all right?"

"I'm fine, Mom. My mind's just on other things, that's all."

"I asked if you wanted any of the furniture or should we try to sell it furnished?"

"Sell the house?"

"What do you think I've been talking to you about for the last ten minutes?" Barbara shook her head. "If you don't want to talk about it then just say so."

"Mom? How did you know it was right?"

Her mother looked at her for a second, then took Carey's hand and pulled her toward the bedroom. "When you start asking questions like that I know it's time for a serious talk."

"But Grace will be looking for me," Carey protested as she was pulled into the room.

"She'll survive two minutes without you," her mother said, closing the door behind them. "How did I know what was right?"

"Mom..."

Her mother pointed at the bed. "Joanna, sit."

Carey wanted to protest but took one look at her mother's face and thought better of it. "We can't be in here long," she said as she sat down. "I don't want Grace to think something's going on." *Why are my hands so clammy?*

"You're walking around with your mind a hundred miles away and you don't think she's going to think something's going on?" Barbara pulled the chair from the desk over to the bed. "Talk to your mother."

"What made you think Richard was right for you? He's not like Dad."

"I could ask you the same question about Grace," her mother pointed out. "Though you seem happier with her than you ever were with Eve."

"I love Grace, very much," Carey said. "She's not like Eve at all."

"You never talked about what happened between you and Eve," Barbara pointed out. "As a matter of fact, you hardly spoke of her at all even when you were together. I ask you how you're doing now and I hear all about Grace." She smiled. "And Richard hears all about you. That girl adores you."

"I know that," Carey said. "That's why I did something really, really crazy. I bought her a ring, Mom. After dinner I'm going to ask her to marry me."

"Marry her?"

"You don't approve?"

Barbara reached over and took her hand. "Oh, baby, I adore Grace. You know that. I was just surprised that you want to marry her when it really won't mean anything."

"It will mean something to me, Mom. And I hope it will mean something to her too. I'm not doing this for any type of benefits that they award to someone that is married in the eyes of the law. I talked to Reverend Pellegrino, and he agreed to marry us. That's official enough for me." Carey leaned forward and squeezed the hand that was holding hers. "I want to give her this special moment to show her that I'm committed to this relationship. That she's the only one I'll ever want. I've sent her too many mixed signals, but this will tell her that I'm really serious. Isn't that what getting married is all about?"

A tear started down Barbara's face and she pulled Carey over for a hug. "Yes, it is."

"Grace," Carey said. "I need to run down to the store and get more milk." She grabbed Richard's arm. "Your dad's going with me. We'll be right back."

"I am?" he asked, allowing himself to be led to the door.

"Yes, you are. The store's just down the road," Carey said, climbing in the truck and starting the engine. "I wanted to ask you something."

"I had a feeling I wasn't here just to keep you company," he said.

"You know I love Grace."

"Ayup."

"I think of our relationship as a permanent thing," she said, taking a deep breath. "And...I'm committed to making it work. I would never do anything deliberate to hurt her."

"Grace is very happy," he said.

"Yes," Carey said. "She seems to be. The thing is...I want to show her how I feel." She rolled down the window, the cab suddenly feeling very hot. "See...that commitment...I want to give her that...for both of us." She passed the store. "And well...tradition...and..." Shaking her head, she reached over and opened the glove compartment, revealing a velvet box. "May I?"

Richard started chuckling and reached for the box. "Finally decided to make an honest woman of my daughter, huh? Good thing too, because you're not the only one around here with a shotgun." He opened the box. "Oh, that's very pretty. I'm sure Grace will love it."

Carey pulled over. "So that's a yes, right?"

"Ayup, if you're asking for my daughter's hand in marriage. Do yourself a favor, though," he said, closing the box and putting it back in the glove compartment. "Just show her the ring. It'll say everything for you."

"What are you doing here?" Carey asked, stepping outside and closing the door behind her.

"You're going to ask her, aren't you?" Gage said. "I want to see her face when she sees that ring."

"Before or after I have my heart attack?" Carey said, sitting down on the steps. "I almost had a stroke just asking her dad's permission."

"You mean your step-dad," Gage said.

"Don't say it like that," Carey said. "I'd much rather think of him as her father and the man who lives with my mother. If I think of him as a step-father then that makes Grace my step-sister, and that's just too weird to be asking my sister to marry me. Funny, I told Grace it wasn't that strange, but at a time like this, the last thing I want to do is think of Grace as my sister."

"Just don't faint before you give her the ring," Gage said. "Come on, let me in so I can watch you make a fool out of yourself."

"Look who's here," Carey said as she opened the door and ushered Sue in. "Mom, you remember Sue, don't you?"

"Of course I do," Barbara said. "It's nice to see you again, Sue."

"Yes, it is," Sue said as she walked over and sat on the arm of the couch.

"Um...I have to get something out of the kitchen," Carey said, turning away from the group of people sitting in her living room.

"I'll go with you," Grace said, following her into the kitchen. "Are you okay?"

"Me? Of course," Carey said, feigning casualness.

"You seem nervous or worried about something," Grace said, moving closer. "Are you sure you're feeling okay?"

"I'm fine." *My stomach's in knots, my head feels light and I'm not sure if I'm going to pass out or throw up. Other than that, I'm fine.* "I think it's just a little warm in here."

Grace put her hand on Carey's forehead. "It seems fine to me but you do feel a little warm. I'm going to get the thermometer."

"No," Carey said, putting her arms around the younger woman. "I'm fine, really." Holding Grace in her arms had a calming effect, ebbing the fear that was playing havoc with her emotions. "I love you," she said, claiming Grace's mouth with her own.

"Mmm, and I love you," Grace said when their lips parted. "You sure you're okay?"

"I'm sure," she said. "Go on, I'll be out in a minute."

Grace kissed her cheek. "I love you."

Carey watched her leave, then turned and leaned her forearms on the counter. *It's time. Just go out there, kneel down next to her and give her the ring. That's all there is to it. She'll say yes. Of course she will. She loves me. She wants commitment. She won't ask to think about it. She'll say yes.* "Oh God," she whispered, clasping her hands together. "Please just give me the strength to get through this...and please let her say yes."

Taking a deep breath, Carey pushed open the louvered door, her eyes locking on Grace. "Um...if everyone could be quiet for a minute. I have something I want to say." She took a step forward, aware of Gage's smirk, Richard's smile, and most of all Grace's concerned look. "Grace, when you first told me you loved me, I couldn't return that love." *That's good, voice is steady, keep going.* She took another step forward. "I told you to find someone else, that it could never be." The room seemed to close in and Carey gripped the back of Gage's chair for support. "B-but you waited for me to see what you knew all along." She reached into her pocket. "That we were meant to be together." Cupping the box in her hand, she knelt down, her eyes never leaving Grace's. "I love you," she said, revealing the black velvet box and looking into teary blue eyes. "I...I..." Tears formed in her eyes, matching those rolling down Grace's cheeks. Opening the box, she held it out to the woman who owned her heart. "Marry me?" Grace didn't say a word, she just held out her hand as tears started down her face.

She watched as Carey slipped the ring on her finger, words still eluding her. Then she placed a hand on each of Carey's cheeks and leaned over for a kiss. "I love you," she whispered, just before their lips met. "I love you."

Barbara started to applaud, and Richard and Sue joined in. Carey turned to them, her face flushed. She looked back to Grace. "That's what I get for proposing in front of an audience."

Barbara smiled and rested her hand on top of Richard's. "Now that she's accepted, all that's left is to do the planning and have the wedding." She looked at Carey. "Then you two can worry about giving me grandchildren."

Grace and Carey shared equally shocked looks. "Grandchildren?" they said in unison.

"Do I have to guess what you're thinking about?" Carey asked when Grace adjusted her pillow for the fourth time in ten minutes.

"We've never talked about having children," Grace said. "Do you want children?"

Carey looked at the clock. "Not bad. One-thirty. I'm surprised you cracked so early."

"So do you?"

"What do you want?" Carey countered, lying on her back and pulling Grace closer.

"Well, since I figured I'd never have sex with a man, children didn't seem to be in my future. Maybe someday, I guess." She kissed Carey's shoulder. "I'm not in any hurry."

"Good, because there's no way we can afford a baby," Carey said. "Not with me giving up my job to move to the cottage."

Grace nodded and snuggled down in her pillow, then lifted her hand to look at her ring again.

"Hey," Carey said softly when she saw new tears. "Why are you crying?"

"Happy tears," Grace said, looking at the ring on her finger. "It's so beautiful."

Carey turned on her side, propping herself up on one elbow. "I'm happy you like it."

"This is why you were asking me all those questions at the mall that day, isn't it?"

"Guilty as charged," Carey said, kissing Grace's shoulder. "Couldn't give my future bride a ring she wouldn't like, could I?"

"I love you so much."

"I love you too, Grace," she said, eminently pleased with herself.

"There's just one thing."

The self-satisfied smile dropped. "What?"

"I have to take it off from time to time," Grace said.

Carey shook her head. "Why?"

"Well," Grace said, pushing Carey down onto the bed. "You see, that's my left hand and that's the one I use..." She pressed her thigh between Carey's legs. "Unless you don't want me to do that anymore."

"Use your right hand," Carey suggested.

"I do better with my left hand," Grace said, reaching into Carey's pajama bottoms. "That way I can kiss you and still have my thumb..." Carey gasped as Grace made contact. "...there."

"I thought you were tired," Carey said, her legs parting in conflict to her words.

"And I don't know why you bother wearing clothes to bed," Grace said, never ceasing with her gentle stroking. "Hmm, feels like I struck oil."

"You always do when you do that," Carey said, reaching up to caress Grace's breast. "Come here."

Giving the sensitive area a final caress, the young woman snuggled into the crook of her lover's arm. "You're the best thing that's ever happened to me," Grace said, sighing contentedly. "I love you."

"That goes both ways," Carey said, taking advantage of their positions, she kissed the top of Grace's head. "I love you, too."

"You have to get out here," Gage said impatiently.

"In a minute," Carey said, rinsing her mouth...again.

"Come on, you big coward."

"You're not helping me," Carey said, shutting the water off and drying her face.

"I think you've got puking down to a science," Sue said from the other side of the door.

Carey looked at her face in the mirror and groaned. "Whose idea was this anyway?"

"Yours."

"Don't remind me," Carey said, slowly straightening up and opening the bathroom door. "I look like hell."

"Nothing a little makeup couldn't fix," Sue said, guiding Carey to the chair.

"I don't do makeup."

"You do today or Grace will think she's marrying a raccoon."

"Who is it?"

"Your father."

"Just a minute, Dad," Grace said, taking the tuxedo shirt off the hanger and putting it on. "Okay."

"Just checking to see if you need any help," he said.

"Yeah." She pointed at the cufflinks on the dresser. "I can't make my fingers work today."

"It's nerves," he said.

"I don't have any nerves left," she said, holding her arm out so he could fasten the cufflink. "I was up most of the night worrying."

"Don't worry," he said as he secured another fastener. "She's here."

"I know she's here," Grace said. "I think it's silly we can't see each other."

"You two are the ones that wanted so much tradition," he said.

Grace picked up the pale blue bow tie and faced the mirror. "Daddy? Were you nervous on your wedding day?"

"Let me," he said, reaching from behind to help her with the tie. "I was absolutely petrified," he said. "Almost passed out before the minister could finish."

"Oh, don't say that," Grace said, picking up the white cummerbund.

Her father chuckled. "You'll do just fine," he said.

There was a knock at the door. "Grace?"

Grace froze. "I'm sorry, Daddy. I didn't know she was coming."

"Don't worry about me, pumpkin. I don't mind her being here, as long as you're okay with it."

Grace shrugged her shoulders. "I'm okay, I guess."

"You're sure? Because I'll be happy to escort her out of here if that's what you want."

"I'm sure."

He could see the uncertainty in her eyes, but she said she was okay. Reluctantly he turned and opened the door. "Hello, Edna."

"Richard," Grace's mother said. "I'd like to talk to my daughter."

"Our daughter," he said. "Grace, I'll be downstairs if you need me."

Grace hugged him. "Thanks Dad."

"Careful," he said. "You don't want to show up at the altar all wrinkled." He left, closing the door behind him.

"A tuxedo?"

"You know I hate dresses," Grace said, picking up the vest and slipping it over her shoulders.

"Well at least button it properly," her mother said, shooing Grace's hands out of the way. "I know how nervous a bride is," she said as she straightened out Grace's vest. "My hands were shaking so bad your grandmother had to button up my dress."

"How did you know about this?" Grace asked.

"You did put an announcement in the paper," Edna said, finishing the last button. "There."

"Tell me you didn't bring him."

"He's not here," her mother said. "He dropped me off and I'll call him to come back to get me."

"I so do not need this today," Grace said, turning away to check her appearance in the mirror.

"Grace, do you want me to leave?"

Tugging her vest, Grace shook her head. "You're here. Oh God, you're going to end up sitting next to Dad and Barbara." She turned around and looked at her mother. "Please tell me you can get along with him today."

"Of course I can," Edna said. "Grace..."

"No." Grace reached for her jacket. "Not a word about it. Not today."

"You stand next to me and don't you dare let me fall," Carey said.

"Don't worry," Sue said. "I'll be the perfect best man, or best woman as the case may be."

Carey pulled on her collar. "Why haven't they started the music yet?"

"They are playing music."

"You know what I mean," Carey said. *"Here Comes the Bride."*

"When Grace comes out. Calm down."

"I can't," Carey said. "I keep having visions of her riding away on Jan's motorcycle."

"She's not going to run away," Sue said. "Now stop it before you give yourself a stroke."

"Why did we pick such a hot day?"

"The day's not hot, you are," Sue said. "It's not like anything's going to change between you. You've been living with her for how long now?"

"Living with her isn't the same as a marrying her," Carey said just as the organist changed the music. "Oh God, she's coming." The temperature seemed to jump even higher as beads of sweat broke out along her forehead and a buzzing sound filled her ears. "Sue..."

"Don't you dare wimp out on me now," Sue said, gripping her nervous friend's shoulders. "Carey, breathe."

"Look at her," Carey whispered as Grace walked down the aisle, her arm entwined with Richard's. "She's so beautiful."

"And I'm sure she's thinking the same thing about you."

Their eyes met and the nervousness that had so consumed Carey suddenly dissipated, replaced with a calm peace. This was right. This was what was meant to be. Taking a deep breath, she let it out slowly and reached for her bride's hand.

"You're not going to pass out on me, are you?" Grace asked softly, squeezing their joined hands.

"I hope not."

"Good, because I feel like I might," Grace said. "All these years, I always wondered if a day like this would come and now it's here."

"I love you," Carey said, bringing their joined hands to her lips. "Thanks for not giving up on me."

"You were worth waiting for."

"Ready?" the minister asked, giving the couple a gentle smile.

"For the rest of my life," Carey said.

"For the rest of our lives," Grace corrected. They faced the minister as they would the rest of their lives...together.

The End

About The Authors

Verda Foster

Verda Foster has worked in and around the art and crafts industry for twenty years, and you can often find her judging at one of the many ceramic and craft shows held throughout Southern California.

She has been teaching the art of painting statuary for thirteen or fourteen years and enjoys seeing a student's eyes light up when they see a piece of white-ware come to life in their hands.

She wrote her first story in 1999 and was hooked. Her first book, *The Chosen*, was published in September of 2000.

She has collaborated with B. L. Miller on several stories and loves working with this wonderful writer.

Verda Foster has a new forthcoming novel, *These Dreams,* which will be published later this year by BookEnds Press and distributed by SCP.

B. L. Miller

B. L. Miller claims to be a hermit by nature, loving to stay at home and partake in her favorite pastimes of reading, writing, and painting garden gnomes.

She was born in Massachusetts during a blizzard in 1967 and was raised in and around Albany, New York. Now a resident of Maine, she still gets teased about drinking "caw-fee." She was a wild child, spent her teenage years giving her mother gray hair and self-destructing. Now she spends her days working for a large telecommunication company and her nights sitting in front of the computer happily writing away and answering email. She loves writing and hopes to continue to do so for a very long time.

B. L.'s other works include an *'Accidental Love'*, *'Josie and Rebecca*: *The Western Chronicles,'* published in 1999 by B. L. Miller and Vada Foster.

B. L. also has a novel *'Court of Love'* that was only published in German.

In addition to Graceful Waters, Verda and B. L. co-authored *'Crystal's Heart'*

New Releases From
Intaglio Publications

Gloria's Inn
by Robin Alexander
ISBN 1-933133-01-4

Hayden Tate suddenly found herself in a world unlike any other, when she inherited half of an inn nestled away on Cat Island in the Bahamas. Expecting something like the resorts found in Nassau, Hayden was shocked and a little disappointed to find herself on a beautiful tropical island undiscovered by tourism. Hayden reluctantly begins to adapt to a simpler way of life found on the island, and her conversion is often comical.

Not only did Hayden's aunt leave her an inn, but the company of her former business partner as well. Strange as she is beautiful, Adrienne turns Hayden's world upside down in many ways. Hayden quickly learns that being with Adrienne will always be an adventure.

The tranquility of the island is shattered with the disappearance of a mysterious guest. Hayden and Adrienne soon find themselves at the center of a murder investigation, fearing for their own safety and the lives of their guests. Eager to rid themselves and the island of a ruthless killer, Adrienne and Hayden decide to conduct their own investigation. The eclectic mixture of guests and staff make their efforts both interesting and humorous.

The Gift
by Verda Foster
ISBN 1-933133-03-0

Detective Rachel Todd doesn't believe in Lindsay Ryan's visions of danger, even when the horrifying events Lindsay predicted come true. That mistake could cost more than one life before this rollercoaster ride is over. Verda Foster's The Gift is just that – a well-paced, passionate saga of suspense, romance, and the amazing bounty of family, friends, and second chances. From the first breathless page to the last, a winner.

Radclyffe - Author of Fated Love, shadowland, and the Justice and Honor series

The Cost Of Commitment
by Lynn Ames
ISBN 1-933133-02-2

"ABSORBING"

Lynn Ame's first novel, The Price of Fame, has been called "absorbing and filled with romance" (Lori. L. Lake, Midwest Book Review). Now Ames is back with the second installment in the lives of Katherine Kyle and Jamison Parker.

SPINE-TINGLING SUSPENSE

Kate and Jay want nothing more than to focus on their love. But as Kate settles in to a new profession, she and Jay become caught up in the middle of a deadly scheme—pawns in a larger game in which the stakes are nothing less than control of the country.

OUTSTANDING ACTION

In her new novel of corruption, greed, romance, and danger, Lynn Ames takes us on an unforgettable journey of harrowing conspiracy—and establishes herself as a mistress of suspense.

THE COST OF COMMITMENT

It could be everything...

Infinite Pleasures: **An Anthology of Lesbian Erotica**
Stacia Seaman (Editor), Nann Dunne (Editor)
ISBN 1-933113-00-6

Hot, edgy, beyond-the-envelope erotica from over thirty of the best lesbian authors writing today. This no-holds barred, tell it like you wish it could be collection is guaranteed to rocket your senses into overload and ratchet your body up to high-burn. This is NOT a book to be read in one sitting—savor, simmer, and let yourself be seduced by these Infinite Pleasures from Ali Vali, C Paradee, Cate Swannell, CN Winters, DS Bauden, Gabrielle Goldsby, Georgia Beers, JP Mercer, Jean Stewart, Jennifer Fulton, Jessica Casavant, K Darblyne, K Stoley, Karin Kallmaker, Katlyn, Kelly Zarembski, KG MacGregor, Leslea Newman, Lois Cloarec Hart, Lynn Ames, NM Hill, Nann Dunne, Radclyffe, S. Anne Gardner, Sarah Bradbury, Stacia Seaman, SX Meagher, Therese Szymanski, Trish Kocialski, Trish Shields, Vada Foster, and Verda Foster.

Visit us at
www.intagliopub.com

or

www.starcrossedproductions.com